A BEND OF LIGHT

A Novel

JOY JORDAN-LAKE

LAKE UNION
PUBLISHING

Text copyright © 2022 by Joy Jordan-Lake

Published by Lake Union Publishing, Seattle

www.apub.com

Amazon, the Amazon logo, and Lake Union Publishing are trademarks of Amazon.com, Inc., or its affiliates.

ISBN-13: 9781542037907 (hardcover)
SBN-10: 1542037905 (hardcover)

ISBN-13: 9781542037891 (paperback)
ISBN-10: 1542037891 (paperback)

Cover design by Faceout Studio, Tim Green

Printed in the United States of America

First edition

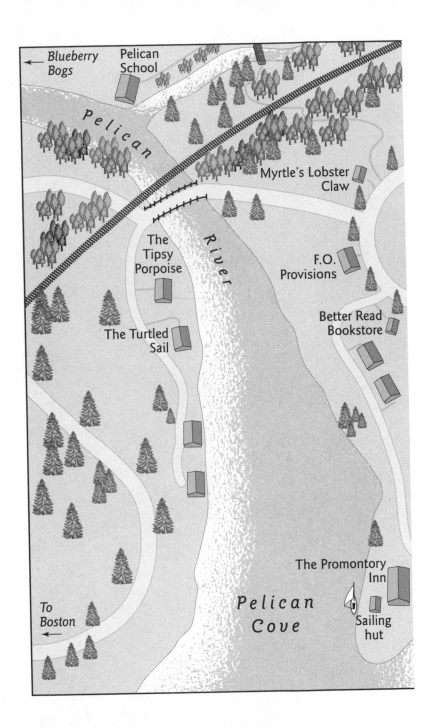

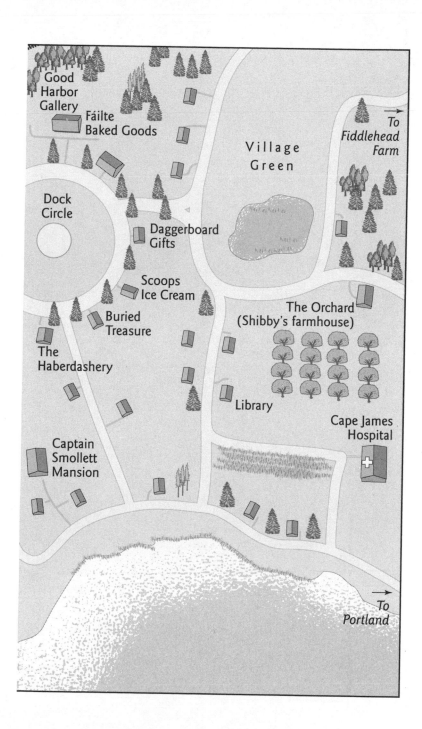

Prologue

The body knocked deep burgundy leaves from the maples as it fell, flailing, from the third-story window of the inn and down past the trees. Rain droplets from the branches caught the light, haloing the shoulders and head on their descent.

Up the slope from the inn, a young woman froze in place where she'd been kneeling, her camera gripped in both hands. Her only prayer until a fractured second ago had been the perfect shot, to capture the beauty of this place on Kodachrome that she'd develop herself. A beauty so stunning. So startling.

Now the young woman found she could not move, the camera still in front of her face as if it might shield her from what she'd just seen. As if she might rewind the spool of film—and time with it.

Even as it landed, the body looked the perfect part of the saint— arms outstretched in a gesture of welcome, face upturned and strangely serene.

Silence. For several long seconds after the fall.

Then nothing but the swoosh of a great cormorant's wings as it dropped from the pines and a whisper of leaves as they spiraled down.

Now two separate sounds shattered the quiet at the same instant: a gasping, choking intake of air from the young woman as she tried to scream and, yards away near the road, the whimper of a young child who'd hardly spoken for days.

Chapter 1

The Previous Week

For all her dread in coming back here to this place, this rockbound, sea-pounded village, she'd forgotten how much she'd once loved it.

Edging the long blue nose of her roadster close to the harbor, Amie Stilwell rolled down her window to listen. After all her training during the war to focus only on what she could see—down to the splinter of a detail—she'd forgotten how much this place's pull on her involved sound.

The bell buoys were tolling, their low tones rolling over the water. A loon called his three notes of longing—the *I'm here, here, where are you?* Waves splashed and fizzed and sucked at the boulders on the shoreline.

The parts of her that the war had damaged and hollowed out slowly shifted a little. Perhaps the sounds here, and the day's waning light on the ocean—*how could she have forgotten that silver?*—were stirring something inside her that had been silent and still for too long, coaxing something dead back to life.

A soft whine to her right made her turn.

Putting out a gloved hand, she opened her palm as the dog lifted his paw to her. "Nope. We aren't looking back, Hopkins. This will be good. A fresh start."

Hopkins barked once, a valiant, full-throated effort for such a small dog. His tail, a fluffy white feather-duster sort of affair, swept back and forth.

"Exactly," she said. Tossing back the blue scarf at her neck, she reached into the camera bag for her Deardorff with its most powerful lens. "And *this* is how we'll survive."

A maroon car purred past, its paint so new it glowed against the wet road. The driver, his fedora pulled low and scarf wrapped high, appeared to be paying little attention. His gleaming right side nearly brushed the roadster's front left as he swept past.

Amie leaned out her window to shout at the man. *"Careful!"*

But the car ahead careened from one side of the road to the other, its driver's silhouette never twitching or turning. Oblivious to how close he'd come to a collision, he'd not heard, maybe not even seen, her.

Easing her car farther onto the road's shoulder, Amie slipped the strap of the camera over her head, and with a flat hand to signal Hopkins to stay, she opened her door. Her boots sank deep into damp leaves as she slid from the car. But at least she'd had the good sense back in D.C., even in her daze, to replace her tweed suit and nylons with wool socks and dungarees.

The suit, in fact, she'd stripped off as soon as she got in last night from the dinner, zippering the thing off right there at her D.C. apartment's threshold—right there in the hall. Still livid after her boss's announcement, she'd marched, in nothing but a slip, to her window to hurl the suit down as if the tweed itself stank of betrayal.

To her, it did. Always would.

Amie scrambled now to the top of a pile of lobster traps at the edge of the shore. Closing her eyes, she focused on the shot she would make—before seeing it. Fog was wrapping the village. She could smell the wood fires of the villagers' hearths, both the lobstermen's cottages and the old sea captains' mansions, the smell of spruce, too, and salt breeze. The taste of cinnamon and brown sugar hung suspended somehow in the air—although maybe that last was just the longing of memory.

Now she opened her eyes, and standing just barely balanced on the shifting pile of traps, she leaned out to the right to capture the lights from the Promontory Inn across the harbor. She adjusted the shutter speed. Her best shots typically came from the most precarious angles, she'd learned years ago.

Shifting her balance, she respooled the finished roll and reloaded the Deardorff with a fresh cartridge of color film from her coat pocket, though the low light this evening would render the scene in grayish blues. She'd have to experiment with the gelatin reliefs and the cyan dye transfer to do this scene justice: the navy swirls of the sea, the charcoal of the rocks, the pale froth of the waves.

She snapped a good dozen pictures, pausing between to advance the film. With the aperture so fully open, she braced her arms against her body to steady her hands. The lights of the Promontory Inn spilled and sparkled across the water. Amie aimed carefully to avoid the sign in the foreground on this side of the harbor that mentioned the inn. Not that its words would be legible in the picture, but she'd know what they said, and she'd rather throw open the door of a darkroom herself and ruin these shots than have that sign appear in them. That sign spelled out in molded metal letters all of this town's elaborate flattery of the Promontory's owner, widely praised here and even more widely despised.

Cradling the Deardorff inside her coat for protection, Amie clambered back down the pile to her car. Inside, mist sifted through the slit in the roadster's canvas roof to land on her lap and the driver's seat. Even with the heater and radio both blasting all the way up Route 1, from D.C. through Philadelphia and New York through Boston, and onto the new Maine Turnpike, her teeth had chattered much of the day.

She glanced in the rearview mirror for the first time since she'd packed the car at midnight. Her hair, glossed for yesterday's dinner into waves worthy of Rita Hayworth, fell now in frizzed, half-frozen curls. She looked, she decided, about how she felt: wild, unruly, and fierce.

"You certainly picked the smart side of the car to sit on," she told the dog.

Standing on his hind legs, Hopkins propped his front paws on the passenger door to look out. His body, with its long, silky white fur, was a reverse silhouette against the fast-darkening ocean as the sun dipped below the horizon.

She'd forgotten, too, how the lights sparkling on the harbor made ugliness—heaps of nets and traps or, in her case, blotches of a messy past—all but disappear.

This village, Amie thought as she steered toward the town center, *is the perfect place after all to start a new story.*

On a stone pathway leading to one of the captain's mansions, a tall, broad-shouldered man was carrying a Saint Bernard with a wrapped paw—hauling the huge dog to the wood-slatted bed of his truck, and then, apparently changing his mind, to the other side of the cab, as if the creature weighed nothing. The man's cap, a gray wool beret, shadowed his face. But he lifted one hand from the wrist and dipped his head at the same time, the cove's signature greeting.

Amie's heart gave a small twist, a squeeze of hope she'd not felt for a while. Not because of the man himself, whoever he was, so much as the wave he'd given, a flash of human warmth across the late-autumn chill.

"Yep," she said aloud, still convincing herself, "it'll be good. Good to be back."

Up ahead, the lights of shops and wharves glittered across the harbor as it narrowed to the Pelican River where a bridge connected the Lower with the Upper Village. A car—the maroon one from before—paused at the railroad tracks that crossed the road just before the bridge. Off to the south, at least a good mile away, a train blew its whistle.

But the train wouldn't stop, Amie knew—not now that the summer tourists had gone. All through the warmer months, the Cheshire and the Pine Tree carried Bostonians and New Yorkers and even weary legislative aides all the way up from D.C. to tumble off at the stations up here and catch trolleys to hydrangea-edged inns and collapse on the beaches all along Cape James. This time of year, though, a train would simply blow its warning to each coastal cluster of town and hurtle past.

Feeling her fists on the wheel start to relax, Amie slowed a good fifty feet back from the car ahead. She was almost to the bridge and the Upper Village. She was in no hurry. She'd rather take a moment to breathe, to prepare for approaching the heart of the cove—and her own past.

From her radio's speaker, giving out more static than tune now, Frank Sinatra was mourning a lost love.

Amie smacked the dial to off. "We're not," she told Hopkins, "going all Sad Sack. And we're not looking back."

The dog cocked his head.

The train tracks shot in two silver lines parallel to each other and, right here, also parallel to the sea before the waves crashed inward and carved out the next harbor. She could picture two children walking in single file here—herself and her best friend Jake—scarves wrapped to their noses, L.L. Bean boots balanced on the few inches' width of steel. In summer, they'd walked the rails barefoot, then raced each other over the boulders to the shore.

Jake.

She felt the stab of the loss, as fresh as it was five years ago when the war ended.

Ever wish, Jake had asked as a kid more than once—and his voice echoed now through the dusk—*you could just disappear?*

Jake.

Being back here made his loss all the more real.

Up ahead, a streetlamp caught the glint of the hood ornament on the maroon car ahead. A silver *B* tilted forward as if poised for flight, a wing on either side. The vehicle's body swept back in perfect, undulating proportions, all in that deep, glowing maroon.

Amie whistled. "Dear God. Who in this cove can afford a Bentley? *Somebody* came out of the war with some pocket change."

But the Bentley only rolled forward a scant few more feet. Then stopped. Directly on top of the tracks.

Its broad headlamps flicked off, even as the train sounded its horn again. Louder this time. Closer.

With growing horror, Amie watched the driver—the brim of the man's fedora just visible—tilt his head back. Not like someone desperately trying to wrench a car out of a stuck gear. Not like someone preparing to leap from a stalled vehicle.

But, rather, like someone waiting. Stoically. Shoulders hunched up. Braced.

Amie felt her lungs contract in panic.

Good God, the man is braced for impact.

Surely he wouldn't knowingly . . .

From behind a line of white-balconied inns, a flash of steel. The train approaching. At top speed. Its whistle sounded again, tracks vibrating, its long, sleek body rushing toward them.

It was going to flatten the Bentley and its driver.

Her heart was hammering in her ears.

"Move," she murmured aloud. "Dear God—*move!*"

The train's brakes shrieked as its engineer must've caught sight of the car—but too late. Much too late to stop.

And still the car did not budge. The silhouette of the man sat still as death.

Move . . . Move . . . Move!

Gripping the steering wheel with her left hand, she lunged with her right for her dog's collar. Her foot stomped the accelerator flat to the floor. The roadster hesitated, tires spitting wet leaves.

But only for an instant. Now, its tires finding asphalt, it shot forward. Straight for the rear of the Bentley.

Amie felt her own shoulders hunch to her ears as the roadster's engine and the train's screaming brakes and thundering wheels all roared in her head.

Straining, Amie kept the accelerator pressed flat to the floor.

As she herself braced for impact.

Chapter 2

Slowly, painfully, Amie raised her head from the steering wheel. From the nose of her Aston Martin came steam rising to meet a gathering fog. Or was it smoke from the engine? And, dear God, how her back hurt.

Her right hand was still gripping Hopkins's collar as the little dog climbed onto her lap and sniffed her neck—assuring himself maybe that she was still alive. She wasn't so sure herself.

Ahead and to the right sat the Bentley, its rear end crumpled where she'd rammed it off the tracks. But still running, still fully intact: a maroon battleship of a luxury car.

Grimacing, she reached to open the door. Her left shoulder and neck would be feeling this for some time to come.

With one foot out of the car, she called to the Bentley's driver, "You okay?"

No answer.

Motionless, the driver slumped over the wheel.

Oh God. What if she'd hurt the man she'd been trying to save?

Amie stumbled out and began limping toward the Bentley. "You okay, mister?" she called again.

Nothing.

Despite the stabbing pain in her shoulders and back, she broke into a run.

But the Bentley jolted into motion. Tires spinning on the damp pavement, the car fishtailed before finding traction.

Amie watched, stunned, as it careened away. "Why, you *bastard*."

Not only had the driver nearly killed himself back there, leaving her no choice but to try to save him, but also he'd surely have derailed the train, taking who knew how many others with him. And now, with not a word of thanks or explanation, he shot ahead, disappearing into the fog.

Chapter 3

Boston, Massachusetts

A sudden crash, a pulverizing crunch of metal on metal, sent Tom Darnay whirling around, one arm flying up to cover his face.

But the sound had not come from nearby. Tom told himself this as he tried to lower his arm. These were no bombs screaming as they dropped from a B-17's belly. No hits to his own engines or wings. No carpets of fire below consuming children on bicycles or elderly men trading thoughts on the weather or women standing in line for their family's bread.

This was probably, in fact, only a construction crane just beyond Boston Common, maybe on Tremont. Just some steel girders of another skyscraper that would dwarf even the Park Street Church steeple.

These types of clangs and crashes, though, so often got amplified in Tom's head—so real at times he could smell the smoke and ash; taste the bitter metal of blood in his mouth; feel his right hand shaking, groping to clutch the lever that would open the plane's lower bay doors so that the laws of gravity, ignition, and combustion could do their merciless work.

Sweat poured now from under his hat as he flipped up the collar of his overcoat—not for fashion this time, or even the cold, but an instinctive protection of the jugular. He turned back toward the statehouse.

Breathe. He had to breathe. All that was over, was finished . . .

A flash of light, blinding, just inches away, sent him reeling. His arm shot back up over his face.

"Now *there*," said a voice, raspy and pleased with itself, "is a hell of a picture."

Forcing his arm down, Tom looked up into what wasn't a shattered B-17 windshield but a face. A reporter stood there smirking, holding his camera and its big silver saucer of flash across his chest like armor.

Tom cursed under his breath. "Why would you jump out on a man?"

"Hell, I think we both know. Your face, Darnay, says *guilt* clear as Trinity's chimes."

Tom recognized the reporter, an old salt from the *Boston Globe*. Tom dealt with his sort constantly but never bothered learning their names. They were all alike, sly and sneering, weaseling their ways in to the Somerset Club, the Algonquin Club, the Union Boat Club, to the back cigar-stub-strewn rooms of the Massachusetts State House: everywhere they didn't belong.

Tom loathed the whole pack of them, part kingmakers but mostly just spies. These days, he couldn't afford to be photographed, ever. The chrome flash just now and the camera attached by a cord might just have scorched a negative onto its film that would look like something it wasn't—something *he* wasn't.

"I'm insisting you not use that picture." Tom held his fists close to his thighs inside his pockets. Still, he could feel their tremor. "Whatever expression you caught is not what it seems. Let's be honest: you have no real story to go with it."

"But I'll damn well get it. You know why? 'Cause I despise—get that?—*despise* your boss and how he runs that empire of his."

Not more than I do myself, Tom thought. But he clenched his jaw so the words couldn't wedge their way out.

The reporter glanced down at the heavy square of his camera as if he could see the film developing inside its accordion-pleated body. "I'm sayin' two columns at least for this pic. Above the fold. It's got your basic juxtaposition of your dark and your light, your evil and your proverbial good."

"You have no idea what the hell you're talking about."

The reporter snorted. "You and that movie-star mug of yours don't fool me one bit. There's lies buried all around you and Fossick. Lies and who knows what else."

Tom made his face hard and did not blink.

"What I got here says plenty for now." The reporter ran his hand across an imaginary page in front of Tom's face. "I could lay it out right now myself, tomorrow's *Globe*: underneath the two-column pic, the cutline'll say—without actually saying, of course, until it's hard facts— that Tom Darnay, minder for the Beacon Hill–based tycoon Fossick, teeters on the verge now of confessing how the corporation screws over its workers and everything Fossick Enterprises touches."

Clenching his fists inside his coat pockets, Tom stiffened his whole body so the shake of his hands might not show. A picture like this that could expose who he was could not be allowed. *"You cannot,"* he said, and heard the steel edge of his own voice, "print this."

"Yeah? Is it you gonna stop me, Hollywood?"

Tom's right hand flew out from the pocket. Still in its fist, it hooked left toward the reporter's face.

Ducking the blow, the reporter tottered backward as if he'd been struck.

Then, recovering, he laughed. Actually laughed.

Just what the weasel wanted, Tom realized too late. Baiting him into doing something, saying something, that would be the story's lead.

Stupid. How stupid to let himself lose control just because of some flashbacks, the past crashing in with that commotion nearby. There'd been a time when he'd never have taken a swing at a stranger. There'd been a time . . .

"You know, Darnay, I've enjoyed our little chat. Look forward to doing it again someday soon. Meanwhile, you give my regards to your family. Oh, crap, that's right. You got no family. Reason why you left Canada, right? That and the war."

The words landed where they were meant to, deep in Tom's gut. Tom tried to breathe, to focus on the gold dome of the statehouse glinting in the last of the evening light.

From the corner of Beacon Street came the laughter of girls in matching plaid skirts and black-strapped Mary Jane shoes, kicking leaves in great arcing sprays of russet and gold. Glancing toward them, Tom scowled. One of the schoolchildren in a pleated, plaid skirt and braids lifted her too-clean, spoiled-rich-kid face to him and returned his glare with a startled look and then a small smile. Brave in the face of his glower.

Tom fell headlong into a memory.

Long brown braids swung around and rested on overall straps, the overalls frayed and threadbare. Had she dressed like that sometimes so he wouldn't feel so self-conscious about the patches at his knees? She was laughing and holding her hand out for him as he wobbled on the log bridge over the stream. Her laughing made the dark circles under her eyes disappear for a moment.

He'd known not to ask if she'd waited up the whole night. Again. For a man who rarely appeared.

It had been snowing that day. The log had been dusted in white, its surface already slippery under their boots. But she'd reached for his hand anyway.

"Come on, now," she'd whispered. "We'll keep each other from falling. Always."

But it hadn't happened like that.

Hadn't happened like that at all.

They had fallen, both of them, and not even fallen together.

Wiping at the sweat under his hat, Tom aimed his steps toward the Park Street Station T stop where the reporter had just disappeared underground toward the subway.

That picture on the *Globe* reporter's camera could not, could *not*, be printed.

Chapter 4

Pelican Cove

"Everybody all right here?" From the driver's side of the olive-green pickup with the wooden slats at the top of its bed, a man called, the truck rolling to a stop.

Before Amie could answer, he emerged: the man who'd carried the Saint Bernard with such ease. In his wool cap and argyle vest and high rubber boots, he looked like he'd just stepped out of the English Cotswolds.

Now with his cap pushed back farther on his head and by the light of his truck's headlamps, the face was familiar, Amie realized. One of those glittering stars in the galaxy of older teenagers on Cape James—the beautiful, the athletic, the ones who required no braces to rearrange teeth. Seth Wakefield had been a sun with his own solar system of girls orbiting him.

Now, though, a scar ran from one temple across his nose to the far side of his mouth, and his gray eyes were guarded.

European or Pacific theater? she wanted to ask.

If his face were an aerial shot during the war, Amie thought, *I'd have had to report the eyes, so changed since the last sighting.*

What she remembered of him, that carefree grin, the swaggering cockiness, all that was gone.

She nodded. "Thank you. My car—long story—but its engine just quit."

He glanced at the Aston Martin, its front badly crumpled, the slits in its canvas roof.

His gaze swung back to her, one eyebrow raised. "Not too big of a surprise it quit, treated like that. Bit of a rough go, looks like."

"You're Seth Wakefield, I think, yes?"

"And you're . . . Sorry. You do look familiar. But I can't place—"

"Amelia—Amie—Stilwell. I was—am—younger than you. I was several years behind you in school."

He blinked. Then the left half of his mouth lifted just slightly. "No kidding? Dr. Stilwell's kid with the pigtails? Definitely couldn't have picked you out of a police lineup now."

Amie raised an eyebrow to match his. "Interesting that was the image you chose for me, a police lineup."

"No offense."

"Only a little taken."

"So Amelia Stilwell Without Pigtails, can I give you a lift since . . . ?" He glanced back at the car. "Never seen one up close, by the way. An Aston Martin."

She could see the question behind his eyes: how she came to be driving such a machine and why it looked just now like a powder-blue battering ram. "It's a long story involving a former colleague, his trust fund, his deep and abiding attachment to gin, and a worse-than-usual hangover that I think he somehow blamed on the car."

She frowned back at the vehicle. "Trying to knock a car off the train tracks back there didn't exactly improve its good looks."

"Car on the tracks?" He extended his hand.

Amie took it, her gaze fixed on his face, on his eyes that bore in on hers.

Beside them, a police cruiser slid next to her Aston Martin. Police Chief Roy, unchanged for the past decade except for a broadened girth, wedged himself out from behind the wheel.

Still shaken from the collision and her futile chase, Amie tried to answer the questions he began lobbing at her: "What was the crash I heard after too many blasts of the train whistle? Where exactly did this other car go? What kind of . . . ?"

She dragged her eyes from Seth. "I'm sorry. You just asked?"

"A *what* kind of a car, did you say?"

"A Bentley. Maroon."

The chief flicked the shiny black brim of his hat back from his face. "Pretty girl like you wouldn't be too likely to know a make of car, now, would you? Nobody here in town owns a Bentley—that's for damn sure. Guessing what you probably—"

Amie stepped forward as she'd learned to do during the war when a general or reconnaissance pilot wasn't listening to one of his photographic interpreters. Crossing her arms, she lowered her voice to a register he might better hear.

"A Bentley. I'm certain. I saw the hood ornament clearly before the approach of the train."

"Uh-huh." The chief wrote something down. "So in the midst of a train bearing down, at dusk, in the fog, no less, a sweet thing like you noticed the hood ornament on a car maybe, what, forty feet away?"

She drew a breath. Held it. Made herself recite in her head what Shibby, the woman who'd essentially raised her, had muttered so often when Amie was growing up: *Blessed are the peacemakers, the damn peacemakers. For God's mercy is a hell of a lot wider toward other folks than most of us want it to be.*

Now she made herself smile—pleasantly even. "My team and I interpreted aerial photos for the Allied Central Interpretation Unit in

Medmenham, England, during the war. I learned to spot camouflaged borders of airfields smaller than a cigarette butt. With all due respect, Chief Roy, I think I can spot a silver *B* on a nice car."

This seemed not to deflate the chief in the least. "So little Amie Stilwell was a WAC, huh? In my son's unit, the boys liked to say the Women's Army Corps gals were mostly all whores. You find that to be true?"

Blessed are the peacemakers, the damn peacemakers.

"Your son's unit had expertise in that field, did they?"

Roy's blue eyes glinted, apparently pleased that she'd fired back.

"You know, Chief, someone tried to take his own life here just a few moments ago. Could very well have derailed the train. Taken dozens of lives."

Jerking his head toward Amie and winking, the chief addressed Seth. "It's what they warned us would happen if we let the dames out of the kitchen too long. They'd try and take charge."

Amie threw up her hands. "I had to *ram my car* into someone else's to knock him off the tracks tonight, Chief. Seems like it might be worth finding out who it was."

"Hell, it shocks me you survived. Wouldn't have figured on it." He pivoted toward the Aston Martin, touching his fingertips to the brim of his cap as if in salute. "You get a look at his face, that driver's? You and your *photographic interpreter* skills."

He was mocking her, clearly. Playfully. But it stung. Mainly because she'd not gotten anything like a good read of the man's face. The hat had been tilted too low, the scarf wrapped too high. There'd been nothing distinctive like a Roman nose or a shrub of facial hair.

The chief nodded at her placatingly. If he'd been standing closer, Amie thought, he might have reached to pat her on the head.

Instead, he asked a half-dozen more questions, jotting notes as she answered.

Now he slid the pad into his jacket's breast pocket with an extra jab, as if to be sure it stayed there. "Well. Guess that'll about do it."

"So you have no idea who it could've been?"

"Not from around here, that's for damn sure. Doc Wakefield here, he can tell you that much."

But Seth's gaze shot from the train tracks to Amie and then quickly away. His jaw tightened with words he appeared determined not to say.

"So . . . ," Amie began. But the set of Seth's jaw said he wasn't ready to talk. She switched course. "So you became a doctor, then?"

The chief barked out a laugh. "To things with four legs and big ole rubbery udders, if you count that."

For his part, Seth Wakefield still didn't meet her eye. "Maybe you oughta try and start your car."

"The engine gave out, but maybe it'll be fine now." Amie trudged back to her driver's-side door and slid in. "It's been through a lot even before it was mine and always . . ."

The engine, though, did not even turn over. Just a single wheezing attempt, and then nothing.

"I might," she called, "need that lift after all. If it's still on offer." She hoisted up Hopkins and tucked him close under her coat. At least the roadster sat well onto the road's shoulder, where it had careened after slamming into the Bentley. "And I guess this is where I'm parking my car." *With no income,* she added to herself, *to fix it.*

Knocking wet leaves from his boots and shouldering aside the Saint Bernard who'd settled in his driver's seat, Seth circled the truck back toward her.

The chief swung the patrol car in a tight U-turn that made his squad car's tires squeal. Amie swiveled toward him from the passenger side of the truck, one foot on the running board and Hopkins under one arm snarling at the Saint Bernard.

"So, Chief, you're going to . . . ?"

But the chief was leaning into a squawk coming from his squad car's radio: "Car One, Car One, problem at the Tipsy Porpoise." Throwing up a gloved hand in a wave and hauling on his steering wheel, he spun away.

Amie watched him go.

Shaking her head, she settled herself into the truck's cab, the rounded lines of its fenders exaggerated, making it look almost soft, like great mounds of moss over the wheels. "Thank you for the ride. I need to get to the Promontory." No point in giving directions to someone who grew up here.

Seth's answer was a turn of his head. A nod. His eyes had gone softer now, kinder. Attention back on the road, he ran a hand over the Saint Bernard's nose, then placed the hand back on the wheel. Seth's head tilted toward Hopkins. "There's a breed I haven't seen."

"Because it's only just now been invented, you know. Some poodle in the stew, I suspect, along with at least one Angora bunny and a mop." She stroked Hopkins's silky ears by way of apology—and as a way of trying not to stare at Seth's face and its scar. "You looked as if you knew who that might've been on the tracks. In the Bentley."

Guiding the truck over the bridge and into the Upper Village, he kept his gaze straight ahead, jaw shifting. Now his eyes darted away as they neared Dock Circle. The truck slowed.

Amie saw on his face that he'd decided to lie.

"Don't believe I do, no."

"It'd be hard to miss—at least, the way I remember this village. Lots of flannel and Ford Model Ts and Model As and Bs. Not so much foreign imports."

He nodded. But offered nothing of what was behind his eyes.

"If the driver wasn't from here," she said, "seems odd he would know what time the Cheshire was due to pass through. And park right then on the tracks."

The truck rolled to a stop, as if his thoughts and the tires had all snagged on something. "Parked . . . you mean deliberately parked on the tracks? As in . . ."

"As in timed exactly to get obliterated." She watched him take a long breath and hold it, along with whatever he knew. He flinched then, as if holding it in were causing him actual pain, but letting it out was not an option.

She could not let him offer nothing at all.

During the war, she'd seen bomber and fighter pilots, sweet boys and good men who were her friends, flying on information she'd pieced together from pictures. Some of those sweet boys and good men had been incinerated overhead. She and the others in photographic intelligence had only gone on by believing there was some sort of higher purpose for all the loss. She'd be damned if she'd sit back now and ignore that someone had wanted to cause carnage here, here in this village where leaves came quietly fluttering down in swirls of soft, faded fall color and lights glowed so peacefully on the water, and where Amie might just be able to start over again. No way could she pretend she didn't see that Seth Wakefield knew something.

"Look, it's okay for me not to know who it was I was trying to help—smashing up my car in the process. But the guy must've been beyond desperate. So whoever might know him might want to help."

What was roiling now in his expression?

"Somehow," Amie said more softly, "you might want to help your friend know there are other ways out than that one. A way that could've killed more people than just him."

She could see Seth's face flushing red, the scar going white.

"Yes," he said at last, his eyes locked on the road ahead as he eased the truck ahead now into the rotary of Dock Circle.

Amie shifted her attention to the shops clustered here at the town's center, their awnings and eaves stippled with frost. "I'd forgotten."

"What's that?"

"How charming it all is. The village."

Most of the shops in the cove's Upper Village gathered around the statue at the center of Dock Circle like children playing "Ring around the Rosie." To the truck's left as Seth pushed the gas again was Myrtle's Lobster Claw, a hut more than a shop and closed in the off-season. To their right sat the general store, F.O. Provisions, followed by a crescent of shops offering what were for Amie all the essentials: clothing, books, and ice cream. On the far side of the circle sat Daggerboard Gifts, with its heavy, door-framing twists of wisteria vine, bare now but sparkling in the mist. And to Daggerboard's left sat a blue clapboard building with a new sign in one window that Amie couldn't read from this angle. Light danced from the lampposts and the entrances of all the shops, as if making up for all those blackout years of the war.

Seth nodded. "Sight for sore eyes when I came home from the service. From . . . over there. You'd think I'd have missed most what the tourists come for in summer."

"The sailboats," Amie suggested. "The hydrangeas. The lobster shacks."

"Yeah. But what I kept seeing was this. Dock Circle in late autumn. Just before the first snow. Like now."

Amie hugged her dog to her as Seth circled a second time so she could view it again. "I see what you mean. Exactly. Although . . ."

"Although?"

She lowered her voice to a whisper. "What I missed most all these years were the sailboats and hydrangeas and lobster shacks."

The left side of his mouth lifted again. The guarded gray eyes glanced toward her—*gratefully, almost,* she thought.

Guiding the truck around the circle, Seth slowed in front of the blue clapboard building at the far side. Half of the building was still glowing inside, its name, *Fáilte*, in neoned green cursive letters.

"Ah," she said. "So that one's new."

"Yep. Best cinnamon rolls on the planet."

Amie rolled down her window a crack. Even now, the air smelled of pine and decaying leaves, of cinnamon and brown sugar. So it hadn't been only memory earlier, what she'd tasted in the air.

"Dear God. I might have to camp out right here."

The other side of the building, though, sat dark, a sign hand-scrawled and taped crookedly on its door. Amie read it aloud.

FOR LEASE.
SEE FLETCH,
DURING BUSINESS HOURS *ONLY* FOR GOD'S SAKE.

"Of course." She laughed. "Of course that would be Fletch."

Her gaze swung away. Squinting at what she could glimpse of the harbor between the shops, its water gone charcoal with ripples of gold, reflecting the electric lights of the shops and the wharves as a thicker darkness was beginning to fall.

She could almost see herself here at thirteen tromping through the snow with her best friend Jake, both of them laughing, both of them running and sliding.

One of them gone now.

She shivered, suddenly cold beneath her blue scarf and gloves and the wool bulk of her sweater.

As the Saint Bernard rested his big head on Seth's shoulder, his eyes dropped to inspect the little feather duster of a dog on Amie's lap—apparently hardly worth the Saint Bernard's notice. The veterinarian swung his truck out of the circle and onto Ocean Avenue toward the inn.

"Some other day maybe," he said, "you could tell me about what you did during the war." He glanced toward her again. "Maybe also whether you're coming back now for a visit or coming back home."

She met his eye. Paused for a moment. So much she could say about why she'd come back, about all she'd left behind. In Medmenham, England, and in D.C.

"Good question. One I need to figure out."

The silence rolled forward with them.

The only other person out on this evening was a woman walking alone. Not pausing to look for cars, she stepped into the street. A belted mauve coat flapped in a full skirt below her knees, her feet covered in dainty mauve boots that buttoned up one side to the ankle. A wide-brimmed mauve hat mostly obscured her face. The woman was more fashionable than Amie recalled most of the villagers being—although maybe that had changed after the war.

On the right side of Ocean Avenue sprawled the harbor. On its left were the Upper Village's share of sea captains' mansions with their widow's walks and steep gables. Amie turned her head away from the largest of these, but not before she'd seen that the Captain Smollett house sat entirely shuttered and dark, withdrawn—just as it had always felt inside back when she had lived there.

Up ahead on the right, visible even through a grainy dusk, three stories of stone and white clapboard gleamed from a finger of land where the Pelican River met the sea. Beside the road sat a giant brass anchor, the inn's name rising beside it in tall, windswept brass letters:

THE PROMONTORY INN

And in smaller letters:

ESTABLISHED 1798
OWNER, DESMOND FOSSICK

Amie frowned. *Fossick.* He'd grown up farther north on the cape, not technically in this village. But he'd plastered his fingerprints all over New England and, she'd read, even beyond that now.

Seth had slid out and was walking around to open her door.

Clutching Hopkins in her left arm and opening the passenger door with her right, Amie waved him back. "You've been so helpful. Thank you."

He stopped. Stuffed his hands in his jacket pockets. "I wonder . . ."

"Yes?"

"I wonder if maybe our paths'll cross again."

There was a flatness to his expression, as if life had taught him to tamp down emotion until it was perfectly safe. If only she could read a face as well as she'd learned to find arsenals and V-2 rocket launchers in a grainy black-and-white landscape.

"In this village, I expect so. Everyone knowing everyone here." She gazed up Ocean Avenue into the darkness where the woman in the mauve hat must still be walking away. Amie turned back to find Seth watching her.

For all his size and muscle, there was something strikingly gentle about him overall. None of the swagger and smirk she remembered from him when he'd been part of the pantheon of sports gods in high school. For all the violence the scar on his face seemed to suggest, the rest of his large frame seemed to have settled now back into quiet.

"But maybe more to your point, Dr. Wakefield, I'd like to hear you answer the same—if you'd like. What you did during the war."

He waited, as if giving her time to study his scar. As if wanting her to read something there—some sorrow, maybe, that he'd rather not speak.

"You're staying here?" he asked at last.

"No. Just meeting a friend."

"Could I reach you at the Captain Smollett house, then? Been shut up for a while, but I guess . . ." He stopped there, seeming to gather from her expression that he'd said something wrong. "Guess your father's not much here in town."

"No. He never was."

The Captain Smollett house.

Everyone here called the captains' homes by the names of the seafaring men who'd built them, no matter how many generations of other families had lived in them. But especially in her father's case, that was fair, his having bought the place for its beauty, like art to be owned and admired. Not lived in or loved.

It served as an investment, and also a place to house his daughter well away from his own world in Boston.

"Actually, you could reach me at the Orchard."

He nodded. "Shibby Travis's place."

"That's right. For the next little bit, at least." She lifted a hand to shake his, but adjusted her scarf instead. "Thank you again for the lift." She paused, watching his face, feeling the warmth emanate from his body. "And I do look forward to hearing about you. Where you've been. What you've done."

European or Pacific theater.

What you've suffered yourself. What you had to watch other people endure.

"Trading war stories," he said. "Literally."

For a moment, Seth stood there, his eyes still on her. His face was a map in itself, but one she had no idea how to interpret. She took a single step closer, then two, not so much a decision as being drawn toward him.

But their silence was broken by a commotion at the inn's far corner. Lifting the free hand not holding Hopkins, Amie stepped back, waved goodbye, and turned to the inn.

She could almost feel Shibby's hug. Almost hear the words *Welcome home, sugar* that Shibby would whisper, throwing open her arms as she had for every lost kid who'd stumbled into her farmhouse over the years and patting Amie's cheeks as if she were a small child. Which, even when you're twenty-seven, is sometimes more than okay.

Nearing the front entrance, Amie slowed, the oak of the inn's double doors polished to a startling shine. A round window was framed in brass on each door like two portholes. Through a large arched window just before the entrance, Amie could see the sprawling great room, the beamed ceiling, the upholstered chairs with maritime prints.

Through the same span of window, Amie spotted the life-size portrait of the owner himself hanging on a near wall of the room, a roaring fire close by in the hearth. Even from this distance and through slightly rippled antique glass, Desmond Fossick looked belligerent—almost gleefully so.

The kind of man, Amie thought, *who'd throw a punch just to see what it broke.*

The lobsterman's son who'd grown into a titan of business, no doubt he'd purchased this inn as a souvenir of his past, a way to gloat.

To her left, just behind a broad stone pillar, a man she couldn't see was raising his voice to rasp just over a whisper.

"Just remember the kind of loyalty I require."

Shifting Hopkins to her other arm, Amie eased back well into the shadow of the pillar before she could be seen. Hopkins growled low.

Two figures walked in the shadows at the far end of the flagstone entrance, swept clean of leaves. In the narrow shaft of light from the window nearest them, Amie could make out little about them, their heads and anything below the waist unlit, but she could see they both wore navy blazers, a gold anchor over the pocket.

The figures appeared about the same height, but the first was powerfully built and moving in jerks. Now as he whipped to his right and his face caught the lights, Amie gasped.

"As always, I expect your discretion," Desmond Fossick was saying, fairly spitting the words. "I'll be needing the room I always use when entertaining a guest."

There was something oddly magnetic about the man, Amie had to admit. Something raw and elemental about him. You found yourself watching him, no matter how hard you tried to look away.

The second figure's voice came low, unintelligible, but it might have been a woman's.

Then Fossick's again: "Of course it's complicated. Do you think I *relish* dealing with her again? She's a simpering fool. A whining, blackmailing fool."

"*Blackmailing*, Mr. Fossick?"

But rather than answer, Fossick jerked forward, the second figure pausing a moment as he disappeared around the inn's far corner. Amie watched as it straightened, the shoulders of its navy blazer thrown back. Then, as if coming to a decision, the second figure followed, a flurry of taps like a woman's high heels on the stone.

Chapter 5

Boston

Tom knew all it would take was a feigned stumble, nothing but that, and the reporter would be dead, his damning pictures gone with him.

Only inches in front of Tom in the Park Street Station underground, the reporter stood looking around—warily, as if he sensed danger. But the idiot didn't look directly behind him where the danger stood tensed and ready.

Tom moved closer still. He could smell the guy's cigarettes, something with a cloying menthol. Cheap aftershave and garlic clung to him, too. Even here in the cold of the subway in autumn, the *Globe* reporter was sweating.

The concrete vibrated under Tom's feet, but he would not, he would *not*, let himself picture the floor of his B-17. Sweat beading across his forehead, Tom reached inside his coat and, ducking his head into the Burberry scarf, took a swig from the small black flask he always carried these days. Just one swig. Really just a touch to the lips, hardly more. But it would help the vibrating concrete beneath not become the cockpit he saw in the nightmares that woke him, made him cry out, in the wee hours.

The wind from the tunnel whipped at his hat as an outbound train approached. A voice from his past spoke in his head louder now, nearly a shout.

My boy, it said, *my dear, sweet boy. Don't let fear guide what you are. Fear can strangle out the person you ought to become, leave only a corpse of a soul. I should know.*

But too much was at risk.

The crowd pushed forward toward the train, closing around Tom and shoving the reporter up past the red caution line on the floor. The hands Tom had just removed from his pockets, palms just two inches from touching the reporter's back, were nearly forced to make contact too early by the press of the crowd.

The irony of it. The crowd's pushing Tom to shove the reporter in front of the oncoming train even before Tom made his own move.

Elbows and shoves from the crowd. The voice in Tom's head at a roar.

The train screeched, blasting out from a curve. Almost here.

This isn't, dear boy, who you are. Fear only . . .

Tom gave his head a sharp shake, as if he could jerk the voice loose from inside.

There, just inches away, stood the threat to the life Tom had so carefully built. There. Already well past the red warning line. Already almost over the lip of the concrete and down onto the tracks.

Now was the instant Tom had to act.

The crowd surged forward again. Suddenly, the reporter was off-balance, stumbling forward.

Tom's hand shot out.

Chapter 6

Pelican Cove

Standing just inside the inn's front doors, Amie let herself be wrapped in a hug, Shibby's thin arms tight—fierce, even—around Amie's neck. The wrinkles of Shibby's sixty-something-year-old, well-weathered face deepening, she pulled back, hands on Amie's shoulders, and beamed.

Framed by salt-and-pepper curls now, untamed as always, her face somehow looked almost younger with wrinkles—or more joyful, maybe it was, as if laughter had etched itself deep into each line.

Shibby paused to slide a brown wool coat—the same shapeless one she'd had for years, Amie saw—over the black dress of her maid's uniform. Glancing down to see she'd misaligned the buttons, she shrugged and spoke over her shoulder as she walked ahead. "Hon, I got enough questions for you to keep us at dinner three days. Did I say it was good to have you home, Amie, sugar?"

Amie laughed, catching up. "Three times at least. And I've loved every one."

Shibby had rarely spoken warmly of her childhood in Texas, but something of Texas had left its mark in her big, open-armed welcomes, nearly knocking a person down with the sheer force of her gladness.

This must be, Amie thought, *what having a real parent feels like. Ridiculous, almost, in its pouring out. Crazy. Unfettered. Ferocious. If there's a divine force in this ugly world, that must be what God is like, too.*

Shibby was charging now toward the village restaurant they'd agreed on—an easy agreement since it was the only one open at night once the tourists left. "I swear this flight of steps up to the Tipsy Porpoise gets longer every year. Which is real strange, me getting stronger and more seductive each day." Shibby winked from under her brown knit cap, a monstrosity she'd knitted herself, the pompon at its end like an explosion of leftover yarn.

She'd knitted Amie's blue scarf and hat and gloves, too, years ago. Scores of stitches were dropped and holes were bunched over with other nearly blue rows of more stitches. But even at sixteen, Amie had cherished these above all the fancy cashmere and alpaca Filene's and Jordan Marsh hats and gloves that Dr. Stilwell's assistants in Boston had been paid to buy for her.

At the top of the stairs just outside the door of the Tipsy Porpoise, a waitress was leaning on the railing for a smoke. Her hand sweeping gracefully from her mouth out beyond her shoulder, the smoke hung like white bunting there in the air before dissipating. Her name, *Kalia*, was stitched in black over the left side of a pearl-gray uniform, and she'd looped a white, gauzy scarf once at her throat like a statement—perhaps that she was a person not to be defined by a uniform.

A hundred shades of black and white just in this one frame. Amie itched for her camera. Ansel Adams couldn't have asked for a better shot.

The waitress was already turning when Shibby enveloped her in a hug.

"Amelia Stilwell, meet one of the newcomers to our fair village, Miss Kalia Clarke."

"Amelia Stilwell," the waitress said, lowering her cigarette and smiling, her tongue light, tap-dancing almost on Amie's name. "*Wah gwaan?* What's going on?"

Amie shook her hand. "You're not from here."

"It was only the accent of the islands that gave me away, was it?" Kalia Clarke's laugh came easy and low, like a warm breeze wafting through the cold. "Otherwise, you'd never in days or extra days have picked a Jamaican out of a crowd of Mainers, no?"

Returning the smile, Amie pulled her own scarf closer around her neck. "This isn't the climate I'd have guessed would be a destination for Jamaicans."

"Brought here by your very government in '42 to pick fruit in upstate New York when most of the farm workers had gone off to war. Then I welded ships in Charlestown Navy Yard—you know it? Then"— she swept the hand with the cigarette toward the harbor—"after the war, I came here. I'm an odd bird to be from Jamaica, it's true. But I like my coasts rocky, I do."

"And your seawater cold to the point of lethal?"

The laugh again. "As I don't swim, that's no matter. Our friend Shibby here has told me so much of you. I welcome you home."

"We've had a few changes here since the war," Shibby was saying. "Meeting Kalia, just that, is worth driving up from D.C. on wet roads."

The waitress opened the door of the Tipsy Porpoise wide. Warmth flowed out, and also music. Billie Holiday was crooning "All of Me" from a jukebox just inside the entrance.

Hurrying out of the cold, Amie paused near the jukebox and pointed at the wall to a framed article, "The Orchardist of Pelican Cove," from an issue of *Yankee* magazine several summers ago. "Look at you, the famous Shibboleth Travis. I'm so glad at least someone's publicizing this village's one claim to fame."

Shibby waved this away. "It was a puff piece of journalism, only because—"

"Because one of your foster kids is an editor at *Yankee* now. Yeah, I know you say that. But the truth is you're extraordinary, what you've done at the Orchard. Even if it annoys you to hear people say it."

"All I did was leave the door open and see who tromped in. Lordy, all you kids all those years. Like putting socks on a rooster."

Laughing, Amie caught up to where Kalia had paused to wait for them. As they passed a small pine bench next to a table of pitchers, the waitress called out to a small figure curled up at one end. "*Wah gwaan*, little man? How are you now?"

She lowered her voice as she tilted her head back toward them. "That small fellow there, he's been sitting on the same spot for too long. Won't speak a word to me, poor little thing. I rang the police station, me not knowing if that was right even, and the chief, he came by a few minutes back. But that sweet child wouldn't talk to him either, no. It's like he's been told he better sit tight to wait for somebody and not say a thing. The chief, he went off looking for who it is ought to be here for that poor child."

That was all it took for Shibby to peel away, walk to the boy, and kneel down. The little boy wore a bow tie, barely visible beneath his head ducked so low. His dark blond hair appeared nicely cut and recently washed. His coat and Bean boots both appeared new.

Whatever Shibby said to the boy, he didn't even look up. Just pulled his knees closer to his chest as he huddled there on the bench.

When Shibby returned, Amie squeezed her arm. "Never seen you fail to charm a child. He must be made of wood and not a real boy."

Shibby turned to Kalia, who'd stopped to gather two menus, on their covers a blue porpoise balancing a frothy pint on one fin. "Let us know, please, if he's still sitting there much longer with nobody coming to collect him. A night this cold's made only for creatures with blubber or fur."

"He's awful cute in that bow tie, those little boots. Got some *broughtupsy*, I'd say. Raised with some money. Surely someone just told him to wait there a small moment, yes?"

Kalia showed them to what Amie remembered as Shibby's favorite table—the few times Shibby ate out in a given year. This one, large and round and thickly lacquered with nautical varnish, hung out over the harbor, the windows nearly to the floor and the water directly below as if the table were launching itself recklessly, joyfully, into open air.

A little like Shibby herself, Amie thought fondly.

"Lordy, the village," Shibby was saying as they took their seats, "it may seem lots the same since last time you visited—the shops and all. The people, though . . ."

"Lots of new faces?"

"Some. Then, too, there are the ones come back from the war looking, or being, different."

They both paused. For the sake of the ones who'd come back so different. And the ones who'd not come back at all.

"I still think," Shibby said, a catch in her voice, "and I know you don't agree, but I still think our Jake'll come home."

"Shibby." Amie kept her voice calm, though her own grief made her want to reach over the table and shake sense into her old friend. "It's been *five years* since the war's end. Nine since you got the letter saying he'd run off and enlisted."

"I've called and written every government office, every *every*where anyone's suggested to me. Been hard to get answers, 'specially with me not being his actual mother and—"

Amie reached out her hand and covered Shibby's. "You *were,* though. You were the woman who raised him. You have every right to know what happened to him. How he died. And where."

"You know I'm not convinced he died."

"Shibby." Amie's voice sounded now like the mother, comforting her older friend as she might a child. "I know you've said that before. But there are so many boys unaccounted for—who never came home. Eighty thousand almost, last time I heard Mr. Murrow announce it. So many bodies never recovered. I know it's awful not to have a date and place. But if he'd somehow survived, we both know he'd have contacted you."

"He might not have . . ."

"You have to hear me. His death was not your fault."

Shibby's eyes welled. Shibby—a woman, Amie recalled, who never cried.

"He might not have come back . . . because I told him not to."

Amie stared.

But Shibby had no chance to go on. Kalia appeared at their table again, bringing fresh baked bread with honey butter and blueberry jam—homemade, Amie recalled, by the owner of Daggerboard Gifts in Dock Circle.

Kalia plucked a notepad from her apron pocket and then the pencil from behind her ear. The sleeves of her gray dress she'd rolled up to her elbows. Amie's eyes landed on Kalia's right arm.

Amie had meant to pursue what Shibby meant, but Shibby herself looked relieved for the interruption. So Amie let her attention swing to their waitress's arm. "Tattoos. Now there's something you don't see every day in Pelican Cove. Good for you."

The waitress shrugged. "Serves me right for hanging out with sailors on leave—*rampin'*, you know—me playing too long in the Charlestown Navy Yard."

Sighing, she held up the underside of her arm where a Celtic cross had been inked above a thistle and shamrock, and above that, the words *You Must Remember This* in an arc. "The boy I was so crazy in love with that night was Scotch Irish, from the South End, by way of Dublin. We'd just seen *Casablanca* at the Colonial on Boylston Street, and I was also in love with Paul Henreid, not so much Humphrey Bogart."

Shibby's brow furrowed. "The Southie boy? Did he stay with you?"

"The maternal instinct never rests," Amie said, chuckling. "If that soldier did you wrong, Kalia, she'll track him down and castrate him before bedtime, followed by a prayer for his soul."

Kalia sighed. "Honestly, I think it was the hot toddies I adored, not so much my Scotch Irish Teddy, you know? For a girl with *You Must Remember This* on her arm, I'm fuzzy now on his face. Also his last name. Every little thing, I'm sorry to say."

Glancing around the pub, Kalia fixed her gaze on a table of younger lobstermen. "Let me check on those boys and I'll be back. *Mi soon come,* as we say back home."

Shibby had regained her composure, the stiffness of her spine suggesting she didn't want to revisit where they'd been a minute ago. Speaking of Jake had wedged open an old broken place in her, the ragged shards that Amie had rarely glimpsed.

Now Shibby was simply matter-of-fact. "I don't believe our Jake's dead. But I've no wish to argue with you."

Shibby's calm, Quaker insistence on peace could be maddening. Especially when her face said, *No matter how wrong you might be.*

Also, she had a habit of lapsing into her old Texas drawl when she thought she was right and you weren't. She'd buoy you up in that drawl's easy current and float a subject away before you could stop to argue.

"In summer, hon, new folks have been flooding in with the resorts back open again, the sailing, the gardens. By now, course, the last of the summer people are gone, but you see how the village is: more picture-postcard than ever. A good town and a good harbor all the year round."

"Good harbor," Amie murmured, suddenly struck by a thought—or several.

"What's that, sugar?"

"Nothing. Just . . . thinking."

Trying to focus back on what Shibby was saying, Amie wriggled off her coat.

"Sugar, you're thinner than a dried-up fence post underneath all those layers."

"Nothing a few trips to that new bakery on Dock Circle won't fix."

"Wait till you meet the owner. Can't be even as old as you. I say bully for him. Real sweet fella." Shibby shook her head. "But fragile as a calf newborn in a freeze."

"I swear, Shibby, you still talk like a Texas ranch hand half the time. The other half you sound like Saint Francis. And the third half—"

"I do like a world with three halves."

"Also like a ranch hand."

"Just trying to keep all the damn saddles oiled," said Shibby.

Kalia spun toward them, a platter hoisted high in one hand. Then, without their having ordered, she set down two steaming bowls. "You didn't order these. But, truly now, if you're not having the seafood chowder on a fall night in the cove, there's not much point in living, no?"

"I'd say you're right." Amie bent over the steam and breathed in: the cream fresh and thick from a farm just up the road, the clams and lobster off this very shore. "Thanks, Kalia. Best chowder on earth."

"Ah, but the pleasure of the thing is all mine."

Blowing the waitress a kiss as she spun back toward the kitchen, Shibby leaned forward. "Tonight, sugar, I want to know, really know, about your life. About what's happened that's brought you back home. In addition to my own loud, obnoxiously fervent prayers."

Amie crumbled crackers into her chowder. "I'll get to all that, the whole ugly story. First, though, I have to check: You keep changing the subject every time I ask who in this village might own the Bentley. Which tells me you might know."

Shibby shook her head. "I was cogitating on it, you're right. Wish I had a guess for you, even one that's more wild than guess." Shibby patted Amie's hand. "I'm just so glad you're okay. In the process of trying to save someone else, you very well could've been killed. Crazy as a bullbat, your ramming him off the tracks."

"You can't tell me you of all people, you in all your Quakerish mercy and light, would've sat there and just watched someone take his own life. You've saved more lives than I can count." Amie waited until her friend looked up. "Including mine."

Shibby poked at great chunks of lobster floating amid the butter and cream. "Cost some lives, too," she murmured.

"What's that supposed to mean? You're the village saint—if saints can be from Texas. Which, I realize, is unlikely. Still: the village saint."

"Saints." Shibby waved the word away like a horsefly. "Nothing but sinners more covered in horse crap than others but don't mind it showing so much."

She propped her elbows on the lacquered table and popped her chin onto her fists. "Now. Catch me up with your life. Who's done you wrong and why? So this old Quaker can start plotting a nonviolent but truly potent revenge against anybody who hurt you."

Kalia appeared, pencil poised above a notepad. "I show up for your order and the first thing I hear is *revenge*? I'm hoping now you don't ask me to leave. Just when the spice gets stirred up in the sausage."

"No need to leave." Amie grinned, shaking her head, then turned to Shibby. "Might as well get the news over with. That dinner at the Occidental, the one I thought was going to be the announcement of my getting a promotion? They announced a newly hired GI would be getting my job. With me sitting there watching and meant to be thrilled. *Because*, the colonel said"—she made quotes with her fingers—"*we all understand that no woman should keep a job from a man with a family to feed.*"

"But you have more experience. The war plus nearly five years after that."

"But I didn't have the foresight to be a GI instead of a WAC. All those years the colonel and I worked together, and that was his goodbye. He announced it at the Occidental dinner, our whole department there, so I couldn't stab him with a steak knife."

Shibby shook her head. "I always did think that man was more hat than cattle. Kalia, we're gonna need to skip straight from the chowder to the two biggest slices of blueberry pie you got back there, the size of slice that heals up a heart. You know, hon, there *is* such a size."

Kalia nodded earnestly before leaving. "I know just the size we'll be needing now."

"It's just that I felt so stupid. So blindsided. *Since you don't have a family to feed,* they said. They were *certain*, they said, that I would join them in wanting to show thanks to our boys who served their country. Which is all well and good, but were any of them giving up *their* jobs to say thanks?"

"Oh, hon. I'm so sorry. What business do they have teaching you how to analyze photos of enemy territory fourteen hours a day, bombs dropping like rain, but then once you're back home and safe, throw you out like cow's milk set out in the sun?"

"A lovely image. And just what I've always aspired to."

Shibby's hand settled over her heart. "You're my dear child. Always."

It was, Amie knew, what Shibby would've said to any of the foster kids who'd grown up and launched out into the world from the old farmhouse, the ones placed there by the state and the ones, like Amie, just needing someone who cared. Shibby's face, and her tone—all of her—somehow invested those words with a warmth that radiated across the whole room, baked down into that worthlessness sunk deep in your bones.

Amie could have sat there for longer, just basking in the moment. But her old instincts for searching were gnawing at her. "So enough about my life imploding."

"Not your *life*, sugar. Your life is so much more than a bunch of old knock-kneed geldings kicking you in the teeth."

"Okay. Not my life. Just my means of making a living, my friendships, my location, my . . ."

Kalia arrived with two slices of warm blueberry pie, the crust crumbling away in crisp golden-brown flakes, the berries big as shooter marbles—and heaped with hillocks of vanilla ice cream the Tipsy Porpoise was famous for hand-churning itself. Each slice was easily a quarter of the whole pie and the berries, Amie knew, grown in a field in the Lower Village just down the road past Pelican School.

"*This,*" Amie burbled through a mounded bite of blueberry. "Okay, *this* makes all the world good again."

Shibby raised her own mounded spoon in a kind of toast. "To a richer, fuller life—in every way."

Taking another bite, they looked at each other now, both dazed for a moment by the burst of the berries' flavor, sweet and sour both, against the smooth comfort of the vanilla ice cream. Amie felt suddenly close to tears—and laughed at her own response. "Honestly, just for that bite full, I was actually happy to have lost a job I loved and my income."

Shibby laughed with her. "Priorities, sugar. You'd clearly gotten yours way out of whack if you'd forgotten the Tipsy Porpoise blueberry pie."

Amie waited until they'd both swallowed again. "And you're *certain,* Shibby, you can't think of anyone who might own the Bentley?"

Shibby's gaze swung away. "Now *there's* a tight bend in the trail."

"I just keep thinking about it. That kind of desperate, despairing impulse seems like it's often that: impulse. Not like something a person would drive to another far-off town to do. And to pick Pelican Cove, of all places . . ."

"Mm-hmm."

"Tell me what you're thinking. Please."

Shibby was taking far longer to consume her next spoonful of pie than it required.

"You have a suspicion, at least."

"Nope, not really. No more'n a grackle of a thought flapping past in my head."

"Desmond Fossick's the obvious answer, right? The only person who comes around here off-season and rich enough to own that sort of automobile."

"Except that man never drives himself anywhere. Ever. Flies in here from Lord only knows where, including Boston—like there's any good reason to fly from just there to here except showing off, and liking to throw money out windows. One of those black cars the inn keeps a fleet of for guests always picks him up, carts him around every time."

"So it couldn't have been Fossick?"

"Not from where I'm sitting."

"Surely whoever it is needs help. Urgently."

"Sounds like it, sure enough. I'm baffled as you. Just not near as banged up."

"So." Amie sighed, then plunged a spoon back into the pie with gusto. "I can't believe you're down to not one single kid at the Orchard."

"With my getting older, and the roof and plumbing along with me, then needing to get a job that, to be honest, brought in a bit more than I had . . ."

"If money's tight, Shibby—"

Shibby waved this away. "Nothing a little hard work can't fix. Anyhow, what with my new employment adventure"—she plucked at the collar of her maid's uniform—"it seemed best not to have a houseful of little ones anymore." Shibby looked down at both arms, as if shocked all over again to find them empty. "Although I'll admit it sure feels odd. Like I'm a largemouth bass who's decided to try living on land, and my tail fin not quite built for walking."

Kalia approached, holding out a thick piece of paper, folded once, a word scrawled on its top. Kalia's eyes had saucered.

"When I went to insist that poor little boy-child on the bench come have some hot cocoa at a table, he still wouldn't speak, not a sound. But he finally stood up."

She thrust the note at Shibby. "It's your name. That child was wearing a note with your name around his sweet, cold little neck. Sweet Jesus."

Paling, Shibby took the note. Read it aloud in a near monotone:

This is Chester, a good and a kind boy, they tell me, though I'd hardly know, God help me.

People say you work wonders with children who need a good home. Please take good care of this boy. It's not his fault.

"Sweet Jesus," Shibby echoed.

For a moment, none of the three of them moved, staring at the note as if its author might rise up from the blurred ink and explain. Then staring at each other.

Stirring, Shibby shook her head as if to clear it of whatever it was she'd been thinking. Now she bolted for the child curled up on the bench just inside the door.

Chapter 7

Amie fought to hold in the tears as little Chester unpacked a tooth-brush from his leather bag, a circle stitched in gold on one side, with gold-stitched ivy running in and out of the circle. Still not speaking, not looking at either of them, he padded to the sink in brown footed pajamas, white moose on them. Hopkins padded after the child. The boy paused to kneel on the black-and-white tile of the farmhouse bathroom to kiss the dog on top of the head.

"Dear God," Amie murmured. "Dumped off with only a note and that little satchel and a Superman lunchbox. Have you heard him say a word yet?"

Shibby shook her head. "Not a one."

"Can you tell if he even *can* speak?"

"Reckon he can. Listen close. He's made some sounds like words to Hopkins. I'd guess someone told him he couldn't talk about how he got dropped off and who did it. Or it's pure shock from whatever happened. I'd calculate both."

Amie stepped toward the bathroom, only this one for all five bedrooms, all those kids growing up here all those years. Now she knelt beside the boy and the dog. "You like this furry little guy?"

Eyeing her, Chester jerked his head yes.

"And do you have—*did* you have . . ." Amie glanced back at Shibby for help. Even asking a simple question was strolling across a minefield. "Have you ever had a dog, Chester? Where you lived before?"

The child's big eyes narrowed a little, as if he were considering the question for tricks. Pressing his lips together, he placed a small forefinger vertically over them.

"Someone asked you not to speak?"

Finger still over his lips, he nodded earnestly.

Shibby touched a hand lightly to his shoulder. "It's okay, sweet boy. You don't have to talk. Not a minute sooner'n you're ready. Hopkins here, he's been at the farmhouse for hours now, and he's not said too much either. But come breakfast, I'm expecting him to speak up if he'd like some bacon. You're welcome to tell me, too."

Chester's eyes widened. But he kept his lips firmly locked.

"Now it's also just fine not to say. Sometimes, I got to admit, I don't cotton to talking over breakfast myself. Just want to sit down and eat me some bacon and slather up a hot biscuit with some good apple butter before I say a durn word. Helps to be brave the whole day, I find, some good apple butter and bacon for breakfast."

Chester inclined his head, considering. He didn't smile, but the barely contained panic that had sparked in his eyes looked a little less likely to burst into flames.

Teeth brushed, he padded back toward the bed and paused. A question in his eyes, he looked up at Shibby.

"Absolutely, this is your own bed, right here. See the airplane posters all over the walls? This here room belonged to another couple of little boys way back when. This room loves little boys, and little boys love it. It's a real safe, friendly place."

As if to confirm the goodness of the room, Hopkins leaped onto the bed. Slipping his footed-pajama legs under the duvet, Chester curled himself around the dog.

"Miss Amie was just telling me that Mr. Hopkins here," Shibby said, tucking the sheets around him, "is about five years old. I'd guess that's about how old you are. That right?"

Twisting only slightly from his tight curl, Chester held up both hands, one with all five fingers raised and the other with one.

Small for his age, Shibby mouthed.

"Well now. Six years old. A wonderful age. My own personal favorite. That'd make you in about, let's see, sixth grade? Twelfth?"

One hand flashed one finger. Then dropped back under the duvet.

"Oh, *first* grade. Of course. What the Joshua tree was I thinking? First. That is one wonderful grade."

Still curled into his ball around the dog, he lifted both hands above the duvet, palms flat against one another.

Shibby knelt down beside him. "I think, sugar, you're telling me you like to pray before bedtime, that it? I like to, too. I just want to make sure I pray the right kind of prayer so you go to sleep feeling loved as can be. Let's see now—"

"Now," echoed a little voice.

Shibby and Amie exchanged glances.

"Right *now* you want to pray?" Amie asked.

A shake of the little head.

"Now," he murmured again into the dog's fur.

Shibby sat on the bed beside him. When he recoiled from her touch on his shoulder, she smoothed Hopkins's fur. "Now," she began softly—almost a question, "I lay me down to sleep."

The child's body, tensed as a coiled spring, relaxed just a little.

"I pray the Lord my soul to keep," Shibby continued as Amie eased down close beside her. "If I should die before I wake, I pray the Lord my soul to take." Shibby tilted her head toward Amie to whisper, "Whoever made up that god-awful grim old prayer for children ought to be hog-tied."

"Tea," came from the depths of the duvet now.

Shibby and Amie looked at each other.

"You'd like some nice hot tea?" Amie asked.

A sharp shake of the head.

Amie tried again. "You like riding the T underground in Boston?"

Another shake of the head.

They tried a number of other suggestions, but the boy only curled in tighter around the dog.

"I'm sorry, hon," Shibby finally said. "We'll figure out the part about *tea* tomorrow, how's that sound? Meanwhile, you and Hopkins here sleep tight. Also . . ."

The boy didn't turn, but his head twitched a little toward the voice.

"I'm god-awful glad you're here, Mister Chester. Can't tell you how happy I am to have you here in this home. *Your* home now if you'd like it to be."

The little boy said nothing, but Amie watched the rise and fall of his body as his breathing steadied—and slowed—at Shibby's words.

"You remember now, I'm right across the hall if you or Hopkins either one need me in the night, hear?"

They could only see the back of his head, but the boy gave one last nod, then buried his face deeper in the duvet and the dog. Hopkins lifted his head and crouched as if he might leap out to join Amie. But she held up the flat of her palm for him to stay. The dog curled back up with the boy.

Shibby eased the door closed as Amie held up the pair of beige corduroy trousers that Chester had shed and neatly arranged before putting on his footed pajamas.

"The pockets had this." Amie lifted two items, the first a folded copy of the years-old *Yankee* magazine article about Shibby and her foster home, the Orchard. They both stared at the visible piece of headline. "Maybe that's how the person who left Chester decided who to trust with him. It's still despicable, leaving a kid all alone like that. But someone at least did research."

Shibby unfolded the article as if she'd never seen it before. "Dear God, to choose where to drop a child . . . over *this*."

Amie held up another item. "Here's the second thing from the pocket."

This next was a black-and-white photograph, a bit blurry and badly creased, as if Chester might have kept it with him in his pocket regularly. The background showed a narrow street tumbling uphill and lined with trees. In the foreground stood the little boy, possibly a year or so earlier, his face a little rounder, cheeks plumper. Beside him stood a slender woman in a belted dress, hair pulled back neatly. Her face was sideways to the camera and shadowed, but she was smiling down at the child. Chester was holding her hand and looking straight at the camera.

"A look of . . . *confidence*," Amie marveled aloud as she and Shibby walked downstairs to the kitchen. "And trust. Nothing like he looks now."

"A child," Shibby agreed, "who's been loved at some point, at least."

"But then dumped off in a way you wouldn't leave a puppy. What kind of mother would do that? Makes no sense at all." Amie held up the picture. "I'd like to study this better. You know, that was the colonel's goodbye gift to me at the Occidental dinner—the stereoscope I used during the war. In his mind, it was probably fair compensation for ending my whole career. But it could come in handy for this. I could also show the picture to some people."

"Except that it's his picture, hon. We can't take something he prizes so much, not when his trust has got all shredded." She pointed to the camera lying in its case in a pile where Amie had unloaded a few of the belongings they'd retrieved from the broken-down Aston Martin. "Didn't you say you sometimes took pictures of pictures and blew up bigger whatever you needed to see?"

Amie kissed Shibby on the side of the head. "You read my mind. You, too, could have been an official air spy for your country." She was just pulling away when Shibby touched a palm to her cheek.

"I'm god-awful glad you're here, Amie. Can't tell you how happy I am to have you here in this home. *Your* home if you'd like it to be."

The words were ones Amie had heard scores of times—for herself, and for all the kids who'd passed under this roof.

But like any good liturgy, the words had not, it turned out, gotten old. Instead, they swelled inside her, filling something she'd forgotten had been painfully hollow before.

≈

Amie heard the *pad, pad, pad* of Chester's footsteps outside Shibby's door. Then the creak of hinges.

Tensed, she waited. A few moments went by with no sound.

Shibby, always awake in a flash at the slightest movement of a child in the night—or the return of a tardy teenager—was not stirring. As if she sensed for some reason it was better for Chester to find her peacefully still and asleep, rather than bolting upright to see what he needed.

Then the soft *pad, pad, pad* again. The creak of the hinges of Shibby's door closing. Then a louder squeal from the hinges of the door to this bedroom that Shibby had assigned Amie, the footsteps growing closer as Chester approached.

Following Shibby's lead, Amie forced herself not to move or even open her eyes. Enough moonlight spilled through the sheers on the windows that Chester would be able to make out her face.

Gently, the little boy bent over her, then lifted a hand close to her face. Amie could feel the warmth of his arm and his hand so close to her cheek and nose.

Still, she didn't move. Didn't speak. Didn't let herself breathe.

A small whimper of alarm came from the boy.

Just as she drew in a breath and was about to turn to comfort him, she heard him exhale in relief. He made his way back to his room.

My breath, she realized.

He'd come here, and he'd gone to Shibby, to be sure they were both still breathing in their sleep.

Dear God. What has this poor child had to face?

Chapter 8

Boston

"Whipple? Tom Darnay here."

Tom leaned back in his chair and waited. The chair was Italian leather, hand tooled, and that should have calmed him, but didn't. Upstairs in Tom's Back Bay townhouse bedroom, a woman was still asleep. It was quite early this Saturday morning, and Tom resented her being there, even though he'd invited her here. Which, he realized, wasn't exactly fair to her. He wasn't so far gone that he didn't know he was being a cad.

Last night he'd swung by the Last Hurrah at the Parker House Hotel for a brandy. There might have also been a Dickens's punch or two in the mix. At any rate, Tom had ended up drunk on self-pity, on top of the brandy and punch, and now he had a woman whose name he couldn't recall upstairs in his bed.

A pause on the other end of the line. Then: "Well. Darnay. Good thing I'm a part of the early-bird staff here at the paper, or you'd never have caught me in." Suspicion sat thick in the other man's tone.

"Pleasure to hear from you. Calling, no doubt, so you and me can meet at the Bell in Hand for a couple of Haffenreffers. Drink to old times in the air corps."

"Yeah, sure. Maybe after a ball game at Fenway next summer sometime."

"Sure, sure, with the Sox about to win the World Series. So, Darnay, you're calling for . . . ? Not to discuss baseball, I'm guessing."

"Some other time, sure. But listen, one of your men accosted me a little while ago on the Common. Thinks he got a keeper of a picture of me."

My boy. My sweet boy. Don't let fear . . .

Tom shut his eyes and tried to shut that voice out of his head. God, what was wrong with a grown man who couldn't get an old voice out of his head? It had haunted him in the subway, gotten louder and louder—finally louder even than the roar of the train.

Tom shouldn't have to be making this call. The accident in the Park Street Station would've been called just that: an accident. At rush hour. One man toppling forward into the ditch of the tracks. These things happened with swarming crowds, too many folks in a hurry. The man probably lived alone in a Hanover Street hovel in the North End and wouldn't be much missed. But no. Tom's hand had shot out.

Not to shove, goddamn it, but to jerk the man back.

A chuckle from the other end of the line. "*My* men, Tom? You forgotten I'm just a lowly writer here, not the editor in chief?"

"Yeah, but you're respected there, Charlie. Ever since you landed that interview with Ted Williams by saying you'd give your right eye for one and then—"

"Pulled out my glass one. Whoever thought an injury would be so damn helpful? So, what is it you need, Tom?"

"Sometimes it's just nice to check in with old pals from our piloting days."

"The Royal Canadian Air Force and the U.S. Army Air Corps back together again, that it?"

"Band of brothers, Charlie. Old pals who'd do anything for each other."

"Yeah, and sometimes it's nice to shoot straight with old pals."

Tom paused. "It's like this. You can't let that picture run."

"You give me too much credit, old sport. I got no power over these reporters, 'specially the ones who've been on the paper forever. Not sure even the page editors do. This guy—I'm guessing I know who you mean—dates back to Paul Revere's ride, I think—probably there to take pictures. Man's got a bloodhound's nose for where to show up with his flash. Also, so what? So your face gets splashed on the front page of the morning, maybe the evening, paper. Who cares? You're still not married, right?"

"I'm flattered that you'd keep up."

"So you get some dames falling all over themselves to meet the guy in the *Globe*. Your look-alike, Cary Grant, is back down to one woman these days, for now, so you get his castoffs. Sounds to me like something a guy like you could work with."

"This reporter of yours thinks he's got a story attached to me and Fossick. He's wrong. Point is, Charlie, I can't have it run. It's that simple. Can I trust you to make certain this guy's camera takes a nice swim in Boston Harbor? For old time's sake?"

"Not that simple, Tom."

"It can't run, I tell you. Period." Tom heard the desperation in his own voice. It wasn't like him to crack with the press. "Look. Charlie. Tell me what I need to do to make sure the picture never comes out of the darkroom."

"You trying to bribe an old air corps pal?"

"Let's not call it a bribe. Just asking what I need to do."

"Yeah, and whose palm you got to grease, right?"

"Look. Charlie."

"No, you look. There's a little thing in this country—I don't have a clue about your Canada and don't care—called the First Amendment."

"I'm familiar with it."

"Yeah? 'Cause it wasn't sounding like it there for a minute, Tommy ole pal."

"*Not*"—Tom bit off the words—"my name."

"Yeah, but it always did get you riled."

"Listen, Charlie, freedom of the press is all well and good—*when* the press is running the facts. But this guy's just digging for a story that's not there."

"Then you got nothing to worry about, sport. Don't know if you noticed, but the *Globe* doesn't tend to run pictures without a story attached."

"Let me put it this way: my picture *cannot* be in the paper."

"You put it that way already. Several times."

His nerves rattled, Tom lit a cigarette, the craving intense. "The *Globe* runs a half-assed accusation against Mr. Fossick tomorrow with my picture attached, and you'll have a lawsuit by afternoon."

Another pause. "Shame we're old pals from our days in the air, Darnay. 'Cause I got to say, I'm loyal almost to a fault, but you've got me thinking now there's a story here worth following up."

Cutting Whipple off with a slam of the receiver, Tom glowered at the phone.

Chapter 9

Pelican Cove

I know he won't say, but he has to belong to someone. Amie mouthed the words across the little boy's head. The early morning squint of sun lit the burnt umbers and deep siennas of the trees behind the child, making his little round face appear even paler, like the unsmiling subject of Renaissance art.

She and Shibby each held one of his hands as they walked in the street—the sidewalk not broad enough for three across. Looped on Chester's arm was Hopkins's leash. The little dog turned back every few yards to check the child's face, and the child bent to touch his nose to the dog's. The progress, even just from the Orchard to Dock Circle, was glacial.

He has to, Amie mouthed again, *belong to someone.* She pictured the woman—surely Chester's mother—in the black-and-white photo who'd looked at her son with such affection.

Shibby adjusted Chester's hat, one of the dozens she'd knitted over the years for the children growing up in her house. Like all the rest, the lines were uneven, one color running out and another beginning in random spots. The stitches purled from tight to loose and back, so that the whole thing seemed held together only by color and hope.

He belongs, Shibby mouthed back, *to God*.

From anyone else, Amie thought, those words would've sounded sanctimonious—sticky and stinking with it. From Shibboleth Travis, though, they were defiant: a warning. Shibby'd staked her flag now in defending this child. All hell could come against her and she would not budge.

"It's okay," Shibby was telling the child, "if you don't feel like talking just yet. Sometimes I don't feel much like talking myself, 'specially on a Saturday morning and, Lordy, lots of the time. All I want you to hear right now is that our whole day, Amie's and mine, is better just having you here."

The child raised his face toward the voice like a late-blooming flower, fragile and all alone, lifting up through the fall leaves toward the sun.

It was just after dawn, the new bakery up ahead the only thing on Dock Circle already open on this Saturday early. In the wash of rose-tinted light from the harbor and the last few minutes' glow of street lanterns, several shopkeepers were just arriving. Almost synchronized, they appeared from the spokes of streets that ended in the circle. One villager stopped to adjust the leash on a dog. Another, holding a brown paper parcel, tromped through leaves toward the bookstore, Better Read, a cottage with black-and-white-striped awnings and, over its front, ivy growing so thickly that it threatened to hide the entrance. Every year, Amie recalled, the bookstore's owner broadened her scope after the tourists left, becoming in the off-season a landlady of stray cats and purveyor of fine wine.

Another villager ambled forward from the direction of the nearly one-hundred-and-fifty-year-old Pelican Congregational Church on the village green. This one called a greeting to the others. But with hats pulled low on foreheads and scarves wrapped to the tips of noses, Amie couldn't make out the faces—only knew them by the shops they were unlocking and lighting up.

"It's a wonder," Amie said, "more crimes don't get committed in New England once the temperature drops. No one would ever be able to identify a face."

"Except that we're all too frugal to own a spare scarf or hat. We'd all get nabbed based on the yarn color." Shibby said this cheerfully. As if even the quirks of her world made her content.

"'Blessed are the owners of only one coat,'" Amie said, quoting Shibby from years ago. "'For they lose no time down the drain of deciding.'"

At that, Shibby glanced down at her own coat, its wool pilled and worn thin. Without looking up, she smiled, as if even its shabbiness was a comfort: an old, familiar friend.

Chester gave a single, small tug to Amie's hand, like a question. She squeezed his back. "Almost there. You warm enough?"

Rather than answer, Chester bent again to let Hopkins lick his cheek.

Maybe it was that: the unspoken language of a child and a dog. Or maybe it was the salt air or the glow of the streetlamps or the steady, reassuring bulk of the sea captains' homes that had stood strong through so many nor'easters and blizzards. Maybe, too, it was the stride of villagers through the morning chill to another day of lighting hearths and switching on bulbs to join the splash of sun now finding its way across the water. Whatever it was, Amie felt her heart lift.

"Good," she said softly. "This will be good."

They were approaching the blue clapboard building that sat on the east side of Dock Circle, the right half of the building the new bakery with the green neon "Fáilte" and the left half with the hand-lettered sign "For Lease" slung up on its door. Beyond its window, smudged and filthy, its wooden platform for showcasing products lay bare, except for crumpled paper and rat droppings.

Amie slowed, rereading the sign. Chester turned to stare with her, then cupped his hands to better see past the window's reflection.

FOR LEASE.
SEE FLETCH,
DURING BUSINESS HOURS *ONLY* FOR GOD'S SAKE.

Leaning in next to the boy, Amie pressed her nose to the paned glass of the door. Squinting through the scrim of dirt, she rubbed a circle clean with the cuff of her coat. Cobwebs and dust coated the floor and the surfaces of the shelving and tables. Litter lay strewn everywhere, including remainders of what looked like past meals, as if the former shop owner had moved his merchandise out, then left with bitterness and Chef Boyardee cans in his wake.

"What do you think, Mister Chester?" Amie asked.

From under his cap and a sheaf of bangs flattened to his head, the child stared up at her. His eyes shot back inside the shop. He seemed to be taking it in, considering, even. Now they returned to meet hers. Beside him, Hopkins stood on his hind legs to peer in through the window.

Shibby's only response was a steepled eyebrow.

"No beatitude for me, Shibs? Here, I'll start it for you. Blessed are they that sweep up after disasters and rats . . ."

"For they shall renew their strength," Shibby offered. "They shall clean and not be weary. They shall scrub and not faint—though this here's looking to me a long stretch past weary and faint."

Approaching the bakery from the far side of the circle marched a man well bundled, a red-and-black plaid hunting cap with flaps pulled over his ears and trotting beside him a golden retriever who, like all goldens, appeared to be smiling, mouth open and nose tilted up toward the happy scents of the day.

Amie remembered the hat, the same one for decades, and the same breed of dog. "Mr. Osgood!" To Shibby and Chester, she said, "You two want to go on inside? Shibby, you can start on your morning coffee."

"No morning coffee for me, sugar. Afternoon only these days. But I'll get you all something."

Releasing Amie's hand, Chester handed over Hopkins's leash, then leaned into Shibby as she led him inside the bakery.

The old man's head had swung up. Now it swung back and forth. "Well now. Amelia Stilwell. Can't be good news, you showing up here."

Bless the man. God only knew how old he must be. The owner of F.O. Provisions, Fletcher Osgood sold everything from brown bread in cans to coffee-flavored brandy for local Mainers. In summer, he sold picnic supplies, sand shovels with pails, and canvas with paints to tourists.

He lifted a hand as his head bobbed. "Ayuh. Heard you'd got in a gaum." That was all: his old Mainer's way of acknowledging she'd seen some trouble lately. He cocked his head as if he found something puzzling. "Jake not with you?"

Amie drew a breath and let the stab of the cold air in her lungs keep her from speaking too soon. "Nope. Jake died sometime in the war. More than five years ago now, remember?"

You wouldn't see him here with me even if he were alive, she nearly added. *Not how things ended with us.* But she gave the old man the closest thing she could to a smile.

Fletcher Osgood, who'd rarely left the village in seventy-odd years, would remember Amie as a scrawny girl in a pricey coat and boots purchased by her father's housekeepers on his credit in downtown Boston's finest department stores. No doubt he remembered that girl as always chattering beside that boy, her best friend, and always having two sloppy braids because none of the housekeepers could be bothered to fix the little girl's hair.

"Heard you'd be coming," Fletch said in response to her smile.

"Shibby must've told you, then. Since I didn't know myself until night before last."

"You here to stay?"

Before she could answer, he answered for her, his words slow and morose, his head swinging back and forth again. "Big city's no place for you now. Maybe all right when you're young and wild. I was once, you know."

The thought of a young, wild Fletcher Osgood made Amie bite down on her lips, a chuckle about to escape. "I'd like to think I'm still not terribly old at twenty-seven."

He jerked his head to include the village. "Time all you young people that served in the war settled down. Saw for yourselves the world wasn't flat and wasn't much good. Reckon you saw plenty enough how folks could massacre strangers."

"Yes." Amie let that hang and then fall between them. Then she added quietly, "And, oddly, risk their lives for strangers, too."

He grunted. Which might, or might not, have been agreement.

"A quick question, Fletch." She stepped closer. "Do you happen to know anyone here in the village—or anyone on the cape—who owns a maroon Bentley?"

Fletch hooked a thumb behind each of the overall straps under his coat. "Nope."

"You're quite sure? It's important."

"Nope."

"Sorry, *no* that you're not sure? Or *no* that you don't know anyone?"

"*Nope*, I don't know anyone that stupid, excepting the rusticators, all them rich folks driving their fancy cars up here to stay all summer 'cause they're wanting the *simple* life." He snorted his disgust. "But all them leave by Labor Day. What'd be the point of buying a set of four wheels only for the hood ornament? Give me a good Model A any day. You take the Wakefield boy, for example. He's come back to town."

"Yes. So I've seen." Amie felt warmth spread ridiculously from her middle at the mention of Seth. She jerked on one end of her scarf, a kind of reprimand to herself. Despite their both growing up here, she barely knew him. And like everyone else, including her, he'd clearly not come back unscathed from the war.

"Got himself a Ford truck that'll still be hauling sick pigs and dogs in a splint long after whatever Bentley you saw's gone to scrap." Fletch poked two fingers at his temple. "People nowadays ought to keep *that* in their fool heads."

He jerked his own head toward the statue at the center of Dock Circle, a granite soldier on a high pillar, its engraving at eye level that read, "Memorial to Our Union Dead." Amie recalled with a smile, though, the story behind it, and the lesson it continued to teach old Mainers like Fletch who passed it each day. The statue had arrived in a Confederate rather than a Union uniform, the sculptor insisting the town had made the mistake in its order so that a replacement would require full payment again. Village leaders refused to pay and instead erected their soldier high so that his enemy garb might be less noticeable. It stood now as a memorial less to the war dead of either side than to unbending Yankee frugality.

Amie nodded as earnestly as she could. "I feel lucky to run into you so soon in the day. I was planning to pop into Provisions later to ask . . . I saw the shop there for lease"—she gestured toward the dark, dirty window—"and wondered if we could discuss—"

"Nope."

"No?" Amie's heart sank.

"Nope."

"No . . . because it's already been leased?"

"Nope, 'cause I won't talk about it before the durn shop's even open. During store hours *only*. Says right there on the sign. Upsets the digestion talking business all hours, anyplace. People nowadays."

"But if I came by once Provisions is open? We could talk?"

"Ayuh." It was more of a grunt of annoyance than friendly assent. But it would do.

Fletcher's eyes scanned the street on both sides of her. "Heard you'd gone and crunched up your car."

"It's still near the tracks, actually, just on the other side of the bridge. I had to leave it. I could use your help with it, assuming you'll let me pay you."

This seemed to anger him, a low growl under the muttering she couldn't fully make out, except for a rumble of *people nowadays, don't,* and *neighbors.* He jerked his head toward Hopkins. "New in town."

"Yes, he was my one good friend in Washington."

"Heard there was a man, too."

"I see Shibby has kept you informed. There was." Amie lifted her chin above the blue scarf. "But he turned out not to be: good, that is, or a friend."

Fletch blinked once. Then gave a single nod as if that settled the thing.

Blessed are the uncurious, Amie thought. *For they shall feel satisfied.*

"Might be a terrible thing, Amelia. This coming back of yours. You and your little white rat." He stabbed a finger toward Hopkins.

Then he and his smiling retriever walked on.

Amie bent to scratch her dog behind his soggy ears. It was true he didn't look his best when wet. "Still," she assured him, " *little white rat* would be harsh."

Through the window, Amie watched Chester reach up for a hot cocoa and stare at the tower of whipped cream. Carefully, he put out a tongue to taste it. Amie held her breath for joy to light up his face.

Instead, the little boy appeared panicked, as if having realized how much he liked the taste of the cream, he was now terrified it might topple off his mug. A tear must've slipped down his cheek because Shibby was kneeling to brush it away.

"Who," Amie whispered, feeling tears well in her own eyes, "do you belong to, Mister Chester?"

Chapter 10

The door of the bakery flew open, a slim figure emerging. He held out a steaming ceramic mug. "Miss Shibby ordered a coffee for you. I'm the owner"—his head jerked back toward the shop—"but clearly not above being ordered around by . . ." He stopped there, as if not sure how to characterize Shibby Travis.

"None of us are above that," Amie assured him.

"She does it in the calmest, kindest way, you aren't even aware you've been ordered around until you're standing outside in the cold shoving coffee at a stranger." Looking flummoxed, he held out the mug again now.

Amie took it. "It's part of the mystery of her. Thank you for this. And for coming out in the cold."

He cocked his head, examining her through the early morning mist.

She stared back at the thin, somber face, dark hair cut short, and sad, dark eyes narrowed on her. Behind him, the cheery green door of the bakery and the bright neon sign made his face appear all the more closed off, withdrawn.

He wore a dove-gray turtleneck above darker gray pleated trousers that had been dutifully pressed, a crease straight down the front of each leg. He surely couldn't have lived here for long if he was still spending that much of his time on trouser creases. His face was young—younger than twenty, she'd guess—and almost delicate. Except for a deep line between his brows.

As if some sort of great worry has knifed itself in there, Amie thought.

"Amie Stilwell," she said, stepping forward, blue-gloved hand out.

His own grip was tentative. Not the bone-crushing grip of most locals here—the legacy of the lobstermen, people said, and of winters that only the strongest and most stubborn survived. This fellow's grip, by contrast, was almost a question.

"Your bakery"—she nodded behind him—"was a butcher's shop when I was a kid."

His eyes scanned her briefly, nothing wolfish in them—just an assessment. Her dungarees were tucked into boots again today and belted at the waist, the same fisherman's sweater tucked in.

"I considered," she offered, "wearing my best Schiaparelli gown and opera gloves, but opted at the last moment for this stunning ensemble." Sweeping a hand from the hand-knitted cap down to the rubber boots, she gave him her brightest smile. A smile that went unreturned like a ball whacked into weeds.

He looked back at her, a long, searching look that appeared to be his trying to make up his mind what he thought of her.

Or maybe, she thought, warming a little to him, *he's searching for what I think of him. One of those delicate souls so desperate for others' approval they first build a wall of defense.*

But she was too cold to stand here outside his door while he settled whatever he needed to settle—about her or himself.

She took in the sign behind him in green neon: "Fáilte."

Then took a running leap at the pronunciation. *"Fayl-tee?"*

"Pronounced *Fahl-chuh*. Part of the Irish saying *Céad míle fáilte*." He said it again slowly, "*Cade mee-yah fahl-chuh*. A hundred thousand welcomes."

"That's . . . some kind of welcome." She chuckled, not meaning to—at the contrast of his stiff, stoical face with the neon glow of the word and its meaning.

He nodded, unsmiling. As if he heard the contradiction himself: his whole body tensed against that name, *Fáilte*. Heard it, but didn't find it amusing.

"So," Amie tried again, "just between you and me, if I were to open a business next door and that business fails and I end up sleeping here on the sidewalk, I wonder if you might toss me out the occasional cinnamon roll. Perhaps a blueberry muffin in season?"

His face did not relax. "What business?"

"Pardon?"

"The business that you might open here. Next door to me. What would it be?"

"Oh. Right. Actually, I only started making a plan just . . . let's see, yesterday. In the wee hours of the morning. Somewhere between the turnoff for Long Island and Cape Cod, it was going to be an art gallery that I'd open. Between Cape Cod and Marblehead, it was going to be a taxidermist. Between Marblehead and Ogunquit, it was a blacksmith's shop."

His eyes narrowed. "I think you're kidding."

"Only partly. Let's just say there've been some . . . endings just lately for several parts of my life. I'm still figuring out how to start over."

She watched his eyes dart away, the sadness in them deepening them to dark holes.

"I know something," he said without looking at her, "about endings." His gaze swung back and settled. "Amie Stilwell. Short for *Amelia*? I've heard stories."

She laughed—couldn't help it. "You know, it's probably not surprising and also probably not a compliment if you've heard stories of me."

But again, his mouth didn't slide into a smile—did not even twitch. "The name is Ian"—he paused—"O'Leary." He flinched as he added that last.

There, she thought, *is part of his own story. There in that name.*

He wrapped a thin black scarf twice around his neck. "So, then." His tone, and the way he tossed the scarf, served as a dismissal.

"So, then." She held out her hand again, her glove bright in the early morning light. "I hope we'll be friends, in addition to possibly neighbors. And sharers of blueberry muffins."

He left her hand hanging there a moment. When he shook it, he gave a quick nod, the crease between his brows deepening.

So maybe *friend* would be a stretch. But she wouldn't be his enemy either. Someone or something else was young Ian O'Leary's enemy. The weight of it in his eyes looked as if it might crush him.

From behind her, Fletch appeared with his signature grunt—and with no explanation. Maybe simply because it was now past eight: business hours.

He thrust a key at her, an antique brass affair, scrolled and heavy. "Figured now was as good a time as any for you to see inside," he said. "Well? What're you waiting for?"

"Now that you put it that way, and now that Ian here has brought me my morning coffee, I guess nothing. Mind if I bring your mug back to you shortly, Mr. O'Leary of the Hundred Thousand Welcomes?" Getting only a slight dip of the head from Ian as her answer, she followed Fletch to the door of the adjacent shop. "This key must be original to the door. Late eighteenth century, maybe?"

The key slid roughly into the tarnished lock, and even as the deadbolt slid back, the door with its more than two centuries of paint and weathered wood stuck in the frame for several moments. Throwing her shoulder into the effort, she heaved it open.

Smells assaulted her senses. Mustiness. Mildew. God only knew what else. Maybe wild-animal urine.

With his leash snapped off, Hopkins bounded ahead to sniff out the room. Scuffling through debris, he lunged at a long, skinny tail just as something small and gray disappeared through a small hole in the wall, its lath and plaster insides exposed.

Filth and holes, though, could be fixed. Lots of restoration work to be done, but nothing impossible, surely. Nothing so hard as fixing the holes in a life.

Outside the small office behind the shop's main room, empty cans lay strewn: Chef Boyardee ravioli, Spam, and Veg-All. Amie found a light switch. A bare bulb glowed yellow halfway up a spiraling flight of varnished wooden stairs, remarkably narrow, built for much smaller feet two hundred years ago. Just behind Hopkins, she mounted the stairs two at a time, the steps creaking but seeming sturdy enough.

From the first floor, Fletch called up after her, "Built like a whaling ship, ayuh, like everything was back then. Nowadays, though . . ."

Reaching the top step, Amie stopped to breathe. Amber light spilled through the two-story windows on the shop's street-facing side. One large room, this loft overlooking the shop comprised all of the living quarters except for a small bathroom off to the left. To the right was an open, galley-sized kitchen of a vintage several decades prior, just a black potbellied stove with a flat iron top large enough for a saucepan, a low-slung Frigidaire that at least gave off a heartening hum, and a deep ceramic sink, thick in grime.

But she was no cook, so this wasn't a blow. Once she'd bleached and scoured it all, she could boil water and burn toast as well here as anywhere.

The square footage in the loft would provide only room enough for a bed, but the bank of windows ahead drew her forward to the loft railing. From here she could spot across the circle a sliver of sea and a copse of pines—which she would pretend to smell instead of mildew and rot before she got the place cleaned. To the far right stood a small door. With a groan, as if it had not been asked to move in many months, maybe years, it lurched open onto a small iron balcony at the side of the building. Amie stepped out. The sun was just rising over a stand of birches, most of them bare, their white trunks stark against the harbor.

"Shameful," Fletch said mournfully from the sidewalk below where he'd just stepped from out of the shop. "Last tenant was here just a few months. Left with no kind of notice at all. People nowadays. No pride in cleaning up."

Amie yanked the door closed behind her and scrambled back down the loft's spiral staircase. "Fletch, about the rent, I—"

"Your dad would be cosigning the lease, would he?"

Amie stiffened. "He would not. Definitely not. My father and I have an understanding: he doesn't offer me money, and I don't accept what he doesn't offer—as in, I wouldn't if he did."

Fletch eyed her, then grunted.

"I have some savings from my work these past several years, but not much. I'll need to be careful with that. So what if I did all the cleaning for the property here myself? Could you give me a break on the first month's rent—a break that would be maybe . . . free?"

Expressionless, Fletch looked back at her.

"Ayuh," he said at last.

Which might be enough, that one word, for a verbal contract in Maine, she thought.

The door of the bakery swung open again, Shibby and Chester, hand in hand, standing on the threshold. The little boy dropped to his knees to wrap his free arm around Hopkins.

"Chester! Come meet our friend Mr. Osgood."

Bringing Shibby with him rather than releasing her hand, Chester inched forward. Big eyes peered up from under his bangs.

Fletch put out his hand, large in general and twice its normal size now in its fur-lined glove—a giant's hand. He wrapped it around the child's tiny mittened one. Eyes narrowing, the older man seemed to be scanning the boy's face.

Waiting for someone to speak, Amie looked from one to the other. But Fletch only went on shaking the boy's hand.

"I like a man of few words," Fletch finally said. Slowly, he let loose Chester's hand, as if it were a baby chick that might drop to the floor rather than fly.

Chester looked at his own hand as if it might have changed since the contact with the giant's.

Amie waved Fletch to one side. "Maybe we can continue our conversation about the shop later, you and I? I don't want to tell anyone else until we're both sure."

"Jake Spitzer was just about that kid's age—couple years younger, I reckon—when he showed up just outside of town. You and him like Dick and Jane, always together. Guess the kid here makes you miss your old buddy Jake."

It wasn't a question, and Amie had no answers if it had been.

Even after all these years, she could still feel her stomach go sour with fury toward him, and she still missed him so much it hurt. It made no sense, the churning of all that emotion. But then grief rarely did.

Yes, she wanted to say. *Yes. Dear God, I miss Jake.* Her cheeks, she realized, had gone damp again with tears she'd not meant to shed.

Just a moment ago, she'd felt the seed of a plan growing inside, and even now, a tender shoot of something new. She watched Chester squat down to hug Hopkins again and whisper something in the soft, floppy ear. In that gesture, too, that hug and that whisper, was hope. Made more precious, perhaps, in this place that would not let her forget what had been lost.

Chapter 11

Boston

Reaching across the woman for a cigarette, Tom began the rest of his day with a lie. He despised liars.

Having finished his phone call downstairs, he returned to her, this woman sprawled in his bed. "They were . . . friends. Not family. I told you already. I don't—"

"Have any family left. Yeah, right. Whatever." She pronounced it *whatevah*, which made Tom cringe. She'd smeared pink lipstick onto her chin, and he reached to wipe it away. How was it he could still be tender like this—she smiled up at him—yet about to be cruel?

She raised herself to one elbow, the picture in its silver frame gripped in her left hand. "All's I'm saying, Tommsie, is that you seem awful close to them. Like you was family."

"Not," he said, "my name."

She sat up. Pink lipstick had smeared, too, on the crisp white sheets she'd pulled to her chest. The whole scene struck him just now as pathetic.

"Jeez. What's got you so dull all of a sudden, babycakes? Or do all the women in your bed address you as *Mr. Darnay*?"

"Put it back, please." He tried to keep his voice steady. Calm. Not quavering at the panic he felt seeing her handle the picture.

She held the picture out from her body. Voluptuous, he recalled. A wonder of curves and soft flesh. He might've told her just that last night. But right now, she was a wonder that needed to leave.

"First, dreamboat, you got to tell me who this is in it. If we're gonna get to know each other like this"—she ran a finger down his bare back, swerving around the largest muscles—"it's only fair I'd know about you like this." She raised the picture again, and cackled. "Come on and tell Betty what's making you crazy, me holding it."

Betty, that was her name. Though, poor thing, not worth committing to memory.

Lighting a match, Tom kept his face turned away. That's what was left of his fierce commitment to honesty: he couldn't look her in the eye and lie. "Nothing much to tell about it."

"Gee, you were a porky little guy, weren't you? But with swell little cheeks, even then."

That struck Tom as a question that needed no answer. A cigarette between his lips, he breathed in and then out, a white plume of smoke.

"You three don't look nothing alike—but you said they weren't family."

There was no question there, so he offered nothing.

"So they got cute little villages up there in Canada, too?"

His stomach corkscrewed with her fondling the picture like that. "Yes. In Canada, too."

"She was pretty, this one." The woman said this with a little pout that was probably supposed to look cute—and convey she was jealous.

Tom ignored the pout and took another draw on his cigarette.

"Jesus, the grown woman with all that wild dark hair. She don't look nothing like the mother of the girl. I mean, she's pretty enough, too, the woman is, if you like that wild kind of hair, which I don't much, but they don't bear even a smidgen bit of resemblance, if you ask me."

He couldn't help himself then. He turned and jerked—not gently—the frame from her hand.

"Ouch!"

On another day, he might have asked if he'd hurt her. But he was already edgy about the photograph the *Globe* reporter had snapped, and his phone call with Charlie Whipple had made his head pound.

The woman stuck out her lower lip. "So, handsome. Who was she?"

"Who?"

"The *woman*. With the wild hair."

Tom slid soft wool trousers—custom tailored—over his briefs and yanked on a shirt, its starch still stiff even after having been tossed on the floor sometime after midnight. "She was nobody," he said.

He heard the slash of the words and saw himself as a kid, standing there at the door.

"So, you've already gathered the eggs from the barn?"

He'd not met her eye, but only slung on his satchel and kicked open the screen door with a fourteen-year-old foot.

"Yep," he'd muttered, surly as a wet cat.

"They're all gathered?"

"I said I did, didn't I? You'll make me miss the bus." He'd jerked away from her hand on his shoulder.

She'd opened her opposite hand, where three eggs sat on her palm. More, of course, still sat in the hay in the shed since he'd not been there at all that morning.

He'd missed the bus that morning because of gathering eggs.

"The truth," she'd said when he was done, as she held his glaring face in her hands, "can feel like a bad fence. Like the barbed wire that wants to keep you in a big cage—away from the fun. Is that how it feels to you?"

Sullen, he'd refused to answer.

"But the truth is what gives us freedom, son. The lie is what causes the tangle." She circled a hand around one arm—miming, he was supposed to understand, the punishing work of barbed wire.

"The lie cuts," she'd said. "Remember. The lie cuts."

Her eyes, brown and deep, were still stormy, but had gone back to kind—and a little sorrowful, too. Which made him madder still.

She'd waved from the porch. "The truth," she'd called. "Always the truth."

Stomping, he'd set off on foot the two miles to school and did not turn to wave back.

The lie cuts. Remember.

But all that was so many years—a lifetime—ago.

Tom turned back to the woman in his bed. "I have quite a long day ahead. I hope you understand."

The silence from his bed told him she was offended. But of course she would be. He was treating her abominably.

"Well, then." Even the sheets rustled petulantly as she rose. "So tell me this, Mr. Big Shot, how come you went all crazy over me touching this picture of just a couple of old friends of yours, huh?"

Tom yanked the tail end of a tie into its half Windsor knot and didn't meet his own eye in the full-length mirror. "People die. It's sad as hell, but then you move on."

He turned. "Please forgive me for asking you to show yourself out."

"You'll call, Tommsie?" she asked as he dropped down the first flight of stairs.

"I'll call. Sure." Another lie. Which she surely had to know since he didn't have her number or her last name. God, he was a piece of work.

His phone was ringing in the front hall. Rarely receiving calls outside the office, he'd never bothered to put in any other extension.

Sprinting down the last flight of steps, Tom snapped up the receiver. "Darnay speaking."

"Just a heads-up," came a voice like shifting gravel.

Tom recognized it, his lungs already contracting.

There in the Park Street T station, Tom had been only an instant away from being rid of the reporter and the story he thought he was sniffing out. Tom's reflexes had responded to snatch at the man's coat and jerk him back from tumbling forward into the concrete canyon where the red-line train would have pulverized him the next second. Instead of letting the man fall—or pushing him, as planned—Tom's yank had saved him.

The reporter had regained his balance. Boarding the red-line train along with a crush of commuters, he'd never known that behind him on the platform was the person who'd nearly ended his life, then saved it.

Even in that moment, Tom had known he'd regret the better angels that apparently guided his reflexes, if not his thoughts.

"How the hell'd you get my number?"

"Just a courtesy call, Darnay. Just wanted you to be the first to know—the first after me—that we did it."

"Did . . . what?"

"Scored, kid. You and me. Your good-lookin' mug and my camera. Front page. Hell, lemme be the first to congratulate you."

The *Globe* reporter paused. But Tom's throat had swelled shut.

"I know I only got a piece of the story. But there's something there, Darnay, and I can be a real bastard of a bulldog when I smell a story. I give you my word: this here's only the start."

Chapter 12

Pelican Cove

Amie shivered in the phone booth as the words—the reality—sank in. Again.

"I'm sorry, miss," the woman's voice said with the huskiness of someone trying to muster compassion when she was truly just tired. "You and your loved ones know that he's dead. You may simply have to be content with that. No body was ever found that could be identified as a Jacob Spitzer, but that doesn't mean his death doesn't hurt, your government realizes." She sounded as if she were reading from a card, a speech she'd given too many times to too many tens of thousands of families left in the limbo of postwar not knowing.

Please. Please tell us the impossible. Tell us our son, our brother, our husband, our lover is still alive. Please.

Amie had left Shibby and Chester in the farmhouse in a sweet, sizzling haze that smelled of vanilla and bacon and the breakfast they were making. For Amie to have used the one extension in the farmhouse would've meant standing in the kitchen where Shibby could hear. So she'd walked the three blocks to Dock Circle.

"Thank you for looking," Amie said into the frigid black metal circle of the receiver. At the operator's interruption asking for additional coins, Amie fumbled in her dungaree pocket and dropped another dime into the slot. "Maybe if I gave you more specific dates? He enlisted in '41."

At the sigh on the other end of the line, Amie felt foolish. Of course Jake had enlisted in '41. Every young male in America enlisted after Pearl Harbor when the country was finally officially at war.

"In December, I assume, Miss Stilwell?"

"Actually, I think it may have been well before that, like in . . ."

Hadn't Shibby once said Jake had left town the day after his eighteenth birthday? But that was in June. Just after his graduation from high school. Amie already gone by then and only talking with Shibby over the phone every few weeks at the time, she'd assumed Jake had enlisted right after leaving home. But he wouldn't have . . . would he? America hadn't been at war in June 1941.

The woman's voice broke into her thoughts. "What branch of the service?"

Amie considered. Jake had always loved the sea. Everyone did who grew up beside it. It was as if the salt water seeped into your blood.

"Navy, perhaps?"

"You don't *know*?"

"Not . . . exactly. Could you maybe look one more time in every branch?"

An exasperated pause. "You know, miss, why don't you call back when you have more *specific* information from your family on precisely when your loved one enlisted, including where, and any letters home he may have sent from particular locations. Also, of course, what locale he was last heard from."

"Of course. Thank you for your time." For a moment, Amie leaned against the folding door of the phone booth and allowed herself two bangs of her forehead against the cold glass in frustration. A few yards away, a sleek black car glided past. On its side, painted in gold, were the words *Promontory Inn* with an anchor, and below that, *Desmond Fossick, owner.* Most of the inns in the village shut down after Labor Day, but a few, like the Promontory, stayed open until the full brunt of winter hit. So maybe a few guests were still being shuttled about.

Hurrying back to the Orchard, Amie was just in time to sit down for French toast. The maple syrup, Amie knew, would've been tapped from local trees last spring. The cinnamon-raisin bread must be from Fáilte in Dock Circle, since Shibby never baked except for birthday parties and "general revelry," as she used to call it. The whipped cream, fluffy and just off the beaters, was piled a good four inches high. Chester's big eyes had fixed on the mountains of white.

"Good thing I had the weekend off," Shibby said in a soft voice as she and Amie ducked back into the kitchen to the percolator for coffee. "Not sure what this next week'll look like, though. Can't be leaving him alone, and it's a mite early to know . . ."

She didn't finish the sentence, so Amie did. "How long he can stay." But that made it sound like the boy had come for a weekend vacation, rather than being dumped off, nothing but a note pinned to his coat.

Amie lowered her voice still more. "Looks like the chances by the start of the week of finding that criminal of a mother who left him—or the chances we'd leave him with her even if we found her—aren't good. You know, of course, Mister Chester is welcome to hang out with me when you have to be at the inn. I'm still figuring out life here, so he can be my partner in crime."

Shibby kissed her palm and touched it to Amie's cheek as she had when Amie was small. "Had a feeling you'd say that, sugar. Blessed are the recently fired. For they shall find their true vocation—and meanwhile can drink extra hot cocoa."

~

After Shibby washed the dishes and Amie and Chester dried them, Amie left the two of them reading *The Wind in the Willows* by the fire. As Chester's arm wrapped through Shibby's, Hopkins curled his furry body into the crook of the boy's legs.

Amie crunched through the woods to the library just a couple of blocks away. She could have taken sidewalks and streets, but cutting through the woods gave her a chance to breathe in the musky scent of decaying leaves. She could feel her blood pressure finally dropping after the earlier phone call with the government office.

No body was ever found . . . but that doesn't mean his death doesn't hurt, your government realizes. Amie felt the words again like a series of punches.

She made herself stop and breathe again. Autumn here arrived with a great, rollicking party of colors, followed by these muted, subtler hues, her favorite. On the breeze now came the bracing swish of sea air, sweet, briny smells, and the tolling of the harbor buoys.

She was still able to use her other four senses, and that alone was progress, a relief to even notice the smells and tastes and touches and sounds. For the last five years of work and during the war years before that, she'd tended to stare down the world around her as if peering through her old stereoscope at photos still damp from the darkroom fixative. Sometimes it still felt as if she couldn't simply live life but had to always be desperately scanning for clues. As if Allied generals and reconnaissance pilots were still peering over her shoulder waiting for a verdict on the progress of the Germans' secret V-2 rocket construction, for details that might save—or cost—thousands of lives.

Pausing at the top of the library stairs, she wiped mud and leaves from the soles of her boots. At the main desk, she stopped to answer the questions of Miss Mary O'Kelly, the same diminutive librarian who'd been there for decades, still with the brown hair streaked in white she'd twisted into a bun at the nape of her neck and with the same greeting.

"What books, my dear, can I help you find today?" The word *find* was always accompanied with a hand over her heart, as if what she really meant was *fall forever in love with.*

"I wish I could tell you." Amie's gaze swept over the stacks, the shelving of periodicals, the row of wooden card catalog drawers.

Asking Miss O'Kelly about the Bentley was pointless. On her librarian's salary, it couldn't be hers, and her memory had always been spotty at best—maybe because few other details in life really mattered outside of books. This woman who could recite countless soliloquies from *Macbeth* and *The Merchant of Venice* by heart without missing a word also stared blankly, owl eyes blinking behind Coke-bottle glasses if anyone mentioned a shop in the village that had been there for years.

Daggerboard Gifts, she'd murmured once. *Seems like I've heard of it somewhere.*

The shop had been named that since Victoria was queen of England.

Amie strolled up and down the periodical section first, flipping through a newspaper or two. She thumbed through *Life* and the *Saturday Evening Post*, even through *Look*, full of Hollywood gossip and carefully curated stories of the stars' lives—what the studios wanted readers to believe, at least.

But nothing struck Amie as helpful. Particularly since she didn't know what she was looking for.

In the fiction section for adults, she caressed the book spines. It calmed her, for one thing, just the contact of her fingers with stories, with words. The usual suspects were here, all in lovely, gilt-spined editions: Jane Austen; the Brontë sisters—Charlotte and Emily but also Anne, Amie's favorite of the three—Wilkie Collins; Charles Dickens; George Eliot . . .

Amie's fingers backtracked to Dickens's *A Tale of Two Cities.* A gorgeous antique, nicely preserved.

"It was the best of times; it was the worst of times," she sighed. How often that applied in life, including today. The thrill of her starting-fresh season, the beauty and quiet of the cove—as postcard perfect as her better memories here had promised—but also a lost little boy and the death of Jake.

Now she ambled down the aisles of the children's section, promising herself she'd bring Chester back with her tomorrow. Meanwhile, she'd check out a stack of books they could read to him. If she could just avoid the ones with mothers. Or fathers. Or siblings.

Amie's fingers brushed over the spines of Mark Twain's *The Adventures of Huckleberry Finn* and *The Prince and the Pauper* and kept going. She paused, struck by something in one of the titles. Something that made her think about Jake.

But what was it?

Her fingers walked back to *The Prince and the Pauper.*

Two children—boys in this case—switching places.

"So it's not swell," Jake had snapped at her one day during high school as they'd walked toward the old Captain Smollett mansion. "So your drip of an old man lives in Boston and never shows up here to see you. But you've never once had to worry about money. Never had to hear what people say about you growing up in a foster home full of rejects. I'd trade places with you any old day."

It wasn't what his heart, at its best, knew: how much damage could be done to a child by neglect, not just a punch or a kick. But he'd been feeling sorry for himself that particular day. That one, and a few others around it.

"Trade places, *really*?" she'd shot back. "You've got Shibby there, right there in the farmhouse with you every single day, but just lately, you act like an ungrateful bastard."

Bastard. She'd loaded and fired the word to hurt, and she saw that it did.

They'd glared at each other as people do who have said more than they meant, but have no intention of retracting or backstepping, or God knew, apologizing.

Trade places with you any day.

What if Shibby's insistence was right? What if Jake was still alive somewhere in this world, but had made up an alternative story for his own life? What if he had, in a sense, traded in his own story for someone else's?

It was awfully far-fetched. And Amie had no earthly idea where to start.

So maybe a thought not even worth wasting time on.

She replaced Twain's novel on the shelf and wrenched her attention back to finding a book to read Chester, maybe a more grown-up story from the adult fiction section that the child could still lose himself in. Amie's fingers retraced their path across spines, then stopped on *A Tale of Two Cities.* She'd always loved its end, Sydney Carton in Paris sacrificing and redeeming himself.

But maybe something lighter and cheerier for a boy whose mother could smile serenely in that old picture, then dump off her own son like a load of old trash. Amie shuddered. She was anxious to get back to the farmhouse and see if he'd spoken again—said anything at all.

Hurrying through the periodicals, Amie riffled back through issues of the *New York Times* and the *Washington Post* and the *Portland Press Herald.* No inspiration struck her.

In the card catalog, her fingers flipped through every relevant topic she could think of related to American soldiers missing in action. There were books on the subject already. New research coming out on the Bataan Death March. About prison camps in the Pacific and in

Germany. About Allied governments still sorting out just who'd been lost on D-Day, and how to honor the dead. But nothing specific enough that it could help lead to a single soldier who'd disappeared—killed while serving in God only knew what service of the armed forces, or what country, or what year.

Hopeless.

She checked her wristwatch, a Bulova with a mother of pearl dial that had survived Medmenham and, in the final weeks of the war, Cairo with her, its crystal scratched now nearly to the point of opacity. It had been her mother's, one of the few things, along with a pair of cross-country skis, Amie had of hers—so, scratched crystal or not, it wouldn't be replaced. Its tiny black hands said she needed to be getting back to the Orchard. Looking around for the gloves she'd left in the periodical section, Amie found them on a stack of the latest *Boston Globe*s. Today's issue featured Senator McCarthy on the front page.

Communists, he insisted, eyes bulging in the photo, *had infiltrated the U.S. State Department. Could be found under every rock.*

Amie sighed, eyes sweeping the library once more. She could see nothing that struck her as relevant to her own search for a young man lost . . . God only knew where. Literally. The scorched ashes of his body probably scattered over an open sea, dolphins leaping up through bits of black.

Amie handed over *The Tale of Peter Rabbit* and *Winnie-the-Pooh* she'd selected for Chester to Miss Mary O'Kelly.

"Wait," Amie said. "I'm sorry. I need to put back the Beatrix Potter."

"Such a sweet story. Are you quite sure?"

"It's just that Peter Rabbit had a mother. And sisters. I don't think he'll do."

Mary O'Kelly nodded as if she understood.

Bastard. Amie heard the echo of her own voice all those years ago.

Oh, Jake, she mouthed to the floor as Mary O'Kelly stamped her books. *I'm sorry.*

Chapter 13

Boston

Tom charged up Park Street to the gold-domed Massachusetts State House where they were waiting for him: the pack of reporters like cannibals, ink pens out and poised like so many spears. Bulky cameras across their chests, they wore the rounded disk that shielded the flash like an oversized silver medal hanging around their necks.

Medals, Tom thought, *for extraordinary annoyance in time of peace.*

This time, though, Mr. Fossick wouldn't be here since he was still up in Maine. In Maine, of all places, when he ought to be at any number of meetings along the Eastern Seaboard or out in Las Vegas. Typically, Tom lived safely in the background, squashing negative press and generating feature articles that fawned more than reported. Today, though, he'd have to be the face of Fossick Enterprises.

Which might be just as well, so long as nobody took a photo. Fossick had the Midas touch for making money, but also some sort of Promethean gift for igniting fires wherever he went—and opened his mouth. Today's paper had no mention of Fossick at all, so maybe the *Globe* reporter was all bluster.

Rather than try to skirt the pack of them, Tom bounded up the statehouse stairs directly into their midst. For a split second, they stood stunned at his sudden—and voluntary—appearance.

He eyed them coolly, and tugged the Burberry scarf precisely an inch higher on his neck. Precision in all things was key.

A phalanx of armed reporters attacked.

He held up his hand. "Just so we can communicate effectively, I'll have to insist on no pictures today." He tried a friendly chuckle. "For some of us, all those flashes and clicks still feel like an air fight about to commence." He let that sit for a moment, let them recall what they surely knew was his past with the Royal Canadian Air Force. He let the jackals feel for a moment—assuming jackals had hearts—along with a brave, still-traumatized pilot, part of the illustrious flying corps that had beaten down Hitler.

It was true enough, the way his brain still froze when camera flashes went off—or any loud, sudden sound. But just now, it also provided a good excuse.

"I thank you for refraining." Tom turned up the collar of his overcoat, flicked the brim of his fedora down, and leaned forward toward the reporters' questions. Whether or not they consciously noticed his aggression, they leaned back.

He'd give the press this much: they'd mostly refrained from taking photos of FDR in his wheelchair or looking physically weak. With the exception of the reporter on Boston Common, the newspapermen here generally kept their cameras lowered around Jake because of his war service. He made sure it stayed that way with his regular mentions of combat.

Fossick, of course, was another story entirely.

They were all talking at once, the herd of them. Tom made himself raise an eyebrow as if he were fully engaged.

Here came a fresh onslaught, a barrage of shouted questions.

"Is it true your client denies any safety violations at any of his . . . ?"

"Some of Mr. Fossick's workers around the country claim their hours . . ."

Tom was good at this: the polished, unemotional answer—unflappably cool. Not cold, of course. Cold would not do when addressing stories of pathos and woe.

He leveled his tone to calm. Compassionate, even. "Clearly, no one could care more about these workers than the man who has offered them employment."

One of them squawked above the rest: "Some have said that Mr. Fossick has complained publicly at every turn about workers' compensation for accidents on the job."

"There've been reports," another barked out, "that to work for Mr. Fossick is like a return to the early Industrial Revolution. No worker protections at all."

Tom gave the reporters a look of disdainful patience.

But the loudest of the jackals, checking his notes, wasn't finished. "There've been complaints of overtime hours without pay and an atmosphere of coercion and retribution for workers who refuse at several of Mr. Fossick's properties."

Other reporters were snuffling and growling from the back of the pack.

"The complaints of . . ."

"An accident at one of his . . ."

Tom raised his hand, as if calming a huddle of toddlers midtantrum. "As for the complaints—"

He was interrupted by a commotion, someone charging through the pack of reporters. Someone too short to be visible yet, but forceful enough to have burly reporters leaping backward.

Which could only be one man. Back too early.

Tom winced.

Popping a reporter's arm out of the way, Desmond Fossick emerged from a sea of khaki trench coats. With the agility of a much younger man, he leaped up the steps to stand beside Tom.

Tom tipped his head to murmur, "Welcome back, Mr. Fossick. I have things here well in hand if you'd like to—"

But Fossick had already squared up to face the reporters.

Shifting his jaw back and forth, he was already relishing a good fight. "Let me just add to what Mr. Darnay noted regarding these claims." He paused dramatically, the reporters all leaning forward, expectant. "Let's be honest, some people would rather have me pay them to lie around and pretend to be hurt than put in an honest day's work."

Tom eased in front of his boss. But it was too late.

Already swarming Fossick, the reporters hurled accusations, thinly disguised as questions, at him.

How they loved to get a guy riled. It sold newspapers, baiting a bear like this, and showcasing the roar that came out.

Tom took his boss by the arm, but the man would not budge. His face had gone red in two points at his cheeks. He raised both hands in fists in front of his chest as if his days as a boxer, earning his South End tenement's rent as a young man, had come back to him now. Reveling in the fight, Fossick was bouncing on the balls of his feet.

"Hard work," he was saying, "that's how I made my way in this world."

"Mr. Fossick," somebody called, "are you calling these people whiners?"

As Fossick rounded on the man, Tom held his breath.

A beat passed in which the gaggle hushed to hear his answer. Fossick slowly drew back his lips in his signature smile, which looked more like baring his teeth. "It was your choice, the word *whiners*. But I'll not argue with you."

Granite-faced, Tom did not allow himself a cringe that might attract a camera's flash. More forcefully now, he reached again for his boss's arm to steer him away from the crowd.

Fossick let himself be led two steps toward the waiting car.

"Mr. Fossick!" a lady reporter called, her voice a jolt in the midst of the low thunder of the men's shouts. "Are you saying there's no legitimacy in the claims?"

Tom propelled Fossick toward his black Delahaye, its driver poised at the wheel.

Fossick had never been one to resist females, and this one was uncommonly pretty—the only dame in the whole newspaper pack. Fossick's eyes ran the length of her, from a brimless Calot hat that showed off the waves of her hair to stockings and black heels. "In fact, young lady, if you're looking for the right word for these types, you might go with *extortionists*. Forcibly taking money from hardworking people and handing it to whatever lazy slob blubbers the loudest."

An electric moment of quiet shot through the crowd as the reporters processed what they'd just heard. Then the pivot back—all gleeful now with that quote—to scrawl on their pads.

Guiding his boss around the Delahaye's hood that seemed to stretch on for miles, Tom ushered Fossick into the car's black leather hush, and nearly slammed the door on Fossick's foot in the haste to send him away.

Fists clenched in the pockets of his overcoat, Tom turned.

"Mr. Darnay! Mr. Darnay!"

The reporters were frothing behind him. They'd smelled blood and would try to go in now for the kill.

Tom braced himself for damage control.

One reporter was shouting over the rest. "Surely after your own role in the war, Mr. Darnay, you can empathize with these workers' complaints. The down and out? Their feelings of being abandoned?"

At that last word, Tom took a step back. He could not help himself.

"We all," he heard himself say, "make our own way in this world."

It was true. Though not what he'd meant to say.

But that word the reporter had used: *abandoned.* As if somehow she knew.

Tom stared, unspeaking, at the herd of journalists. He felt the fangs of the past take their hold, the rip and the tear of what he'd tried so hard to forget.

A boy sat there, knees tucked under his chin, on the side of a road near a blueberry bog that stretched out for acres, a farm stand beside it, rain pelting down.

He was shivering hard, the Tootsie Pop his momma had shoved at him gone a good hour ago. He'd soiled his pants, and the smell sickened him.

But his momma had walked away here.

She hadn't said where she was going, but she had to come back. Even if they didn't want the kid, even if the kid made them feel mad and cheated by life, didn't mommas still have to come back?

So the boy sat there in the storm, the wind wrenching a branch off the tree straight over his head and sending it to crash just inches away beside him.

Hours went by. Or it might have been days, even years, the boy's body so cold he was certain he'd frozen in place.

He was alone—would always be, he felt sure.

He was unwanted. Unmissed.

No one was looking for him. Nobody cared if he was found.

His face was down on his thighs, his arms hugging tight to his knees. The lightning flashed over his head.

Even now, he could smell the soiled pants, feel the fault line inside him crack open, the fear he'd lived with every day of his life quake into full terror.

Tom shook off the image.

Turning, he faced the reporters. Once again, he'd have to round up the usual scrum of editors who'd assign slick, full-color features on Desmond Fossick, Achiever of the American Dream.

"Let's remember who we're talking about here: the boy who started out life in a three-room cottage under a pine in a little fishing village, the shack and the pine leaning hard away from the winds off the sea."

The crowd quieted under the power of the story, the lull of Tom's voice telling it. Now the next step: he would compliment one of their number. "Frank, you recently included Mr. Fossick in your excellent *Forbes* feature on self-made men."

"Forbes," the reporter called back, "has estimated Fossick's net worth well over three hundred million, yet—"

Tom cut in before that *yet* could do damage. "A real accomplishment from a boy born into a family of a simple, honest lobsterman, wouldn't you say?"

Fossick's net worth was well above three hundred million, Tom could have told him. Some days, the man's creation of mind-boggling wealth was the message: Titan of Industry. Lion of Wall Street.

But the message today was Fossick's peace and goodwill to all. Despite some damning evidence to the contrary.

This was Tom's value as a mouthpiece for Fossick: the suave, polished young man who could buff out his employer's rough edges. Though Tom rarely appeared in public beside Fossick, the two of them must have made quite a contrast together. The older man, short but powerfully built, had his nose broken in three places during his pugilist days, yet he was somehow still strangely attractive—in that way that rock cliffs attract awe and fear. The young man always appeared tall, sleek, imperious, impeccably groomed. People mostly found Tom Darnay arrogant, which was, Tom knew, far better than their finding the truth.

"Thank you for your interest in the way in which Fossick Enterprises continues to provide employment and prosperity." Tom turned on the heel of his oxfords, and strode not around them but straight through their midst.

They were shouting questions after him as he walked. But all he could see was the crossroads near a sprawling bog and a farm stand. All he could hear was the one word from before, still echoing in his ears.

Abandoned.

Chapter 14

Pelican Cove

The Orchard seemed to have expanded somehow. Muddy boots stood at attention all across the front porch and lined the walls just inside the front door. The farmhouse's two stories of windows glowed gold in the evening gray, making even the worn, faded paint of the porch railing and trim look charming. Here was a place, the house seemed to say, where no one and nothing was perfect—or would ever pretend to be. But warmth: that was something you could count on in every way that mattered.

Amie was just arriving back from her rounds of the village, having gone door-to-door describing the picture of Chester with his mother and asking every household she could think of what they might know of the little boy and how he came to be left at the Tipsy Porpoise. Nothing. Only blank stares of concern. Followed by offers to help.

Earlier this morning before Chester woke up, she'd snapped several shots of his out-of-focus, creased photograph. Amie would develop them herself, just as soon as she had a darkroom set up somewhere, and dug out the chemicals from the trunk of the Aston Martin.

Her feet having gone numb in the phone booth on Dock Circle, she'd asked Fletch Osgood if she could borrow the phone in Provisions. Even though Chester's clothing suggested he'd not been living with anyone on the streets, she dialed the Salvation Army in Portland and Boston to see if they'd seen a woman with a six-year-old child, maybe in a bow tie. She called on and on, including one of Shibby's foster children who'd become a social worker. Amie called the Maine Children's Home Society, the New England Home for Little Wanderers, the United States Children's Bureau—all for any possible leads. Nothing.

When she tried after an hour to leave change on the Provisions cash register for all the calls, including long distance, Fletch growled at her.

"Nowadays, folks act like helping a neighbor'd be some kind of a choice. It ain't a choice." He'd thrust the coins back at her so abruptly, almost violently, she'd taken them.

"Thank you," she'd said. "And I promise not to tell too many people what a soft heart you have inside the hard shell."

Now she unlaced her boots and added them to the infantry already in line. Her muscles burned from hurrying back from Dock Circle— but it was exhilarating, too, as if breathing that hard was burning off the tangled underbrush of her brain. Even the windburn of her cheeks felt like another sign she was coming back more fully to life. It had been too long since she'd had this feeling: launching into the near darkness of not knowing, but driven forward one grainy sighting, one detail, one gut sense at a time as she connected fact to fact until a full picture formed.

Now the front door flew open, Shibby standing there, arms open. Amie let herself be pulled inside.

The living room throbbed with music from the old upright piano, Ian having sat down to play Nat King Cole favorites at twice their normal speed, so that even "Mona Lisa" spun out as toe-tapping dance music.

At one end of the living room, a stone fireplace hulked up the wall, and a fire roared in the hearth. Overhead, the ceiling's rafters were rough, untreated timbers. Amie recalled when children had tumbled about on the floor, little dustings of rafter wood sifting down from above—as they did now with a roomful of people and Ian's gleeful pounding of the piano.

Fletch arrived just behind Amie. Kalia Clarke was just emerging from the kitchen carrying a trayful of cream cheese Danishes and chocolate pastries that Ian, it turned out, had brought from Fáilte.

Several former foster kids of Shibby's from all over New England milled around, some with children of their own now giggling and rolling about with Chester and Hopkins on the living room floor. At one end of the big room, some of the adults had flopped back the old rug to dance as Ian spun out his tunes.

Shibby loved nothing more than a good party of the rafter-shedding sort, Amie recalled, one of the Orchard's "general revelries." When Amie was young, Shibby's kitchen had never been a place of gourmet delicacies, usually smelling instead of lobster or cod—they'd both been so cheap and plentiful then—and of some dutiful, overboiled vegetable. Tonight, though, aromas of buttered pastries and chocolate and almonds and spices that Amie could only guess at drifted through the house.

Seth Wakefield stood at the long pine table sampling the pastries already there. Hopkins was standing on his hind legs beside the vet.

"I can be rather clumsy sometimes," Seth said, glancing up with a shy smile. "He's clever to stand there and take his chances."

Here, indoors under the beamed ceiling of the farmhouse, he seemed even taller than he had outdoors—maybe quieter, too, against the boisterousness behind him in the living room. He wore the same argyle vest smelling faintly, pleasantly, of leather and hay and damp wool.

Amie fought back the urge to bury her nose in the vest and breathe in. She crossed her arms over her chest to be sure she didn't reach out and touch the vest—or him. "I'm afraid he doesn't know he's a dog."

"No reason he has to be told. The name Hopkins?"

"Named for a poet I like. No one's ever heard of him."

"Gerard Manley Hopkins?"

Amie cocked her head. "Except, apparently, veterinarians on the southern coast of Maine."

"'Whatever is fickle, freckled (who knows how?)

"'With swift, slow; sweet, sour; adazzle, dim.'"

"'Pied Beauty.' Very nice, Dr. Wakefield. Not what I would've guessed from a high school baseball star: a lover of nature poetry."

"He wasn't. That guy back then almost never cracked open a book, any book, least of all poetry. It was the years after that." He didn't say the word *war*, but it sat between them, heavy and dark. "I was in the South Pacific. Looking for ways to keep from being terrified every moment. A buddy I met there discovered Hopkins at Oxford. Had a thin little collection he kept in his pocket." He looked away. "Gave it to me before he died of malaria."

"I'm . . . so sorry," Amie began. But those three words, pathetic and flimsy, covered so little of those years. The losses that still ached.

Seth turned back, and the corners of his eyes crinkled, a dimple showing through the stubble of his cheeks where he must not have shaved lately. "But a party's no place for swapping those sorts of stories, yet. Tell me something I've always wondered about, and I'm guessing you're just the person to ask: Where did Shibby get her name?"

"Ah. I'm happy to help you with that. First, you probably know she grew up in Texas."

"That's hard to miss knowing her more than five minutes."

"Second, her daddy was a Pentecostal preacher somewhere south of Fort Worth. He was the one who named his sweet baby girl Shibboleth Shiphrah Travis."

"Dear Jesus."

"Exactly. There's a fight going on in all three of the names, Texas and Old Testament both. It's no wonder she's got some spine to her. Have to, to have stood up under the weight of those names all these years."

Chuckling, he held her eyes.

"Actually," Amie added more quietly, "something hard made her leave Texas, I think. Honestly, I don't know what it was. When you're a kid growing up, it never occurs to you to ask an adult what it was in the past that sent them running from home. Until, maybe, you're old enough to have run yourself. Maybe even come back."

Amie felt him searching her eyes, as if he were trying to recall something he'd heard about her long ago. He'd have left the village by then for college. She looked away.

In the living room, the little ones, including the children of Shibby's former foster kids, as well as Chester and Hopkins, tumbled about, only sometimes landing on the rug's padding. Occasionally, somebody yelped, but mostly they squealed, plunging their faces into Hopkins's long fur. Beside them, several of the adults danced, their feet somehow sliding and spinning among the small, tumbling bodies. Ian's fingers bounced over the keys into "Take the A Train" as Hopkins bounded in a circle.

Amie found herself seeing the puppies from years ago that someone let out of their box in the corner nearest the hearth. With ears too long for their heads and legs too short to be goldens, they were creatures no one had planned for or knew where to put, except to dump on the side of the road.

"Strays," a nine-year-old Jake had muttered, "like all of us here. Unwanted strays."

He drew back a foot as if he might kick one. But one of the smaller children dived for the puppy just then, and Jake stopped his foot just short of connecting with the child's head.

The little girl rocked onto her back, the puppy sprawled over her chest, and stuck her lip out. "Jakie, no!"

"I wasn't gonna hurt the stupid dog." Jake kicked the leg of a wooden high-back chair instead.

"Shibby!" the little girl wailed. "Jakie said *stupid* again!"

Before she could finish her tattle, Jake caught her up by both ankles and flipped her upside down, the girl's face an oval of shock, then delight as he spun her around.

The other children scrambled forward. "Me too, Jakie. Me too!"

As if the spinning had shaken off his own darker mood, Jake held up a hand. "You little ingrates will all get a turn, I promise. But *after* I grab something me and Shibby made special." His eyes had shot toward Amie, sitting on the floor quietly, pensively, arms wrapped around her bent legs.

He'd disappeared through the kitchen's swinging door, loud on its ancient hinges, and emerged with Shibby, who balanced a platter of towering, sliding tiers of chocolate. A cluster of candles blazed on top.

"Jake made it all by himself," Shibby announced.

Amie could still recall holding her breath, afraid to stand, afraid that the moment might not really be hers.

"Happy birthday, Amie!" Jake and Shibby had called together, the younger children jumping about.

Like little frogs in pajamas, Amie had thought. *Precious, precious frogs.*

"I've never had one," she'd whispered.

Jake's jaw dropped. "What the hel—?"

"Hill," Shibby corrected. "What the Sam Hill."

"What the holy *hill*, then. With all his mountains of dough, your daddy doesn't get you a big ole bakery cake with fancy roses all over the sides?"

Shibby had been watching her face—Amie remembered that clearly—and was quick to add, "I reckon her daddy'll send something later."

Amie had felt the weight of Shibby's expression, the concern there. It served as confirmation for what Amie had been suspecting: that her experience of home was different from other children's.

"I . . . don't know if my father knows when my birthday is, actually." When a roomful of faces turned silently, pityingly toward her, a hot flush of humiliation rose through her neck. Dear God, these were the lost children, the rejected, abandoned, pathetic ones of the village, pitying *her*. "Because," she'd blurted, "he's a busy and important man."

That had been the moment she'd been exposed, beneath the Jordan Marsh coat and Bean boots, for the poor, lonely child that she was.

That had been the moment, too, when Shibby had claimed Amie as one of her own.

If not by the state of Maine, Shibby had come to say, *then by the state of grace, which has its own rugged coastline.*

Jake had gone chattering on about the cake, how he'd doubled the icing's butter because who doesn't love extra butter, but maybe that was making the layers slide, and would she please blow out the candles now before the flames went all sideways onto the floor?

Amie had let herself be hugged by Shibby and by all the children. She'd eaten a slice of cake nearly as big as her face. She'd laughed till she hurt.

And she'd known herself to be home.

For all the betrayal he'd dealt her years later, the week she'd left town, it had been Jake who'd first remembered her birthday.

Jake.

Standing here now, Amie heard in her head the voice, strained and exhausted, of the woman at the defense agency: *We have more than seventy-nine thousand cases still open like yours, Miss Stilwell. Although I will say, it's rare we can't find a name for enlistment, at least. I'm sorry. I wish we could tell you more.*

Plucking her out of the past now, Shibby approached and laid her palm on Amie's cheek. Then with the other, she handed Amie a platter of ham sprinkled with cinnamon and brown sugar and smelling of maple syrup as she addressed Seth. "You're just in time, you know."

"In time for . . ."

"We were just wondering what we would do with the too much food we made. How lucky for us that you've come!"

Seth reddened and rubbed the back of his hand across his stubbled chin. He looked as if he'd like to say something, and also as if his throat had suddenly closed shut.

Chester scrambled up from the floor to stand beside Shibby.

"Mister Chester!" Amie called.

At her greeting, he reached out a hand to take hers. His eyes, still sad, appeared less hollowed out than last night but still one-dimensional, mostly lifeless, like a sketch by a novice artist yet to study the art of eyes.

Behind them, the kitchen door swung open again, Kalia now holding aloft a platter that left the scent of banana and brown sugar in her wake. Chester took in a breath so deep his nose pointed up to the ceiling.

"Plantains!" Kalia announced as she set it down. "You, Mister Chester, must be the first to try the things, yes? It would be a great favor to me, to see if I've remembered my grandmother's recipe right."

The little boy's eyes rounded as he sampled a bite. Considered. Then nodded, fixing on Kalia a look of abject adoration.

"Precisely," said Kalia, "the thing on your face I was hoping to see."

Amie stood with Chester at the rough-hewn table as Shibby motioned the guests to gather around.

The children waited for the prayer, forks gripped in their fists.

Shibby bowed her head. "Well, God. Where do we even start? We're just all bowled over with gratefuls for this food and the whole bunkhouse of hands that prepared it, mostly not mine. We ask, please: give us your light to see by and keep us keeping this table long and wide enough for all who'd ever want a seat. We give thanks, we surely do, for the long and the wide of your love that found a seat for the rascally likes of all of us here."

A pause. Amie watched the children's eyes spring open, sensing the denouement of the prayer.

"Amen." Shibby threw open both arms. "Now, children, you may begin."

By *children*, Amie recalled, Shibby always meant anyone there. And for a moment, the faces around the room all seemed to shine with childlike delight, the worries of bills and bad health lifting.

The entire group swelled toward the table, mounding their plates and balancing them on their free hands as they moved about the first floor. Shibby stood beaming over the platters as they emptied—as if somehow she saw a world Amie couldn't see, one where there was only goodness and kindness and plenty. Platters that always refilled. Tables that lengthened and widened no matter who came stumbling by.

After eating, Amie wandered back to the living room, where Shibby sat cross-legged on the floor beside Chester. They were gluing a black yarn beard to a glass mason jar. A few feet away, a young woman who'd not taken off her coat, a mauve full-skirted affair, stood watching.

With a jolt, Amie recognized her from the street when Seth had driven Amie to the Promontory the night before. Stella Lapierre, another one of Shibby's former foster kids—though only briefly.

Stella put out an elegant, long-fingered hand. "Well, if it isn't little Amelia Stilwell, all grown up."

Amie stared back at her—and felt the old stab of insecurity. Because here were movie-star-perfect features: unblemished skin, a beauty mark, perfectly penciled in, hair a sunny, Marilyn Monroe blond. Back when

Stella had been sixteen, glamorous even in a simple calico dress and leaving for a date with yet another boy in a letterman's jacket, Amie and Jake used to gaze up, starstruck, from playing Monopoly on the Orchard floor.

"Stella," Amie said now. "You look . . . exactly the same."

The truth Amie didn't add was that Stella's looks had, if anything, improved. Which ought to break some sort of universal law: that the unblemished elite of high school should have bloomed early and begun shriveling by now.

Stella cocked her head. "You're pretty much the last person I'd expect to come back to the cove. Though to be fair, I'd have said the same thing of myself."

"I remember you lived here at the Orchard for a year or so."

"Toward the end of high school, yeah. The year my parents decided to take their private squabbles to the streets, to the racquet club, to the general store. It was humiliating."

Amie recalled that now. Stella had been from a well-to-do family, but with no relatives nearby. Her father's leaving and her mother's nervous breakdown had caused quite the stir.

"Anyway"—Stella shrugged an elegant shoulder—"Shibby stepped in. You were here at the house more than me, it felt like. You and little Jakie, the bookworm valedictorian two of a kind. Everyone called you 'the smart ones' in the house. Like the rest of us weren't."

Amie was startled to hear an edge of bitterness there. "You were 'the beautiful one,' which must've been nice. The rest of us with broken-out skin and braces."

Stella's face, though, did not soften with the memory.

"Unless"—Amie inclined her head, watching Stella—"it wasn't as nice as I always assumed. Also, not that it matters, I wasn't the valedictorian."

"Weren't you? Oh. That's right. You went kind of crazy that last year, then took off out of town. My God, I'd forgotten all about that."

Stella stepped back to consider Amie head to toe. "Anyway, you're prettier now than you were then."

And that, Amie thought wryly, *would be what really matters.*

"My God, Amelia. Top of the class, then you just disappeared into nowhere. All of us who passed through the Orchard had our stories, didn't we? Heard you've been living in D.C. or somewhere since the war. You married?"

Amie crossed her arms like a shield over her heart. "I had . . . There was a pilot. During the war. But . . . no." She offered no more than that—and even that was too much. In Amie's head echoed the solitary call of the loon, mournful, unanswered: *I'm here, here, where are you?* "Not married."

"By the look of your face, I shouldn't have asked." Stella glanced away—out past the living room window into the dark. "Honestly, I don't recommend it."

"You're married, then?"

"Was."

Amie waited for more, but Stella only plucked a cigarette from her purse, lit it, and took a long drag, her lips marking the white with a bright red band. "War took a lot from all of us in one way or another. At any rate, I'm seeing someone quite seriously now. We'll be getting married soon, I feel sure." She added that last, Amie thought, with a lift to her chin in that way people do when they only wish they were sure. "Guess you'll be staying at your old man's place?"

Amie shook her head. "It's closed up for the winter." *And my father and I hardly ever speak.*

Now it was Stella's turn to wait for more explanation.

Apparently seeing there'd be none coming, she nodded. "At any rate, surely you'll be inheriting that gorgeous old place one of these days. My mother recently moved to Florida with her new husband and just deeded over their place here."

Amie nodded. "The Captain Cavin house, just down from the Promontory."

"Exactly, and while it's not nearly so grand as that Captain Smollett home of yours—"

Not mine, Amie wanted to say. *And never a home. Just a house my father owns.*

"Still, it's been gratifying to bring the place back from years of neglect and poor taste."

Stella straightened her shoulders. Then pointed down at the home-made manger scene displayed on a sideboard—apparently left up all these months since last Christmas. "I remember Shibby would leave this thing out the whole year until one of us kids complained it was too hard to dust around."

Amie's mouth twitched at the memory of Jake at fourteen or so, staving around the sideboard where the manger scene was splayed.

It's embarrassing, he'd muttered. *Nothing but cardboard and construction paper and glitter. Piece of crap. Whole thing ought to get tossed.* He'd reached for it.

Amie had grabbed his arm first. *Don't, Jake. I love it this way.*

Now Stella lifted a shepherd made from a cardboard toilet paper tube, its arms brown pipe cleaners and its robes an old washcloth. Then lifted a wise man crafted from a tin can, gold braid glued at strange angles all over its grand silvery self, and a tennis ball left on the Promontory Inn's court painted gold, with more braid for a crown.

Stella shook her head. "It's grown even since my day. Must be thirty shepherds here. Probably—what'd you guess—thirteen wise men, and even some wise women now, it would appear?" She lifted one paper towel tube with a painted face, its lips crayoned red with full brown yarn for hair and strips of terry cloth strategically placed like a bikini. "Surprised Shibby didn't monitor this little hussy."

Shibby looked up from where Chester had moved on from the mason jar and was completing another addition, this one an old brown sock stuffed with pine needles. Its face was a bright Picassoed nose and eyes with no mouth.

The lines of her face crinkled. "You may've noticed: not every piece is quite to scale."

For an instant, Amie found herself seeing through the young Jake's eyes: the mismatched, misshapen ugliness of it—like a huddle of Frankenstein's monsters gathered around a cardboard manger. Above it all sat a silver menorah.

"It always drove Jake crazy," Amie said. A flush of pain washed crimson across Shibby's face.

But Stella broke the silence with a laugh. "It is an awful lot of shepherds, and they seem to keep coming."

"But," Shibby asked in that voice of hers that was quiet and calm, yet somehow filled up the room, "how could we turn any away?"

Amie squeezed Shibby's shoulder as she joined Stella by the fire. They exchanged pleasantries for several moments.

"So that's great," Amie said, "you were able to move into your folks' old place. Great views out there on the point."

"They are that. So long as I can keep the Promontory guests from tromping across my backyard all summer. People with money to burn like that think the whole world is theirs to tromp on. Some of us work hard for what we have."

"As a nurse you must see a lot of what's going on. Behind the scenes, I mean."

Stella shot her a look. "You have no idea."

"I'm sure Shibby probably already asked you this." Amie made sure Chester was occupied with his shepherd. "Any idea who his family might be?"

"Poor little guy. What kind of a monster treats a kid like that?"

"The police have no clue—no one seems to. Part of the mystery of the whole thing is he doesn't appear to have been mistreated before coming here."

"Thank goodness at least he's in good hands for now."

"While I'm being nosy, and since you probably see more than some others in the village might see . . . There was a maroon Bentley here my first night in town—last night, in fact. Goodness, it seems days ago. I wonder if you'd have any idea who around here might drive a Bentley. Or maybe you know someone in Portland who does."

Stella swiveled to face Amie full on. "A Bentley. Maroon."

"Sound familiar?"

"I may have seen it once before, though I'm not sure."

"And did you know who it belonged to?"

Stella hesitated. "You'll understand when I say it's a bit classified. Too much gossip already in a small town, you know?"

She clearly wanted to say more. Was weighing how much she could.

"This much I can tell you: it could concern"—she glanced both ways—"an affair. Quite possibly with an out-of-towner." She raised a carefully penciled eyebrow, as if to say she couldn't decide which was worse: the sordidness of the affair or that it involved someone from outside Pelican Cove.

"What if I told you this person, the driver of the Bentley, seemed to be a danger to himself and possibly others?"

Stella smoothed back her hair. "I'd say I wasn't the least bit surprised."

Chapter 15

A commotion from the top of the staircase startled the occupants of the living room, all the tumbling and jitterbugging suddenly stilled, Ian's fingers on the yellowed keyboard plinking to a stop. A ghostly figure began descending the flight of stairs—with a thunk on each step.

As they watched, the wraith continued its thumping approach. At the bottom, Kalia and Seth stepped from behind the bulky figure they'd been carrying, its height and breadth fully covered in what Amie saw now were old canvas sails. Kalia motioned for Shibby to join her at the center of the room as the crowd circled around them. Seth ducked his head and stepped back. Catching Amie's eye, he flashed a half smile.

"I'm not much," Kalia was saying, "at the speeches and things. But I wanted to thank our friend Shibby for welcoming me when I was new here and still missing my island, my home. Still thinking that it was much too cold here. Imagine."

The crowd laughed with her and pressed closer in.

"But as a small way of showing my thanks, and thanks for all the others here that she's welcomed, I wanted to present our friend Shibby with this." Gently, Kalia lifted the canvas.

Crafted in driftwood stood a sculpture of a woman with her arms open to a child. The woman's hair was made of both dark and bleached-gray wood curling in waves up from her head as if caught in a sea breeze. Her skirts swirling around her legs, she reached toward the child with such energy and delight, it felt as if in the next instant she would sweep the child up into the air.

The entire sculpture was crafted from wood, and only found wood, at that. Just what Kalia had gathered from the shore.

It was exquisite. Every curve, every muscle, every limb of the inter-twining branches was perfect. Somehow those bare lines conveyed a kind of joy so intense, it was hard to look at—and harder still to look away.

For a full moment, nobody spoke. Amie's eyes shot to Chester, who was gazing at the sculpture with the kind of rapture he'd given the plantains.

Frozen in place, looking, for an instant, less lifelike than the art, Shibby stared. "How did you . . . ?" she murmured. Eyes brimming, she turned to the other faces. "Did you ever think you'd see such a talent in all your born days?"

Applause broke out as Shibby threw her arms around Kalia. The crowd jostled to see the sculpture more closely.

Waiting until everyone there had spoken to the sculpture's creator, Amie approached. "Kalia, this is amazing. Honestly. That you could craft fine art and not just some cheesy bundle of sticks out of driftwood . . . I wonder, do you have any more sculptures like this?"

"None like this one, no."

Amie's heart sank.

"But I do have other sculptures if that's what you mean. I don't make any of the two just alike."

"You . . . Really? That's perfect—fabulous, actually. If they're half this good, Kalia—"

"You're welcome to see them, you know."

"I'd love to. As soon as you're ready." Amie lowered her voice. "I want to ask you this: If I were to open a gallery to sell some photographs of the Maine coast, and if I took in some other New England artists to sell their work on commission, what would you think of including your sculptures? We could discuss percen—"

Amie stopped there. Because a few feet from the piano where Ian was pounding out an old show tune, Chester was sitting on the floor playing with a brown sock shepherd and a tin-can wise woman—and singing. After hours of hardly making a sound, he was belting out the song. Every word.

Just tea for two and two for tea,
Just me for you and you for me alone . . .

Amie approached the little boy slowly, afraid to spook him. Shibby, already beside him, looked up to meet Amie's eye. They sang along, others in the crowd picking it up.

One by one, guests were entering the room from all over the house.

Nobody near us, to see us or hear us,
No friends or relations on weekend vacations . . .

"Tea," Amie whispered near Shibby's ear. "That's what he must've been trying to tell us last night. His bedtime ritual: that grim prayer and this song."

Shibby was nodding, apparently having already reached the same conclusion.

Ian finished the song with a flourish, then leaped into a number of Frank Sinatra hits, none of which seemed to capture the child's attention, much less call up his little voice. Ian launched into other songs now, his head twitching back to see the boy's reaction. The older the song, Amie noticed, the more likely Chester was to at least look up. Even light up a little. On "When Irish Eyes Are Smiling," the child's mouth moved to each word, and he looked up again from his play.

To Amie's left, Fletch grunted. "Irish. Maybe that's who the kid's people were. Nowadays, world's so jumbled up you can't tell the micks from the Brits."

But Amie's attention was fixed on the child—watching his mouth. His eyes.

Guests were beginning to leave, stuffing on boots and ramming fists into coats. Arms thrown about Shibby, they kissed her on the cheek or the forehead or on top of her wild, waving hair. Stella, bundling back up in her mauve coat and lifting a hand to Shibby, swept out the door.

Seth bent to embrace Shibby now. His eyes lifting to Amie's, he turned to her. Standing close in the departing crowd, Amie could sense the other figures blurring as his eyes locked on hers. He seemed to be deciding whether to speak.

Suddenly, though, at the sound of Chester's small voice again, everyone turned.

"'Danny Boy,'" Amie whispered. "Dear God. He's singing 'Danny Boy.'"

This time, Chester rose and stood beside Ian at the piano. The two of them sang together, the young man's tenor and the little boy's pure, sweet soprano sending out notes weighted with beauty and sorrow:

> *But when ye come, and all the flowers are dying,*
> *If I am dead, as dead I well may be . . .*

Tears pooled in Shibby's eyes, and in Ian's, as everyone sang along.

> *Ye'll come and find the place where I am lying,*
> *And kneel and say an Ave there for me . . .*

The little boy's head tilted back toward the ceiling, and his face soaked with tears, he sang to some trusted face the rest of them could not see. Amie could feel her own eyes brimming.

Whatever this child's story, she thought, *he's been acquainted with death.*

She knelt by the child and slipped an arm around him. "Did your mother sing that to you, Ches?" she asked gently.

Blinking up at her, he shook his head. "No," he whispered. Then earnestly held his forefinger across his lips.

Chapter 16

Boston

Tom Darnay woke in a panic.

He'd left four stories of lights blazing last night in his Back Bay townhouse when he'd fallen asleep on the couch—its leather top grain and aged to a mottled whiskey brown, but uncomfortable as hell. Freud might have said those four stories of lights left on said that his subconscious was dealing with feeling alone.

But far from the aloneness becoming a fetter, he'd let it drive him forward, hadn't he? To push through flight training with the Royal Canadian Air Force, and then through the hell of war. To survive the purgatory of recrossing the Atlantic and going to college when, in his head, bombs still dropped from his bay doors all day long. Anyone could see all he'd achieved: this prime piece of Marlborough Street real estate, for one thing, and the beautiful women who came here on his arm.

If his conscience pricked sometimes at Fossick's take-no-prisoners approach to business, well, that was the way corporate empires grew.

Only children could hope to live in a world where kindness was the rule of the day.

Still, something inside him ached at times for the child he'd once been.

On his front stoop were only brown leaves, no Sunday edition of the *Globe*. The paperboy must be shirking his duty again—but also maybe it was a sign. Maybe there was no photo, nothing for Jake to fear. He'd buy a paper on Tremont this morning, together with a stiff drink. He'd look then, when he was ready, but meanwhile he could still breathe.

Cutting through the Public Garden on his way to work, Tom strode past the centerpiece pond. They'd put away the Swan Boats for the colder months, the willows bending bare and grieving over the water.

There on a park bench was an abandoned Sunday edition of the *Boston Globe*. Approaching slowly, Tom made himself look.

On the front page of the *Globe* above the fold, his own face grimaced back at him. Features contorted. As if he were confessing some unspeakable crime.

Tom jerked it up for a closer look. The expression on his face was bad enough, but also the photographer had caught the gold-domed outline of the Massachusetts State House behind him—like a farce of a halo. The dome's glow only seemed to highlight the shadowed face in the foreground, Desmond Fossick's sleek young lieutenant looking as if he had something to hide.

Tom scanned the cutline, a masterpiece of imagination:

> Thomas Darnay, second in command for one of Boston's wealthiest—and most controversial—moguls, considers the claims of improper conditions at several of Fossick's properties.

The paper clenched in both hands, Tom skimmed the story. It included a fresh accusation by a worker who'd reported unsafe conditions at a factory and reports of repairs delayed in essentially ten-ement housing. Few details given. Nothing but a photograph that made the whole pitiful story appear to be drawing to some sort of epic climax.

Mind spinning, Tom launched out into Charles Street without waiting for traffic to clear. A Mike's Pastry delivery truck screeched to a halt three inches away, its driver leaning out the window to flick his fingers from under his chin.

Tom was barely over the threshold of the fourth floor of Fossick Enterprises when his secretary, also apparently working on a Sunday, punched her arm toward him, receiver gripped in her manicured hand. "Mr. Fossick for you, Mr. Darnay."

She didn't have to say that Fossick on the other end of the line sounded irate. Her eyes, wide and alarmed, said that for her. She'd probably already fielded any number of profanities.

"Thank you. I'll take it in my office."

Tom squared his shoulders. Ridiculous how one man could inspire so much fear in so many.

"Good morning, Mr. Fossick."

"I rise, Mr. Darnay, at four o'clock sharp each morning."

"I believe you've mentioned that once or twice." *Every day.*

"I've checked the price of gold, silver, as well as the share prices of Ford, Bethlehem Steel, and General Electric on the stock ticker before the sun's up, then later the whole damn Dow Jones. I've studied the day's performance of the London Stock Exchange before the slackers on our own coast begin to wake up. Typically, I've finished the *New York Times*, the *Times of London* and the *Wall Street Journal* before most of Boston has had coffee."

Tom braced himself for what had to be coming.

"The *Globe*, Mr. Darnay, I save for last, the paper of record for the general region of my birth—which, typically, is often hardest on me. Still, even the *Globe* rarely insults me on its *front page*."

"I'll be calling the editor to demand a retraction."

"I don't have the damn patience to hear mewling excuses over the phone. Be at Mount Vernon Street in ten minutes."

"Actually, Mr. Fossick—"

"*Ten minutes*, Mr. Darnay." The line went dead.

Fossick's butler, Byers, was at the black double doors of the Beacon Hill home on Mount Vernon Street when Tom arrived. *Townhouse*, Fossick called it, despite its being a mansion. Fossick himself would have happily flaunted his riches, Tom knew, but the caste of wealthiest Boston Brahmins he tried so hard to imitate were famous for amassing material comforts even while scorning any display of them. Thus, *townhouse* rather than *mansion*.

Byers held out a gloved hand to take Tom's hat, then realized that Tom, who'd hurried from the office with only his coat, had arrived bareheaded. The butler looked past the visitor to the medieval tapestry that covered one wall of the foyer, as if it might offset the obvious philistinism of the visitor who stood there, hatless and clearly sweating.

"Mr. Fossick is in his study."

In hopes of the offer of coffee or something stronger, Tom turned. But Byers had already marched back, chin stoically high, through the foyer and disappeared.

Fossick was pacing by the study's only window. Mahogany bookshelves spanning each wall, the room was dark. A small fire burned in the hearth. On top of the logs was the front page of the *Globe*, Tom's own face succumbing to flames.

Sweat breaking out on his forehead and neck, Tom's vision suddenly went dark. Now the fire in the study hearth appeared to leap forward, tongues licking the walls, fire beneath him, above him, all around him, an engine roaring in his ears. Tom's right hand slipped to his coat pocket, the tin of the flask cool, comforting to his touch. But Fossick was only a few feet away.

Folding his hands together behind him to disguise their shaking, Tom crossed the Persian rug to one of two leather chairs by the hearth. Fossick shifted in place, a phone receiver in one hand and its cord wrapped around his fist like a boxing glove.

Now he bellowed into the phone. "How the *hell* is this still a problem, Miss Michaud?"

Tom tried not to watch his own face on the logs twist and then char, tried not to feel the tremor of his own hands.

Fossick listened for a few beats. He appeared to be gathering air for his next blast, which came in a gale of disgust. "I'd thought a woman at the helm there might actually work. I suggest, Miss Michaud, you don't prove me wrong!"

With that, Fossick slammed the received into its cradle.

From a small wire structure with a single candle burning beneath it, he lifted a brandy snifter warming over the flame. Three words, *the Promontory Inn*, had been etched into its glass.

"That sounded," Tom began, "like something I should know about."

"I'll tell you what I'd like to discuss with *you*, Darnay." Fossick jerked his head toward the fire.

Like yesterday when he'd faced the reporters, Fossick's cheeks were lit with two tiny circles of red. Which was never good.

Behind Fossick, on the floor-to-ceiling shelves, sat books purchased by a designer for the leather of their bindings and gold-embossed titles of classics that the old monied class of New England all seemed to own. If anyone here in Boston actually disliked Hawthorne or Melville or Thoreau, it could not be uttered aloud.

So far as Tom knew, Fossick had never read any book ever. But he'd done well in collecting fine bindings.

"Mr. Fossick, my facial expression in that photo has nothing to do with our work here. I'd simply . . . recalled a memory."

"A memory."

"Yes."

"Exactly what memory, pray tell, completely unglues a man—*in public*—whom I pay very well to remain *glued*?"

"It wasn't exactly in public—"

"It certainly seems to be now. I've no interest in why you'd allow yourself to be distressed. That, I assume, is your own business and mercifully not mine. The photo, however, suggests a vulnerability in our approach to business. As if anyone who scrapes a knee roller-skating can come sniveling to my doorstep and demand compensation."

"I understand, Mr. Fossick."

"Do you, Mr. Darnay? Because I grit my way through the Handel and Haydn Society's rendition of *Messiah* here every damn year just to contribute to this city's perception of me as a man with a heart."

Tom nearly laughed here, the idea of Fossick as a man with a heart being so completely absurd. But Fossick was railing on.

"I cannot bear Handel, do you understand? *Cannot. Bear. Him.* Yet I press on, and do you know *why*?"

"To present the warmer, more civic-minded face of Desmond Fossick."

"Tell me this: Do you have any idea how much damage this one photo has done? Your becoming emotional, Darnay, in an unguarded moment means now we must take action. *Firm* action."

Behind Fossick on a grand piano that, so far as Tom knew, had never been played sat a platoon of elaborate brass frames parading pictures of Fossick with important people. The incorrigible Mayor Curley beamed, appearing downright boisterous in his corruption, alongside the boyish newcomer John Fitzgerald Kennedy, waving after he took Curley's congressional seat. Inside one elaborate brass frame was Frank Sinatra, beaming his signature smile and lifting a glass to Fossick beside him, palm trees behind the two men. On one end sat a photo with

President Truman—though Truman was glancing sideways at Fossick as if watching for a snake to strike.

Only one woman figured in any of the photos. Unlike the others in black and white, this one was in color. Tom didn't recognize the woman as a celebrity, and she wasn't wearing a blouse cut as low as was generally required to make Fossick stand still, but she was attractive in her well-cut navy blazer with a gold anchor on its pocket.

Fossick's arm was around the woman's waist—or, actually, lower, as if he'd let the moment of the camera's flash allow him to run a hand over her curves. The woman's gaze was confident, but also . . . what? Calculating? Whatever she was actually thinking about the placement of Fossick's hand, she'd learned to freeze in place for self-preservation like a wood frog.

Other photos showed Fossick as a young man flaunting trophies. Tom squinted at a probably twenty-year-old Fossick in sepia tone, his boxing gloves on, his chest bare, and his face already showing a desperation—the mounting torrent of smarts and energy that had grown up in a small town and not yet found their channel. Boxing must have given him something to hit, but no worthy opponent.

Not a single other woman graced the piano's splay of frames. Except, now that Tom looked more closely, one grainy candid photo framed in simple pine at the back, the young woman's hair cut in a bob, her arms holding a toddler. A stack of lobster pots teetered beside her, a stand of pines towering in the background. Even in black and white, the woman looked alarmingly wan and exhausted.

"Your mother?" Tom asked. Then wished he could swallow the words whole, even if they gashed his throat going down.

Fossick rounded on him, boxer's hands raised to waist level: ready.

"Sorry. Just hit me. I've never"—Tom scanned the pictures on the piano—"seen a picture of your mother before."

It was shaky ground, and Tom knew it. Shaky like the edge of an active volcano.

Fossick's gaze was searing. "Tumor," he said. "They said it could be taken out. Said she might live if it was. 'If she'll live,' we told them, me and my dad did, 'then whatever the cost. Whatever the goddamn cost.' The hell they knew."

Tom waited. It was safer not to make a sound.

"Mortgaged the house, the boat, took out a goddamn mountain of loans to pay for the treatments. You know, she was the only woman I ever really trusted. Ever. You know what happened after all that?"

Tom shook his head. Though he could guess.

"We goddamn lost her." Glaring, as if Tom had forced the confession from him, Fossick flexed his arms. "Destroyed my old man," he added, turning away.

And you, Tom thought. *The destruction just came out looking different in you.*

"I'm so sorry," he offered at last.

"Yeah, well. Clearly, I don't need your pity, Darnay."

"I wasn't implying . . ."

Waving away whatever Tom might have said, Fossick snapped a letter from his desk, its paper thick and smelling of lavender. "I presume you recall the little matter of a certain"—he lowered his voice, though they were alone—"Mrs. W."

Tom tried making his face impassive but wondered if a cringe showed through at the edges. Of course he remembered. It haunted him. A sorry business. Fossick might pride himself on keeping a woman in every port, but this was another, messier matter. "The reply I sent her on your behalf wasn't sufficient, I assume? Shall I send another reasonably small check to the same post office box?"

"You know how women can be. A man has a fling, nothing more, maybe a few pleasant months together, and suddenly this sort assumes they're owed something. It's blackmail, I tell you." The right side of his upper lip curled. "Perhaps I should ask her to marry me—or let her think that's my intent. A good ploy, yes?"

"Only if you intend to follow through."

"If I want," Fossick exploded, "a damn choir boy for an assistant, I'll hire one."

A pause. The mahogany panels of the room seemed to crush inward. "Of course. Would you like me to try and negotiate a higher sum that might satisfy her?"

"Honestly? What I'd *like* is for you to make her disappear. For good, Darnay."

Tom did not move, the crackling of the fire, of his own face, to his right amplified in his ears.

"'Make her go away,'" he repeated, forming the words with care as if they might explode in his mouth. "You don't mean . . ."

"What the hell do you *think* a man means when he says that?" Fossick shook the letter, its handwriting shaky, its lines uneven. "We'll discuss this more fully later."

Tom put out a hand for the letter slowly, as if he feared its thick, perfumed paper might scald him.

Pacing forward, Fossick shoved the page at Tom's chest and stepped back, arms flexed. Predatory. Tom could see why his boxing opponents would've been cowed: not by the man's size, but by the ravenous hunger that emanated from him, a panther ready to sink teeth into the neck of his prey.

"We," Fossick snarled, "are taking a trip."

"Sir?"

"Are you *completely deaf?* You've got a half hour to pack."

"May I ask where we're going, Mr. Fossick?"

"You plan on piloting the plane? Didn't think so. Just be at my personal hangar at Logan Airport within the hour. By God, we'll give them a story."

Tom knew saying a thing was potentially suicidal, Fossick already a lit fuse. "It's not that I'm unwilling to go, of course. But it would be helpful to know—"

"Of course you're willing. You owe me your damn current existence."

Fossick stood with his hands clasped behind him as he stared out the window. Mount Vernon Street's linden trees glistened with a sheen of mist and bowed toward each other, forming a near tunnel of sequined brown arms. There'd be snow on them soon. Tom tried to think about snow.

He knew Fossick wasn't admiring the view. The pose was just that: a pose. One meant to convey a man of power deep in contemplation.

The head twitched to one side. "*Darnay*. I suggest you get the hell to it. You might begin by calling my pilot before he thinks he's taking a Sunday off."

The study door slammed behind Fossick so hard, the picture frames on the piano trembled, the one with the woman in the navy blazer falling onto its face.

Those eyes that had stared out with such calculating calm.

Chapter 17

Pelican Cove

This, Tess Michaud knew, was her time. Her place. No one was going to ruin that for her.

This ocean—this view—had been her inspiration when she'd first come to the Promontory at eighteen as a waitress. Then secretary. Then several more steep and wobbly rungs to general manager. She'd known from the first time she'd set foot on the flagstones of the entrance here that she would work at this inn the rest of her life. One day, she would run everything here.

"Run *everything*," she murmured aloud, "including its owner."

Men might be the tycoons and presidents and prime ministers and appear to take charge, but as a whole, she'd found, men were easily led. She'd learned the story of Samson as a girl watching the figures line up on the flannel graph board of the Cape James United Methodist Church. It might not have been the lesson the sweet gray-haired teacher had meant her to hear that morning with Nabisco Vanilla Wafers and watery punch, but Tess had taken the lesson to heart. A good-looking woman with a functioning brain could make men bend to her will, even men with remarkable strength.

Especially, in fact, men with remarkable strength.

Tess smiled to herself at the thought.

She'd often marveled at how often people failed to plan their own lives. Instead, they let their days career forward, one bump and crash after the next.

Then there were men like Desmond Fossick who thrived on the illusion of control. Not seeing how much they, too, were merely spinning their wheels. Ready—at the right time—to be undone.

Tess had left her office door open—intentionally. Everything Tess Michaud did was strategized three steps ahead. Her secretary—*so few women have their own secretaries,* Tess liked reminding herself—was prone to eavesdropping. The girl's mind gorged on a steady diet of *Photoplay* magazine. Last month she'd made her life goal becoming Jimmy Stewart's next wife. The month before it was Gary Cooper's.

Today, she'd pored over a *Photoplay* feature, been so immersed in it she'd been slow to answer the phone. Finally, Tess had snapped the distraction up from her desk. Pictures of lady golfers, swimmers, and tennis players in action lay against photos of Hollywood beauties, posed and perfect. This was supposedly proof that becoming an athlete—and also, the article implied, becoming college educated—made a woman nearly ineligible for marriage or a movie career, either one.

Tess had bent over the girl. "Do something, please, with that flabby mass of gray between your ears."

Tess did not hate men. On the contrary, she simply understood her own power, and wielded her Max Factor Clear Red No. 2, what Elizabeth Taylor wore, without shame. But she had no patience with women, pretty or not, who insisted on being dumb as a stump.

Marching back to her own office, she surveyed her domain: a corner second-floor space she'd earned every inch of. Its forward-facing view overlooked the inn's grand entrance of stone and clapboard. Its left windows overlooked the croquet grounds and lawn tennis, the maples that edged them gone mostly bare, a handful of leaves hanging on, brown and bloodred.

Bloodred. Odd that she'd thought of the trees' color that way. Rather morbid but also understandable, given the man she worked for.

Tess often imagined her boss as a spider, a blood-sucking spider, spinning a web of cast-off women and unhappy workers and evicted tenants so vast, he was bound someday to be strangled in it himself.

"One can at least hope," Tess added aloud, feeling a thrill at the sound—the rebellion—of her own voice.

Through the office door she'd left open, Tess saw a maid racing past.

She lifted the receiver she'd set on her desk, though the line had gone dead. But Tess's secretary, and more importantly, the Audograph recording device for executive offices, wouldn't know that. Slipping her hand into the drawer, she punched the Audograph's switch to record.

"Shibby Travis just passed by my door, Mr. Fossick. If that's who you meant." Tess enunciated the next words, and even opened her desk drawer an inch wider. "I treat all of our workers with consummate fairness, of course. But, I agree, she somehow seems to know private details of our guests' lives. Even"—she paused here for dramatic impact—"of your own personal life. It is most disturbing."

She could imagine how he'd looked a moment ago when he'd yelled at her over the phone. His thin lips would've been pressed into a still-thinner line.

As if he were there in the room with her, Tess stood taller, glad for the extra height of her new peep-toe slingback heels. She crossed her arms over her chest. Even without Fossick's being physically present, her instinct was to be on the defensive, to protect from those hands of his, which tended to rove.

"She does have, as you recently learned, Mr. Fossick," Tess said to the machine, "a disquieting way of knowing things that she shouldn't. Clearly, this is unacceptable."

Some people as focused on their work as Tess Michaud might not have noticed what a member of the housekeeping staff said or did. Shibboleth Travis was only one of many maids, after all. Eminently replicable and unremarkable, really. Except for her seeming to know—or maybe sense—things about people, to be a person that complete strangers seemed drawn to, told secrets to, even. Adding to that was the maid's unfortunate habit of speaking her mind.

Most general managers wouldn't have known intimate details about a lowly member of the housekeeping staff, but Tess missed nothing.

It was what she excelled at—one of the many things, actually. But one of the few assets that didn't have to do with her looks. Her male colleagues were always willing to praise *those* out loud. With her in the room. Or just as she was leaving.

Damn. Now that *is some kind of pair on that one.*

As if her chest and backside and legs were all as open for comment as the inn's quarterly profit-and-loss statements she'd just set before them.

Tess did not have women friends to ask how they handled this sort of attention. She suspected some despised it and fumed silently into the coffee they fetched. Maybe, Tess thought, a few basked in it.

She, however, did neither. She did not return their flirtations. Nor did she complain when their eyes wouldn't fix on her face but kept drifting down. Instead, she used their distraction to her own advantage.

While she went right on not missing a thing.

Now, finishing her end of the call with a pretend Desmond Fossick, she cracked the drawer wider, the Audograph disc still spinning inside.

"Indeed." She placed a hand over the embroidered gold anchor on her navy blazer's pocket. The fact that Fossick wore the blazer himself when in town only made her despise the uniform more—his way of creating his workers in his own image. "Miss Travis's outspoken behavior could certainly mean unpleasantness for the peace—and profit margin—of the inn. Better safe than sorry these days. I agree with you, too, that her claiming to possess certain information about you could be construed as a threat. Pardon? Yes. I'll be sure to keep an eye on her. All right, then. Goodbye."

Tess switched off the Audograph. She'd learned much from her years here at the Promontory, including the art of listening well—eavesdropping, if necessary. Like everyone, Desmond Fossick had his weaknesses, and one of his weakest was women.

How fitting, how wonderfully fitting, if what he tries to ensnare in his own web might, in the end, be his own undoing.

Chapter 18

Amie was still trying the next morning to shake the image of Chester from the previous night, his big eyes tragic, a finger pressed over his lips. Stella Lapierre had been right with her word choice: What kind of *monster* had dumped the child off, apparently even demanded the boy not speak a word of whatever had happened?

But yesterday evening had also hinted at hope. Chester had sung his heart out, and Kalia Clarke, with her extraordinary sculpture hidden beneath the old sail, had given Amie the idea to approach someone in charge at the Promontory Inn. Here was a chance to move forward with the plan for how she might earn a living here.

The mist from last evening had turned into snow, a front coming through overnight—quite early for this many inches. The radio station WCSH out of Portland hadn't predicted more than a dusting. Now amber and russet leaves fell onto a blanket of white. Amie closed her eyes for just a moment and let herself breathe in the scent of the first snowfall and the fire she'd just set in the farmhouse's woodstove.

From the Orchard's front porch where she'd unloaded them, she lifted two long narrow planks of wood. She'd barely fit the cross-country skis into the Aston Martin the night she'd left D.C., but they'd been her mother's and not something Amie would leave behind, even when it meant abandoning a box of kitchen utensils there on the curb in D.C. as she'd loaded the car. No question which she'd use more.

The hickory of their construction made them not terribly light but sturdy, and their cambered design, arching up in the middle, distributed the skier's weight across the length of the skis. The poles from her mother's young womanhood were lengths of bamboo with leather wrist straps on one end and five-inch "baskets" with leather edging on the other so the pole tips only thrust so far into the snow.

Amie positioned her boots onto the slim width of skis. The buckles over the toes were stiff with age, as were the buckles of the straps that ran behind her heel, but her boots were securely fastened now. When they were kids, Jake had fashioned door hinges to hold the toes of their boots to their skis.

Jake.

Every corner of this village, nearly everything she touched, held reminders of him. Of the loss of him.

Amie admired the gleam of the wood against the snow, like the way she remembered her mother's hair, a light brown against the white fur of her coat's hood. She'd died when Amie was young, but that one image stayed vivid.

Pushing off, Amie found her rhythm, the kick, glide, kick, glide, skate forward. Most people here preferred keeping their arms parallel. But Amie, as impatient as a child as she was now, had found her own way of reaching a place faster than anyone else. Now each of her arms swung up as the opposite foot shot back. Muscle memory. Something elating about her body working, pushing, sleek and fast—without seeming to circuit commands through her brain.

Approaching Dock Circle, Amie slowed to herringbone uphill strides in front of Fáilte. She waved at Ian, staring out the front window of his shop and standing rigid, arms crossed tightly over his thin chest as if he needed to guard his insides.

Maybe he does, she thought.

Maybe whatever hurt in life that had come hurtling at him just kept coming.

If he saw her, Ian didn't wave back. From behind him, a woman stepped close to him, her back to the window. The woman's hair was pulled into a tight chignon, but she didn't appear to be old.

Whatever the woman said to Ian, his face contorted with . . . Was it grief? Shame? He dropped his head into his hands. The woman, too, seemed distraught, her head shaking back and forth as if she'd just disagreed with her own words.

It was no business of Amie's. Still, that expression of Ian's and the drop of his head . . . The sorrow heavy in that single gesture. She saw it again and again as she glided on up the edge of Ocean Avenue. As she passed the Captain Smollett house on her left, she kept her eyes straight ahead.

Amie left her skis propped against the Promontory entrance and launched herself into the main parlor straight to the concierge desk. A young Brit there, Collin, listened to her request and motioned to where the general manager, a Miss Michaud, was standing near one of the fireplaces surveying the room. The concierge chattered on for a moment—about the manager, the inn, Maine. Amie could imagine the guests here would be charmed by the accent, a hint of Cockney that felt reminiscent of the brave United Kingdom saved from the Nazis, a voice that seemed to have in it mulled wine and Saint Paul's Cathedral and Big Ben: things not entirely lost in the rubble of bombs.

"But first"—Amie placed a hand on Collin's arm—"could I ask a strange question?"

He grinned, his accent deepening. "The stranger the better, love."

"Is the portrait"—she gestured with her head toward the oil rendering of the inn's owner—"a new addition? I don't recall its hanging there when I was growing up here in the cove."

Collin cocked his head at the painting. Then leaned in to whisper, "I'm afraid it's a bit dreadful, really." He stopped there, apparently realizing he'd chattered himself onto thin ice. "But you're asking is it a recent addition. It is."

Amie squinted at the thing and found herself agreeing with the concierge's assessment. It was a bit dreadful, not because the artist hadn't managed to replicate the owner's face remarkably well, but precisely because the artist had—and in doing so, captured something in the man's eyes, the set of his jaw. Even through oil and canvas, something flammable, something dangerous, burned there. Studying the portrait, Amie could feel the general manager studying her.

So crossing the main parlor, Amie approached. The woman, though, spoke first.

"Tess Michaud." The general manager offered her hand to shake. She wore the Promontory Inn's standard blazer, but with the addition of a silk scarf at her neck, its navy-and-yellow pinstripe elegantly arranged.

"You're working on a Sunday, I see."

"I work *every* day, nearly. I take pride in my work. Now how might I help you?" Even asking to help, the woman conveyed power.

"Amelia Stilwell. I worked here a couple of summers in high school cleaning the docks and the sailboats that you keep for guests. I've recently come—"

"Welcome back," the general manager interjected, her tone cool.

"Thank you. I'm considering a new venture or two, and it occurred to me this inn might be the perfect place to see if I might take your old sails off your hands—the ones that can't be repaired. Back when I worked here those summers, there were inevitably some sails that had seen better days or that a guest had somehow slashed on rocks when a boat capsized, that sort of thing. You know how the guests can be."

The general manager eyed Amie as if any admission of difficult guests might be a trap. "You'd like these cast-off sails for . . . ?"

"For upholstery, actually. For the gallery I'm envisioning. The former tenant left a few couches and chairs, but they're horrifically stained." Amie leaned in. This appeared to be a woman who prided herself on good taste. "You'd be appalled. But I feel certain I could arrange the canvas to fit a nautical theme. And if this inn is run anything like to the standard it was back when I worked here, no sails in inferior shape would ever be allowed out with a boat."

A bit of a cheap shot—to appeal to snobbery. But it worked.

Tess Michaud tipped her head toward the long expanse of snow that sloped down to the harbor. "Follow me."

~

Amie followed the manager through a back corridor past vast shelves of linens and a closet apparently dedicated solely to the Promontory's extra navy blazers for staff. Just beside the blazers hung a line of keys with a sign beneath it that read, "Check Out All Cars in the Fleet from the Manager. NO EXCEPTIONS." Amie recalled seeing the sleek black car with the Promontory's name on its side cruise past her when she'd been in the phone booth.

Outside, picking their way down a shoveled path to the docks where the sailing hut perched, Amie waited for Tess Michaud to spin the combination lock. The numbers had not changed: still 1-7-9-3, the founding year of Pelican Cove.

Inside the hut, the general manager, who'd paused to slide boots over her slingbacks but wore no coat besides her blazer, appeared stiff with cold—and hurried. Finding several sails with rips and worn places, she navigated around the hulls of the boats and masts and daggerboards covered in tarps. But her eyes continually darted to the side of the hut. Approaching Amie, she handed over a stack of canvas.

"You're sure, Miss Michaud, you can spare these castoffs?"

"I'm sure that the Promontory Inn presents only the finest for our guests, including the sails on our boats."

"Well, then. Thank you. I'm so glad to see the inn's standards are being maintained so well under you."

"Yes. Well. I wish you success in your business endeavor. Next to the bakery, you said?" The woman suddenly lurched closer to Amie, causing her to stumble back, and Amie's foot caught on something rounded jutting out just behind her. Tess Michaud reached out to help steady her, even as they both looked down for what had obstructed the path.

Old sails lay draped over bundles of masts at all angles, and judging by the gleam of polished wood, more daggerboards and rudders had been stacked sloppily over a long, rectangular base. And on the hut's floor . . .

Amie studied the sand floor of the hut, the faintest outline of tire tread barely visible there among the footprints. There were no boat trailers here, each hull being carried and stored by the summer staff.

Tess Michaud, rather than apologize for all but shoving Amie backward, merely watched, as if curious to see what she would do next. Amie lifted a corner of an old sail. And found herself staring at half of a whitewall tire and a luxuriously rounded wheel arch of shiny maroon.

"The Bentley!" She breathed it more than spoke it aloud. Whirling, she yanked the canvas farther back and reached to catch the toppled masts that had disguised the vehicle's shape beneath. "This is the car I've been searching for!"

Unblinking, the general manager met her eye.

"Miss Michaud, I have more than a few questions. I had to ram this car from behind to keep it and its driver from being flattened by the evening train."

"Indeed?" The woman's face did not change.

Something too still there, Amie thought. *Something calculated, like a decoy missile left as a trap.*

"What a shame, Miss Stilwell. However, it's not my vehicle. I can assure you of that."

"It's Mr. Fossick's, I assume."

"No."

"No?"

"No. Of that, too, I can assure you."

"Honestly, Miss Michaud, I find that hard to believe. Desmond Fossick is one of the few individuals for miles around who could afford this sort of automobile. Not to mention that it happens to be stored on property he owns."

Also, Amie wanted to add aloud, *who's to say you're not lying for him?*

The general manager shrugged. "You're free to believe what you like."

Her face the very picture of bland indifference, this Tess Michaud appeared to be an excellent liar, in fact. As well as loyal in the extreme.

"Miss Michaud, whoever was sitting there on the train tracks that night was trying to take his own life. And someone needs to know who that is in order to help."

The general manager gazed back at her impassively.

Amie returned the gaze without blinking. "So you're not going to tell me."

"I already have. It's not mine. Nor is it Mr. Fossick's. That is sufficient for you to know."

"You realize there are times when keeping a secret is risking a life."

Amie watched the general manager take this in, then mentally bat it away.

"You realize, Miss Stilwell, that Mr. Fossick never drives his own car when he is in town."

Just what Shibby said.

"Furthermore, the car could belong to any number of people."

"Any number of people associated with Desmond Fossick, since it's being stored here. Any number of people who can afford a machine worth more than most people in Maine make in a year. I'd say that number isn't so very large, wouldn't you?"

The general manager stood at the sailing-hut door—her posture, Amie noted, strangely at ease, given what had just been exposed.

"Miss Stilwell, I have work to do. Our time in here is over. I assure you—and I regret I don't know how to put this delicately—it is no business of yours. Let me recommend simply that you leave the issue of this car alone."

But even as she said it, the general manager smiled. As if she were counting on her command—that the issue of the car be left alone—becoming the last thing Amie would do.

Chapter 19

———— ❧ ————

Pacing across the shop's wide-plank pine floors, Amie passed one of the open boxes she'd hauled from D.C., the books she'd not been able to part with. One finger running over the spines, she scanned their titles—like viewing a list of old friends. At the *W*s, she paused, then pulled a black leather edition with gilt-edged pages from its place. The portrait of a young man, Dorian Gray, in formal white tie stared back from its cover.

Like the portrait on Oscar Wilde's novel, Fossick's likeness surely showed more than the painter intended: not just the taut muscles and keen eyes of a man who kept fit and kept sharp, but also a kind of coiled-up ambition, ready to strike. She tucked the book into its box and turned back to the task at hand: the renovation of this half of Fletch Osgood's building.

Picturing the crumpled back of the Bentley there in the sailing hut, Amie dipped her brush again into the paint and tried to sound casual. "So, about Desmond Fossick. Does he come back to the village very often these days?"

But if Fletch heard, he ignored the question. "It's the colors of the sea we're after, is it?" He stepped back to survey their work. He was trying, Amie could tell, for his usual tone, the gruffness of an old salt.

Not to be kept away that afternoon, despite giving her the first month's rent and the paint for free, Fletcher had rolled an entire wall of her shop in the time she took to finish the doorframe.

Back as far as Amie could remember and long before that, F.O. Provisions was the general store where tourists stopped not only for their wine and sandwiches—what Mainers called Italians—for a picnic, but also the watercolors and paintbrushes and board games they wanted when a storm squalled through and ruined their afternoon plans for the beach or boating. Fletch was also the best handyman in town.

Already, Amie sensed, her project had become his. Fletch owned the whole building, but his investment in her shop went now beyond property value.

"The sea's what I'm trying for, yes. What do you think?"

He lifted his head, as if letting the Kohler Cerulean Blue wash over him.

"What I think is you'll have whole armies of kids in here dripping ice cream cones"—he jerked his head across Dock Circle toward the pink-and-brown triple-dip-cone wooden sign for Scoops—"and these couches of yours will be all chocolate and muddy paw prints by day two."

"Since what the former tenant left here was already more coffee stains than patterns, I'm covering the couches and chairs with old sails from the Promontory." She paused, wondering whether to mention having found the Bentley.

But Fletch was already swinging his hoary head back and forth. "People nowadays eat everywhere but a table."

"I plan to spill lots of Rocky Road on them myself. What else do you think?"

"Those pictures, all that glass, and those driftwood things, whatever they are"—he nodded toward three of Kalia's sculptures partially covered in sails—"they'll be broken, all in a hundred thousand splinters."

"Fair enough. And?"

He snorted, then frowned, like she was trying to yank loose an admission from him that he'd rather keep folded close to his chest. "We'll see. Might yet be a bust."

"Let me ask you this, Fletch. What do you think of Good Harbor for the name of the gallery?"

A single grunt.

From Fletcher Osgood, it was a ringing endorsement.

Amie smiled as she poured more cerulean blue into the bucket. If only a paint color could set the mood for this place, for the people who walked into her shop. If only a paint color could wash away fears with the illusion of the tides.

The door bonged open—its bell buoy hung above the doorframe being one of the few undamaged items left by the former tenant. Both Amie's and Fletch's necks craned back toward the sound.

Ian O'Leary stood there, three drinks clustering together in his two hands. "One coffee with more cream than coffee so what's the point, and one coffee black, which is how it should be," he announced, not smiling, and plunked them down on a board propped up between two cardboard towers of boxes. "Plus one for me."

Amie set down her brush. "Thank you. Wow. Coffee and judgment, both. Delivered together."

"I can tell by looking ninety percent of the time."

"And I look like I drink my coffee wrong? With boatloads of cream?"

"Well? Do you?"

She laughed. "Since I'd rather not admit you were right, let's just go with your being not entirely wrong. Let me pay you for these."

Ian's head drew back. "God, no. Are you kidding? Then I'd feel the need to offer to help with the painting. *That* is not going to happen."

He'd spun back out the door and away before Amie could insist.

Fletch raised an eyebrow at the slammed door. "No idea where the kid got the funds to run his own place."

"Is he a good tenant?"

Fletch rolled through his thoughts for a moment as if he were straining to recall something negative about Ian O'Leary the baker. Fletch grunted at last. "I got no complaint," he complained.

Now he brightened, apparently having thought of something. "A lighthouse." He jerked his head toward the bakery. "Just painted it on his shop window—of my building. Underneath the word *Fáil-whatever-the-heck-chuh*. A word nobody but leprechauns can pronounce. Lighthouse doesn't work with the name. Does he know that?"

"Maybe to represent a warm welcome."

"Does he know, this landlubber Ian O'Leary from Southie—"

"It's part of Boston, Fletch. The T runs straight from there to the wharves if that counts."

"Does he know the purpose of a lighthouse is to keep ships *away*, not lure them in? Nowadays, people want lighthouses and angels all over things, like they're sweet."

"They're not sweet?"

He snorted his disgust. "Lighthouses and angels are signs you're supposed to be scared as hell about what's coming for you. *Then* you get the 'fear not' or the 'steer clear.' *After* you're scared as hell."

"Let's hope Ian's customers aren't thinking as clearly as you."

Fletch tugged his hunting cap lower. "I'd a kept to the cunning little clovers myself."

Amie glanced his way as she sent her paintbrush up and down over another door's trim—this one leading to the little office that would become her darkroom. Now was as good a time as any to press questions on one of the oldest residents of the village—who kept tabs on everyone here.

"Fletch, about Desmond Fossick. I saw him at the Promontory briefly the other evening speaking to a staff member just outside the front entrance. The conversation seemed awfully tense. Does Fossick cause trouble here in the village, even though he lives most of the year in Boston?"

"Ayuh. Been up here more often just lately. He grew up the son of a lobsterman on the far side of the cape, Fossick did."

Lobstuh. How Amie had missed this accent.

"Grew up poorer than most. With more loss, too, maybe," he added.

"More loss?"

He rolled through another couple of minutes. "Makes some people 'specially hardworking. Made Fossick that, but also him needing to steer every ship."

He stared for a time at one of Amie's photos, this one a dry-docked vessel with a cracked hull. "Don't s'pose a man like that changes direction without some sort of crash."

His tone was brusque as always. But his head with its buffalo plaid bobbed once at her. "So, then."

Like a priest, Amie thought wryly, might make the sign of the cross as a blessing.

"So then," she echoed. Their own liturgy. "And, Fletch, while we're on the subject of questions, who in this village might know about Chester? Where he came from. Why his clothes look like he came from money. On the same night the Bentley appeared."

Fletch's head swung side to side. "Nowadays, people act like they have more money than they got sense. Bentley, my eye."

"So you've no idea at all about Chester?"

He grunted at her rather than answer.

Without explanation, he set down his paint roller and stepped outside. Amie set down her brush and followed.

For several beats, she let Fletch study the great cormorant on a wharf piling visible between shops on the other side of Dock Circle, the bird's large black wings folded. Maybe the two of them, both coastal males, were warming themselves in the sun before the next dive.

"Nope. I don't." Tugging on both earflaps of his hunting cap, he slogged across Dock Circle toward Provisions.

Amie caught up and walked with him to his shop. "Tomorrow, I won't make you talk to me while we both work."

"Talk all you want. Makes no difference to me not listening."

Late the next morning, with Hopkins curled up at the foot of one of Kalia's sculptures, Amie answered a thumping at the shop door. Fletch stood there saying nothing, but jerked his head toward the front of Provisions—where he'd towed the Aston Martin. She began thanking him even as she slid on her boots.

Muttering, Fletch stomped toward the car as she joined him. "Tinkered with the carburetor this morning. Pounded out the worst of the damage. Don't make machines like they used to."

"To be fair, though, I slammed the poor thing into another car. That's not normal wear and tear."

Fletch frowned. "Needs plenty more work."

"Story of my life these days, apparently. Meanwhile, I've got a small trip I need to make."

Even the buffalo plaid of Fletch's hat looked reproachful. "Drive out in the willy-wacks like you're saying you'll be doing to take these pictures of yours, you're liable to hit some slick roads, stave the car up on a tree, and then where'll you be? Stranded."

She smiled at his old Mainer phrases: *willy-wacks, stave up*. "Thank you. Truly. I don't know what I'd do without you."

He waited until she'd circled the car.

"He might be," he said suddenly. "Behind it, I mean."

She turned. "Sorry?"

"Fossick. Who else? Behind the Bentley. Somehow."

He was already throwing open the door to Provisions. "'Nough said," he lobbed at her and did not look back.

~

If there was such a thing as a divine presence or a muse, Amie knew one thing for sure: something or someone spoke through a camera lens and developing fluid.

As a child she had filled her hollow world with books and her camera, in addition to Jake and Shibby. As an adult in the turmoil of war, she turned to books and her camera again—along with her memories of the sea.

Maybe this gallery, Good Harbor if she kept that name, could be a place of refuge for other people needing rest. Needing the sea.

After feeding Hopkins and tromping with him through the snow as the little dog made his rounds of Dock Circle's shops and its people, Amie settled him on his blanket. "If dogs were welcome in the library, as they should be," she told him, "I'd take you with me."

Inside the library, Amie stationed herself with a view out into the pines. For years, maybe decades, Mary O'Kelly had walked from the ten o'clock service at Pelican Congregational at the far end of the green to open the library by noon. Today, Amie saw, she'd swung by Fáilte for a pastry, and looked a little wild with pleasure at this new debauchery, flakes of golden brown at the corners of her mouth and the tip of her tiny nose.

In the card catalog, Amie's fingers riffled through stiff paper to the name *Desmond Fossick*. These pointed to chapters on him in a couple of books, one apparently decrying the heartlessness of capitalism and one lauding the ideal of the self-made man.

A number of earlier newspaper articles questioned his ethics. In interviews in *The Nation*, tenants called him a slumlord. Former employees at his factories complained of the bleak working conditions, of safety inspectors bribed.

The library's door swinging open interrupted Amie's thoughts.

"Here to deliver a precious package to you, if you're ready," Shibby said from the threshold. From behind her, a small head appeared.

~

Staggering under the load of children's books they'd checked out and waddling a little in his snowsuit, Chester entered Good Harbor. Carefully, he set his books on a sail-covered chair before Hopkins leaped into his arms. Boy and dog watched Amie unpack her darkroom chemicals. She'd brought the cyan, magenta, and yellow dyes, the paper, the filters, and everything necessary for the complex dye-transfer process with her from her apartment in D.C. When the chemicals and equipment had taken too much space in the roadster, she'd opted to leave a whole pile of dresses and a box of high heels behind to make room.

Chester pointed at some birch branches.

"It's just some tree branches I cut from . . ." Amie paused there, not wanting to give the entire story behind saying *my father's property*.

Technically, she probably didn't have legal access to those trees, Captain Smollett's land firmly in the grasp of her absentee father. She had no desire to inherit a house where there'd been so little love and no reason to believe he'd leave it to her someday. Still, without a pang of conscience she'd cut the birch branches from the backyard where she grew up.

Amie helped the boy climb out of his snowsuit. "I cut these because they're such interesting textures and shapes. We'll string fishing wire from them today and then hang them up high from the loft so they look like they've magically grown through the wall to the inside."

The two of them gazed straight up at the exposed beams, aged oak with wooden pegs for nails—and a white bunting of cobwebs heavily draped. "How about I get two brooms and we rig up really long handles to clean the ceiling better?"

Amie let Chester flip through the records left in a dusty stack on top of an ancient, paint-spattered record player the former tenant had left. "We're working with somebody else's taste here, my young friend. Wait, whoa, what's this?"

Chester held up a battered record sleeve.

"The Mills Brothers?" Amie cocked her head. "Sounds good to me."

Chester fumbling with the turntable, Amie helped him steady the phonograph's arm over the outermost song. The two of them blasted the music and, long handles duct-taped to brooms, made a game of swatting cobwebs down from the old beams.

"We used this during the war," Amie told him, pointing to the silver tape that stretched and held just right. "Fixes every darn thing but a broken heart."

They swatted at cobwebs in time to the music. By the second round of the chorus of "It Don't Mean a Thing," they could belt out the words together. After that record finished, Amie helped steady the little boy's hand again to lower the needle onto his next choice, a single with a label he seemed to recognize, both a bluebird and a dog on it. Amie and Chester spun with their long-handled mops to Glenn Miller's "In the Mood" as they swatted down cobwebs but mostly just danced, replaying the song over and over again.

When they took a break, Chester stuck his head out the front door and threw it back for a long sniff. "Minacen."

Afraid for a moment to make a sound in case she broke the spell of his speaking a word that wasn't a lyric, she whispered back. "What, Ches?"

The little boy wiped one hand under his nose, then pointed next door. "Minacen."

She reached for Chester's hand. "Ah. Cinnamon. Think we can run next door without coats, even though it's maybe a thousand degrees below zero? We could freeze like statues"—she struck a dramatic pose of running, right leg high—"before we get there. And they'll have to thaw us back to life in April."

He giggle-snorted.

That laugh, she thought. And homemade cinnamon rolls. And ripples of hope.

Fáilte's door jangled as Amie and Chester entered.

She called across the crowded shop to Ian at the counter. "Would you sell two hungry workers some cinnamon rolls? And you should know: money is no object. A hundred thousand bucks each is just fine. We are *that* ravenous."

"*Rabe*nous," Chester repeated, hopping on one snow-booted foot.

A smile played at one corner of Ian's mouth. "Savvy businesspeople, I see."

To Amie, he raised an eyebrow. *He spoke,* Ian mouthed.

Chester skittered to the far end of the bakery case.

"So"—Ian nodded at the floor—"you're going to track snow into my shop instead of yours?"

"You have a better cleaning service, I heard. Mine's only me, and I really stink at it. Also, do you always have this many people in here on a Sunday afternoon?"

Amie braced for two friendly figures rushing at her. Both threw their arms wide, their loose, flowing skirts making them look like a festival of summer kites just catching the wind.

Amie gave herself up to the hugs and answered as briefly as possible all their questions about her living these past years "away." That last word, *away*, these two women spoke in a whisper, as if leaving this village could not be other than a serious misstep in life, a shame best quickly forgotten.

Ian approached with a coffee, heavy on cream, held out to Amie. Or more like a cream light on coffee.

"Everyone new in town gets the first cup free. Fáilte policy."

"Except you already gave me my free one, remember?"

"From here on out, you pay through the nose. Double if you keep tracking that much snow into my shop."

Amie took the mug and lifted it in a toast. "To Fáilte, then. May it prosper for years to come."

"I've decided I'm going to stay on your good side, if you stay on mine."

"A hundred thousand thank-yous, Ian O'Leary. And please tell me this one's Sanka. Unless you want me so full of caffeine I'm swinging from your lovely historic rafters."

As he lifted his own mug to toast hers, his eyes swept to the door. As she followed Ian's gaze to the front, she froze. A tall figure ambled into the bakery.

"The usual, please," said the man, a wool beret pulled low and his jacket zipped to a jaw not recently shaved. He plucked the cap from his head.

Seth nodded at several neighbors perched at tables and stools around the bakery—putting off the moment they'd have to lumber back out into the cold. As his eyes swept past Amie, he stopped. Held her gaze.

Lifting a hand to him, she checked to be sure Chester was still fine, one knee pulled to his chest as he nibbled slowly, ecstatically, at his cinnamon roll.

Ian set a cup on the counter. "The Country Vet Special."

"Thanks so much," Seth said to Ian, eyes still on Amie's.

Fletch appeared, thumbs hooked behind his overall straps. "Got a question for you, Doc." Laying a hand on Seth's shoulder, Fletch steered him to the bakery's front, where Fletch's golden stood just inside the door—smiling.

Ian looked at Amie and gestured with his head. "You knew Seth Wakefield before?"

"Knew *of* him was more like it. He was older. I'm surprised he's come back here."

"Same's been said about you, trust me."

"So you *have* heard stories about me."

Ian held up a hand. "You get to tell your own stories about yourself." His eyes narrowed on her, but not unkindly. More like they were drilling in for the truth.

Amie returned the look. "Fair enough. But it's a longer story than *No, 'cause I'm years out of contact with a father who owns a house here.* You?"

He paused before answering. "For me, it's a longer story than *No family here in the village.* Which was the point of coming."

Amie's eyes traveled to a hand-painted sign on the far wall, the whole Irish saying: *Céad míle fáilte.* "Not exactly a hundred thousand welcomes back there in Boston—in Southie?"

The two wells of sadness staring back at her were her answer.

"So, then," she said, "you're making your own story. Good for you, Ian O'Leary."

Ian didn't smile, exactly. But his eyes warmed, his mouth relaxing above today's turtleneck. "You know, I might decide I like you after all."

"In spite of the stories you've heard about me?"

"*Because of* the stories."

She laughed. Then didn't. "Just don't believe everything you hear. Only ninety-five percent of it's true."

"Fair enough. So, Amelia Stilwell, you were saying about the cove's own version of Dr. Dolittle over there?"

Amie felt fluttering in her middle, which was ridiculous. She wasn't a pimple-faced preteen anymore sitting with Jake at the ballpark eating snow cones. "Seth Wakefield left for college when I was a kid. Some big scholarship as a pitcher."

Approaching again now, the veterinarian must've heard his name.

Amie wondered, too late, if she smelled like the faint scent that still remained in the shop: mildew and dust and wild-animal droppings.

"Nice to see you again." His cheeks flushed above a brown flannel shirt.

She felt her own blood rise to her cheeks. "Nice to see you."

Ian pulled on the ribbed neck of his sweater. "I was about to tell Amie here about what you did—playing ball, I mean, with the . . . wherever it was. Sorry. I'm not so great at knowing baseball."

"Not to worry," Seth said. "Baseball's good, but not anything life-and-death important."

"Tell that," Ian murmured in an accent Amie could barely make out, "to me ole da'."

From staring down at his coffee, the veterinarian lifted his head to study the younger man's face, pinched and drawn. Seth seemed to be waiting to speak out of respect for the story Ian had begun—but only begun.

"I played a couple of years," Seth told Amie after a moment, his voice quieter now, "with the Yankees' organization, a sin that Fletch Osgood will never forgive."

"I'm afraid I'm with Fletch on that."

Seth's dimples dug in. "I was only ever really farm-team good. Then, yeah, the war."

They all paused again there. That word, *war*, had a way of elbowing all sound aside for several beats, always demanding its space of silence.

Seth brushed the stubble on his chin with the back of his hand. "After the war, though, I started doing what I'd always wanted to do."

"Which was?"

"Raise Clydesdales."

Amie laughed. But his brown eyes blinked earnestly back.

"I'm so sorry. It's just . . . such a specific dream. You actually raise Clydesdales? Like the Budweiser horses?"

He ducked his head back down toward his coffee. "You'd be welcome to come meet them sometime. To a horse, they're perfect gentlemen. Though, admittedly, they're mostly all gelded."

Ian tilted his head so the vet couldn't see, and winked.

Amie ignored this. "I'd like that. Thank you. And maybe . . ."

Seth's eyes lifted an instant.

"I wonder if I could bring a friend."

The vet flushed. "I should have said that right off. If you have . . . someone special. Sure."

She nodded toward the chair where Chester was still relishing his cinnamon roll. Glancing up, brown sugar all over his cheeks, he ran a tongue around his lips. "That would be my someone special."

"Right. Of course. Chester's welcome any time." The shy half smile again. "Heck of a job he did singing the other night."

"He did." Amie smiled back as Seth's gaze flitted down, then steadied on hers. His irises were a light gray, lines radiating from the corners of his eyes as if they'd seen too much and aged before the rest of the face.

Behind her, Ian raised an eyebrow again.

Seth glanced down at his watch. "I should go. Bit nervous this next house call could be a red bag birth."

Jamming the cap back over the thick straw-colored mass of his hair, he yanked the old door behind him and jogged toward the green Ford parked just outside the bakery. The parallel wooden slats of the truck's bed gleamed with ice.

Avoiding Ian's eyes, Amie poured more cream into lukewarm coffee. "Do. Not. Speak. Not a single word."

Ian held up a flattened palm. "I wouldn't *dream* of it."

∽

Back in Good Harbor, Shibby's having poked her head in to announce dinner at the Orchard would be in an hour, Chester watched the record spin, mesmerized.

Tell you what, Ches, Amie had said. *I've got some pictures I need to develop, and I'm not sure how well this new darkroom will work. You're in charge of our music, okay? I'll be in there for the next few minutes if you need me. Just don't open the door without my giving the all-clear, or we'll have a bunch of dye-transferred nothingness.*

Amie listened to the records Chester chose to put on—chosen, she couldn't help but think, for being the oldest covers, and therefore the oldest songs.

A six-year-old with the taste of a sixty-year-old, she marveled as she dipped the next paper into the magenta bath.

Even there in the dark with nothing but a red light to see by, Amie could make out something new on the page where she'd enlarged the bottom portion of the picture she'd snapped of Chester's photo with his mother. With the image enlarged and replicated, two new prints of it placed overlapping under the stereoscope, the road became nearly three-dimensional—and appeared now to be something other than asphalt or concrete. There were rocks here, not just the pebbles of a dirt road. The street where Chester and his mother were standing appeared to be cobblestone. And the fallen leaves of the trees that lay on the ground, now seen through the scope, might just be lindens.

"Acorn Street. On Beacon Hill," Amie said aloud to the red light of the darkroom. "In Boston."

Chapter 20

─── ⚬≈⚬ ───

Fossick's Piper Cub bounced heavily on an air pocket, the jolts sloshing Tom's Bordeaux onto the file of documents he'd just opened in his lap. He'd be annoyed, except that this gave him an excuse to hold it up for the Cub's private stewardess to refill his drink. It was his third of a short flight so far, but the stewardess was well trained enough only to smile as she tilted the bottle's neck down toward him.

He'd kept the shade of his window down in order to focus, but also so he didn't have to see the cities his brain might tell him were blazing beneath the plane. He'd tried reasoning with himself since boarding, tried three glasses now of Bordeaux, and still in his mind the ground beneath them would be in flames if he let himself look.

Across the broad aisle, Fossick reached for the brandy snifter warming over a candle just like the set in his Beacon Hill study. This glass had *the Promontory Inn* etched in front of an anchor, too.

Odd. Considering how minuscule a part of his investment portfolio that inn accounted for, Fossick seemed to care about it more than most any other. Maybe for all his bluster, the man still desperately wanted people in his home state to admire him. Or at least admit they'd been wrong in thinking the scrawny lobsterman's son would never amount to a thing.

Swirling his brandy, Fossick muttered under his breath. "Survival of the fittest. It's about who takes the risks."

Make her go away, Fossick had said in his Beacon Hill study. The words still echoed in Tom's head as he tried not to think of burning cities below. Was that what Fossick meant by *survival of the fittest,* making anyone who threatened him . . . disappear?

"Yes, sir."

"Who's got the moxie and strength to create wealth? By contrast, by God, who ought to just be grateful for a job created by somebody else?"

"The story," Tom said, glancing up from his leather document folder, "that'll run in *Life* next week depicts you as the smartest businessman east of the Alleghenies."

Fossick needed regular infusions of praise. For a man who prided himself on toughness, he could be fragile as a paper lantern.

"Damn right," he grunted.

Tom risked a sidelong glance at his boss. A man who was soulless. Rapacious. Insatiable.

But working for him hasn't changed me, Tom thought, defending himself from no one present. *Except that I'm not dirt poor anymore.*

Now Fossick was surveying the landscape below with that look he got during all confrontations—a mixture of hostile and hungry, eyes twitching.

The pilot called over his shoulder from the cockpit. "About to touch down, Mr. Fossick."

Touch down? It was far too soon to be in descent.

Tom raised the shade of his window. No desert stretching for miles. No dot of a city with a brightly lit strip. "This isn't Las Vegas." Sweat poured from his forehead.

"Nope," Fossick said, "there's been a change. We have a new potential crisis brewing at one of my properties. The fallout in public relations could be ugly if I—meaning you—don't address it in person. Immediately."

"New crisis? Mr. Fossick, I believe I keep abreast of all—"

Fossick popped Tom's jaw in what might have been meant to be a playful right jab. The older man's mouth twisted into a smirk.

"It's why I hired you, Darnay. That pretty-boy face of yours that rarely shows a damn thing of whatever the hell you're thinking. Although sadly not *never*, as we have recently learned." He turned toward the cockpit. "My face, on the other hand, always looks like I'm wanting to tear somebody's head off. Am I right, Sann?"

The pilot chuckled rather than venture an answer, and Fossick shrugged. "Which, for the record, is always exactly the hell what I'm thinking."

The Piper Cub braked to a smooth stop, and the cabin door swung open. Fossick patted his private flight attendant at the back of her waist—then dropped lower.

Fossick was in a bullying mood today. Less clear was whether he was simply feeling especially belligerent, which came and went like sea currents, or whether something particular was bothering him, giving a murderous glint to his eyes.

Tom watched the pilot lower the Cub's stairs to a one-runway airfield. The smell of salt air whipped over the surrounding fields of an early snowfall.

His heart hurled itself at the walls of his chest. He could not get off here. Could not be seen. This was the last place on earth he'd have come if he'd known.

Desperately, he flailed for excuses as he kept his head down to gather his files. Hand shaking, he reached for a cigarette and a light.

"Not time for that now, Darnay. Have your damn smoke in the car they've sent for us."

Tom straightened as he turned to Fossick. "I'm sorry, sir. But I can't disembark."

"Is it all Canadians or just you wound so goddamn tight? Of course you'll get off the damn plane."

"I understand, Mr. Fossick, this might seem peculiar, my insisting—"

Fossick leaned in so close Tom could see speckles of dust in the felt of his boss's fedora, see a single crinkle in the band of brown ribbon that ran its width. Tom could smell, even taste, the brandy on his boss's breath.

"Get the hell off the plane. And welcome, Darnay, to the state of Maine."

Chapter 21

"Dangerous," Fletch said. He'd frowned up at the pewter-gray sky. "Breezed up and snowing hard before you've got back."

Amie raised her hand to show him she'd heard, then turned her back. It was his phone in Provisions she was using—again. But this call was too important to mishear the voice from the administration offices of the Boston Public Library.

"Honestly, Amelia, I'll try to be thinking who else you could call—who might be chummy with the oldest families on Beacon Hill. I know you were only at Radcliffe two years, but there has to be someone besides me who'd know more of the tony set."

"I'm not sure it's more of the tony set I'm after. Just a mother and a sweet little boy about six—maybe living on Acorn Street, if that's the one that still has its cobblestones."

"That'd be your tony set."

"Also, for what it's worth, the mother could be Irish—at least from an Irish background, or who just loves old Irish songs. Old songs, in general, in fact. 'When Irish Eyes Are Smiling,' 'Danny Boy,' 'Bicycle Built for Two' kind of thing."

"You have got to be kidding. Could the kid have been taken away just based on the mother's taste in music?"

"'Sweet Adeline' was another one he knew all the words to this morning over breakfast. The little guy perks up with all the oldies, so she must've sung them or played them a good bit."

"Poor little chap. You say he was just left up there?"

"Left with a note for exactly the person she wanted to take charge of him. So she'd done her research, apparently. She left a magazine article in his things that must've been what led her to the exact person in town—in all of New England—to trust with a child."

"*Still*. Research or not, she left the kid, right?"

"I know. *Still*. At any rate, please do let me know if you think of anyone else I should call."

"Will do. And you gave me the number you're telephoning from. That's where you're working?"

Amie's eyes shot to Fletch as she turned. "It's where I can be reached, at least, if you ask for the message to be passed along. And here's another." She gave Shibby's number, too. "Thanks so much again." She hung up.

Fletcher was frowning.

"*Please*, Fletch, let me pay for my calls. I'm leaving change under the counter and you can't stop me."

His head swung back and forth. "The weather's breezed up."

"You're probably right." She swung the strap of her Deardorff over her shoulder and slipped outside to the roadster, Fletch scowling as he followed. "But thanks to you, I won't have to walk after all. Truth is all my best shots are from days I was afraid to go out or angles I thought were too precarious. Having some more dramatic photos could be the difference in whether Good Harbor makes it as a gallery, or I have to beg to be your cashier at Provisions."

"You wouldn't be any good at it." He stomped back into his shop.

~

A wet snow was falling again now with huge, lovely flakes sifting past onto the last of the russet and amber leaves that refused to let go: a battle of the seasons, autumn with no memory that it lost every year. Amie pulled off the road to admire the leaves and lift her thermos of coffee in salute. Tenacity even in the face of certain defeat: that felt like her life right now.

Ahead on this bend of shoreline, black and silver rocks reared up fearsome above the waves, the gulls soaring in circles over the cliffs as if it were not bitterly cold or the wind almost unbearably stiff. Maybe they were too brave or too strong or too busy to care. Maybe, like Kalia, Amie would get her own outlandish tattoo, hers of a brave, stubborn gull soaring.

Opening her door, she breathed in the scent of seaweed and fresh snow and fir. She let her head clear.

The little bundle of black metal on the passenger seat represented her chance at survival now. For Amie, this one metal box with shutter and lens felt like her only paddle upriver.

The years of scanning pictures for weapons and troop movements had trained her to see a photograph before she snapped the shutter. The sand that in summer would be a warm cinnamon sugar like Shibby dusted across buttered toast was today coated in white. Crunching through frozen sea grass to the cliff's edge, Amie lay down full length for several shots.

These, she thought as she balanced her weight against tumbling off, *these will be good.*

Back in the roadster, she downshifted as the wharves of the next town, Cornwall, eased by, the outdoor seating of little restaurants and lobster shacks quiet here in late autumn. Only gulls held vigil outdoors on the pilings. At Cornwall's last wharf, light glowed through frost-ed-pane windows where locals huddled inside a diner.

Parking several yards above the wharf on a hill, Amie snapped a good dozen photos of the gray-shingled diner framed by a dark, frothing sea. Realizing suddenly she was hungry—*rabenous*, as Chester would say—she made her way down a rocky path and found a seat at the counter where she could read the hand-chalked menu hung over the grill.

A slim figure in a hacking jacket and jodhpurs sat on the stool to Amie's right. *Surely she hasn't actually been out riding in the snow,* Amie thought.

Or maybe this woman was one of those people who never felt they belonged except when in the uniform of their group, whether that happened to be army fatigues or a suit or jodhpurs.

Amie tried not to stare.

Come to think of it, was this the same woman she'd seen talking with Ian in Fáilte?

She thought of Chester's picture with his mother—maybe on Beacon Hill. But this was definitely not that woman in the belted dress and the adoring smile.

This person smelled faintly of hay, an odd contrast to the gleam of wealth she gave off, pale hair pulled back, sleek and shiny, into a barrette, her skin and teeth and posture all perfect.

To her left on the counter, the woman had set her purse, a satchel with a wide drawstring opening. Her face, as she lifted it to meet Amie's eye, was as hard and as aloof as any mannequin's.

Amie studied her profile: something too perfect in the small nose and slightly drawn mouth that said she had no inclination to speak to those beneath her. Which, Amie assumed, was everyone here.

The woman set down the black crushed-velvet helmet she held. *She looks,* Amie thought, *like she's walked out of a Trollope novel—or maybe a Stubbs painting. And why would she be carrying a riding helmet into a diner if not to set herself apart from the common folk?*

Amie dropped both elbows to the bar. As she did, her right arm accidentally jostled the woman's leather purse, toppling it down onto the polished oak boards.

Amie slid off her stool. "I'm so sorry. Let me get it."

The woman scrambled to her feet, then dropped to her knees. Frantically, she began shoving the items back into her purse: a wallet that matched her riding boots, a ring of keys.

Amie reached for a small cylindrical metal can with a bright red label that had rolled beneath her own stool. Its front showed a black ink sketch of a horse's hoof and over that, the words *Carr & Day & Martin* in an arched banner.

As Amie stood, the woman snatched the can from her hand. "Thank you." The words came forced, as if she'd pressed them out of her mouth.

Amie inclined her head. "That was clumsy of me."

A hesitation, the woman's fingers curling around the can. "Don't mention it."

Without the instinctive move to cover the label, Amie might not have thought twice about the little can. As it was, though, the gesture suggested something the woman was trying to cover up.

Amie thrust out her hand. "Amelia Stilwell. I grew up on this coast—though a few miles south of here."

The pause that followed was heavy with indecision, the woman looking as if she weren't sure how much to say.

"In Pelican Cove," Amie offered.

She'd offered it as much to see the woman's reaction as to be friendly, and she got her reward. The woman flinched at the name of the village.

"Gertrude Winthrop," the woman said. Two words tossed out. More like scraps to a stray dog—to make the thing go away—than a civil exchange.

But Amie's interest had been piqued now. She saw that Gertrude Winthrop wished she would do like any other good New Englander and keep to herself.

But this made Amie want all the more to draw her out. "I grew up knowing practically everyone on the cape—off-season, at least. Not in the summer, of course, when the tourists came back."

Gertrude Winthrop gave a curt nod. But said nothing. She turned mostly away, only her profile visible.

And that profile . . . Was it the one from Fáilte when Ian looked so distraught?

"I'm guessing you're a visitor to this area. Are you staying in one of the inns that keeps its doors open in winter? Not many do."

Nothing.

Amie took a stab. "The Promontory is one of the best known if you've not tried it."

Again, that slight flinch. Whatever this woman's relationship with the inn, she knew the name.

"If you want to try the best cinnamon rolls in Maine, maybe in all of New England, it's absolutely worth the drive down to Fáilte in Pelican Cove."

As if recoiling from the word *Fáilte* or maybe *Pelican Cove*, Gertrude Winthrop jerked up. There in her hacking jacket and jodhpurs, she stood regally beside her stool, like Princess Elizabeth preparing to survey her mounted Life Guard. "Lovely meeting you. I wish you a good day."

Now there, thought Amie, *is the triumph of etiquette over emotion. She no more thinks it was lovely meeting me than it would be having all her teeth pulled. A real Mainer would've been more authentic—and just left without saying a word.*

Amie held out her hand to shake and was surprised by the grasp of the other woman: firm, but also with a tremor. A woman who was an athlete, but also who, right now, was afraid—terribly so—of something or someone.

Including, perhaps, Amie thought, *of herself.*

∽

Amie took the first curve on the way back too fast and felt the roadster's wheels slide on ice. Reining in the instinct to tap on the brakes, she maneuvered, just barely, through the turn.

For now, she could only see what was here: the blackened stalks of the roses through fallen leaves and now snow, a gray ocean churning under a white, menacing sky. Big, wet flakes fell, coating the windshield of the Aston Martin as fast as her wipers could heave them off. Snow leaked, too, through the slit in the roadster's canvas onto her head.

But Amie hardly noticed. Her mind was focused on Jake—the old ache in her gut. But also on Shibby's insistence that he was still alive. And on the U.S. government's having no record of him.

Which surely meant that if he *were* still alive, he'd changed his name from the start and disappeared to go work somewhere for those months until the U.S. entered the war in December of '41, as Shibby had always assumed. It was possible he'd crossed the border into Canada to enlist months earlier, as thousands of Americans had apparently done. Or both: crossing the border and changing his name.

Even if that were true, though, more than forty thousand Canadian soldiers alone died in the war. Who was to say Jake, even if he was fighting for another country, wasn't one of their dead?

But what if . . .

What *if* he'd survived? What if he'd traded stories with someone?

Amie drove slowly back to the cove, wrapped not only in the white squall of the snowstorm, but also in her own fog of possibilities. Rather than steering toward Good Harbor or the Orchard, she let the roadster roll to a stop on Sandpiper in front of the library—minutes before closing.

Mary O'Kelly smiled her usual nearsighted smile and asked the same question she'd asked just a few hours ago: "What book can I help you find today?" The librarian seemed in no hurry to shoo Amie back out into the storm.

Amie thumbed through the card catalog under Royal Canadian Navy, which seemed the most likely, then the Canadian Army and the Royal Canadian Air Force. She scanned old magazine articles. More than a million Canadians served, she read. About nine thousand others were Americans who joined with Canada to fight before their own country declared war. She jotted down the phone number of the Canadian governmental office charged with keeping service files of the war dead. She'd call tomorrow to see if there was any record at all of a Jacob Spitzer or any name like it.

Feeling nearly cross-eyed now, and knowing Shibby would be worried if she didn't appear for dinner, Amie stretched the tension from her shoulders and back. "Thank you, Miss O'Kelly," she called across the little library.

Mary O'Kelly put one finger to her lips. Though there was no one else there.

Standing near the periodicals, Amie rewrapped the blue scarf three times around her neck and stuffed her arms into her coat sleeves. One of her gloves dropped to the floor. As she bent to retrieve it, she glanced at the *Boston Globe*'s front page.

A picture of a man in a dark overcoat and fedora covered two columns above the fold. The man's face was partially turned away, his face contorted with something that looked like guilt. Or anguish. Or both.

The face—what she could see of it—looked strikingly like Cary Grant's, though that seemed more likely for the front page of the *Los Angeles Times* than the *Globe*, which liked to view itself as too sophisticated to follow the hysterical drama of Hollywood. Curiosity roused, Amie checked the caption, just in case.

Not Cary Grant. Just some man named Tom Darnay who worked for . . .

Here was a name in the caption she recognized: Desmond Fossick. Amie's heart missed a beat. And then two. She'd quit breathing.

Darnay. An unusual name, at least in New England. The same one as one of the main characters of *A Tale of Two Cities:* Charles Darnay, who switches places with Sydney Carton at the end to save Darnay's life. And the name *Tom*: the pauper boy who switches places with the prince in *The Prince and the Pauper.* Both books that she'd loved growing up.

And so had her best friend Jake.

Hands trembling, Amie held the newspaper up to the light as Mary O'Kelly watched from her desk. The librarian placed a finger again over her lips, as if she sensed somehow the cry rising up through Amie's middle.

The man in the photo, Amie saw, had a lean face with high cheekbones and a firm jaw—nothing like the round, almost doughy face of her old friend growing up. Still . . .

Tom Darnay's eyes.

There was something in them besides only guilt or anguish.

Their shape. The way the left lid drooped ever so slightly. But especially that expression, that hurt deep in them that had not changed since he was a boy, rocks being thrown at him from the rich kids in town.

Spitzer, one girl had cried. *Jew Boy hasn't even got parents!*

Amie stared at the newspaper's photo. "My God," she whispered. "Jake. Is that you?"

Chapter 22

Jake shuddered. This was a disaster.

No point continuing the charade of Tom Darnay anymore—at least in his own mind. Stuck here in the village, what were the chances that no one would recognize him? It was only a matter of time now before Fossick knew the whole truth.

Cracking open the seal on his former life would surely let in a whole fetid river of memories and emotions Jake hadn't planned to deal with. Not ever.

A black Allard sedan—an anchor and *the Promontory Inn* painted in gold on its side—that had picked them up from the tarmac now waited for them outside the inn. Fossick's name appeared—*of course it did*—in only slightly smaller script below the name of the inn.

"For a driving tour of the area," Fossick had said. "To eyeball how the village and the cape are faring economically—and if they're up to the Promontory's elite standards." He'd smiled maniacally, as if enjoying some sort of private joke.

Wearing a black trench coat and sunglasses, the driver looked like a bit player straight out of a James Cagney gangster flick, the character who could pull a revolver from his pocket at any moment. Gunning the engine, the driver took the two-lane road up the coast with gusto.

Tensing, Jake made himself crack the window and draw a deep breath. He'd forgotten that you could smell the snow and the salt and the balsam firs all at once. Crisp and clean and tangy—also sweet. Something about the ocean.

He'd forgotten, too, how the hemlock branches shot out long from slender trunks and draped green layer on layer. The driver watched him from the rearview mirror, his mouth twitching up on one side.

"Smells good, right?" the driver asked in a deep Maine accent. "Like no place else."

As they looped back toward the village, Jake could feel his back tensing, the whites of his knuckles on the Allard's back-seat door handle. Then, there it was: a sign. Not the one from his childhood, but something new. A mound of boulders and the wooden sign braced at the top by wrought iron announced it:

WELCOME TO
PELICAN COVE

A low sun glinting off the snow and the last of deep crimson leaves, the bells tolling across the harbor, Jake felt his heart seizing up in his chest.

He pressed his face to the glass of the Allard's back seat to see out better—and wondered if he looked as much like the kid that he suddenly, uncomfortably felt: Nauseated. Insecure.

Abandoned all over again. About to watch the life he'd constructed for himself implode and burn like the city of Dresden he'd seen below his B-17.

Dusk was just dropping like silver silk over the roofs of the town center as the Allard rolled forward, its driver mercifully silent. Lights blinked from inside the shops of Dock Circle and glowed from inside the homes. Much of the town looked repainted since the war. Looked ready for a new start.

For Jake, though, the village might as well have been charred remains—all that was going to be left of his life.

"So, Darnay. We'll get dinner back at my inn in the Helmsman. Your never having been to Maine before, you should enjoy a taste of local cuisine. Tomorrow, we'll take care of business."

Now Fossick nodded toward what appeared to be a historical marker Jake recalled being erected before he left town at eighteen. He caught Fossick's name on it as the Allard swept past. "I'm a veritable legend here, you know, Darnay."

Jake could hardly make himself speak, his air cut off. "Of course, Mr. Fossick," he said, his voice hoarse, unfamiliar. Just the choked-out words of a stranger.

Chapter 23

───── ⟡⟡ ─────

"Fossick Enterprises International," snipped the voice on the other end.

It was Monday morning early, and Amie was surprised anyone answered before eight o'clock. But maybe that was how Fossick ran things. Amie cleared her throat. "Yes. I'm trying to reach Mr., um, Tom Darnay."

The phone booth's glass panes were frosted opaque. As she watched another of those black sedans with *the Promontory Inn* on its side and a green truck, likely Seth Wakefield's, roll by, Amie was grateful for a few moments of privacy.

"Mr. Darnay is a very busy man," said the secretary, whose accent, nasal and fast, steamrolled its *r*'s.

The words tumbled out before Amie had planned what to say: "It's about Mr. Darnay's family."

A pause. Then, a little petulantly, "Mr. Darnay's got no family still living. He's from Canada." The secretary said this as if being from Canada explained his being alone in the world.

Amie leaned heavily against the phone booth's glass door.

"No family?" Amie repeated.

She closed her eyes.

There they were at the back of the old barn behind the Orchard. Sweat trickling down the side of his face from the August heat, a young Jake cupped both hands gently around a ball of trembling fur.

Their heads tipped together and a blue summer dusk falling, they'd marveled at the enormity of the eyes peering out from between Jake's fingers.

"It's been two days," Amie whispered.

"You sure?"

"I counted careful. What? Don't you trust me, Jakie?"

He'd met her eye. "You're one of two people in the whole world I trust." The brown cowlick at the top of his head bobbed. "It'll be that way for always."

He made his way barefoot from the barn to the house, careful even crossing the gravel, sun-seared and sharp-edged, not to jostle the kitten.

At the screen door to the kitchen, Amie stood by his side as he held out his hands.

From a steaming pot on the stove, Shibby had turned. Brushing dark tendrils of hair back from her face with her forearm, she smiled at them. "What is it you have there, sweet ones?"

"This kitten's momma," Jake said, "hasn't come back for two days— me and Amie, we've watched. We figure she's got herself trampled by a moose."

Amie jumped in. "So now, she's got no family at all. Like—"

Like Jake, who's got no family either.

She'd almost said it aloud—and could still, after seventeen years, hear the words she'd nearly delivered just then. She could feel the edges of them to this day, like jagged tin.

But Jake had finished her thought: "Who'd understand better than me? Me and Amie thought we'd best bring it in here to you."

Shibby had stepped from the stove. Over the top of Jake's head, bowed to the cat, she'd given a slow, private nod to Amie, like Shibby had heard somehow what nearly got said, the *like Jake, who's got no family either*. Like Shibby was absolving the girl of the damage she'd almost done to the boy.

Then Shibby had kissed Jake on top of the head. "You have a family that you can share. You and Amie did right to bring it straight home."

"About his not having a family," Amie said. "That isn't true. He does. So it's imperative that you have him call me. *Immediately*."

Amie gave the Provisions' number to the assistant. "My name is Amelia Stilwell. And you'll be sure that he gets it? It's urgent."

"Ur-gent," the secretary repeated in a tone meant to convey she was writing it down as dictated. Without believing it.

"Yes. Something urgent in his hometown, Pelican Cove, please tell him."

"Mr. Darnay is from Toronto, Miss Stilwell. Which tells me you have the wrong man."

"Was his late mother killed in a boating accident north of Cuba, did he say?"

"Yes."

"His late father, by any chance a prominent surgeon?"

"Why . . . yes."

"Then I have the right man."

Because he traded in his own story for mine. And maybe pieces of someone else's. Jake Spitzer is alive, but his whole life is a lie.

"So if you could just give him the message."

"I'll let him know that you called, Miss Stilwell. He'll receive it when he returns from a business trip with Mr. Fossick, unless he checks in for messages. Good day to you." A click on the other end of the line.

Amie stared out to sea and tried to imagine a time when the winds here would be warm again, the air soft and full of the scent of the wild beach roses growing along the cliffs above sapphire-blue water. Because right now, she was cold right down to the bone. The blood drained from her head and her limbs. So cold.

And so very, very angry.

Chapter 24

If she couldn't get in touch with Jake right now, she would somehow. And soon.

Meanwhile, she needed to think what she would even say to him—after what he'd led Shibby and her and everyone else to believe, and mourn over. She needed time, too, to speak to him herself, to be sure it was truly, actually Jake, and to blow out the worst of her fury at him directly before she told Shibby.

She'd also pursue the man he must work for: Desmond Fossick.

Shibby had called in sick to work in order to take the day with Chester. The two of them had joined Amie in working on the shop all day—with Amie running back to Provisions every couple of hours to see if there'd been a call from Fossick Enterprises for her.

Nothing.

She wouldn't mention her possibly having found Jake until she knew for sure. She would spare Shibby this next climb and plunge of the roller coaster, at least.

Now, just after dinner, Amie swung the roadster into the Promontory's entrance. Inside, she lifted a hand to the woman with impeccable posture standing near the stone fireplace in a navy blazer with a gold anchor over its pocket.

Miss Michaud approached. "I see we meet again, Miss Stilwell."

Amie held out her hand but froze. She stared up at Fossick's portrait, its face grotesquely changed. Unpleasant before from the vicious glint in the subject's eye, the painting had now clearly been vandalized. Fossick's face had elongated, was melting down into his shoulders, his eyes vertical ovals of white, like a farce of Edvard Munch's *The Scream*. "Oh my God."

A mask dropped over the general manager's face again. "Yes. Clearly, there's been a crime. Likely some local hooligan teenagers."

Not what the general manager actually thinks. Amie could see that in the too-high tilt of the chin. *But she has no intention of telling me whom she really suspects.* "Do your guests not find it just a little . . . distressing? Thinking maybe this is your taste in art?"

Miss Michaud frowned as if this possibility bothered her more than the vandalism itself. "The police have asked that we not touch it until it can be dusted for prints. Analyzed properly. It is, I admit, most unfortunate. Now. How may I assist you?" The general manager clipped out her words so that, despite what she said, what she meant was *Feel free to leave. Now.*

What was it Stella Lapierre had said about the Bentley? *An affair. Involving an out-of-towner.*

Villagers here tended to consider anyone not born and bred in the cove an out-of-towner. Which could mean Miss Michaud.

An affair . . .

If Tess Michaud were involved with Desmond Fossick, or had been at one time, could that be motive enough for her defacing his portrait?

Could it have been Fossick himself in the Bentley that first night—Fossick with a sudden, overwhelming sense of guilt, perhaps?

"Hullo," came a voice from a few yards away.

A tall figure in an argyle vest was just removing thick gloves and a wool beret. The general manager excused herself as the vet took a couple of hesitant steps toward Amie.

"Hullo," Seth said again, shifting his weight. "I was just swinging in here to the Helmsman for a Narragansett after a long day."

"Our paths, Doc Wakefield, seem to keep crossing."

A duck of his head. "The times before, yes. Truth be told, this time I saw you come in. Thought I might . . . Could I buy you a drink?"

Two men in suits that stood out in a village of flannel shirts and knit caps were just walking out the far side of the Helmsman as Amie and Seth wandered in. The shoulders of the taller man, Amie noticed even from behind, appeared hunched.

His profile struck her as distinctly different from the one she'd seen in the Bentley that first night.

But a similarity in the posture.

Braced, she thought. *For some sort of crash to come.*

~

With a series of war-era love songs in the background, Amie listened to Seth describe the horse he'd just treated—a serious case of colic.

"Owner bought the gelding on a whim—think he wanted a lawn decoration more than a horse. Rode the poor thing hard today till they'd both worked up a lather, then shut him straight up in a stall."

"Ah. Like Black Beauty."

"Well remembered. That book's probably why I wanted to become a vet. That, and the fact that our livestock when I was growing up always seemed to be needing veterinary care we couldn't afford. I learned to do a good bit of bringing calves into the world even as a kid just to help out the family."

She raised her wineglass. "Here's to doing what we have to do—and learning to love it."

Seth raised his pint, his eyes settling on hers.

Amie was the first to look away as she leaned toward the pub's window. "The lights on the water, and the harbor fringed with the last of the autumn leaves . . ." She turned back to Seth. "What's your favorite season in the cove?"

He chuckled, a warm tumble of sound. "I'm embarrassed to say."

"Why?"

"Sounds indecisive."

"Go on."

"Truth is my favorite's whichever one I'm in." Under his five o'clock shadow, he flushed.

"We said we'd trade war stories. Though I'm not sure this is the time."

He searched her face for a moment. "Bataan," he said at last. "That's where the scar across my face was from. Trying to help load another prisoner of war onto a stretcher. He was crazy with pain. Both legs with gangrene. Delirious. Pulled a knife out of his pocket."

Now it was Amie's turn to look away.

"The other one's from Boston," he said.

She inclined her head.

"My other scar—the one you can't see. Got back home after the war, and the girl in Boston I'd married two days before I shipped out didn't much like how I looked when I came home. To be fair, my face was even worse then. She broke things off."

"I'm so sorry."

He ran a hand down the side of his pint. "Probably for the best. The war changed both of us. Anyway, just thought you should know before we . . . that is, if we . . ."

"Go on sharing drinks looking out over the water?"

The corners of his eyes crinkled. "Thanks. I wasn't sure how to get out of that sentence."

Amie nodded toward the open span of hardwood floor in front of the bar. "Seems a shame to waste this song."

He said nothing, his eyes on hers. But stood and offered his hand.

Unspeaking, they swayed to "I'll Be Seeing You." The lyrics and the tune had a way of reaching down deep, dredging up so many memories, so many faces that were gone now.

"So, Amie Stilwell Without Pigtails," he said. "How about your war stories?"

She waited several beats, then a whole chorus of the song before answering. Seth waited, his cheek to hers.

She pulled back now just enough to see his eyes as she spoke, but not enough that she couldn't still feel the breadth and the warmth of him, his face—and its scar—just inches from hers. "There was Medmenham. Fourteen-hour days on what used to be a splendid estate, Danesfield House, turned into a headquarters for the Central Interpretation Unit. Some of the top brass weren't too keen on having women there—a hundred and fifty of us at one point, just as PIs. Photographic interpreters," she added before he could ask.

"Sadly, I can imagine they weren't too keen."

"We more than earned our keep, though. A British PI, Constance Babington Smith, was the real star among us. But we all worked hard. Learned to recognize scorched grass from several thousand feet up." She cocked her head. "You'll be shocked to learn my skills aren't so much in demand as they once were."

They rotated a few more times. "I'm sorry," she said again, "about your . . . about the girl in Boston."

"Truth is, she'd have hated it here and *despised* the phone at three in the morning when some farmer was trying to deliver a calf breech. Truth is, too, I'd have hated life in the city. What about you?"

"Times I've delivered a calf breech or number of tragic wartime romances?"

The words already out of her mouth, she cringed at her own flippancy. He'd given her raw honesty, and, in return, she kept veering away from anything sad.

But one of his dimples appeared. "Either. Both."

She looked up at him, then away as they swayed to the music. "There was a reconnaissance pilot. British. Shot down over the North Sea. Trying to bring back pictures to me and our crew of where we thought some subs were being built. We weren't engaged, but . . ."

I'll be seeing you . . . , Billie Holiday crooned.

They spun several more turns, her head easing down to his chest.

"But it was a loss," he finished quietly for her. "A terrible loss."

"Yes."

Amie felt his heart beating against hers as they swayed.

"I'm sorry," he said.

They rotated to several lines of the music before she spoke again. "And Bataan. I've read . . . It must've been horrific."

His answer was a single, slow nod. As if all words fell short.

Amie dropped her left hand from his shoulder down to rest on his upper arm—the hard contours of it beneath his shirtsleeve. His eyes locked on hers. Her other hand was lifted, resting lightly on his in dance position. Now, though, he laced his fingers with hers.

His face lowered slowly, his lips brushing across her cheek—the two of them slowly turning and swaying, swaying and turning, as Billie Holiday sang. Stepping in closer, Amie felt his breath shorten, along with her own.

Lifting herself to her toes, she pulled his head gently down until she could kiss his right temple, where the scar began, then, more softly still, the left side of his jaw, where it ended. Seth's feet came to a stop—his breath, too.

He pulled her in tight, his lips finding hers as the music spiraled around them, through them, beneath them, and the floor seemed to have fallen away.

Suddenly, he sprang back. "Oh God." Yanking at the cuff of his shirt, he stared at his watch. "Gwendolyn. She . . . I didn't intend . . ."

Amie stood speechless. It was not the way she'd expected this dance to end.

"Gwendolyn Weld," Seth said, rubbing the back of his neck. As if the full name somehow explained his behavior. "Amie, I . . . Forgive me. Please let me give you a ride home. At least let me drop you off . . ."

He reached for her hand, but she drew it away.

"Gwendolyn Weld," she repeated. Her breath had not even steadied yet from the kiss, and that made her angrier still.

"Yes. I'm meeting her now. Already late. Let me drop you off at the Orchard."

"On your way to Gwendolyn Weld?" she asked, incredulous. "No. Thanks."

Out in the main parlor, the vandalized portrait of Desmond Fossick seemed to leer. She squared her shoulders against it.

Gwendolyn Weld. Gwendolyn Weld.

Which sounded so very much like another name she'd come across recently.

An idea triggered in Amie's head. Unlikely, certainly. Adding two and two and getting fourteen, maybe. Still, she was remembering the way the woman in the diner in Cornwall had seemed repulsed by the mere mention of the Promontory . . .

"Before you go, a question." She drew herself up. If she couldn't finish the dance, she'd at least keep her dignity, and what her mind was suddenly mulling on.

"Again, I'm sorry, Amie, I—"

"Hoof oil."

He cocked his head. "Was that a question?"

"What is the name of the hoof oil, the kind that Carr something and something makes—"

"Carr and Day and Martin. From England. Been around forever."

"What ingredients would it contain? And would it be normal for horse owners to carry it around with them?"

"Can't imagine why—outside the barn. Typically made of pine tar—that's the old farmers' treatment for hooves—and mineral spirits."

"Mineral spirits," she repeated.

"Flaxseed oil. Linseed oil. That sort of thing."

"Like artists use. To clean brushes. And thin paint."

"Hadn't thought about the connection, but, yes, I guess so."

"Gwendolyn Weld," she murmured.

"Did you say I could give you a lift?"

"No." She heard the stiffness in her own tone.

For several beats, they stood awkwardly facing each other.

"Good night, then, Amie. Thank you . . . for the dance." He stepped closer. Reached to brush a hand down her arm.

But Amie stepped back. He was the one, after all, who'd ended their dance by dashing away to this woman, whoever she was. "Good night, Seth."

Looking pained, he stepped away, but turned back suddenly. "Unless you'd like to come and take photos."

"Of you and Gwendolyn Weld? No. Thank you."

"Her Westphalian's showing signs of being ready to drop—that is, foal. It could be twins—hard to know for sure in horses. Twins are rare and the birth usually doesn't go well. The mare's at my barn. Both of us on high alert, as you might imagine."

"Oh." Amie nodded slowly, processing this—their urgent meeting over a horse. Or at least partly over a horse. "Yes. I can imagine."

"Gwen's a private person. But I think she'd cherish the photos of this birth—especially if it is, in fact, twins. If you'd like to grab your camera and come when it's time. I could contact you. If you'd like."

"I'll . . . have to think. Those might be quite some pictures, you're right."

"Fiddlehead Farm. My family's place. You remember where it is?"

She nodded.

"No idea yet if it's time. I'll be in touch. If I can."

He raised both arms and leaned slightly toward her in a light, uneasy hug.

Patting his arms as she pulled away, she could feel the muscles even underneath his thick coat. Using a calf jack on a laboring cow probably did take some strength.

Waiting until he'd slipped out the double doors, Amie turned to stand before the defaced portrait of Fossick. The eyes had gone huge and hideous in their staring.

As if reacting, Amie thought, *to some sort of horror it had just seen. Or some sort of horror to come.*

Chapter 25

A movement from the back of her shop stopped her breath. An intruder.

Amie froze where she stood at the threshold. Hopkins was crouched, growling, near the closed darkroom door, but now at her entrance ran barking to her, then frantically back toward the darkroom.

Amie had checked back in at the Orchard with Shibby and Chester for bedtime stories. Then come back here to Good Harbor to develop more close-ups—of Chester's mother, her face or her clothes . . . any sort of a clue.

But just now, someone was here. Inside. Snarling, Hopkins paced outside the door.

Amie straightened, the brass key between her knuckles. Not that she knew how to throw a good punch, but the brass key couldn't hurt. She forced out a voice that sounded tough, unafraid. "Who's here?"

Fletch stepped from her office darkroom. "Your little white rat's awful loud."

"Good God, Fletch. You scared me."

"Guilty conscience, then."

"Always."

Stopping to scratch Hopkins roughly on the head, he sauntered into the shop and began inspecting the paint. Only after a full round did he reach into his overalls pocket and withdraw a crumpled scrap of paper. "Message for you."

Amie scanned the words Fletch had scrawled:

Mare in labor.

We're at my farm.

"Wakefield." Fletch added this like a complaint. "Said he tried to catch you at the Orchard but Shibby said you'd just left."

"I'll need to get my own phone here at the shop."

"Or you could keep using me as your full-time answering service."

Despite the sarcasm, he continued inspecting the shop, apparently in no hurry to return to Provisions.

Amie rewound the scarf around her neck. "I've never photographed a birth of foals before—or the birth of anything except maybe spring. Not that I need to explain my comings and goings to my trusty landlord."

"Who's also your answering service."

"That *is* kind of you. Truly. I assume you don't mind locking up—since you managed to lock *in*?" She patted his shoulder and paused to feed Hopkins before dashing back out the door.

Steering the roadster through the falling dark past Pelican Congregational and its aging clergyman strolling across the town green, Amie braced herself for the blast of cold as she rolled down her window to wave. Accelerating out of each turn, careful to downshift and not brake, Amie guided the car over roads the snowplow hadn't yet reached.

At the sign for Fiddlehead Farm, a Clydesdale painted beneath the words, Amie turned left into the long drive. Though the house, a two-story saltbox clapboard that looked like it could easily date to the colonial period, sat on a hill, the drive wound past it down the hill's opposite side. Above the Pelican River sat a long red barn, its weather vane a running horse.

She looked out over the fields, their undulations of white in the moon like waves that were all froth. Slamming the roadster into park, she sprang out and slid through an unshoveled path of others' footsteps to the barn.

Inside, the air no longer hurt her lungs. Lining each side of the corridor were the giant horses from the Budweiser ads, their massive heads swinging toward her. The first was asleep standing up, his cream-colored forelock flopped over one eye, others shifting nervously in their stalls at the grunts from the stable's far end. All around: the scents of oats and manure and leather and hay. And pine. Always in Pelican Cove, pine.

Amie felt a little unbalanced with the sudden warmth and the aromas. Knocking snow and leaves from her boots onto the sawdust floor, she forced herself forward.

In a stall at the end larger than all the rest, Seth bent over a mare on her side. Her belly bulged so big Amie marveled the black hide didn't split. Her body, heaving, glistened with perspiration.

Glancing up, Seth gave a fleeting smile to Amie, then swung his attention back to the mare. "It's the only part of my job I dislike—being pulled from a warm house when it's twenty degrees out."

He rubbed the mare's neck in long soothing strokes. "But the births. These make it all worth it."

Thrusting one arm deep into a duffel bag, he pulled out two rubber gloves and yanked them on, rolling them past his elbows. He shifted closer to the mare's hindquarters.

Amie watched, dizzy and unsure where to stand.

On the other side of the horse, a woman crouched. In tight-fitting tan jodhpurs and a white blouse, high-necked and crisp, she bent over the mare's head. The woman from the diner in Cornwall.

Her hair now, though, fell mussed from her barrette. She raised her head, her eyes rounding as she recognized Amie.

"Amelia Stilwell," Seth was saying without looking up from the mare, "this is Gwendolyn Weld. Gwen, I should've asked your permission to let Amie photograph the birth. I thought—hoped—you'd be pleased to have a few shots."

Gwendolyn Weld's pressed lips said she would not have given permission, but the veterinarian, his whole right arm inserted into the mare and pulling on something, didn't appear to notice how the silence had gone tense and strained.

Amie stepped forward and held out her hand. "Gwendolyn Weld. Good to meet you. I wonder if you're related to a woman I met recently, a Gertrude Winthrop? You favor one another. *Strikingly* so."

"Distantly," the woman said, looking away. The dark circles that had puffed under her eyes had grown darker still, as if she'd not slept since they'd met yesterday.

Quietly, Amie knelt at the edge of the foaling stall and focused her camera. She knew little about horses, but traumatizing a creature giving birth seemed a bad idea, so she'd left the flash in her bag. She'd have to be creative with her aperture and shutter speed, her use of existing light. The mare rolled to her back now, kicking her legs and grunting as she fought the pain.

Gwendolyn shot a look of worry to Seth. "It's been such a long labor already."

"Her vitals are still good. She's doing well so far, Gwen."

Gwen.

Amie chilled at the familiarity between them, this woman who'd lied to Amie about who she was. Was it only the bond of veterinarian and horse owner? Or something more?

Again, Seth spoke to the woman. Spoke tenderly, even. "Need to let anyone know where you are?"

A look passed between them. An understanding.

"I have a car here."

"I hope you know you can stay here again if you need to."

Stay here again?

Amie felt the hair on the back of her neck stand up, the two of them passing some sort of unspoken words to each other. Amie wanted to slap Seth for kissing her as he had—or had she kissed him? And right before he ran here—to her.

She wanted to slap Gwendolyn Weld for being a liar, and for being the person he'd run to. Amie wanted to slap herself, too, for letting herself be pulled into that dance, into that kiss . . . and now this. Only her pride kept her here, pretending to examine her camera's lens, pretending she'd come only out of professional interest.

Gwendolyn's eyes dropped to her mare, then lifted once more to meet Amie's gaze. Her face, which had struck Amie as pretty when they'd met in Cornwall, was streaked and knotted still worse today with something like fear.

Still, she was lovely—or maybe arresting—in that way a valuable painting damaged by fire or water or time could still retain beauty that drew the onlooker. Amie's father had bought several such paintings, including a Vermeer cared for poorly by its previous owner. Even before Dr. Stilwell had paid thousands to have it restored, Amie had stood before it enthralled.

She adjusted her aperture and shutter speed in preparation for the birth, both Seth and Gwendolyn engrossed in the mare's breathing.

She's doing well so far, Gwen . . . You can stay here again if you need to . . .

The intimacy between them.

Seth was stroking the mare's neck with one hand while the other plucked out a stethoscope from the duffel. Fitting it to his ears, he bent over her belly.

The mare rolled and thrashed again. Then she lay still, heaving, as he leaned in to listen.

Seth closed his eyes as he worked, as if needing to shut down all his senses to one. "I'm touching a hoof," he murmured, "and now . . ." His words jumbled, a mix of comforting sounds for the horse and maybe some for himself as he worked. "She's got two babies in here all right."

Seth tipped his head back, his hair, thick and uneven as if he cut it himself, catching the light of the bare bulb that hung from the rafter. "Got things shifted around best I could. Could be a while still. No hurrying this, bringing new life into the world."

The bare yellow bulb illuminated his face—the rugged lines of it going softer as he turned to look at Gwendolyn Weld with . . . What was it? Concern?

Tears trickled from the woman's eyes.

Again, exchanged looks between the woman and Seth. Again, some sort of understanding.

Gwendolyn hooked her body over the horse and hid her face in the mare's mane. She might have stayed that way indefinitely if the mare hadn't suddenly thrashed onto her back, legs kicking, her whole body writhing.

Seth guided the tiny hooves inside their sac as they appeared. Staying out of his way, Amie knelt to focus her camera. *Snap. Snap. Snap.* She shifted position for a better angle. Then the rest of the first foal's body. The second followed a few moments later, Seth clearing both foals' nostrils with hay as Amie, surprising herself with the emotion, the awe the birth had welled up in her, continued to snap photos.

Rocking back on his heels, Seth passed an arm across his forehead. "Two healthy foals: one filly, one colt. Extraordinary. They're whopping for twins. No wonder the poor momma'd gone wild with hurt."

But Gwendolyn Weld didn't appear to hear him. Her face should've looked relaxed now, bent over the foals—but seemed to be seeing something besides new life. Her tears had moved from trickles to streams down her cheeks. And maybe not tears of joy or relief, it appeared. She'd folded in her lips and was biting down on them as if she were afraid to let out the words that might come.

For a good half hour or more, the three of them remained in the stall, Seth checking on the three horses, Amie snapping pictures, and Gwen watching from a few feet away. When the mare rose to her feet, Gwen stood, too, but then, as if she were the one who'd just given birth, sank back down in her corner of the stall.

"Look at that," Seth said.

The foals were both making valiant attempts to leverage themselves up on top of those spindles for legs. The filly found her mother's milk first.

Seth stroked the mare's neck. "She did great."

Letting her camera swing loose from its neck strap, Amie sat back onto the hay. "Some kind of nice work you did here tonight."

He shook his head. "I just rearranged legs a little so things could get moving."

The mare's head, though dropping, still hooked back to her foals, as if to assure herself they were okay.

The vet held up a plastic bag to the lantern light—bulging, bloody masses inside. "I need to take these home."

"Well *that*," Amie said, "is a disturbing thing to announce."

"I'll lay them both out in the daylight to be sure they're completely intact." He swung the bag of bloody pulp closer to Amie's face. "It's the placental sacs, one for each. Got to be turned right side out and examined to be sure nothing's missing. A piece gone'd mean something's left inside the mare's uterus, which could mean infection."

"And you enjoy this?" Amie touched the bag, the soft warm mass of it, and recoiled.

Lifting the placental sacs up to the light again, Seth marveled. "To think something grows in sacs like this for three hundred forty days, and on the same day it slides out the canal, can stand on its own legs and walk."

From where Gwendolyn Weld sat in the hay, her knees drawn to her chest and her arms wrapped tightly around them, her voice came strained. "She did well."

Seth was wiping the filly's coat down with a burlap sack. "It's nature's way."

A sob seemed to catch in the woman's throat.

Seth turned. "Gwen." His voice had gone tender. "I can see to the foals and the new momma if you need to go now."

Gwendolyn Weld teetered to her own feet.

There, Amie thought, *is that terrified look again.*

"Yes. I do need to go now."

"Gwen, get some rest. Don't worry right now about all the other."

Amie stepped with her toward the barn doors nearest the mare's stall and watched the woman slide one panel back to walk ahead toward a car, barely visible in the dark.

Gwendolyn turned back once as if she might say something.

Amie held out a hand. Her jealousy toward the woman had given way to genuine alarm at the pain on her face. The woman's eyes reminded Amie of the fighter pilots headed up in their Wildcats and Thunderbolts, their Hellcats and Corsairs to an airspace they knew they might not come down from in one piece.

"Gwendolyn," Amie said.

Slowly, as if unsure she wanted to hear whatever was about to be said, the woman turned.

"I don't mean to intrude. But are you all right? Can I help?"

Joining Amie at the barn door, Seth strode forward suddenly, the barn's lantern in one hand. "Damn it all, Gwen. One of *his* cars?"

Gwendolyn Weld hesitated at the driver's-side door of a sleek black sedan. Throwing it open and herself inside, she slammed it so hard a row of icicles fell from the barn's eaves. She rolled down the window to defend herself plaintively. "You don't understand. If you knew the whole story . . ."

"You could've asked to borrow my truck. I could've picked you up."

"He owes me."

"Damn right he does. But why be obligated to him? Why keep taking the crumbs he offers when he owes you the world?"

She shook her head. "He's softened. He wants to talk again soon."

"The hell he has! You can't possibly believe his crap."

"I have no choice." Her voice rose now, more desperate. "You know I can't go back to the house in Brookline, not after . . . If you knew the half of it . . ."

Before he could say more, Gwendolyn stomped the accelerator, the car's tires spinning, then finding traction.

In the shaft of light from the barn door, Amie could see the side of the car as it flashed by: *the Promontory Inn* painted in gold on its side, Desmond Fossick's name beneath that.

The Allard crunched away through the snow, sliding first right and then left until it reached the more firmly packed drive.

Amie and Seth stood for a moment watching the taillights disappear up the hill toward the road. Suddenly, Seth whirled and kicked the barn door with such force the horses along the corridor swung their heads up and around, startled. Gathering himself but not meeting Amie's eye, he yanked the barn door closed and walked back toward the end stall. Squatting beside one of the foals, he watched the colt still sorting out his four limbs.

Amie lifted her Deardorff from around her neck, twisted off its lens, and arranged it in its bag. "I should go."

Nodding, Seth rose and walked with her in silence to the far end of the barn where she'd parked. The vet paused to check a Clydesdale here and there.

Hauling the far door open, Seth turned to her.

Amie waited until he met her eye. "She seems . . . vulnerable."

Pausing before he answered, he looked away. "She's not thinking straight. Someone needs to shake sense into her."

And you, Amie was tempted to ask, *would be that someone?*

"You seem, Seth, to know her well."

Another pause. "I've cared for her mare for some time now."

Just for her mare? Amie wondered, feeling suddenly angry again—and confused. "And you care for her, too," she said. A statement. Not a question.

Seth rounded on her. "She's a wreck right now. She's playing right into his hands. *Again.*"

"If your . . ." She searched for the right word. "If your friend Gwendolyn Weld is involved in some way with Desmond Fossick, could you talk about it?"

Amie saw his throat constrict as he swallowed.

Seth neither spoke nor moved for a moment.

Which, Amie knew, was at least part of an answer.

Chapter 26

"Extraordinary that you'd ask." The voice came fuzzed in static over the line.

It had taken Amie a couple of days to track down Eunice Kennedy through their mutual friend at Boston Public Library, all three of them having been students together for a short time at Radcliffe. Eunice's voice sounded as bright and eager to help as it had all those years ago when their paths had crossed for a few months in Cambridge, Massachusetts—Eunice fresh from Stanford and Amie about to leave for England. "A woman with a young child living on or near Acorn Street on Beacon Hill—with a possible Irish background, is that right?"

Amie felt her hands go sweaty on the receiver and had to grip it more tightly to keep it from tumbling to the Provisions floor. Several children, too young to be at school on this Tuesday morning, huddled around the candy aisle. A woman one aisle over was filling the basket she carried with deviled ham, Sunbeam bread, and oleo. Amie kept her voice low and tried to ignore Fletcher's watching her as he rang up a sale for another customer. "I've called everyone I could think of from our circle of friends back then with connections to Beacon Hill."

"You and I overlapped only those few weeks," Eunice said, "so I'm pleased you'd consider me even part of your circle. It's so odd you should broach this subject this week, of all times."

"Of all times?"

"Mother and I were just planning a special dinner for my father—pulling out old photographs, letters, awards, that sort of thing. It would seem that my father had a way with the ladies at one time."

"Did he really?" Amie hurried to ask. The fact that Joseph Kennedy, father of many children and married to Rose for many years, *still* had a reputation in New England—and in Washington, too—with "the ladies" would need to be politely ignored.

"Anyway, I was having lunch with Margaret yesterday near her office at the library. She mentioned you'd called her about trying to track down the mother of that poor, sweet kid who'd been abandoned up there. When she described the two of them . . ."

Eunice Kennedy was a straightforward woman. But just now, Amie wanted to reach through the phone line and speed up the flow of her words. "You think you might know who his mother could be?"

"I'm afraid I have only a few thoughts to offer."

"I'll take any you have."

"Among my father's old love letters—heaven only knows why he saved them—were quite a few from a woman he called Addy."

"'Sweet Adeline,'" Amie murmured.

"Apparently, the love of his high school years was this Addy."

"You don't know a last name?"

"Not yet. But I'll see Father tonight. The thing that struck me in connection with you, though, when Margaret mentioned your search, was that this woman, whoever she is, apparently grew up on Acorn Street. I can't imagine, though, that Father is still in touch with her in any sort of significant way, their lives having gone different directions."

A pause here, as if Eunice Kennedy herself harbored doubts about her father.

"But they did happen to see one another at a dinner for Mayor Curley not too long ago. Mother mentioned that this Addy person, the old flame of Father's, was the only one who'd not brought a spouse."

Amie held her breath.

"This Addy-whomever did, though, bring a child with her, of all things. It's not much to go on, I know."

True, Amie wanted to agree. *Just a random mother and child on Acorn Street hardly narrows things down.*

"But here's the one other thing Mother recalled, Amie. Addy's child was a little boy, and he looked as if he might be about five or six." She paused. "Mother recalled he wore a bow tie."

Amie emerged blinking from the darkroom she'd created in the shop's office. The photos of Puffin Beach in snow and her drive up the coast had come out better than she'd dreamed. One of the triumphs of that roll had been the arctic tern who'd flown directly toward her, wings outstretched so that he'd looked like an angel with a flaming tongue and full head of black feathers.

Another triumph from that same Kodachrome roll had been the diner in Cornwall. She'd meant to capture it with no human movement. The gray-shingled diner sat perched on its wharf, sad and desperate looking as if it were wading into a cold winter sea.

Now Amie examined it closely. Through the window, only the outlines of human forms showed. But there was Gwendolyn Weld, appearing, from the hunch of her shoulders and the drop of her head, to be in a similar emotional state to the diner itself.

The hunch of her shoulders . . .

Amie held up the photo.

She'd been assuming lately the Bentley she'd knocked across the tracks that first night in town belonged to Fossick. But what if it belonged to a woman—or at least had been driven by a woman wearing that man's fedora?

Last night, when she'd looked at Gwendolyn Weld just before she drove away from the barn, Amie had felt as if she were looking into the face of a soldier just back from combat. That sadness, that numbness, a darkness where light and logic could no longer reach.

Gwendolyn Weld had been driving an Allard from the Promontory. Desmond Fossick must surely be the *he* of her exchange with Seth. The man who owed her the world. The man she shouldn't be begging favors from.

Amie turned toward the wall that separated her shop from Fáilte. Hanging the wet prints up to dry from the twine she'd secured yesterday between posts, she wondered if Ian next door could tell her something about this Gwendolyn Weld that Seth could not—or would not—last night.

❧

"There ought to be a door here," she muttered aloud. "If only so I don't need to put on my coat to walk what could, with a little sledgehammering, be ten steps."

Shoving on her boots but not the rest of her gear, she dashed the few yards through the cold next door and flung herself in the door.

Ian raised an eyebrow. "Did you travel by slingshot?"

Shaking wet leaves and snow from her boots, she flopped down her things at the only available table next door. Making her way to the counter, she surveyed the milling group of villagers.

"You okay, Amelia? Because your neck looks like it's stuck in a quarter turn of the head."

She needed to launch in with something besides her actual question so he didn't freeze up. "If Fletch approved, since he owns the building, how would you feel about our busting a cute little Hobbit door—"

"A what?"

"Like the book. *The Hobbit.* You know, sweet little creatures who live in these charming burrow-like—"

"Never read it."

Amie laughed. "Then I have a new reason for living. I'm lending you my copy tonight. Meanwhile, you could imagine a charming little door—think Old World England and creatures who eat meals between meals . . . Which reminds me, why do I never see you eating your own pastries? Ever?"

Ian ignored this. "So a *door.*"

"With an arch, and I could string lights—"

"Whoa, back up. I think maybe the hundred-thousand-welcomes idea has gone way to your head. You're saying you want to bust a door . . . *where* exactly?"

"Between Good Harbor and Fáilte. It could be locked when one of us needs to be closed. But it would be open most of the time since my customers—"

"Which you don't currently have."

"True. But in theory. My Imaginary Friend Customers of the Future, let's say, are people who love photography and nature and locally made objects of art and blueberry muffins and fresh-perked coffee and running into other people interested in those very things. Don't you think?"

"I think first of all that paint fumes have impaired your judgment. Second, I think you're too lazy to put on a coat and scarf to get coffee."

"Absolutely right on both counts. But before you say it's nuts . . ."

"It's *totally* nuts. Like my South End Irish cop dad didn't think I was embarrassment enough already, you want me to help build a Hobbit door."

"Okay, then, before you say no"—she held up a flattened palm in front of his face as he formed the word—"just *think* about it.

Meanwhile, I plan to charm Fletch with the idea, and I'll present it as if you're totally on board. Hope that's all right."

As Amie turned with her coffee in hand, a small child bolted toward her from the door.

"Lordy-howdy it's cold," Shibby called from across the shop as she hurried in. "Ian, I sure could use a shot of Texas whiskey in my muffin this morning, hon. I mean, Lordy, don't give it to me really. But I sure could use one." She sent an air kiss his direction, and he blew one back. Striding toward Amie, Shibby kissed her on the cheek.

"Are Texans ever *un*friendly?" Ian asked. "I keep wondering when you'll crack."

"Unlike some of my dearest and most valued friends here"—she beamed in Fletch's direction as he jangled through the door—"we don't feel the need to express our every ugly, unfiltered thought."

"For those who like phony," Ian said over his shoulder from the percolator.

"For those, sugar," Shibby shot back, smiling, "who think some dose of sweetness, phony or not, helps with the spooning out of life's castor oil."

Bending to hug Chester, Amie stepped to an open space beside the percolator and spun him in a circle. Pausing for a moment, she said quietly over her shoulder to Ian, "I need to speak with you about how you might know a woman who was in here talking with you the other day."

"That's about as vague as it comes, don't you think?" But his eyes, she saw, had narrowed. As if he had a feeling what she might be wanting to ask and was already preparing an answer.

"The thing is, I don't mean to be nosy, but I saw you talking with her one morning when you were alone—except her—here. You looked awfully upset."

His voice had gone hard. "That would seem to be the very definition of *nosy*."

"I don't want to pry into your personal business. Truly. It's just that I met her myself up in Cornwall under one name. Then last night under a different one—with Seth Wakefield at his barn. She'd apparently borrowed a car from the Promontory."

"You want to know about her because you have designs on Dr. Dolittle and you want to know what their relationship is?"

"Designs?" Amie's hands fisted on her hips. "Are you *really* as old-fashioned as that? Give me a little credit for caring whether or not someone is so bad off she'd park her car on train tracks!"

They glared at each other.

It was Chester who broke the standoff by tugging on Amie's sleeve.

Shifting, she spun Chester once more.

Maybe it was the little boy's giggles that softened Ian. Amie caught a glimpse of his face as she let Chester's feet sink toward the floor.

"My family," he said quietly as Amie steadied herself. "Let's just say she knows them. She was . . . worried about me. Also, yeah, I'm worried about her. We've all got our secrets, don't you think, Amelia Stilwell?" He let her full name sit there, almost aggressively so, a spear-tip sort of reminder of any secrets she might have of her own. "That's all I can say. Because I promised."

"But—"

The bell on Fáilte's door trilled again, Seth Wakefield standing at the threshold.

Looking, Amie thought, a little wild—deranged, almost. His straw-colored hair stuck up almost straight from his head and he was casting his gaze about desperately. He snatched his beret from his head and was wringing it.

Clearly ready to change topics, Ian raised an eyebrow at her. "Dr. Dolittle arrives. Imagine if there were an open door between our two businesses, and I could just call over my every unfiltered thought, day or night."

Later, Amie promised herself, *we'll finish that earlier conversation.*

"You make a point. But I still think a nice little Hobbit arch with cute little lights is the answer."

"The answer. To everything? Including your not having to put on a coat to get coffee?"

"And the answer to sharing your customers. Also to world peace."

Seth took a step forward but stopped, his eyes still darting about. Even beneath his windburned cheeks, he looked pale.

Fletcher, Kalia, and a good dozen others were all milling about the bakery. Stella Lapierre was just buttoning her mauve coat over her nurse's uniform. Amie waved a greeting, and Stella, taking a final sip from her coffee, waved back. Fletch, easing down at a table with steaming cinnamon buns, stretched out his long legs. In overalls again today, he looked as much like a custodian as the owner of the whole building.

With a hand on Chester's shoulder, Amie ambled toward the front door where Seth still stood unmoving, as if his eyes had not yet focused. "Chester, you remember Dr. Wakefield. And, Seth, you recall the finest young man you've ever met."

Chester blinked up at the veterinarian. Shibby was headed in to work a ten o'clock shift at the inn today. She and Amie had discussed this morning whether Chester might not need to start Pelican Grammar School—both for the routine and to make friends while they continued their search for his mother. But today, he would stay with Amie.

"He still doesn't talk much at certain times," Amie offered softly. "He's super smart, though."

Seth, looking down at the child as if he'd never seen him before, turned to go without speaking. Brushing past on her way out the door, Kalia greeted Amie and him, but unlike Amie, he did not respond.

"What on earth?" Amie touched him on the arm. "Seth, what's gotten into you?"

He turned only halfway back, but didn't appear to be actually seeing anything in the bakery.

Crazed, Amie thought. *He looks like he's gone stark raving mad.*

A black sedan was rolling through Dock Circle, *the Promontory Inn* on its side. In the front sat a driver and in the back seat, two men, both with their heads turned away.

Slamming his cap back on his head, Seth swiveled, then dashed out Fáilte's door in the direction the Allard had gone.

At the grunt behind her, Amie turned to find Fletch frowning, arms crossed over his chest. Beside him stood Chester, arms crossed in perfect imitation.

Fletch muttered something mostly inaudible and mostly profane.

"Was that Fossick already back in town?" Amie stepped to the bakery window.

Across Dock Circle, Seth had thrown open the door of his truck. Pausing, he bent to do something Amie couldn't see. Headed in separate directions, Kalia and Stella both hurried past his truck, each raising a hand in greeting—neither of which Seth even seemed to see. He stood still only an instant before leaping into the cab and spinning away.

"The man's gone down the cellah behind the axe," Fletch was saying.

Annoyed at Seth's behavior, Amie half grinned at the old Mainer phrase. "That bad, huh?" She held a hand out to Chester. "I need to run a quick errand with my young friend here. But, Fletch, if I could just ask one more question."

Ian, passing with a tray of cinnamon buns and coffees, steam rising from the cups, rolled his eyes. "She's hoping to bust a door in your lovely wall over there, Fletch. It's just a play for free coffee all day."

"Actually, this is a different question. Though after I leave, do get Ian to tell you about the Hobbit arch. He's been kind, saying he and I could do the sledgehammering work ourselves if you agree."

She tilted her head at Ian, then turned back to Fletch and lowered her voice. "What I wanted to ask was whether you know a woman named Gwendolyn Weld."

"Who the hell is Gwendolyn Weld?"

"Or maybe named Gertrude Winthrop?"

He swung his head back and forth, scraggly chin brushing over his overall straps. "Sounds like Boston Brahmin names to me." He did not say this with reverence.

"Never mind, then. I'm also wondering if anyone has bought linseed oil from you lately in Provisions. I know you keep it in rainy-day stock for the summer tourists. I know it's a long shot but . . ."

"Ayuh. Just one." Fletch jerked his head back toward where Ian stood near the front door, where a villager was bustling in.

Ian was turning, greeting new guests. Now he paused to read something on a piece of paper just handed to him, his face going pale.

He gripped the paper in one hand. With the other, he jerked his white Fáilte apron up over his head and shoved it at the owner of Daggerboard Gifts.

"Just for a few minutes while I run out," Ian was telling her. Flying past Amie and Fletch without a word, he grabbed keys from beside the cash register and disappeared out the back.

"Sold a can to him," Fletch said. "Which'd be strange. Didn't buy any oil paint."

～

Amie turned to be sure Chester was settled in the passenger seat of the roadster. She tried not to convey the hurry she felt.

"F-A-R-M, farm," Chester spelled as she steered left into Fiddlehead Farm's long drive.

"*Farm* is exactly right. And it's so nice to hear you say it out loud."

At the far side of a pasture, someone was hurrying toward the road. Amie squinted but, at this distance, couldn't be sure who it might be. Definitely, though, the person was too short and too thin, even under a coat, to be Seth.

She eased the Aston Martin into the drive as she reached to pat Chester's leg. "Listen, sweetie, I want you to stay in your seat, okay? I'll just run into the barn for a minute."

Pointing back toward the sign with the Clydesdale, Chester looked stunned at the injustice of the request. "Please, may I see the big pretty horse?"

What could be so bad, after all? Seth, and possibly Ian, too, probably both would've gone flying to help Gwendolyn Weld, even if the trouble was only the foals not nursing well.

"If you'll stay right with me, okay?"

The sky today was striking: a high banner of cirrus clouds above a brilliant swath of sapphire blue and, beneath that, the snow of Fiddlehead Farm's pastures—*like the alternating stripes of a Greek flag*, Amie thought. With the red of the old barn and the towering hemlock beside it, the scene looked as if it had been Technicolored beyond real life.

Amie took Chester's hand as they entered the barn. "Seth? Anybody home?"

From the middle of the corridor, a slim figure emerged from the tack room, where Amie caught sight of the blankets and bridles, along with a whiff of leather and grain.

Shadows hid the figure's face. For a moment, it stood unmoving, as if paralyzed by fear or indecision. Or both.

"Amie?"

"Ian! What . . . ?" They stared at each other a moment.

Ian shifted uneasily, then approached a few steps. Clearly, he'd not planned to be caught out here. "Got a note a few minutes ago to come out here. *Emergency*, it said."

But there was something she couldn't read about his face, something desperate in his eyes, eyes that wouldn't meet hers.

"Your note was from Gwendolyn?"

Ian half turned away. "No. Seth."

"Seth?" Amie recalled the dash to the green Ford. She looked around. "But he's not here?"

"Nothing but equine." Ian moved as if he might leave.

"Ian, maybe it's none of my business—I realize that. But maybe you should tell me how you and Gwendolyn know each other. Or how Seth knows her."

"Seth is her vet."

"And?"

"You'll have to ask him. I have to go."

"Look, regardless of what secrets you or Seth are keeping for her—or about yourselves, for that matter—isn't it time somebody tried to help the woman? If she was the one I saw on the train tracks that night, she absolutely is dangerous—to herself and others."

"That couldn't . . ." But he stopped there. "I need to get back to the bakery." Yet he didn't move. As if he were waiting for her to leave, too.

As they stared at each other, Chester trotted down the barn's corridor. Leaping up at every stall door, he got a quick glimpse of each horse before dropping back to the sawdust. He'd reached the last one on the left now. "Little horses!"

"Yes!" Amie called back, breaking eye contact with Ian and walking toward Chester. "They were just born last night."

Leaving Ian standing there unmoving as if stuck in place, Amie jogged ahead, standing beside the child and bending to pick him up for a better view into the foaling stall. But she stopped dead.

Oh God. Oh dear God.

Her eyes flew from the stall back to Ian. Instead of lifting Chester, she placed a hand on either side of his head.

Like a helmet, Amie thought. *Like I could protect him from some wreck ahead.*

The mare munching her oats and the foals nursing, Amie braced herself for opening the stall door—if she could spare Chester somehow from what was inside.

In her peripheral vision, Amie saw Ian approach step by reluctant step as she stood with her hands helmeting Chester's head. She moved her body between Ian and the child.

Stepping alongside her, Ian followed her gaze down.

There on the floor splayed across sawdust lay Gwendolyn Weld. Unmoving. Her head, lying near the mare's front hooves, had been gashed open just over the eye. A black velvet riding helmet lay upside down a few inches away.

Amie threw an arm around Chester. She could hear the strain, the false cheeriness, in her own voice. "Just a minute, Ches, sweetie. Looks like the foals aren't ready for a visit just now."

Chester gazed up, an accusing look.

He heard fear, no doubt, in her voice. And she'd gripped his shoulder, she realized, too hard. "I'm sorry, Ches. But we'll need to come back later to see them." Even to her own ears, her voice sounded too tinny and panicked.

Face gone ashen, Ian was still staring down where the body lay. His mouth ovaled in what looked like the start of a scream.

"Ches, big guy, can you just stand here a minute? Tell you what, you close your eyes really, really tightly, and that'll help me get this one thing checked fast." Heart pounding so hard she was afraid Chester might hear it, Amie slipped past the boy into the stall. Closing its door swiftly behind her, she dropped to her knees beside the body. Lifting Gwendolyn's wrist, she felt for a pulse.

"Oh God," Amie whispered. "Dear God."

Looking up to meet Ian's eye, Chester too short to see, Amie watched the young baker mouth only one word: *No.*

But for all Ian's near paralysis at the scene, something about his expression made Amie wonder. He appeared horrified having to look at the still face of Gwendolyn Weld, yet . . .

Ian O'Leary had just received a note from Seth Wakefield. And Seth had looked so upset in Fáilte just a short time ago, then disappeared—a dead body now in his barn.

Amie studied Ian's face an instant longer.

He looks terrified, she decided. *But he does not look too surprised.*

Chapter 27

Chester must've known something horrific had happened. The child sank back into his silence, a thumb in his mouth.

In the Wakefield home, left unlocked, Amie held Chester's hand as she called the police first, then Shibby at the inn to come pick up the child. Until Shibby pulled up in her ancient DeSoto, its engine coughing, Amie sat with her arm around the boy as she pointed out birds. "There's a herring gull. And there's a great black-backed gull . . ."

Holding Shibby's hand, Chester allowed himself to be led away, head down. Not looking back.

"I told Miss Michaud," Shibby called over her shoulder, "I need the rest of the day off, so you take your time here."

The undertaker and the ambulance driver were the same person in Pelican Cove—the only man to own a vehicle long enough to stow a body, alive or dead, lengthwise and covered behind the front seats. He arrived with a blare of a makeshift siren—the siren more, Amie suspected, because he enjoyed the sound than because he hadn't been told the victim was already dead.

Along with Ian, Amie was answering the police chief's questions—or trying.

"Kick to the head, looks like. Damn shame," the chief muttered, jotting notes.

"Could be," Amie said—without conviction. "But that's not—"

"I got plenty more questions for you later, Miss Stilwell, you being one of the last people to see Mrs. Weld alive."

"'Mrs.'?" Amie asked, and could've smacked herself. That was hardly the most urgent question just now.

The chief rounded on Ian O'Leary, standing mute nearby, staring as the body disappeared into the mouth of the ambulance-hearse. "I got more questions for you, too, O'Leary. Same goes for our local animal vet when he shows."

It was, Amie thought, *awfully convenient, the timing of Seth's disappearance. Emphasis on the awful.*

"I have no idea," Amie heard herself repeat, monotone, to the chief. "No earthly idea."

Ian appeared, if anything, worse, hardly able to speak. A woman was dead, one he'd been seen talking with in Fáilte—seen not just by Amie, but also by the owner of Daggerboard Gifts. Worse, Ian had been there at the barn—on the scene.

And acting suspiciously, Amie could have added.

The chief finally stuffed his notepad in his coat pocket, huffing as he did. "It's clear the woman's been kicked in the head by her own horse."

He swiveled toward Amie. "You want to tell me why you're shaking your head, Miss Stilwell?"

"She'd already left the barn. After her horse gave birth and the foals were clearly healthy and nursing. She left. In one of the fleet of Allards that Desmond Fossick keeps at his inn."

"So what are you saying? That she couldn't come back for one more look? Gotten too close to the momma's hind end, maybe come between her and her babies? Horses kick, you know."

"They do, yes, I suppose. But . . ."

"Tell you what. Why don't you save us both time and say whatever it is you're thinking?"

"The wound strikes me as odd."

He sighed, a long-suffering blow of air. "How so, Miss Stilwell?"

"It's a head wound. I had one myself when the Luftwaffe bombed Medmenham."

"So?"

"Head wounds bleed. Profusely. This one didn't. Hardly any blood. As if she were dead before she was hit in the head."

"Which is ridiculous."

"Which is odd," she countered. "And the wound itself isn't filled with bits of wood shavings or hay as you'd expect from a wound caused by the mare's hoof."

As if demonstrating, the mare shifted her weight, lifting her back left leg to rest, toe down, in a cocked position. Bits of wood shavings and hay clung to the hoof wall and its iron shoe.

"So what? So the debris came off when she kicked."

"Maybe." Amie's eyes scanned the stall, all the browns and tans and golds of the shavings and hay and three dark bay horses. Now she stepped back into the corridor, a row of pitchforks and shovels hanging neatly along the near wall. Again, the pine boards and the shavings, the blades and tines of the tools: a blend of browns and tans and grays. But at the far end, something bright caught her eye. Something red.

A can just like the one in Gertrude Winthrop-Gwendolyn Weld's purse that day at the Cornwall diner. A kind of oil, Amie reminded herself, that could protect equine feet. But what if its pine tar and linseed oil properties could make other substances pliable? Melt them, almost. The oil paints of a portrait, for example.

She turned back to the stall, her eyes still on the ground. There, near the stall door, was something cylindrical in the hay and sawdust.

Amie bent for it. Straightening, she was still registering what it was: a needle, surprisingly long, attached to the glass vial that delivered medicine through a shot.

"What's that you've got?" came the chief's voice from a few feet away. Instinctively, Amie turned her back to him.

Even before she'd had a chance to weigh what this meant, her reflexes took charge to hide what she'd found. She was protecting Seth, she realized—in the same moment she realized he might not deserve protection.

But it was too late anyway for making that decision, the chief straightening up from where he'd been bent, easing himself well clear of the three horses as he kicked at the sawdust and searched for clues. Part of her was relieved to be given no choice.

She shifted her eyes to Ian, who blinked back at her. He was frightened, all right: that much was clear.

Even as she watched, he sank down in the barn's corridor and buried his head in his hands.

Amie opened her palm as Chief Roy leaned in.

"Damn," he said. "Wouldn't have a needle that size poking me in the backside."

Amie bit her lip as she watched the chief's face.

Most country vets here in New England, if they operated like the one she'd known near Medmenham in England, carried a pentobarbital mix with them for euthanizing livestock that required putting down. Her vet friend in England had once described having to put down the day's favorite at Ascot when the chestnut broke his front leg at the water jump.

"It probably," she suggested, her stomach already gone sour, "was here from before. Some other horse that needed a shot of some sort. Tranquilizer, maybe. Painkiller. Something. Just got lost in the hay."

The chief's mouth was working now—priming a pump, it seemed, for his voice to come out a few seconds later.

"Probably," he echoed, blinking at Amie while she held very still, her palm wanting to close over what she not only did not want him to see, but also didn't want to see herself.

Chief Roy plucked his handkerchief from his back pocket and spread it out in his left palm for Amie to drop the syringe onto. Amie could see from his eyes that his mind was circling the same questions as hers.

"Probably," he said again, meeting her eye, "just lost in the hay."

∼

Amie lowered her voice as she spoke into the Provisions phone to the police chief. "So you're saying the lab determined the cause of death was definitely not a hoof to the head." She turned her back to where Fletcher was watching her from a row of snow shovels, children's mittens, rock salt—and also nylon-webbed lawn chairs still in stock from the summer.

"Yup. Like you guessed somehow. Which is the only reason I'm making this call."

Trying to focus on something other than her mounting panic, she watched the gulls outside Provisions' side window soaring over the harbor, the gray of their wings against the clouds like pencil on paper. Amie tightened her grip on the receiver.

It was warm inside Fletch's general store, yet her hands and feet had all just gone icy cold. "So the wound on her head . . ."

"Likely a shovel, the coroner said."

Amie squeezed her eyes shut against the image of Gwendolyn's face. "But there was too little blood."

A huff at the other end of the line. "Yup. Me and the coroner said the same thing."

"Would you be willing, Chief, to let me know what else the coroner finds?"

A pause—in which he was probably swallowing a sarcastic remark. "Seeing how you helped me out there in the barn, maybe I'll share what I can. How 'bout we board that boat when we get there?"

"Fair enough. But let's just say the autopsy results come back showing a substance in her system that killed her. Not a shovel. Not a hoof. Just made to look that way. What then?"

Best to let the chief take credit for a few ideas now.

"So, obviously, I got to entertain the possibility of that Ian O'Leary fellow."

Amie glanced around Provisions. Empty. Except for Fletch rearranging canned bread. "Why on earth him?" She knew several reasons why. But didn't know how much the chief knew.

A pause. "He was there, obviously, at the scene."

"Although you'd think he'd have made an effort to hide if he'd been the perpetrator."

"You said yourself he looked surprised when you drove up unexpected."

That much was true. She'd not even offered to the chief just how rattled Ian had looked, even before she'd found the body.

"Also, him and this Gwendolyn Weld woman both come from Boston families with names to protect. Hers because the Welds have been there forever. Her husband or ex-husband—we're not sure which yet, but they weren't on good terms—has some big place in Brookline."

Brookline. Gwen had mentioned that posh part of Boston just before she'd left the barn. Something about not being able to go back to that house after . . . after something she'd not been able to name.

The chief was rattling on. "The O'Learys, they got a name to protect 'cause they're new—and the Irish been on the rise down there lately. Kennedys and that crowd finally making a place for their sort in politics and business."

"What does that have to do with suspecting Ian?"

"Let's just say Gwendolyn Weld knew Ian O'Leary."

"Yes. He told me as much himself. I don't know that that was any secret."

The chief snorted. "As in, she knew the guy's a damn fair—"

"Fairly new owner of a bakery here?" Amie said over him. "I think that's what you meant to say, wasn't it?" If he could hear the anger in her voice, good.

"Whatever the hell you want to call it. I got to say: People do crazy things, violent things, when they think their secrets are gonna be spilled. Defend the kid if you want, but Ian O'Leary's got himself secrets that made him leave Boston."

Amie's head throbbed. "You'll call me—or call Fletch to find me— as soon as you hear back from the coroner? And has Seth Wake—?"

But the chief had hung up.

~

Still feeling shaken, Amie watched a scrum of three men, including the town's mayor of many years, charge down to the street, their backs to her. Still, though, she recognized the shortest of the three. His walk, more like a panther stalking its prey, and the way he held his arms well out to both sides as if braced for attack, was unmistakable. As they bolted away, she noticed, too, the tall, slender man beside him in a dark overcoat and hat, wingtips buffed to a bright sheen—ridiculous here, especially in this weather. Someone *from away*, clearly.

She was feeling her own sense of urgency. She needed to call Fossick Enterprises again since she'd heard nothing back. Jake, she imagined, would be less than pleased to hear she'd found him. No telling how he'd react. *Badly* was a safe assumption.

She eased into an empty stool at the bar. The Tipsy Porpoise was nearly full, its being the only restaurant open for lunch in the cove this time of year—yet the vaulted interior was nearly silent.

News must've spread of the death in the Wakefield barn. It didn't take long in this village. Even though not every household had a telephone, word spread as if carried by seagull.

Amie watched the other diners shift uneasily in their seats. Some turned and stared at her. So word had spread also that she'd been there.

She gazed out over the harbor, the bright-colored lobster buoys hanging from several buildings, all dusted in snow, the old gray-brown wharves reaching out into the ice-puzzled edge of water. A red-breasted nuthatch balanced on a limb of red spruce growing close to the water.

Shibby had taught all the kids in her care, including Amie, to identify local birds. This one, with his apricot—not really red—chest, white throat, and bold black stripe through his white face had always been one of Amie's favorites: the look of him and also the little bird's name.

The nuthatch is good luck, Jakie! she'd told her best friend when they'd spotted one. *It's delicate looking, but strong and tough,* she'd said. *Just like us.*

Amie sighed now and looked around. Oddly, still no table servers or bartenders were circulating at all, as if the entire restaurant staff and all its patrons were as stunned into silence as she was.

"Kalia." It was as warm as Amie could manage just now as the waitress appeared at the kitchen door.

Approaching, Kalia studied Amie's face. "You're looking a bit like the last fish left alone with the gator. Any little thing I can get to make you feel better now?"

"My kingdom for a glass of white wine."

"One white wine in exchange for a kingdom coming right up."

Amie sipped her wine, probably a little too fast, then fished for a handful of change from her coat pocket. "So, Kalia. I guess you heard."

"Whole village jabbering. Somebody said you were there at the barn. Some woman from away kicked by her own horse, somebody said. But you saw a thing no one else did, yeh?"

My gift, Amie thought. *And my curse. To see what no one else does.*

Amie spoke carefully. Chief Roy hardly trusted her now as it was. She didn't need to be talking too much. "We'll see what the coroner says."

"I'll ask this thing, then: Is it true Seth's disappeared?"

Amie stared at her. "Meaning you suspect him of something?"

Kalia turned quickly away. "I don't recall saying that."

"No. You didn't have to."

Chapter 28

Jake saw a woman hurrying out the back of the Tipsy Porpoise as he and Fossick approached. At a distance, the blue knit hat she wore looked a little like the one Shibby had made for Amie, but Amie lived in D.C.—he'd done his research—and would not be here in the cove. He was simply on edge being back in this town and seeing ghosts behind every corner.

Now if only he could think up his own way to flee. So far no one had recognized him. He'd grown a good five inches since age eighteen, his face changing shape from pudgy-cheeked to lean and chiseled.

Also, he was supposed to be dead.

No one would be looking for an awkward, pimple-faced kid in an out-of-towner's well-groomed face above a Parisian silk tie. He and Fossick had mostly stayed in the inn yesterday, meeting with that manager Tess Michaud, making phone calls, going over documents.

Then he'd done what Fossick had demanded of him, the dirty work that would keep Fossick's hands clean, though always fisted and ready for the next fight. Once again, Jake had been Fossick's mouthpiece.

This time, though, Jake had done more than that. Jake had been Fossick's hands.

Jake's head throbbed, dark spots floating in front of his eyes.

But now they were out here. In public.

If Shibby walked by . . . or Fletcher Osgood. There were people here who wouldn't be fooled by the expensive wardrobe and extra inches of height and lost weight. Their recognizing him would send the whole house of cards crashing down—what hadn't crashed already. To say that Fossick would be enraged wasn't nearly vivid—or lethal—enough.

Jake might just yesterday have done Fossick's bidding on a whole new level and now Fossick had gotten his wish, but even that wouldn't buy the mogul's mercy. If Fossick discovered he'd been lied to about his right-hand man's background . . . Jake's life as he'd rebuilt it would be over.

Jake smoothed his tie across his freshly starched shirt. Part of him wanted to leap onto the table. Get it over with, what had to be coming.

Just as something crashed back in the kitchen, a deafening clatter of metal on metal, the waitress plunked down their water glasses. Jumping, Jake felt the room rotate, as if the outer wall had become the ceiling and the floor a wall. The clatter from the kitchen became the roar of turbines now as he turned upside down, his left wing exploding in flame, black smoke swaddling the body of the B-17 as it spun earthward.

Lowering his face toward the menu, Jake steadied his arms against the table. Instinctively, his right hand dropped to the inside breast pocket of his coat. The smooth, nickel-sized roundness of the flask's lid should've helped calm him, but just now, not being able to draw the thing out felt like a taunt. Jake's heart hammered against his chest cavity.

The waitress, watching him with one eyebrow arched high, stood now tapping her pencil on her notepad. "You fellas ready to order, yes?" She rolled up the sleeves of her blouse to the elbows, a tattoo of some sort on one arm: a Celtic cross and a few words.

You Must Remember This, Jake read.

The waitress, who had a Caribbean accent of some sort, was staring—though not at him anymore, thankfully. Her eyes narrowed on Fossick.

"My name," she said stiffly, "would be Kalia, and I'll be your waitress. Two of our specialties would include the lobster bisque and the French meat pie with pork, cinnamon, and cloves—quite lovely. Our beer, you'll want to be knowing, is brewed right next door at the Turtled Sail."

Fossick wrinkled his nose. "Next door? Hell, since when can just anyone brew beer wherever they feel like it?"

"Since Lower Mesopotamia," Jake murmured, probably too low for Fossick to hear. Still, Jake felt his reserve slipping.

The mayor of Pelican Cove, who'd joined Fossick and Jake, raised his hand. What was the pompous fellow's name? Something Lawrence. He'd been the mayor forever.

"I think, gentlemen," said the mayor, "that I should order, if I may, for us all. There are several additions to the menu you simply must try."

Fossick rolled his eyes. "Fine. You order."

The mayor did, including three beers brewed next door. But the waitress only listened, hands still on hips. Then she turned to Fossick.

"You're the owner of the Promontory. The millionaire fellow, yeh?" The waitress's voice punched out one word at a time with mechanical force. "Desmond Fossick? Of Fossick Enterprises International?"

"Guilty as charged," the mayor assured her.

Interesting choice of words, Jake thought, *given that death in the barn. That horrible death in the barn.*

The mayor swept an arm toward Fossick. "It's your privilege today, young lady, to meet one of the great business giants of our time."

Fossick arched his neck back to survey her. "You would be?"

"Kalia. Clarke." Both words sounded like the cocking of a pistol.

Fossick locked his hands behind his head, elbows spread out like wings. "Kalia Clarke. Who is, I believe, supposed to be turning in our orders right now. Is that not right, *Kalia*?"

Fossick had turned the waitress's name into a sneer. An obscenity.

The mayor flinched at this, adding, "Yes, well, thank you, Kalia."

The waitress returned with the three beers. She set them each down with a plunk on the lacquered wood and splashed amber liquid across the table. "Another thing I need to ask: You own many rental properties in Boston, too, yeh?"

"Again, I hardly think a list of my business holdings merits a delay in our being served our lunch. Do you, *Kalia*?"

If she felt the sting of this, the waitress did not blink. "During the war . . . ," she began, nearly spitting her words.

But the mayor held up his hand. "Forgive me, Kalia, but we have things here to discuss. Perhaps Mr. Fossick would be happy to chat with you later."

Still trying to steady his breathing, Jake was only half listening.

On his third glass from the Turtled Sail, Fossick's voice rose over the soft rumble of conversation beneath the restaurant's central cupola. Even after several brandies or multiple beers, Jake had marveled, Fossick's words never slurred—a wonder of alcohol absorption that somehow detoured around the tongue. But Fossick always grew louder and more belligerent, as he was doing now.

"I'll say this. I'm glad that you, Darnay, would appreciate working for a man like me who came up from nothing and nobody, and worked his way up by sheer grit." Fossick's eyes locked on Jake's. "I appreciate a man who remains loyal and grateful to those who helped him along the way."

Sweat beaded Jake's upper lip. "Of course. What else would I be?"

Jake made sure he kept his face its usual cool. The unflappable Tom Darnay.

The waitress was just bending over Fossick's right shoulder, a fresh pitcher of Turtled Sail beer balanced on the tray in her left hand.

"You know, Mr. Fossick," she was saying, "here is the thing: During the war, you doubled the rent on the tenants married to soldiers being shipped out. One of those, in fact, was my sister, and her with three children, all *winjie*—so little."

He shrugged. "It was probably one of my people who made the decision."

"So this is how you behave, then? To let your underlings do the dirty work for you? To take no responsibility for yourself?"

You don't know the half of it, Jake thought. Dear God, did he say it out loud?

Fossick's eyes rolled back in his head. "How the hell do we make you go away, huh?" His legs short but powerful, he shot himself back from the table.

Whether or not Kalia Clarke had planned to do what she did or was simply knocked off her feet was unclear.

Although Jake did see her profile go hard before Fossick's push.

And he did hear her mutter *"Bastard!"* as she stumbled on Fossick's chair leg, her arms shooting forward for balance.

Jake could admit to himself later that he saw the pitcher tilt before it actually spilled.

She could have stopped it.

For that matter, *he* could have stopped it.

But she didn't. And neither did he.

He must've chosen not to, reflexes slowed by a sudden, bone-deep revulsion for his boss. He watched the pitcher lurch sideways. Its entire foaming, golden contents cascaded over Fossick's head, onto his arms, and into his lap.

With a shriek, Fossick leaped to the balls of his feet, his fists in boxer-ready position.

But there was no time for throwing a punch.

"You clumsy little whore!" he raged, hurling obscenities after her as she walked calmly away. The words echoed inside the vaulted room as every diner at every table turned. "You'll be *fired* for this, I'll make *damn* sure of that!"

The waitress rotated slowly. Jake could imagine the Celtic cross pulsing on her arm, keeping her hands by her sides with effort. Her voice, though, had the lilt of a steel drum, cheery and light. "I doubt that thing, Desmond Fossick. But if so, it was very, very much worth it."

~

Jake kept the brim of his hat pulled low as he hurried after Fossick. They'd just finished at the Haberdashery, the cove's only clothing shop open after the tourists left. Fossick strode ahead, clad now in an entirely new shirt, coat, tie, and pants. A nearly blubbering, apoplectic Mayor Lawrence had insisted on paying—out of village funds.

"Don't you worry, Mr. Fossick," the mayor was saying—*unctuously,* Jake thought. *You can almost see the oiliness drip from the man's ears.* "We won't let any sort of negative publicity leak out from that little scene."

Fossick leveled a glower at him.

Desmond Fossick, Jake knew, despised toadies—even as he demanded toadying treatment from everyone in his path.

The mayor scurried to catch up. "Not that there *is* anything negative to leak out, of course."

"So what exactly," Jake demanded, not caring who overheard, "was the waitress talking about?" He heard the challenge in his own voice, and knew he'd crossed a line. He knew the kind of man he was working for, had seen it more starkly than ever today, Fossick's delight at the news of the death in the barn. Somehow, though, seeing a waitress, of all people, be the one to tell Fossick off had triggered something in Jake.

Fossick slowed and tensed, like a tiger measuring the leap to its prey. The mayor paled—his face already an oyster white—and made a mumbling excuse for a return to the Haberdashery.

Neither Jake nor Fossick acknowledged his scuttling away.

Fossick turned, and his words came from low in his throat: a snarl. "Not that I owe someone who's paid by me, and paid goddamn generously, an explanation. But part of my genius, Darnay, has been to seize on opportunities to rid my properties of undesirables."

"'Undesirables,'" Jake repeated, aware that he'd lost control of his face, probably reflecting now the utter disgust he was feeling for Fossick. "Like the families of soldiers risking their lives to fight fascism? Like women who feel used and tossed out by a man?"

"Don't go the hell all sanctimonious on me, for God's sake. You know what I mean. Foreigners." Fossick moved in closer, a fox putting his face to the mesh of the henhouse. Something hungry, almost gleeful, there in his eyes. "Your being *from Canada*, in fact, this village must seem foreign to you."

"It . . ." Jake felt the wharf shift beneath him. There was Shibby's face again, unyielding, her finger pointing to the barn for Jake to begin finding eggs, since he'd lied the first time.

"Let me remind you, Mr. Darnay, should it *ever* enter your head that you're in control of your own fate: your fate and mine are tied *inextricably* together. Now more than ever."

Fossick squared off in front of Jake. "Let me remind you, that this"—he swept a hand to Jake's tailored Italian suit—"is the damn life you lead."

Jake gazed out over the harbor, its edges laced in ice that would widen and thicken as the long winter set in.

I'm living in my own long winter, Jake thought. *How long has it been since my life wasn't perpetual winter?*

But Fossick wasn't finished. "Now you're trying to push me against the ropes. Let me remind you: *I do not like* being pushed against the ropes." Fossick pitched forward still closer. "As I'm sure a man raised how—and *where*—you were would understand, Mr. *Darnay.*"

Jake heard something shift in Fossick's voice. It was the snarl that turned to frothing—just before the lunge.

"You look a bit scared, Mr. Darnay. Like maybe you did when you were young. When you would never give out the address of where you lived to your classmates because you couldn't bear to have them know where you lived."

No words would form on Jake's lips, his tongue limp, inert in his mouth.

Fossick threw both palms flat on either side of his face in mock imitation of a female voice. *"Poor little guy, just abandoned there on a street corner to rot!"*

Fossick's voice dropped now to low and grating, full of danger—like tectonic plates moving. "Did you really think, *Darnay*, that I didn't have your background thoroughly vetted before hiring you? That I wouldn't know if you'd created some jackass backstory for yourself. That you'd *lied?*"

Jake could not move.

The world seemed to have suddenly turned impenetrably dark.

Except for the image of Shibby's face, so sad, so disappointed in him. Her hands full of eggs.

Chapter 29

Jake tried to steady his breathing and focus, not on Desmond Fossick's small head in its dark hat, but beyond that, to the last of brown and gold quivering on the trees—shaking as if they were listening in.

Jake made himself focus on an old memory of Amie and him as kids tromping through the leaves, laughing . . .

If he could just keep thinking of that, maybe Fossick's face, purple with rage, in his own would disappear.

At the end of the wharf, Fossick whirled. A herring gull soaking up late-autumn sun there on a piling shrieked at the sudden movement and launched. Fossick glowered after the bird as he bit off his words. "How could you not suspect that I've known all along about your actual past?"

Jake cringed. But said nothing at first.

"Spitzer. Jake Spitzer. Which sounds, doesn't it, like a lawn sprinkler coming on. *Jake Spitzer. Jake Spitzer.* Like a man who'd work as part of my grounds crew at one of my properties."

"The name—my name, Spitzer—is German. Ashkenazi Jewish roots, which, for obvious reasons in the past several years—"

"So you didn't know which was worse after the war, being a Kraut or a damn Jew, that it?"

Jake heard the right hook of the word the way Fossick had punched it—*Jew.* "Let me explain. It wasn't a lie, really."

"Wasn't it? Hell if that damn reporter at the *Globe* doesn't think he's sniffed one out. Why do you think he's been on your trail, *Spitzer?*"

"Not a malicious lie. Or even intentional, really. It just . . ." Desperate, Jake reached for the truth. Or a piece of it. "I was raised Quaker. That is, by a woman here in town who's a devout one. You may know this by now."

"Damn it, you idiot, *of course* I do."

Jake let the explosion blow past him. "She took the part of her faith about nonviolence deadly seriously. That is . . ."

"Poor word choice, I'd say."

"She was hoping I'd claim conscientious objector status. Said there were plenty of ways one could help the war effort without killing. Said no child she'd raised would take human life. Ever." Jake drew a breath. "But I fought. Enlisted early. Left home the day after I turned eighteen. I hitchhiked and walked across the border to Montreal, joined the Royal Canadian Air Force."

Fossick's eyes bored into him. "How the hell does that lead to a whole house of lies?"

"I didn't just fight, I flew a bomber. I didn't just kill soldiers on the other side of a field. I dropped bombs." Jake tried to keep the tremor from his voice, but it edged its way in. "On Dresden. Incendiary bombs. Women and children. Innocent—"

"Hell, it's what happens in war. You expect me to cry for you now? For *them?*"

Jake looked away. Steadied himself. "Just hear me out. There were other reasons I thought I'd never come back here. Other reasons it seemed better to start over again. For everyone's sake. So when a fellow RCAF pilot ended up in Stalag Thirteen with me, and then when he died, I used his dog tag numbers but made up a name from stories I liked as a kid. I used some details from his life, and one other."

Including hers.

I just traded stories.

Fossick seethed, pressing his lips into a line before he spoke. "Did you really think I'd be such a damn fool to hire a greenhorn without knowing he could be molded to precisely my wishes?"

Jake swallowed. "There was also my pilot's training. Surviving a war. A German prison camp."

Fossick waved this away. "Like I give a rat's ass about any of that. It's experience on the battlefield of business I value. What you brought to the table, when I learned about you, was that background of yours."

"Sir?"

"Scrappy. Hardscrabble. Hard-bitten. I knew what you were made of because I knew where you came from—the same stretch of coast I came from myself. The place where my mother was sick and my dad sold everything to keep paying the bills."

It was that piece of Fossick's well-publicized story that never got mentioned for the slick magazine features. That piece that Fossick had alluded to in his study on Beacon Hill.

"She died anyway for all that mountain of bills, leaving my dad to die the next year on the deck of a goddamn boat that wasn't even his anymore. Bank owned it by then—along with the house, everything. Taught me how the world works, how it'll crush you if you don't control it first."

Fossick's entire career of cutthroat business, Jake thought, *and at its heart a scared little boy.*

Jake looked into Fossick's eyes and saw himself, the Burberry scarf at his neck, an expressionless face looking back.

"So when I got the report on you, who you really were, I knew you'd work longer and fight harder than any silver-spoon-up-his-ass polo-mallet-swinging playboy."

Fossick was beginning to bounce on his toes. He'd shed his imitation of upper-crust Beacon Hill–bred enunciation, his voice like the swing of a fist now. "But it served me well at the time, *Tom Darnay*, to let you play your privileged Royal Canadian Air Force hero role with investors, with me as the rags-to-riches story."

"So you hired me, despite knowing I'd misrepresented my background."

Fossick's laugh came out as a bark. "I hired you *because* of it. Another reason I chose you: No family. No competition for your attention. A man as focused as I am on what matters: commerce." Fossick leaned toward him, eyes burning like the blue depths of a flame. "Undistracted by a sniveling world. A man like me."

No family. No competition for your attention . . . A man like me. Jake felt himself shudder.

Hadn't Jake done yesterday exactly as Fossick had ordered?

A man like me.

Maybe, in fact, Jake was the more vile of the two since he still had a conscience, or the remnants of one.

"Remember, *Spitzer*, it was no accident, my handpicking you, still green around the gills, you with a past to hide and good reason to be grateful to me for paying you three times what you're worth."

Jaw clenched shut, Jake kept his eyes on the harbor.

"You know, the media could depict this foster mother-son thing as a kind of noble story. Might have a lot of schmaltz to it. The public eats that crap up. Point is I can't afford to be seen as a cold-blooded blowfish. Neither can anyone associated with me."

Jake swung slowly to look at Fossick. But still said nothing.

"So you'll go see this woman Shibboleth Shiphrah Travis—*God, what a name*—who ran the foster house or kennel or whatever the hell it was where you grew up. You'll go public with your life story, and it'll be touching as hell. Play it up right and Frank Capra'll direct the film version."

Fossick paused for breath. "You look distracted, Spitzer. Did I mention needing you to look distracted? Because I *do not*."

"I just need to . . . think."

"Yeah? Well, I'd advise you to think what'd happen if the story gets spun out wrong about how you lied to your employer about your background. I'd like to see you get another job *ever, anywhere*, after that." Fossick thrust out his hand—more like a challenge than a handshake. Slowly, reluctantly, Jake extended his, the older man's hand cold as a boat tiller in winter.

Winter, Jake thought. *My life is already and always winter.*

Fossick leaned in, and Jake tried not to wince at his grip, the ratcheting down of a steel wrench. "I'll be taking the Piper back to Boston after we meet again in a few moments, you and me, with the general manager of the Promontory. Then you'll stay on for a couple of days at the inn. Miss Michaud will see to details so you can do what you *will* do."

He leaned closer still, the Turtled Sail beer sour now on his breath. "Just keep in mind what the future looks like. And who's holding it for you."

Chapter 30

Amie watched the image beneath the developing fluid emerge: another close-up of the face of the woman in Chester's picture. This time, though, she'd managed to keep the image sharper in the enlargement. Here was the same face with its delicate features, but now, Amie could make out lines around the corners of the woman's eyes, across her forehead.

This woman was surely too old to be Chester's mother.

Come to think of it, if she was Joseph Kennedy's high school sweetheart, shouldn't she be around sixty? Amie cursed herself for just now realizing that.

"Who are you, then?" Amie whispered. "And what's happened to you?"

She'd ventured out early this morning to snap more pictures, mostly of the village's sea captains' mansions and historic inns. Several of the Promontory Inn came out better than she'd expected, she could see now, the light landing at intriguing angles across the white clapboard and windows, the hemlocks and maples, the pillars of stone.

Suddenly, the door of her darkroom flew open, Police Chief Roy standing there. He glanced down at the image beneath the fluid. "Did I ruin anything?"

"You did, yes. It's called a darkroom for a reason. There was something here I wanted to show you. About Chester's mother—or the woman we *thought*—"

She stopped there. "You have something urgent to tell me."

"Just heard back from the coroner, yeah. Figured I could share this much with you."

Amie pulled her gloved hands out of the developing fluid. Let them drop, limp, by her sides, liquid dripping on the floor. "I'm ready," she said. Which was not true.

"Turns out we were right about something other than a hoof to the head that killed Gwendolyn Weld."

Amie gave the smallest of nods and let the *we* pass.

"Lab says it was a pentobarbital mix in her blood. Injected, looks like."

Amie felt the ground go wobbly under her feet. Felt her knees going spongy.

She saw the face as it had been at the threshold of Fáilte: the eyes crazed and desperate, unfocused, the hair sticking up nearly straight.

The chief let his right hand rest on the butt of his holstered gun. "It's what's used—"

"By vets to put down horses," she finished for him.

"Yup. Which is why, soon as he shows his damn face or I hunt him down, Seth Wakefield is under arrest."

Chapter 31

Amie stepped outside the shop to steady herself, to breathe fresh air that was not laced with developing fluid—or heavy with that news from the coroner's lab.

The snow melting around Dock Circle looked less friendly now. Less like a lovely fresh start that covered the mess of the past and more like the photo the chief had just overexposed by flinging open the darkroom's door. All the world right now felt too starkly white and washed out and blurry.

A tall, slender man in an overcoat, dark and impeccably tailored, was crossing Dock Circle. Hurrying, he looked about.

Seeing her, though, he stopped. And stared. As startled, it appeared, as she was.

Amie studied this stranger's face. The same one from the *Boston Globe*'s front page last Sunday. The picture that had prompted her phone call.

Would she have recognized him if she'd passed him on the streets of Boston? Possibly not.

The face was leaner—by quite a lot—so that cheekbones and a firm jawline showed in what had been a decidedly baby face. The hair swept away from his forehead; the cashmere scarf, a Burberry plaid; and the wool overcoat: all of it made the face refined—and starkly unfamiliar.

It was one of those faces you could be sure belonged to money. To country-club soirees and lawn tennis and yachts.

Except for the eyes. Just a flicker of the old little-boy vulnerability there.

She scanned him in a glance: the fancy shoes, the tailored coat and cuffed pants, the haircut, the fedora he held in one hand. By contrast right now, she must look exhausted and frazzled, hair rumpled and frizzed from hard work with scents of Pine-Sol and darkroom developing fixatives, her face probably splattered in paint.

Unable to move, she waited while he approached, picking his way over ridges of plowed snow. Now she managed to cross her arms, but her feet would not budge. She was watching a ghost saunter toward her, but this one was suave and polished—no shame, no regret, no emotion at all on his chiseled face.

She wondered if he could sense the anger rolling off her.

He stepped quietly forward. "Hullo, Amie."

"Is that really the best you can do after being *dead* all these years?"

He held out his hand—tentatively, as if he weren't entirely sure whether she'd shake it or smack it. "Kind of a lot to say once we get past hello."

"So," she managed at last, ignoring his hand. Rage was making her voice tight, as if she were being strangled. "Looks like you got my message, *Tom Darnay*."

"Message?" He looked at her blankly. "I never got any message from you."

"But then why . . . how are you here?" She was fighting the urge to either throw her arms around him or deck him.

"Maybe first let's get to why are *you* here? You work in D.C."

229

That caught her up short for an instant, that he'd tracked down where she'd lived. She held up a palm. "Let's start with you, shall we? It's got to be a more interesting story, your having *expired*."

"Look, I'm sorry just to show up with no warning. I didn't know myself I was coming."

"My *God*, Jake. You let us think you'd been killed. Do you have any earthly idea what you did to Shibby? To all of us? Or how angry I am right now?"

"That's fair."

"Damn right it is."

"I realize I've got some explaining to do."

"And some apologizing. The sackcloth-and-ashes, shave-your-head sort."

"That, too. But if we could start with Shibby. Does she know . . . ?"

"That I just happened to figure out the scam you've pulled off for years?" Amie shook her head. "I was planning not to tell her until I made contact with you in person to be sure it was you. Also, I thought if I really found you alive, you and your lies, I might kill you myself. How could you be so cruel to Shibby? To all of us."

He turned away. "Where is she now?"

"Home at the Orchard today. If it hadn't been for the . . . for what happened today, she'd be at the Promontory."

"What? Why would she be at the inn?"

"Like most people working most jobs: she needed the income."

"I wasn't . . . I was just startled by her working . . ."

"At the very place that your boss owns?"

He must've heard the challenge: she could see that in the way his head jerked back. "It's just that I would never have pictured her being there, that's all."

"I'm surprised you ever bothered to picture Shibby at all. God knows, she talked about you enough all during the war. And since."

Jake stared back at Amie a moment before speaking. "So you kept in touch with her, I take it. Even though you left in a blaze."

"Oh, no, you're not going to pin this on me, Jake. I left, you're right. Hurt. Furious, in fact. Broken. But I kept in touch with Shibby."

"But not in touch with me. Me, you told—"

"To never speak to me again. I meant it, sure. As much as a mad, messed-up seventeen-year-old can mean anything."

"You went to war, too," he said quietly.

She blinked at him, startled that he would know this, too. "Yes."

"I made an effort to find out where you went. After Pearl Harbor. Once war was declared. You weren't the type to stay wherever you were and roll bandages."

"No," she said quietly. "I wasn't." She studied his face: too self-consciously refined, too distant for the boy she knew.

Something simmered there in his eyes . . . a desperation. Or maybe guilt.

"Help me understand, Jake. How exactly could you have done this to her? After all those years of her trying her best to be there at every turn for you, for all of us, despite all the ugliness of life."

He crossed his arms to match hers. "My plane was shot down. I was in a prison camp—in Germany. I just didn't happen to die. Does that help?"

She drew a long breath before answering. "I'm sorry for what must've been horrible. Truly. But it doesn't explain how you could've been cruel."

"Look, maybe you'd be interested to know what Shibby told me before I left. We act like she was a saint, and maybe she mostly was, but by God, for a woman who believed so much in peace, she could handle her end of a fight. She yelled. We both did. Told me she'd raised me to live justly, love mercy, and walk humbly with God, and that sure as hell did not include killing."

"So that was the worst thing she said to you in that temper of hers, that she'd raised you to love mercy? You poor thing."

He ignored this. "She begged me—then tried demanding—I register as a conscientious objector. I told her I was going to join the war. Not just enlist but sign up to carry the most guns or the most bombs I could. The whole world was coming undone, the Nazis rolling over one country after another. You leaving, then Shibby throwing all that nonviolent crap at me . . . I exploded. Told her I'd kill as many Nazi bastards as I possibly could. String them end to end to stretch from the White Cliffs of Dover to Berlin, just the men that I'd shoot with my own hands, up close so I could see them bleed. It was . . . ugly. Anyway, she kind of snapped at some point. Told me to leave."

Amie could see there was more. "And?"

"Told me killing would eat at my soul. Told me it would be killing a part of myself. Then she told me not to come back, ever, if I did what I said."

Looking toward the harbor, he shook his head. "We were both right, in the end, Shibby and me."

Amie weighed this. And waited.

"You were there, Ames. We were part of the winning side. The good guys that beat the bad guys—the evil guys. We shut down the death camps and set the world free from a monster. More than one of them. Fighting was the right thing to do."

He ran a hand back through his hair. "When I dropped those bombs onto Dresden, I heard Shibby all over again. I did what I thought was right by enlisting. But I killed people, Amie. Lots of them civilians. It mangled a part of me that feels like it won't ever be right again. Not ever."

Amie stood there in silence. Her eyes welled, not for this man who'd deceived Shibby—deceived all of them—but for the loss all over again of the sweet, trusting boy that she'd known.

After a few moments that felt stretched into years, he turned. "I have to wonder why you've come back here. Of all places. You."

"We can deal with all my mess later. Right now we're talking about you. How you went to war to do the right thing and not be a coward. How you did it bravely. But then came home and became a coward by lying. By hiding. Because why, you couldn't face the sixty-something, ninety-pound Quaker who raised you?"

He waited until she met his eye. She'd triggered his anger, that much was clear. The remorse and anguish had dropped from his eyes, leaving only a smolder now. "As I recall, Amie, you did your share of running away."

She was braced. Partly. But not for what he was about to fire.

"Or didn't you deserve your last year's reputation around here as the girl who'd go upstairs with just about anybody?"

Chapter 32

The slap Amie delivered was no feminine brush of the cheek, but a whole-arm, well-muscled wallop straight to his jaw.

Jake staggered back.

For a moment, neither of them spoke. Just glared at each other across a ridge of snow.

"That," he said finally, "was rude of me."

The hand that had hit him, he saw, was trembling. With rage, he knew, not with fear. The Amie he remembered had never invested much time with fear.

It was a nine-year-old Amie Stilwell that Jake had been expecting to see some day—if he'd expected to see her ever again. Though certainly not here. Not now.

How much she's changed had been his first thought.

Followed the next instant by *How much she hasn't*.

No little girl with long braids stood there, faded Levi's and new Bean boots. Instead, here was a young woman in her twenties with waving hair the color of honey, trousers tucked into wool socks and boots, smudges of blue paint on her forehead and nose. Even now, paint-stippled with no makeup, she was beautiful—even more so than back then.

Back then he'd loved her, though he'd only admitted that once aloud. He wouldn't be making that mistake again, not ever.

He tried extending a hand, but it was ignored.

"I'm sorry, Ames."

Nothing. She was livid.

"I think maybe," he said, "I should go find Shibby."

"Yes. You absolutely should go. And probably stay very gone."

Jake steadied himself at the door of the farmhouse. Nothing around him felt stable just now, not the peeling boards under his feet, not the pine door he held his hand up to knock on, and certainly not his own life.

By all rights, Shibby should slam the door in his face.

That, in fact, would be a relief, her sending him back into exile.

In answer to his knock, Shibby's voice called from the kitchen. "My hands are deep in cream. Come on in!"

Which was like her, of course. Never cautious enough. Giving the welcome no matter what sort of wolf might be at the door.

Jake paused, at first not removing his fedora, its brim helping to hide his eyes. But no mere hat could save him now.

Inside the farmhouse, Shibby was partly turned away—making chowder, it seemed, from the smell of butter and lobster and cream. Turning with that old smile of hers—same as always, though quite a few more lines at her mouth now and a feathering of gray at her temples—she froze, ladle in hand. The smile disappeared. Mouth dropping open, she stared at him.

She can read it all on my face, he thought. *Of all people, she can see straight through to what I've become.*

"I understand," he said, "if you'd rather not see me. But I wanted to let you know—"

He stopped there, his mind churning with all the defense of himself, all the explanations he'd planned to give.

"I'm not," he heard himself choke out instead, a sob escaping his throat, "not proud of what I've become."

With a cry, she tossed the ladle up into the air and ran to him. Arms wide, her small, wiry body somehow enveloped all six feet of him.

"Welcome home," she whispered, as cream dripped from the ceiling down onto their shoulders and heads. "Dear, dear boy, welcome home, welcome home, welcome *home!*"

The words swelled and crested and broke over him, taking his breath, knocking him off his feet in the warm flood of them. His custom-made suit crumpled as Jake huddled there on the pine floor of the kitchen, Shibby beside him, and wept.

Her whispered *Welcome home, welcome home* kept coming in waves. Shibby held him as he sobbed like a child, and she did not let go.

Chapter 33

Standing outside the little shop that must be Amie's gallery, Jake replayed what Shibby had told him about it in the hours they'd spent together. This was one of the few shops on Dock Circle that hadn't been the same business for decades. This and some new bakery.

Just inside the door he'd propped open with his boot, Fletcher Osgood was bobbing his head toward the sidewalk—and not bothering to lower his voice. "You know there's a fellow out here seems to be waiting on you?"

Amie's voice came loudly from somewhere in the back of the shop. "Can't be for me, Fletch. Chester's with Shibby. Ian's at the station being questioned again. Seth Wakefield's still . . . God only knows where."

Fletch craned his neck. "Could be a bad case of more than one *he*, then, ayuh?"

As Amie emerged, rolling up her sleeves, Fletch spoke over his shoulder to her. "Just remember: never put up with the dubbahs."

It wasn't a compliment in Maine, Jake knew. Fletch had recognized him beneath all his big-city finery, had apparently weighed him in the balance and found him wanting.

Jake expected nothing less from Fletcher Osgood. Raised in Aroostook County much farther north, he'd always been ferociously loyal. Jake had not only violated that code but drawn and quartered it.

Skirting well around Jake without speaking, Fletch stomped through the snow toward Provisions.

"Amie," Jake began as he stepped over the threshold, "I've just come from seeing Shibby."

"Actually, I'm just finishing up for the day." She turned her back to him.

Crossing the room, Jake laid a hand gently on her arm. "May I just admire a moment? What you've done with this place?"

Birch branches hung from the rafters, along with glass birds in blue and green that caught the light. Couches and chairs, canvas-covered, sat in friendly clusters, interspersed with standing sculptures made out of driftwood, of all things. A rearing horse. By the far wall stood a small figure beside a larger one with its skirts swirling and hair wild and arms flung wide for an embrace.

Shibby and me, Jake thought, tearing up all over again. He'd shut all that out for so long, he'd forgotten his heart could feel this many feelings at once.

On all three of the walls not taken up by the front's two-story windows were color photos, framed seascapes and landscapes from all over Maine. Close-ups of textured birch bark behind brilliant gold leaves, scarlet lichen on sea-splashed rocks, a blaze of vermilion sky above a blue sea, a red-and-white-striped lighthouse beaming its warning through a silver mist.

"Amie, this—all of this—is stunning."

She stood with arms crossed.

"In Boston, these photos, these sculptures, they'd go for God only knows how much."

"The sculptures are Kalia Clarke's. She's magnificent."

"Your photos, Ames. Your nature photography is . . . amazing." He stepped back to survey several others. "These of the different inns in town. They're remarkable, too."

"The nature shots are what I love. The ones of the inns are mostly mercenary on my part: counting on each inn's guests to absolutely have to own one to take home. I just took more of the Promontory, but it could take several tries to capture the light, the weather, the time of day all just right."

"You realize no one is using color like this outside magazine ads."

"Eliot Porter is."

"Who?"

"The Ansel Adams of color photography." She crossed her arms tighter over her chest and spoke stiffly. "I'm using his developing methods. Experimenting some on my own."

"I remember your camera was your escape, even as a kid."

He held her gaze there for a moment.

But turning abruptly, she crossed to the front door and rattled her keys in the lock like she wanted to disrupt the moment—shove away the closeness of the past that had bound them together for that instant. "Let's just hope the tourists come back to Pelican Cove before I run out of light bill payments."

"Amie, I'm wondering if we could talk."

"Thought we already had. It didn't go well."

"I mean without me losing my temper. Or getting insulting. More like catch up. A world war. What we both did in it. What we didn't. Just . . . spend time together."

"I should go." She held out her hand to shake. "Have a good trip back to Boston, Mr. Darnay." She tried to withdraw her hand.

But he held on. Gently. "Actually, I'm here for another couple of days. I'd love to hear more of your new business. What you hope life will look like here. Little details like that."

Amie gave a yank that pulled her hand away. "Jake . . ."

"About what I said earlier: I deserved the slap. Which, by the way, had some muscle behind it."

"It wasn't just what you said, Jake."

"I realize I have more explaining to do. More apologizing, too."

She eyed him carefully. "But also you've changed."

"You'd rather I stayed the awkward kid with the holes in his Keds?"

"That kid, Jake, was my *friend*. I loved him. This guy who lies to people who are mourning him, and who works now for Desmond Fossick . . . To be brutally honest, I'm not sure I want to 'catch up' with the person you are now."

"Then give me a chance to redeem myself."

She shook her head. "Believe it or not, I'm busy, Jake. What with trying to get the shop up and running, and needing to hang out with a sweet little six-year-old . . ."

"I met him. At the Orchard just now. With Shibby. He reminds me a little—"

"Of you."

"Yeah. Exactly. Though he's cuter than I was. Or we can sit and not say a thing. We used to be able to sit for hours out on Puffin Beach, just watching the pelicans dive. Remember?"

"Why are you pressing for this, Jake?"

"I'd like to try and explain. By not coming back, I thought I was doing what Shibby wanted. What she asked for."

"The hell you did, Jake. You knew she was scared for you, and you knew she was completely convinced there is never a justification for violence, ever. But she saw like everyone did what the Third Reich had done. She saw—or came to—the different ways people had to respond. You want to know what I think?"

"I have a feeling just like when we were kids, you're going to tell me."

"I think you were just being selfish. That you were wanting to remake your life as a rich guy with no past, nobody but his slick

240

handsome self to worry about. And now you show up here wanting us to be best pals like old times? Like you can waltz in here and sweep me and everyone else off our feet because you look like some Hollywood—"

"That's how I look to you?"

"Shut *up*, Jake, and listen! The boy we all loved, the one Shibby raised, was kind and honest and sweet. A little sulky sometimes. But also funny and humble and *ferociously* loyal. Until he wasn't."

She stopped there as if she expected him to recall something. Understand something.

He blinked at her. Pained. The tide of fathomless love he'd been floating on from Shibby was draining fast now, a great stopper pulled from the floor of the sea.

"Show me *that* man, Jake, the grown-up version of the boy who was kind and honest and loyal, *then* we can have a conversation about finding time to catch up."

"Maybe being back here . . ." His gaze swung from Dock Circle out toward the harbor. "Seeing Shibby again. Seeing you. Maybe it makes me—"

"Nostalgic? Maybe that's some kind of start. Although I think I'd rather hear *Sorry for the selfish bastard I've been to the woman who raised me.*"

"If it helps, I did say that. To her."

"Good. I hope you also kissed her feet."

"Tried. She wouldn't let me."

"Of course she wouldn't. 'Blessed are the merciful,' Shibby would say. But you know what? I've got a new ending: But, lo, they shall infuriate the rest of us who need our pound of flesh before we calm down."

"If you need to hear me say it, I will: I was stupid, you're right."

"And outlandishly selfish."

"And selfish. Outlandishly so." *Also brutal,* he wanted to add. *You have no idea.*

"Look, Jake, I've got to go."

"Amie, I'm not in the habit of begging."

"No, I don't imagine you are these days."

"I'm asking you to just give me some time. No pressure other than that. Just time to maybe learn to be friends again."

He'd promised himself years ago his blurting out his love for her would never happen again. But here he was pleading with her, trying to hold on to her like a rock in the storm that was his life now.

She walked backward toward the door of Fáilte. "The truth is, Jake, I'm not sure we have enough in common these days to be friends at all."

"Just coffee, then. Looks like they could brew a decent cup next door. Please. For the sake of the kids we used to be. Both of us owing Shibby . . . a lot."

"Our lives, Jake. We owe her our lives."

He saw softness break over her.

"Our lives," he agreed.

~

Jake reached for his coffee from Ian. "That's right. I grew up here."

"But you live in Boston now? You didn't come back here after the war?" The bakery guy cocked his head at Amie in mock horror. "Imagine looking for more in life than lobster rolls, sailboats, and blueberries. Oh, and Moxie, the only drink you'll ever need. Besides all that, what else *is* there in life?"

"I cannot think"—Amie moved to stand beside him—"of another thing."

Jake looked from one to the other of them. "Both of you have lived other places, seen some of the world. You know what I mean. I wanted—"

"Jake"—Amie leaned over the oak counter close to his ear—"for God's sake, *stop talking*."

He obeyed, turning toward her. "I was hoping maybe you and I could walk—"

"I agreed to coffee, Jake. We're doing coffee. As I speak."

"Just to the town pond. Or just"—he looked her square in the eye—"to the river and back."

In the midst of wrapping her scarf around her neck, Amie froze.

Rotating slowly, she stared at him. He could see from the glazed-over look in her eyes what she saw now wasn't a tall young man standing there drinking coffee but the two of them, maybe six years old at the time.

Without saying a word, she slipped past him, her coat still on, and walked out the door, passing the entrance to Good Harbor. She was aiming her steps toward the river that cut through the town's center.

Wordlessly, too, Jake followed, only stopping when she did, at the bridge that crossed the Pelican River and led to the Lower Village. Together they looked upstream, away from the harbor and toward the pine forest. He knew she was seeing, and remembering, what he did.

Jake had been walking home by himself, satchel slung over his shoulder, head hanging, hair flopped thick over his eyes.

Amie had sidled up beside him. "Want company?"

"Nope. Don't need anybody."

Hey! Spitzer!

The voices came from the cluster of maples that Jake and Amie were approaching. Accompanying the voices were both giggles and snorts.

Jake could still see the boys' freshly pressed shorts, the girls' hair bows that matched their dresses. The blond and brown ponytails bobbing. These were the kids whose parents belonged to the Cape James Golf and Racquet Club in summer. The kids who sneered at his hand-me-down clothes that never, ever fit right.

Hey, Spitzer, do you guys have fleas at that house for strays where you live?

The voice had come disembodied from out of the trees. It could have belonged to any one of the children snickering there.

Hey, Spitzer, people like you *aren't welcome here, d'ever notice?*

Jew Boy!

A round of guffaws followed.

Amie spun toward him, her voice low. "You'd better take off. I'll meet you where the log crosses the river."

Jake had stood his ground at first, planting his feet and glowering into the trees.

But the volley of rocks that followed sent him diving to the ground, arms covering his head. Then he was back on his feet, running.

Amie had bolted, too, but at a perpendicular angle from him.

He'd run until the stitch in his side doubled him over, just at the edge of the far woods. Amie had reached the baseball fields, nearly to the path that ran alongside the river.

But rather than disappearing inside the woods, she was circling back. Running. Still running. Approaching the cluster of trees from its thick-limbed far side.

Suddenly, from outside the copse of old maples, rock after rock flew toward the children ensconced in the trees.

Amie had compassed back in a perfect half circle to send a good dozen stones sailing just below the trees' lower branches toward the legs of the assailants themselves. Then she was gone, blazing back toward the river so fast, she'd ducked inside the wood before the children inside the cluster of trees quit howling and started looking for who had attacked from behind.

Amie had hardly been out of breath when she strolled a few minutes later to the log that ran over the river where Jake was waiting.

"No crying, Jakie, remember, we said. Can I walk home with you tomorrow?"

"Guess you can, sure." He'd not wanted to go so far as to say thanks to a girl for playing the part of the hero.

But he'd stuck out his hand for a shake.

Which she'd waved away. "You can trust me, you know."

"I know." He'd kicked off his shoes, and he'd sat down beside her on the log, the river gurgling beneath their bare feet. He'd managed a smile, which was surely better any old day than a cheap *thanks*.

"I trust you," he'd said. "To the river and back."

"To the river and back," she'd agreed.

That had been that, their friendship cemented by a river and rocks.

Maybe, he thought now, *I became a bomber pilot not because I'm braver than others but because I'm angrier—maybe more heartbroken, too—at a world that requires rocks and explosives to supposedly bring about peace.*

Amie thrust both hands in her pockets and did not turn to look at him. "To the river and back," she said softly.

"You were always the brave one back then."

She shook her head. Then turned and walked into the forest. Jake didn't need to ask where she was going.

Following, he joined her at the stream—*their* stream—that ran behind Pelican School and fed into the Pelican River, just where the trunk of a fallen pin oak still made a mossy footbridge over the water. As if she were still ten, Amie walked out onto the log, arms out, balancing, boots planted carefully one in front of the other.

She settled herself onto the log, legs swinging over the water, and looked up as Jake inched his way, the soles of his dress shoes slick, traitorous, on the moss. Suddenly, it mattered immensely that he not slip and plunge down into the stream, not only because the autumn day was frigid, but also he found he desperately, frantically did not want to look clumsy in front of Amie.

She lifted her face to watch him approach. "Those really your best shoes for Maine?"

He inched his way closer. "If I'd known this was where I was coming . . ."

"You wouldn't have come," she supplied for him. "So Fossick arranged it."

"Yes." No point in lying about that, too. "But seeing Shibby, seeing you . . ."

She held up a palm like she used to when they were kids and they needed to change subjects before she lost her temper with him. "It must've been terrifying for you. In the war. Flying, I mean. All those German Focke-Wulfs and Messerschmitts coming at you from all angles."

He eased down beside her. "You want the truth?"

"Now there's a good idea."

"I have nightmares after all this time. Sometimes during the day, too, a sound or a smell, something will put me right back there. Sometimes I'm seeing a Messerschmitt coming at me, the swastika crashing into my face. Sometimes I'm seeing my copilot with half his head gone."

Amie put a forefinger and thumb to her eyes as if she were seeing it, too, and the vision was searing.

"Sometimes"—he paused, embarrassed to hear his voice going husky—"I dream I'm down in Dresden smoking a Camel, sitting on a bench surrounded by little kids playing jacks, and I look up to see the B-17 opening up its bay doors with a payload of incendiaries. Then everything around me's on fire."

Amie waited several long seconds to answer. "All this while the whole country's supposed to be celebrating, the soldiers home and business booming. That must make it even harder."

Gently, she lifted a hand to him, slipping it through the opening of his overcoat and his suit jacket, her fingers passing over his ribs.

Jake's whole body went stiff, electrified.

Slowly, she pulled out her hand now holding his flask, and met his eyes. "So, then. This."

"That." He looked away.

Just as gently, she slipped it back into the inner pocket of his coat. She seemed unaware of what her touch had done, heat shooting through him.

He kept his eyes ahead on the birches, a flurry of brown leaves letting go, swirling down onto the stream. "I haven't pulled it out around you. Not where you could see."

"They trained me to see more and better than you'd imagine. And I've known you longer than forever, Jakie."

Her use of the old name wasn't lost on him.

"Forever," he echoed, his body still stiff from her touch.

They sat still together in silence for some time, the only sound a moose nearby crunching through leaves.

"Like old times," he said at last. "Sitting here. Not needing to talk."

"'Blessed are the quiet,' Shibby used to say. 'For they shall hear God—and also when they're called for dessert.'"

He laughed. A real laugh, he realized with surprise, which rumbled its way up from his gut.

"To the river and back," he said—softly so as not to break the spell, both of them staring down at the stream, their feet swinging beneath them.

Amie's head tipped toward his.

"I remember," Jake said, shifting to face her, "you and me lying stomach down on the barn floor for hours. Shibby bringing grilled cheese out to us and hot chocolate with a dash of—"

"Maple syrup and whipped cream."

"Yeah, that was it. We stayed out there all night until Elsa had her calf, the thing all covered in gunk and us freezing cold—I hadn't felt my own feet for an hour. You sat there all glazy-eyed and said, *Jakie, wouldn't you rather be here than anywhere else in the world?*" He laughed. "And I was pretty sure that sealed it: you were certifiably nuts."

"It wasn't till then that you knew?"

He waited until she met his eyes again. "Speaking of calves being born . . ."

"I cannot imagine where you're going with this sentence."

"Someone at the inn said the big guy with the tall boots in the Helmsman I saw dancing real close with some dame I only saw from the back was the veterinarian on the cape now. Never occurred to me at the time the dame might be you since you were supposed to be in D.C."

Amie said nothing.

"The two of you looked pretty chummy."

"Did we?" Her smile had gone. "What exactly are you saying, Jake?"

"So you just got back here, what, a couple of days ago, and you're already . . ."

Gathering her legs underneath her, Amie prepared to rise.

Jake touched her arm. "Wait. I'm sorry. It's probably none of my business. Please don't go."

One leg still folded knee to her chin as if ready should she need to pop up again, she let the other leg dangle back down. Even with her face turned away, Jake could see the hard set of her jaw.

"Ames, what happened to our being friends?"

"You honestly don't remember."

"Remember . . . what, exactly?"

Something like dread—or maybe shame—washed over her face. "You'd think after all this time I wouldn't still be blaming myself." She crossed her arms over her chest. "We were seventeen. Both trying just to fit in."

Now it was Jake's turn to look away and then back. "I'd always been the outcast, the kid who lived in 'that house with the lady who took in strays.'"

"I was a mess in my own way, trying so hard to get the attention of guys, any guy, maybe since the guy who was supposed to be my dad was never around. And you, you were trying so hard to outrun that feeling of being . . ." She stopped there.

"Go ahead. Say it. *Abandoned*. By a mother who may or may not have even told my father I'd ever been born."

Amie sighed. "It's sad. You're right. Both of us by that senior year, we both got stuck on what we were missing. We couldn't let go."

"Let go?"

"For you, of the hurt of not being wanted by the woman who gave birth to you and start focusing on the woman who *did* want to raise you—the other people in your life who cared about you."

"It was a houseful of waifs, that's what we were—the castoffs. The Orchard: Farmhouse of Misfit Kids."

Amie threw up her hands. "Yes. Including me. So what? So the misfits survived and grew up to be people who knew how to set a big table for anyone, *anyone*, who showed up. People who knew what it was to feel broken and also feel mended—and grateful—in a world where most people walk around looking polished but are just shattered inside. Is that such a bad thing?"

Jake turned his face to study hers for a moment.

"Jake, even now when you're asking me honestly what happened to us, to all those years of being best friends, we can't get past *you*, all your past hurt."

"There was one particular night." He managed that much, not wanting to remember. "I told you how I felt about you. How I'd felt for a long time. You walked away, as I recall. Danced with three guys from some high school hockey team up in Portland. Not one guy but three. That was your answer to my stupid, stumbling confession. I don't know which I was more, humiliated or heartbroken."

She slid her hand over his, looked him in the eye, and lifted her chin. "No, Jake. You're not remembering what happened next."

He lowered his head so his forehead touched hers. They stayed like that for a long moment.

"I remember," he murmured, "what I wished at the time happened next."

Tilting his head, he kissed her, what might have been a long, tender kiss, full not just of the longings of the moment, but also of the loss and the pain of the years they'd walked through together—the long years of trust. Before all that collapsed.

She pulled back, though. Her eyes, not angry but sad, stayed on his. "Jake . . . no."

"Ames . . ."

"I don't want to do this. At least for now."

He searched her face. "I've missed you, Amie. I'd forgotten"—his voice hoarsened again—"how steady I feel with you. How . . . *whole.*"

"Jake." She shook her head. "Don't." She leaned in close, placing the flat of her hand over the left side of his coat. "This can't make the nightmares stop, not in the long run. I can't be that for you, either." She shifted her weight away to rise.

"At least let me see you tomorrow." He reached for her hand. "Please. For the sake of old times."

Just as gently, she withdrew it. "I moved on, Jake. Went to hell and back in the war. Like you did. I moved back here because my life in D.C. caved in, yes. But also I realized I once loved this place and still do. I want to be here to help Shibby with Chester. I want to see him grow up to be strong and fearless, no matter how much reason he has to fear. I want to start a new chapter in an old place. Not write version two of the past."

She straightened, stepping over him, somehow perfectly balanced there on the log, then backed three steps away, her eyes not leaving his face. "We don't need to try to be friends or anything else right now. Especially when you're still running so hard from the past you haven't yet turned to remember and face it all down."

"Ames, at least give me the chance to earn back your trust."

"I'm so grateful, Jake, that you're alive. Honestly, more glad to see you even than I'd have imagined. But also still angry, so incredibly *angry* with you."

And you don't even know the whole story, he thought. *What I've done for Fossick. You'd despise me even more if you knew.*

He stood, wobbling on the log, regaining his balance just in time.

But she'd turned and didn't look back as she walked off the log and away from the stream.

Away from me, he thought, feeling foolish, so completely and utterly foolish standing there in his Italian leather shoes slipping on some old moss on a half-rotten log.

She's walking away from me. Again.

Chapter 34

The chime over the gallery door that mimicked the bell buoys out in the harbor gave its low gong as the police chief walked in. Amie jolted back behind the bookcase, sending the rearing horse sculpture tumbling, front hooves pawing the air, to the floor.

Which makes me look guilty. Great. Just great.

"Chief Roy!" she called out—with a cheeriness to compensate, maybe, for the jumpiness he must've seen.

Knocking slush from his boots, he looked around, floor to ceiling. "Nice work. Didn't expect you'd be this far along. Or working this early."

She righted the horse and held out a hand.

He shook hers, but his eyes kept scanning across what she'd hung on the walls: the boat oars, the ship's wheel—from an actual dry-rotted boat near Old Frigate Beach. The birch branches hung suspended from the ceiling as if they were reaching in from outside the walls, and small lights twinkled from the rafters.

"About the investigation," she ventured.

"Draws a person right in." He stopped in front of the life-size sculpture Kalia had just finished yesterday, this one of Lazarus only just staggering to his feet, his grave clothes still hanging in tatters from his arms.

In anyone else's rendering but Kalia's, Amie thought, it would have felt trite. But here it felt like breath blowing fresh air into your lungs. Like a hand to your own, pulling you up out of despair.

Passing the back of his gloved hand quickly over his eyes, the chief turned toward the wall and stopped at a particularly large print of a seascape near Camden. Amie had reprinted that photo of hers at least seven times, each time adjusting the gelatin reliefs, the washes of cyan and magenta.

The picture had actually been a mistake, her shutter speed slower than she'd intended, the exposure too bright, the images of the cliffs and the surf bound to be fuzzy, she'd thought at the time. Now its swaths of blue and green and white and gold shimmered, seeming to swirl off the wall, to catch one up in the color and light and currents of air.

The chief tipped back his head. Closed his eyes for a moment. "Good Lord."

"What is it?"

"Only every summer day at the beach as a kid all breezing by me at once. Every lobster roll I ever ate. Every goddamn religious impulse I ever felt. Lord, how does one picture do that?"

She watched his face. He'd not walked in meaning to even notice her work or Kalia's, she realized. But he'd not been able to help himself. The best compliment of all: the praise that came spilling out from the grudging.

"Hell, you oughta be stripping the tourists of their cash fast enough."

Now she laughed. "Ah, the secret goal of everyone in the arts who tells you they care only for the art and not at all for making a living."

He crossed the room to the fireplace, which Amie had blazing this morning, and bent to warm his hands. "Up there in the loft'd be . . . ?"

"I've been mostly staying at the Orchard, Shibby Travis's place, but that's where I sleep when I work so late here I just drop. Though I'm always at the Orchard for dinner and bedtime stories."

"Aren't you a little old for that?"

"You're *never* too old for bedtime stories, Chief Roy. Also, there's—"

"The kid Chester."

"Exactly. About the investigation . . ."

But he eyed the loft. "Wouldn't be the most private setup." A question—maybe even a challenge—there in the words.

"Not much in my life to keep private."

He considered this. As if to say that *he* would be the judge of that. "Won't keep you long. Just a couple of questions."

"Coffee?" She gestured toward the percolator and a chair.

He shook his head. Oddly, he seemed intent on wandering her shop just now—or maybe on ferreting out more information before she was aware she was being questioned.

"Gotta say, Miss Stilwell, I'm intrigued by your arrangement. Not that I know your business—"

"Neither do I, yet. I want this to be a gathering place, a place to admire local artists' work, not just my own pictures. A place to be inspired, to connect."

"You'll be adding to the art?"

"I've mapped out a route to a potter in New Hampshire, painters along the Maine coast, and the creator of those blown-glass seabirds. In a weekend—once I've saved up—I can make the whole loop and come back with plenty more to sell." She tilted her head at him. "Assuming you've not decided that I'm the prime suspect to be carted away in handcuffs."

Pouring himself coffee, he sat. "I'm wondering about any recent contact you may've had with Jake Spitzer. I recollect you two were close."

"Jake? Sorry, I thought you were investigating Gwendolyn Weld's death."

"I am."

"But . . . why Jake?"

"You thought I'd be here to ask about Seth Wakefield, that it?"

"Well, yes."

"Or maybe Miss Travis."

"*Shibby?* You can't be serious."

"I got a witness, that lady manager at the Promontory, says Shibby was seen talking to Mrs. Weld at the inn last Friday afternoon before Shibby was off for the weekend. The manager recalled it was midafternoon 'cause Shibby was holding the coffee she has every day at that time. Says Mrs. Weld looked real upset."

"What? How could they have even known each other?" But the words weren't out of her mouth before she heard their flimsiness: Shibby talked to everyone, and everyone wanted to talk with Shibby. Pour their hearts out, even. If Gwendolyn Weld had been staying at the Promontory and had been under duress, and if Shibby had stopped to ask in that way of hers if she could listen or help . . .

"Now, back to my questions about little Jake Spitzer."

"He left town after high school. Just after I left, actually."

"One of Miss Travis's foster kids. I assume he's kept in touch with her."

"Nope. Not for nine years."

Amie could hear her own tone, dismissive and mad.

"We've recently learned," he continued, "that Spitzer survived the war."

"You're well informed."

"Extraordinary powers of deduction. Also, Fletch told me. So Spitzer arrived back here when?"

"The day or two before . . ." She stopped. "Before Gwendolyn Weld was killed. But no connection, obviously."

"Interesting, don't you think? Both living in Boston. Spitzer's been lying for years about where he was—hell, *who* he was, even. Then shows up a day or two before this poor broad gets mysteriously killed?"

"Coincidence doesn't mean evidence, surely."

He ignored this. "Any idea why Shibboleth Travis asked you to find him?"

"She didn't. I started searching for him on my own, maybe just so she could move on—if I could find evidence that he'd died. She'd been insisting he could be alive."

"So you found him?"

"Found where he worked. But he'd already left town. With Fossick."

The chief choked on his coffee. "Sorry. Did you say Fossick? As in Fossick Enterprises?"

Fossick's right-hand man. But she'd let him discover this for himself.

Pulling his pad from his blue shirt's pocket, he wrote something down. "So. Works for Fossick."

Fossick, Amie thought, mind churning, *Jake's boss. An unscrupulous man with some sort of ties to Gwendolyn Weld.*

"Then suddenly, after all these years, Jake Spitzer shows up here just a day or two before Mrs. Weld's tragic demise. Crazy timing, wouldn't you say?"

"Chief Roy, I assume Desmond Fossick is on your list of suspects?"

His eyebrows grew together in one long gray stripe, like a visor over his eyes. "Should he be?"

"I'm guessing it was Gwendolyn Weld's Bentley stored in the sailing hut of Fossick's inn. The night before she was killed, she was driving one of the fleet of Allards he keeps at the Promontory, the ones to shuttle guests of the inn. I can't imagine he gives permission for just anyone to drive them outside of staff."

The chief tapped his fountain pen against his lips. "The general manager, that dame with the great legs . . ."

Amie raised an eyebrow. "Tess Michaud, your witness. I took the liberty of asking a few questions myself. She told me she was the one to loan Mrs. Weld one of the cars. It could be Miss Michaud has some sort of personal connection with the late Mrs. Weld herself. Or could be that the loyal or ambitious—or both—Miss Michaud is covering for her boss."

The chief narrowed his eyes at her. "You know, for a kid who raised all kinds of hell around here in high school, you aren't a bad thinker, Miss Stilwell. Or looker. Not, I mean, how you look. Though that, too, I reckon. Hell, I'm talking about what you see."

She tipped an imaginary hat. "Trained by some of the best."

The chief stepped toward the door.

"Before you go, Chief, there's something else. This might sound, well, wacky."

"Most of this case does so far."

"The portrait of Desmond Fossick in the main parlor of the inn."

"I've seen it, sure."

"It's changed."

"As in . . . been moved?"

"No, I mean it's been vandalized. I think someone on your force might have been notified of it. But it's changed the expression on Fossick's face, and I think it might be related." She smiled at the expression now on the chief's. "I told you it would sound wacky. Very 'I read too many novels.'"

"Meaning?"

"Did you ever study Oscar Wilde's *The Picture of Dorian Gray* in school?"

"If it was assigned in school, nope. I had some hockey to play."

"This won't do it credit, but the story begins with an artist painting the portrait of a handsome young aristocrat, Dorian Gray. Over the years as Dorian ruins lives and commits multiple crimes, his face doesn't change at all. Doesn't even age. Meanwhile, the portrait, which he's stored in the attic, reflects all the brutality of the man's life that never showed on his actual face."

"Lemme get this straight: You're suggesting the portrait of Desmond Fossick is magically reflecting that he's guilty of killing Gwendolyn Weld?"

"How it was vandalized, I've no idea. My earlier theory was that someone put some sort of paint-thinning substance on it—like an artist's linseed oil. Or, I've wondered lately, a moisturizing agent like the safflower in hoof oil that might make the oil paint in the portrait liquefy again. Hoof oil like Gwendolyn Weld carried in her purse."

"Hoof oil? So like Wakefield would have, too?"

Amie nodded once. It wasn't a direction she wanted the conversation to go. "But as far as we know, not just anyone would have a motive to deface Desmond Fossick's portrait."

The chief wrote this down. "We'll check her belongings again. Damn well didn't figure on hoof oil being a clue."

"Maybe it was her silent revenge. Or someone else's."

"Or maybe linseed oil, you said. What, like Fletch Osgood sells?"

Amie nodded again. She couldn't bring herself to add Ian O'Leary's name as someone who'd bought it recently. The chief could dig that up for himself.

"So, Miss Stilwell, I'll tell you this. We learned Mrs. Weld hasn't been seen in public with her husband for quite some time, though they never divorced. Plenty of bad feelings there on both sides, sounds like. One of their neighbors in Brookline told police there that Mrs. Weld would tell close friends—get this—that if something strange ever happened to her, no matter where in the world, to 'check Boston first.'"

"Did the neighbor seem to know what that meant?"

"Said he assumed it was a reference to Mrs. Weld's husband."

"Or what if," Amie mused aloud, "Gwendolyn Weld was involved with Desmond Fossick romantically, let's say an affair that destroyed her marriage—or was the final fracture in a marriage already broken? Then what if she became an inconvenient piece of his past that he wanted gone?"

"You telling me you think one of the most powerful—and recognizable—men in New England would walk into a barn and knock off some dame with his bare hands?"

"Wouldn't a man like Fossick have people to do things for him?"
The chief's eyebrow lifted. "Like Tess Michaud."

"Yes."

"Or Jake Spitzer."

Amie hesitated. Angry as she still was with Jake, she'd not meant to
lead the conversation to him.

*Even with all his lying, even with how he's changed, he wouldn't com-
mit murder for Fossick.*

Would he?

"I'm only suggesting it's worth keeping an eye on the painting.
That maybe someone wants us to *think* it reflects Fossick's guilt over
something."

The chief appeared to be doodling on his notepad.

"Lemme ask you this, Amelia." His blue eyes bored in on hers.
"What if it's Wakefield *and* Fossick—Wakefield having a fling with
Fossick's old lover Mrs. Weld, who, convenient for a big-animal vet,
apparently spent all her time in barns?"

Amie had already thought of this—not wanting to. She gave a
terse nod.

"What if it was Wakefield vandalizing the portrait to make Fossick
look bad? Wakefield, jealous that she was making noises about talking
with Fossick again, so Wakefield knocks off the victim with the drug he
carries to put horses down."

"But even if that were all true, would Seth really have killed her in
a way that would point most clearly to himself?"

"You got me there. Though, I got to say: in my line of work, any
time an investigator starts defending one particular suspect . . ."

"I'm not defending him."

*Though I don't want him to be guilty. Really don't want him to be
guilty.*

"No? Sure as hell sounded like it to me." The chief stood now,
jostling the coffee he'd hardly touched except for the sip he'd choked

on. Brown liquid splattered the front of his navy trousers—though he didn't seem to notice.

With only a nod of his head, he was out the door before the bell had finished its low, echoing call.

Unnerved, Amie stood for a moment staring after him.

As the bell-buoy gong over the door quit sounding, Amie saw an envelope that someone must've shoved through the brass mail slot of the shop door late yesterday afternoon. She'd been busy, and it had landed a bit to the side, so she hadn't noticed till now.

It was a telegram, she saw as she bent for and opened it. Not exactly delivered into her hands as it should've been, but there, in fact, was her name.

Hyannis Port, Massachusetts, the location read. Amie knew only one person who would be telegramming from that town on Cape Cod: Eunice Kennedy.

It was on the long side for a telegram, but still not as detailed as Amie might wish.

> More digging on this Adeline. Never married. Retained affection for my father consummate Irishman. Irish herself. Died recently. Heart failure in sleep. Guardian great-aunt to little boy. Child may never have known identity of his mother.

Amie paused, spinning again in her mind the timing of the Bentley's arrival in town, and of Chester's. Chester had been there some time already at the restaurant. Could he have been dropped off in that public place with a note for Shibboleth Travis by the person driving the Bentley, who then circled back toward the railroad tracks with the intent of suicide? Chester must have been made to promise not to speak of what happened or of who dropped him off—but also, perhaps he didn't even know himself who his driver had been.

Amie saw that scene in the barn again, Gwendolyn Weld doubled over at Seth's words about the horse being a good mother: *It's nature's way.*

The anguish on the woman's face.

One hand over her heart, Amie's whole chest cavity aching, she made herself read over Eunice's final sentence:

Child may never have known identity of his mother.

Chapter 35

"It would help, you know, if you could tell me," Amie said. She'd rarely spoken to Shibby this forcefully. "About whether you ever talked with Gwendolyn Weld."

It was already late, Shibby exhausted from work, from caring for Chester, and from some additional emotional weight Amie could see she was carrying.

"Tomorrow," Shibby said, turning away, "our Chester is going to try going to school. I called over to Pelican Grammar today so they'd know to be looking for him."

"That's good. He'll be needing friends his own age. But you didn't answer my question: if you can tell me about Gwendolyn Weld."

Shibby let out a sigh. "Lord knows, it would help if I could. Lighten my saddlebags a good deal. But I reckon I ought to start with Chief Roy tomorrow."

She began climbing the stairs of the farmhouse to bed.

"So Gwendolyn confided in you when she stayed at the inn. Because people confide in you everywhere, like a priest in an always-present confessional. But maybe especially where people are away from their normal lives."

Shibby stopped. Now she met Amie's eye. Said nothing.

Which was enough.

"And she told you at some point she was having an affair with Fossick. Or maybe once did?"

Still, Shibby did not move.

Amie drew a deep breath. "Did she ever mention she had a child?"

Here Shibby shook her head. "She did not."

"Though she said enough you wondered if that's what her guilt was about."

"For all she poured out," Shibby said finally, "she sure as shooting said nothing about having a child. Maybe I was too slow matching the right straps to the harness. I thought all that guilt crushing her flat was other decisions, like the affair."

Amie joined her on the stairs. "But finally, it occurred to you she might've had a child."

Closing her eyes, Shibby hardly even whispered. "Hit me like a hay baler rolled over my head. Yesterday when I got word about her being dead—dead after watching her own horse giving birth. I got to rewinding the thing."

"And came up with?" Amie's eyes followed Shibby's up to the top of the stairs. To the room where Chester was sleeping.

"That poor tortured soul confiding in me, a near stranger, and me too dense to hear what she was trying to say. It wasn't so much what she'd *done*." Shibby's eyes filled, still focused up there on the door. "The real torture for her, the thing that was so hard for her to believe she could be forgiven for, ever, must've been what she'd left *un*done all these years."

Amie mounted the stairs to stand beside Shibby and gaze through the crack in the bedroom door to Chester's form curled up with a ball of white on the bed. Hopkins opened one eye but did not stir from his post with the child.

Had Fossick, Amie wondered, *done away with his former lover? Could she have been demanding something—financial payments for Chester, perhaps? But why now?*

From the bed, Chester sighed in his sleep and rolled to his other side.

"All she'd walked away from," Amie whispered. "She realized it too late."

~

Her mind on that conversation last night, Amie was distracted as she stepped to the counter of Provisions with two more gallons of cerulean blue. The cash register dinged open just as the store's phone rang.

With one hand, Fletch thrust away the cash she held out as he lifted the phone's receiver in the other.

"Ayuh," he groused into the phone. "But I won't need to cross the circle. Amelia's right here. Told her yesterday she'd be needing more paint. People nowadays don't listen."

A pause. "Both her hands'd be full with handles." He thrust the phone out to hold it to Amie's ear.

"Amie, hon," Shibby was saying. "Wanted to let you know I need to work a little later this afternoon. Miss Michaud is asking if I can see to a couple more things somebody else left hanging. Also, I might as well say, I need to meet with someone here at the inn. Ask a couple of real hard questions face to face. But Chester's getting off the school bus here at three, before I'll be done. I walked him through where to get off right on the road in front of the inn, but his first day . . ."

With both hands occupied, Amie tilted her head closer to the receiver. "I'll be there to meet him. Happy to. Who's the someone you need to talk with?"

"I can tell you about it later. Let's just say I'd rather walk barefoot over three fields of milkweed. Thank you again for meeting our boy, Amie, dear gir—"

A click on the line severed the end of Shibby's last word before Amie could ask anything else.

Thanking Fletch, Amie hauled her cans to the threshold, where Chief Roy stood with his right hand on his gun holster. "About Wakefield."

Amie's heart thudded hard in her chest. "You found him?"

"Seems he took off for Boston—looks awful guilty, just that, if you ask me. We've got men there on the lookout for him."

The paint cans felt impossibly heavy in both Amie's hands. "Honestly, I'm still trying to process it all."

"Actually, I'm here right now to ask you about someone else looking suspicious. Last person *you'd* probably guess."

Amie heard his emphasis on the *you'd*. "No clue."

He looped his thumbs behind his belt. "Just got word from some hotshot lawyer in Boston that Mrs. Gwendolyn Weld's will—just remade a couple of weeks ago, mind you—leaves most of her money not to her husband—they'd separated, like I said. Leaves it instead for the care of Master Chester Weld to Miss Shibboleth Travis of Pelican Cove. Tell me *that* don't sound suspicious."

Drained of all words, Amie could only stare back at him.

"Does," she finally managed, "she know this?"

"Lawyer couldn't say for sure, but damn hard to believe she didn't. Shibby's line about never meeting the woman until Friday . . ." He grunted. "Never meeting, my ass."

∾

Dazed to the point of clumsiness, Amie slogged across Dock Circle with a paint can on each side. She dropped them just inside the door, the bang reverberating in the gallery.

Settling Hopkins with a blanket and water in the shop's raised window display, Amie scratched his neck, her mind whirring.

So many pieces. Too many to fit in this one puzzle.

Something was gnawing especially at her insides now after what the chief had just told her.

For some reason, she was hearing Fossick speaking to the second shadowy figure outside the inn.

Just remember the kind of loyalty I require.

Amie swallowed, an urgency swelling inside her. Cresting.

The image of Shibby's kind face.

What if, Amie thought, *someone else knew about the will that left Gwendolyn Weld's money to Shibby for the care of Chester? Could Shibby's safety be in danger, too?*

Amie's stomach twisted.

Or what if someone—Seth Wakefield, for instance—knew nothing of Chester's existence and became friendly with Gwendolyn Weld in hopes of sharing her wealth? What would happen if someone like Seth, or even Fossick, who had designs on Gwendolyn Weld's money, learned of the bequest in her will?

Chief Roy, after all, was not much of a secret keeper, and this was a small village where everyone knew everything about everyone.

Amie had to get to the inn. Not just to meet Chester, but also to warn Shibby. Suddenly, nothing seemed more urgent.

Or am I only on edge because of the death in the barn? Maybe it's only that.

Sliding into the roadster parked on Dock Circle, Amie kicked powder from last night's snowfall from her boots. Shivering, she slipped the key in the ignition and turned.

Click.

That's all the engine gave her.

"No! *Nonono.*"

Springing back out, she plucked the brass key from her pocket, unlocked the gallery door, and lunged for the wooden skis she'd left propped nearby. Her fingers closed around the cold metal door hinges that Jake had fashioned years ago for securing the toes.

Ski hinges still sturdy after all these years. Jake a liar after all these years, too.

Grief speared her again—no longer for the loss of him now but for having found him. And having found him so strikingly handsome, so not to be trusted—so sadly changed.

Grabbing her camera from the roadster's passenger seat, she slammed the door with all the strength of her anger and grief. At least the Promontory sat surrounded by hemlocks and maples and fir, and the light was gentle today with a bit of mist. If she could just calm down about Shibby, and if everything seemed okay at the inn, she might get some interesting shots. If nothing else, focusing on the details of a scene—how the light could wash purple over the snow, how the brightly striped lobster buoys hung like party décor on the somber, gray-shingled sides of a hut—might distract her from this gnawing fear in her gut. Amie began a herringbone step across the half-plowed Dock Circle.

An afternoon late-autumn sun, golden and soft, tendriled over the snow. And yet this dark sense of urgency was growing inside her.

She bent her knees down the slope where the ski trail nearly converged and ran parallel with the footpath for a few yards.

Aiming her camera across Ocean Avenue to where hemlock branches swooped low over snowbanks gone almost blue in the afternoon light, she stopped, annoyed, when one of the inn's Allards rolled through a shot. She might be desperate enough to try to sell photographs of Fossick's inn to tourists since it was, after all, a historic structure, but she'd never stoop so low as to let a picture include the man's name painted there on the side of a car. Giving it time to pass, Amie adjusted her lens to play with the color and the exposure, then snapped several more.

At the crest of a slight hill sloping down toward the inn, Amie knelt. She took several quick photos of the harbor just past the inn's maples, then of the inn itself, the way its stone and clapboard seemed to tell stories: the droves of tourists in bustles and top hats, the flapper dresses and tuxedos it had seen come and go over the years. The summer regattas that had sailed by, the celebrations it had toasted, the sorrows it witnessed, the storms, too, it had withstood over the years.

The Promontory from this angle looked like a Hollywood set. *Like a scene in a Victor Fleming movie, the snow and the light so perfect, so appealing. With no people appearing—none of their secrets and fears to spoil all that perfection, that light.*

Maybe her sudden fear for Shibby's sake had been only that: just fear, fierce but unfounded.

A yellow school bus was pulling to a stop, its door leveraging open. A little boy, feet together, hopped happily down its stairs. The Superman lunchbox in one hand and the bow tie he'd insisted on wearing visible under his chin, he landed on the ground with snow poufing up to his eyes. The hint of a smile lit the child's face.

Snow can do that, Amie thought. *Lift the weight of all that is heavy and hard, if even just for a moment, in a good spray of fluffy white.*

"Coming!" Amie called, waving. "Meet you at the bottom of the hill!"

He waved back with one hand. Then both hands.

She raised her camera again for a final few snaps.

On the third floor, a window had been thrown open, a worker in a maid's uniform cleaning the inside and outside of the glass.

Squinting against the brightness of the snow, Amie could see now through the lens that the maid was Shibby, discernible partly for the wild, waving curls but also by the quick, broad swipes of her cleaning, the same way she'd swept crayon from the walls when the Orchard had been full of children. Like she did everything—with gusto, as if she worked to some rollicking song in her own head, Shibby was cleaning the panes like she was having fun.

She leaned out over the sill, apparently to reach one particularly dirty corner on the window's outside. Her head had swiveled at the squeal of the school bus's brakes, and, beaming, she lifted a hand now to Chester.

Amie felt her pulse quicken. Which was silly, of course. Shibby was a grown woman who'd raised a good dozen kids all on her own. She knew how to lean out a third-story window. Still . . .

Shibby, Amie wanted to scream. *Shibby, be careful!*

Shibby balanced at the sill, carefully wiping a lower pane from the outside, then jumped as if something had startled her from inside.

Teetering, Shibby grasped for the window frame to steady herself. But part of the old frame seemed to come away in her hand, the window sash, too, appearing to shift.

Amie watched in horror as her friend pitched almost drunkenly forward, one arm flailing backward. She seemed to find her balance, almost. Then lurched again.

Now as Amie stood frozen in place, Shibby was falling, arms spread fully open. Deep crimson leaves from the maples fell with her, raindrops from the leaves refracting the light so that Shibby's head—her whole upper body—appeared to be haloed against the inn's clapboard and stone.

As if in a moving picture's slow motion, time seemed to tick forward at only half speed. As if to draw out the horror.

Shibby fell like the swoop of an angel on a movie set, the safety ropes hidden.

Except this was real. Shibby falling. Three stories down to the white-dusted flagstone below.

Chapter 36

Things had gone wrong, so horribly wrong, Tess knew. Yet there was no turning back now.

Needing to lean hard into the railing, she made her way down the back stairs of the inn, all three floors. On a typical day while traversing these stairs, she could hear nothing but the smack and suck of surf on the rocks where the Promontory's back lawn met the harbor. Just now, though, the hammering of her own heart drowned out everything else.

Yet Tess's brain felt as if it had slowed, straining, shifting into some sort of lower gear—like a vehicle's engine climbing a very steep, slippery hill.

Hard to say who might have witnessed the fall. Certainly not the bus driver, who had other things to focus on.

Which was just as well.

Just moments ago, all had been as it should be: One quiet, pristine village. One quiet, prestigious inn.

Surely she should run now, if only for the look of the thing. Should race inside and dial for the ambulance—or the hearse, rather, that also served Pelican Cove as the shuttle to the hospital. Appropriate, no doubt, in this case that an ambulance doubled as a hearse.

Yes, that's what she would do.

First, though, she had to gather herself. Because the sitting rooms just through the back garden doors of the inn were full of guests who'd have no idea of the fall. At all costs, they must not be disturbed.

Guests at the Promontory, especially this time of year when most other inns had shut down, came in order to escape their own lives, the noise and distress of their jobs and their families in Boston and New York and Portland. Those few who came here in late autumn did so for the seclusion, the guarantee of any fine inn: that no lobster would be overboiled, no duvet sullied, no wine of an inferior year, that no crashes or sirens or cries would fracture the quiet.

Tess heard the tap of her own heels across the wide-plank oak floors, waxed to a high sheen, thanks to her constant vigilance with the staff. She moved quickly now through the sitting rooms—but did not run. Running might distress the guests, might remind them of problems outside these stone-and-clapboard walls. Might remind them also of the pain of a world that had been consumed by war just a few years ago and, thanks to the wiliness of the Russians, perhaps never really our friends, could be at war quite soon again. Those reminders could not be allowed here.

The concierge, Collin, bowed and waved pleasantly, as if nothing had happened. But then, the young man and his affability missed a good deal.

"Beau'iful day, miss, idn't it?"

"Yes. Fine. Call for the ambulance, please, Collin, and keep your voice quiet as you do so. I want no one to hear."

She brushed past him now. Ignored the slack-jawed look he gave her.

Without breaking into a run, she passed where the portrait of Mr. Fossick had hung before the police had hauled it away for tests. She would not allow panic.

What just happened has already happened. No time for regrets now.

Still, the clench and twist of her insides. For an instant she paused, certain she'd vomit the cinnamon bun from Fáilte she'd eaten just a half hour ago.

Raising her left hand to the handle of one of the massive front doors, she drew herself up. With her right, she adjusted the twill front of her Dior skirt, newly purchased. That helped steady her, just the tactile feel of well-tailored fabric.

There now.

Sweeping out from the oak doors—the glass of their portholes a little dirty, and that would have to be fixed—Tess took in the scene at a glance. Holding her breath, she stifled the shriek in her throat that would surely dismay the guests.

Just inside to the left of the main sitting room, the town council was meeting. Mr. Fossick was often in attendance when he was in town. Which he wasn't just now, of course. At least, those were the instructions he'd given her: to tell all who might happen to ask that he'd gone back to Boston already.

"Boston," she'd already told at least one person who'd demanded to know yesterday. "Mr. Fossick has left for Boston, I believe."

I believe, she'd tacked on carefully to the sentence, just to sound vague. As if she didn't keep meticulous track of these things in her inn.

But it gave cover to her, that vagueness did. Not her fault if Mr. Fossick lied to his staff. Not her fault either, really, if she'd been compelled to do things she did not want to do.

Now she forced her gaze down. Forced her mind to take in the scene. Stifled again the scream that formed in her throat.

273

The maid, wild, curly hair and black dress and white apron, lay all crumpled there on the flagstone. She was bleeding from the head. Profusely.

The apron might already be beyond what bleach could redeem, Tess thought. Which sounded a bit callous even to her.

But the world was a balance of those who *felt* things and those who *did* things. For better or worse, she was one of the latter.

As she approached, one of the grounds crew workers who must have been clearing away snow—*God, what was his name, something foreign and strange, some refugee from the war*—was bending now over the body, his shovel tossed to one side. He was shouting, black eyes gone wild. Shouting in that foreign tongue, whatever it was.

Tess placed her forefinger of calm across her lips. "Let's try to be quiet, shall we?"

Someone else—a guest, it must be—had collapsed beside the still body. The young woman cried out as she'd knelt and pulled a small boy down beside her with his face pressed into her side so he couldn't see. Her son, perhaps. The little boy, at least, made no sound.

This would not do, a child at the scene. Even now—*good God*—this pool of blood on the snow. The fresh dusting of white might make it faster to clean up the blood, snow being fairly easy to sweep swiftly aside, but stone being so terribly porous.

Tess shuddered at her own thought, but there it was: the truth—and no fault of hers if it was ugly. Unsettled guests who'd witnessed something unpleasant did not give gushing reviews of where they'd stayed to their bridge partners and golf foursomes and fellow yacht-club members.

Tess felt herself sway, and reached for a square white pillar of the porte cochere—its late-eighteenth-century wood repainted at her insistence just last month. The blood was immense, the snow going red in a circle around the head—and now the whole body. Like the target of a shooting range.

Tess fixed her eyes instead on the firelight she could glimpse through the window and across the main sitting room toward the inn's pub, the Helmsman—well reviewed in *Holiday* magazine, only because she herself had raised the standard. The writer had been assigned to cover the best seaports of the Maine coast, and despite Pelican Cove's being so small and lesser known than its swankier sister ports Camden and Boothbay Harbor to the north, Tess had single-handedly rerouted the writer to include the Promontory and its surrounding little village in his feature.

All that, though, could be thrown away with a sole misstep: a single, unthinking scream, a commotion that attracted a horrified crowd. Even one traumatized guest might relay to his social circle that this was no place to relax.

Out on Ocean Avenue, a couple of cars passed quietly, including one of the Allards, delivering some guest to the town center, no doubt. A pedestrian passed and then a green truck, as if nothing at all had changed.

Tess made herself breathe. A person in her position could not fall apart. Could not lose her head. The young woman kneeling had already instructed someone to run and call a doctor.

No harm in that, a doctor. Though surely too late.

The town's ambulance driver, to his credit, typically came fairly quickly—if he wasn't in the middle of an embalming.

Also to his credit, he asked few questions.

Tess knelt by the maid and felt for a pulse—though perhaps someone else had already done so. She sensed a distant, feeble beating—or was that only her own heart, an echoing throb?

The young woman stood now, stricken, as if she had some sort of stake in the scene. Which was odd for a guest.

But then Tess caught a glimpse of her face: That gallery owner who'd asked for the cast-off sails to use as furniture covers. Who'd asked too many questions about the Bentley stored in the sailing hut. Who'd seemed oddly intrigued—nosy, even—about the defacing of Fossick's portrait. Who, by the narrowed, analytical eyes, had appeared to think Tess was lying when she'd insisted she had no idea who could've done such a thing.

Tess had known then this young woman was chillingly like her: The kind who missed nothing. The kind who trusted few people or no one. The kind who meant trouble.

A long black Willys-Overland careened into sight now, shooting out of the tunnel of hemlock and fir near the main road. Tess cringed, its compensating for a weak, makeshift siren by blasting its horn. No one escaped from the cares of the world to a seaside resort in order to sip wine by the fire with the blaring horn of an old Willys.

But perhaps even that could be spun later: *Dear valued guest, observe for yourself how swiftly help will arrive, even in this quaint little village.*

The young woman was cupping both hands around her mouth now, shouting something that Tess couldn't make out.

If she was telling the undertaker-ambulance driver and his son to hurry, her words were a waste, the son already leaping out of the hearse before it fully stopped. The young woman had dropped to her knees again and, oddly, picked up the maid's hand. Held the hand, even, up to the young woman's cheek, sloppy and soaked with tears.

The little boy dropped down beside her again, a pale fellow with a bow tie. He let the young woman hold on to his hand—so tightly, Tess saw, that the young woman looked as if she might twist the little hand off its wrist.

Tess steadied herself for the undertaker's approach. Now was no time for a person in her position to faint.

The maid did not open her eyes as the undertaker and his son began easing the limp weight of her onto a stretcher made of canvas stretched between two slender pine poles. Already her pallor had gone from its usual shade, something one step closer to brown than just white—a shade Tess had wondered about more than once—to horrifically gray.

Perhaps she was already gone.

To Tess's astonishment, the maid's eyes fluttered open, but for only an instant, then closed. Her mouth moved, her words just scraps of whispers.

Thank heaven her words can't be made out.

Tess bent down toward the stretcher. "You will be in our thoughts, Shibby."

But the little woman did not respond to Tess's gracious remembering of the maid's name. The young woman—*Why, come to think of it, does she keep popping up here, and what does she know?*—bent over the stretcher.

The maid's next words came hoarse, but slightly louder. "Amie . . ."

Her head falling now to one side, she was being lifted slowly toward the square mouth of the Willys. "Amie, please . . . care for . . . Chester."

The next words came only as a riffle of sound: "And please. Also . . . for Jake."

Tess stood unmoving as they shoved in the stretcher.

Jake?

Tess had heard there'd once been children in the maid Shibby's household, a long line of children, other villagers said—villagers who, oddly, adored this woman. They treated her, some of them did, like some kind of peculiar, unholy angel with calloused hands and those oddly unblinking brown eyes. The eyes stared at you like they knew all your secrets and, Tess often thought, maybe like she'd suffered over a few of her own.

It had been Shibby's aloneness that fed Tess's molten trickle of guilt when she tweaked the pay scales—that Shibby was the sole working adult in a broken-down tinderbox of a farmhouse, the place at one time, people said, full of kids that weren't hers. God only knew whose they were.

But it was part of the job for a person in Tess's position to cut costs wherever she could. Fossick had made it abundantly clear that cost-cutting was in all circumstances a virtue—and Tess Michaud, the goddess of virtues.

He'd used that exact word, in fact: *goddess*. Tess had had to stand still too long to let him touch the front of her waist, his hand always, as ever, too high. Moving upward. Already rewarding himself for the compliment with his general manager's stillness. The glide of his hand below her breasts.

Even now, Tess gritted her teeth.

Still, that molten trickle of guilt toward this maid.

So who in God's name, then, is this Jake that has to be found?

As the undertaker stepped past her, Tess grasped at his sleeve. "I need you to refrain from blasting that horn again. Our guests, you see, expect—"

He gave Tess a look of utter disdain.

Some men would not do a woman a favor, no matter how handsome or poised or well positioned the woman, and this startled Tess when, rarely, it happened. He jerked away with such force that she let the sentence hang there, unfinished.

Tess's gaze darted back toward the cluster of people who'd just burst through the door, all of them stunned to a horrified silence.

Yes, there was the town council emerging from where it had been holding its meeting in the front room, its broad span of windowpanes just washed yesterday—at Tess's direction—so an utterly unobstructed view of the disturbance. Even if they'd missed the fall itself, they must've seen the ambulance racing up the inn's drive. Or heard, *dear God,* its obnoxious horn and pathetic excuse for a siren.

Nothing had gone today as she'd planned.

Yet still . . . Still, she could have her revenge.

Chapter 37

Amie had knelt frozen beside the pool of blood and kept her body bent over the little boy, shielding him from being able to see.

"It's all right," she heard herself whisper. "It's all right." She repeated the lie again and again as tears streamed down her face and she held on to the limp hand of her friend. Amie's coat unzipped, she'd bunched the middle of her sweater into a ball and pressed it firmly to Shibby's head.

Taking the sweater off to apply pressure would make more sense, but was there even time?

They'd just lifted Shibby's form onto the stretcher and up. Amie leaped to the rear of the ambulance that was also a hearse—and tried not to think about that.

"I need to ride with her," she told the undertaker. "I have to." She reached for the little boy a few feet away. "And so does Chester."

The driver inspected her from under heavily hooded lids. "Amelia." His eyes dropped down to Shibby, to the blood soaking the canvas-sail stretcher and the front of Amie's sweater. "Just let us get her settled."

Under his breath he added what he might not have meant her to hear: "Likely be the last ride you take with her."

Amie didn't wait for permission before she climbed past him into the cavern of the ambulance-hearse, pulled Chester in behind her, and reapplied pressure to the wound with another balled portion of her sweater.

Oh God, dear God, don't let her . . . please.

With her free hand, she lifted Shibby's, limp and cold, and held it to her own cheek.

Please, Shibby had said, *care for Chester.*

Of course Amie would do that, whatever it meant.

She squeezed her eyes shut to hear that last part of what Shibby had asked.

Also for Jake.

But right now, all Amie could do was hold the rough hand to her cheek, and keep the words coming in waves of hope—with the undertow of her own fear.

"Shibby, can you hear me? You've got to hang on. You've never let go of anybody you've loved, no matter how hopeless or hard or ugly things got. So hear me now: I am not letting you go."

Chester clung to Amie with one little hand and to the side of Shibby's stretcher with the other, his big eyes blinking above the bow tie.

Of all the children who shouldn't have to be here, on top of everything else.

Now a figure that had been walking toward them from the road broke into a run, a mauve coat flapping from the waist, a flash of white skirt and white tights underneath. Stella Lapierre reached the ambulance just before its driver closed the rear door.

"What's happened?" she cried. "I was just walking back to my . . . Who . . . ?"

But there was no need to answer that last. Shibby was only covered up to her chest by the ambulance-hearse's sheet, her face—and bloody head—fully on view.

Hand flying to her mouth, Stella addressed the driver. "My shift begins in a half hour. I'm coming with you. Have we stopped the bleeding?"

"Trying," was all Amie could offer, jerking her head down to where she held her sweater against Shibby's head. "I don't . . ."

I don't know what I'm doing, she wanted to cry aloud. *I don't know how to help her. I'm so scared she's already . . .*

Even as Stella scrambled in, the stylish mauve hat blew off her head and landed back in the snow. If she noticed, she gave no sign, two fingers already feeling for a pulse on Shibby's neck. Sliding out of her coat, she nudged Amie's hand aside and, using the coat's soft inner lining, applied more pressure to the wound, deep red staining the mauve.

The ambulance-hearse spit pebbles and ice from its tires as they spun and then gripped.

Amie kept Chester's face tucked close into her side and stroked his hair. "Her pulse. Is it . . . ?"

Stella bit her lip hard, shaking her head. "What on earth *happ*—?" Glancing down at the child, she stopped, gave another agonized look to Amie, and fell silent.

There would be time—too much of it, Amie thought, *for trying to answer that question.*

~

Tears would be coming, Amie knew as she stood by Shibby's hospital bed. But for now, she felt that strange, stiffening calm that often comes in crisis—only to cease helping later, like a cast falling away from a leg that hasn't yet healed.

For now, though, she needed to stay calm for Chester, who was sitting, knees pulled up to his chest, noting her every move to know how to gauge his own fears.

She straightened, trying to recall how long she'd been bending like that. What was it about hospitals that suspended all sense of time?

In the same rectangular room lay five other patients, all of them silent and still at the moment, eerily so. Far too much like a morgue.

Shibby still had not moved. Not so much as a twitch. The doctor was spooling off words that possibly were meant to stitch meaning together, but lay for Amie in broken threads. She caught snippets—*albumin solution discovered helpful during the war. . . intravascular volume . . . hemorrhagic shock*—but little that stayed connected, much less made sense.

What useless things I keep noticing, Amie thought. *The huskiness of the doctor's voice. His white coat smelling of the cigarette he just smoked. The old wax on the wood floor. Noticing this when Shibby might be dying. Or essentially already dead.*

Amie's mind kept pouncing on irrelevant details—the heavy starch of the sheets, the ragged edges of Shibby's nails—and clung to them like a rope over a canyon. She'd done the same thing during the war: the task of noticing every photographic detail often holding her up over the chasms of tragedy all around.

"So, again," the doctor was concluding, "the prognosis is not good, I'm sorry to say. Dire, in fact, would be fair. Do let me know if you have any more questions."

Questions? She had nothing *but* questions as he hurried out.

Out in the hallway, rubber soles squeaked on the wood floor. A woman's voice—a nurse apparently—pitched itself low, but not low enough that Amie couldn't make out the gist of it.

"Doctor, with all due respect, I told them that cannot be right. The lab could report alcohol in anyone else's bloodstream and I'd believe it, of course. Just not hers."

The doctor's rejoinder was more muffled.

More squeaking on the wood floor, as if someone had turned and walked abruptly away. Stella burst into the room.

Stopping when she saw Amie, she held out her arms and pulled Amie into a hug.

Finally, pulling a handkerchief from her pocket and swabbing at tears, Stella stepped back and retucked the sheets. "I can usually keep my professional calm, but in this case . . . I hope," she added more quietly, "you didn't have to hear that. In the hall."

Now she smoothed the sheets around Shibby. "I see a lot of sad cases here with my work. But *this*."

"I can't imagine how hard this will be for you to do your job with her here."

Stella turned slightly back. "Please tell me you didn't see it actually happen."

"I'd just arrived." Amie nodded toward the little boy huddled in the corner. Lowered her voice. "He'd just gotten off the bus."

"Oh God." Stella glanced up sharply from where she'd lifted Shibby's wrist to check for the pulse. "Poor little guy."

She drew the back of her hand over her eyes. Then, addressing the child, she nodded toward Amie. "You know, both me and her were raised by Mama Shibby. Or, at least—" She lifted her gaze to Amie. "No offense, but it felt like you were."

"None taken. I was at the Orchard more than my own house."

House, not home. Amie looked back at the unmoving form in the bed. The Orchard had been home.

"You and little Jakie. You two were inseparable. My God. I just remembered what I heard. Is it true he's in town?"

Rather than answer, Amie studied the formations of the sheets, Shibby's thin body causing only a small rise in their middle.

Like, Amie thought, *the plaster-of-Paris three-dimensional maps we made of Normandy before D-Day*. Back then, Amie had focused all the pain and confusion of war into helping get right the details. Here in the hospital room with questions and silence and the specter of death, she could feel her mind again straining to cache and line up details.

Stella lowered her voice. "You figured out yet what to do about this sweet little guy?"

"I'll stay at the farmhouse with Chester."

A small sob escaped from the corner. It was more sound than he'd made in the past hour.

"No!" It came out like a fire hose suddenly cranked on. "Not without *her*."

It took Amie a moment to recover from his having said a full four words not in a song or that grim little prayer.

"Or Chester"—she moved to put her arms around the boy—"can stay with me in the loft over the shop I'm fixing up." She gave him a quick hug. "Chester, you can help me. Lord knows I need it."

All three of them stared at the woman lying still under the white sheets.

Stella paused to brush Shibby's hair back from her forehead before stepping toward the threshold. "About whatever you might've overheard us say in the hallway. Before."

"About the alcohol in the bloodstream? I knew that couldn't have anything to do with Shibby. Her one shot of her precious Texas whiskey only once a year on—"

"New Year's Eve," they finished together.

Stella shook her head. "Exactly. So the lab report has to be wrong."

"They surely can't think . . ." Glancing toward Chester, Amie dropped her voice. "Whatever the lab report said, they can't think that's why she fell out a window. Whatever problem she had in the past back in Texas, that was years before you or I knew her. She only ever told people about it so they—all of us—wouldn't keep trying to pin a halo on her."

"Exactly." Stella put a hand on Amie's arm. "So, please, don't repeat what you heard, not to anyone. Not until they get it cleared up. It could make what happened look like Shibby's fault."

Suddenly cold, Amie wrapped her arms tightly around herself as Chester stood on tiptoe to kiss Shibby's cheek.

"Wake up," the child whispered, his little voice fierce and defensive—full of barbed wire and flares. "Pwease."

Chapter 38

In the hospital parking lot near the front garden, Jake stopped, feeling his heart race. A cluster of pale boulders rose above the fall leaves and the melting snow like a pod of beluga whales moving through a churning sea. Jake looked both ways to be sure no one could see him wipe wet from his cheeks.

Climbing out from behind the wheel of the Allard he'd borrowed—demanded, actually, from the Promontory's manager—he stopped in his tracks.

At the other end of the lot, crossing beneath the streetlight, a slim form without a coat was moving quickly. Only once did the man look back over his shoulder, his face above a gray turtleneck catching the lamp's glow.

The bakery guy who worked next door to Amie. He'd somehow beaten Jake here. He might know what the news was on Shibby.

God, I'm being a coward, Jake thought. *I've just seen Shibby Travis for the first time in nine years, and suddenly now if she dies, or if she's already dead, it will . . .*

"Kill me," Jake heard himself say aloud. "It will kill me." Because her death would be his fault. Something he should have seen coming. Something he should have known.

Jake hurried toward the bakery guy. Maybe he could at least warn Jake what to expect.

Jake had just been inside Fáilte, in fact, earlier today, the place full of people. There'd been some sort of fire in the kitchen, it seemed, smoke everywhere. The bakery guy had made them all clear out for a while until, after a time, he'd stepped out to wave them back in. Jake had recognized several of the villagers in the bakery—then milling around Dock Circle, waiting. The owner of Daggerboard Gifts had been there, periodically announcing she needed to get back to her own shop but not leaving, as well as the owner of the bookstore, a blond in a nurse's uniform, the founder of Myrtle's Lobster Claw, Fletch Osgood, who'd grumbled about the price of a cup of coffee, and several others. But Jake had kept his distance, even as they all filed back in after the fire.

None of them, he realized, recognized him. Except Fletch, who'd glanced his way only to scowl.

Jake had only gotten the message about Shibby when he'd returned to the inn. Tess Michaud met him at the front entrance to say Amelia Stilwell had called the front desk from the hospital where Shibboleth Travis lay in critical condition.

Shibby must have been falling, Jake stood there calculating, just as the fire broke out in the bakery. All of them standing in Dock Circle assuming that a bakery fire was the worst tragedy of the day here.

As the reality broke over him, Jake had demanded use of an Allard. The manager, knowing his position with Fossick, did not argue and handed over a set of keys. Which had brought him here to this hospital parking lot. Terrified to go in.

"Hey!" Jake called to the bakery guy. "Hey, you!"

But if he heard, the young man only ducked away from the street-light's pool of yellow.

Jake sprinted to stop him. Over the patches of ice, Jake's slick-soled wingtips found little grip.

As Jake reached the far end of the lot, the bakery guy flung himself into a rusted crate of a Ford Model A, then slammed the driver's-side door and spun away. Which made no sense at all.

Dread slowing his stride, Jake made his way inside. To where the woman who had made so many children like him feel whole lay apparently shattered.

The Cape James Regional Hospital didn't appear to have been updated since before the war. It was a sad affair, even as small hospitals went. Jake's wingtips echoed on the pine floor, gouged and dark with the buildup of old wax.

The information-desk staffer penned a room number and offered Jake a shred of paper. "So you're here to see poor Shibby Trav—"

But Jake was already striding down the hall.

Nurses swept past on either side of him. A youngish one smiled, pretty and pink-cheeked in all her white.

But that's not what he'd come for.

Jake paused only at the door of room 12. Chest so tight he could hardly breathe.

Popping open the door with the palm of his hand, he swallowed down the lump swelling now in his throat, and stepped forward toward the half-dozen beds lined up ahead.

I'm more afraid, he realized, *than I've been in years.*

She'd been all joy and forgiveness at his coming home, which made this moment so searing. Now she lay utterly still.

Shibby's face, lined, cheeks sunken, began to blur as Jake's eyes filled. Impulsively, he took her hand, too lifeless and cold. Amie was standing there to the left of the bed, but he kept his eyes on Shibby's face.

Suddenly, it was as if his taking her hand pulled him out of time, spinning him backward through years.

The rest of the room came loose and fell away. Her face looked younger now. Ruddy. Full of life.

She turned to greet him. Behind her, the percolator hiccupped and hissed, the smell of coffee and cinnamon and cloves filling the room.

"Good morning, Jake. You slept well?"

He was thirteen and not feeling warm toward the world. "The baby kept me awake half the night. Too many stupid kids in this stupid house."

A few wisps of gray hair had grown in at her temples. That made him mad, too—that she would work herself to the bone like this, still young but worn to a small stack of bones.

She gave him a smile, slow and sad. Which made him madder still.

"Which ones of the children do we send out in the wind today, hmm? Shall we decide based on who is the most grumpy this morning? Or maybe we start with the shortest. I agree with you: the little ones cause more trouble all through the night. Though I must admit, they wake up wanting to give me a kiss." She turned back to the counter, adding over her shoulder, "Blessed are the cheerful. For they shall receive waffles with maple syrup."

She set a plate of steaming blueberry beauties on the table. Then turned her cheek for him to kiss. He'd given her a cold, angry peck. But the smell of warm maple and blueberries came from the table, and the smell of vanilla came from Shibby.

He'd watched the butter melt on the stack of waffles, and he'd melted himself. He'd turned his head to her.

"It's not such a stupid house really," he'd whispered.

She'd taken his face in both her hands, her eyes dark and playful. "Good Saturday morning, dear boy."

Amie had been standing there for some time silently, studying his face, apparently, before she spoke. She whispered so softly, in fact, it took him a moment to realize it wasn't the low, ragged gasping of one of the other five patients in the long room. Or the wind outside the hospital window.

"You got the message."

But right now he was fixed on the face too still on the pillow, a bandage circling the forehead. His throat had closed nearly shut.

Jake shifted closer to the bedside, his face turned from Amie. She'd tagged him as a heartless brute, which he knew now he was. But a brute who still, it turned out, could be devastated by the message that Shibboleth Travis had fallen three stories—and was probably already dead.

He bent. Feeling his hands trembling as he reached to balance himself, he kissed Shibby's forehead.

His next words came shredded and raw: "How is she?"

A pause before an answer came—maybe Amie trying to steady her own voice. "They aren't holding out much hope."

Straightening, his gaze drifted to the window, frosted at its edges, and through it to the village green and its frozen pond. To the right, blocked by a stand of spruces and firs, sat the Orchard. Only the half-rotted cupola of the old barn showed above the tops of the trees.

As he turned back, he and Amie exchanged a look—that they were both seeing the top of the Orchard's barn, that they were both reeling as if they'd jumped from its roof. The kind of fathoms-deep expression that only two people who have grown up together can share in grief.

They might not have spoken for some time to come if the nurse hadn't bustled in at that moment. Eyes landing on Jake, she screeched to a halt.

The nurse who'd been at Fáilte earlier. He looked at her straight on now: Stella Lapierre. As striking as she'd been more than a decade ago, she looked in her starched cap and white uniform like Doris Day playing the part of a nurse. The kind of woman he'd have flirted with, and probably taken home, on any other day.

Her makeup streaked from crying, she blinked twice, as if trying to place him. Straightening, she hurried to swipe at the smeared black under her eyes.

No, he thought. *She doesn't recognize me as that awkward, insecure boy who watched her come and go that one year at the Orchard.*

"A new visitor for Miss Travis?" Stella asked, retucking the sheets with her eyes still on Jake. "My goodness, she *does* draw an auspicious crowd. Wait a minute." She stared at him. "It's not . . . It can't be."

Amie swung her satchel up to her shoulder. "*Mr. Darnay* here probably won't be able to make it back after today, I imagine, Stella. Given his terribly busy life down in Boston."

Chapter 39

How exactly, Amie wondered, do you look a kid in the eye who's already lost everything else in his young life except one woman who only recently even became his hub—the center around which all other chaos could spin but not touch—and then tell him that, yet again, life as he knows it is surely ending?

Slogging with Chester through leaves heavy and wet with the last of the snow, they reached the farmhouse together. Stopping at the front door, Amie was about to ask if Shibby still kept a spare key under the steps when Chester swung open the door, unlocked. At the old red couch, Chester opened his arms for the little white dog. Holding Hopkins in one arm, and a blanket in the other, Chester stood sucking his thumb—which he was maybe too old to do, but who could blame him today? Plenty of grown people held on to worse things for comfort.

Amie lifted the boy and the dog and the blanket into her arms. She waited for the wriggling out, his way of reminding her he was too big for holding.

But there was no protest today.

His eyes filled. "Has she *died-ed*, Amie, while we're gone?"

Amie's mouth dropped at that whole sentence from him. Setting him down, she stroked Chester's hair. It was a full moment before she could press out even a whisper. "She hasn't died . . ." The *yet* hung there between them, and she could see on the child's crumpling face that he'd already read the unsaid on hers.

She took his small hand. "We have to hang on to hope, now don't we?" Now she heard herself echoing Shibby from all those years growing up: "'We love and we hope.'"

His lower lip trembled as she brushed two big tears from his cheeks.

As she bent to him, she felt the little boy shudder. And herself shudder back.

"Will she die," he whispered, "like Aunt Addy?" Fear tightened the grip of his little hands at the back of her neck.

Aunt Addy.

It was the first time he'd said her name.

Was that, perhaps, the woman in the photo who'd filled the role of a mother to him? Who'd died, maybe. Leaving his biological mother to . . . What had she done? Panicked? Despaired? Whatever she'd thought or felt, however she'd struggled, she'd apparently delivered this boy to Pelican Cove with a note and then tried to take her own life on the tracks.

Amie could not look him in the eye. Now she was addressing not just the question he'd asked, but also the questions that raged at the edges of her own mind.

"I don't know, Chester, sweetheart. I don't know."

The child's bottom lip jutted as tears spilled from his eyes. "Bad window."

"It was just an acc—"

But she couldn't finish the sentence. As if that last bit of comfort she wasn't at all sure was true refused to roll off her tongue.

Now the tears that had not come as she'd stood stoically in the hospital poured down Amie's face as she sank with him and the little white dog to the couch.

~

With the bedding she'd hauled from the Orchard under one arm and Chester holding the leash, it took Amie five stabbing tries to ram the brass key into the lock before she and Chester and Hopkins could stumble into the shop. Chester blinked at the gallery's main room, lit only by the gaslight of the sidewalk, its sail-covered couches like ghosts in the gloom.

"Fair warning, Ches: I've not had time to fix up the loft upstairs much yet. Mostly just a pallet I've been using when I fall asleep here late at night. But I'll make you a good place to sleep out of the blankets we brought from the farmhouse."

He removed his thumb long enough to speak. But then didn't.

Poor little guy. So much loss for someone so young.

Amie hugged him again. "It's safe here. You and me, we're gonna have our own adventure here at this shop we'll be fixing up together, okay?"

Thumb held poised and ready to plunge back into his mouth, he gave a small nod. "Will that make Shibby get bettered soon?"

Amie stroked his head. "It might if we go to her room every day and tell her about what we're doing and how much we want her to see it."

Deadbolting the front door of the gallery, she tried not to let herself wonder if Chester really was, in fact, safe, given what happened to his mother—if Gwendolyn Weld was, in fact, his mother. Amie groped her way to the nearest lamp. Then led the child by the hand as he led the dog by the leash past the canvas ghost couches.

Even through his grogginess, Chester pointed to the stairs.

"You like those twisty stairs, Ches? You get to sleep up there at the top of them." Scooping up the boy in one arm and the bedding in the other and letting Hopkins run up ahead, Amie hauled herself and the child up the narrow steps.

Exhaustion added lead blocks to her feet. "Now, let's get you tucked in. I'll make another pallet for myself beside you. Sound good?"

She dropped two more rolled blankets onto the wide pine planks. At least the place no longer smelled of rat droppings and rancid Chef Boyardee.

Shifting aside his leather satchel, Amie collapsed on the floor beside the child. The design on the satchel's side, she noticed, looked as much like the letter *O* as it did just a circle with leaves intertwined. *But* O *for . . . what?* Rolling to tuck Chester's blankets under his back, she felt his little body heave with a single sob, yet not make a sound.

"Here's a game," she whispered, "that Mama Shibby taught me. You go back and forth naming everything you can think of you're glad for—from the silliest little thing to the biggest."

No response. But he seemed to be listening.

"You don't have to talk if you don't want to. So, let's see. I'm glad for your being here with me in Good Harbor. And I'm glad for those two tallest pines outside the window and glad for the moon that's letting us see them at night. And speaking of pine, I'm glad for the cleaner Pine-Sol and a shop that doesn't smell as much anymore of rat pee."

This earned a small snort from the boy.

"I'm glad for hot cocoa, and for watching you eat your whipped cream with the fluffy white mustache it gives you. And speaking of fluffy white, I'm glad for Hopkins here with us, and how he likes to sleep at our feet—'cause my toes are still icy—are yours? And I'm glad for the woodstove downstairs that'll be keeping us warm, at least part of the night . . ."

As Amie went on, her voice rising and falling in the rhythm that Shibby had used with all the kids at bedtime, Chester's breathing steadied at last into sleep.

But not Amie's. Images flashed through her head of Shibby's fall. The blood haloed around her head.

Shibby had asked two things of her, and those might have been her final words:

Please care for Chester.

Also for Jake.

That first part, Amie was doing. Not letting herself think further than one day ahead, she would do whatever it took to protect Chester.

But Jake. How could she take care of a man who had the world by the tail—or thought he did? A man who'd once earned her trust as a boy, but lost it years ago. A man who, whatever the details of his life these days, had apparently sold himself body and soul to Fossick.

Chapter 40

Jake had the man cornered and still unaware. Fossick, who'd claimed he was leaving for Boston and been driven away toward the airport, was still here in the cove, Jake felt certain. Everything about this crisis stank of Fossick, and Jake had had enough.

He knew too much. Had done too much himself in service of the man. It was time Fossick paid for the pain that he caused—and ordered others to cause.

Stiff with rage, Jake paused at the Promontory entrance, so quiet early this Friday morning. He pitched his head back toward the stars: bright pinpoints of light against brushed-velvet black.

He'd not seen the stars for years. Not since the war. Pinpoints of light back then had meant only possible—probable—danger, the enemy prepped to attack, the bombs or the bullets that would rain down.

Which had meant, if you were a civilian, time to run for the bunkers and underground train stations—wherever you could for shelter. But if you were a pilot, those little lights signaled you were about to be ordered back up into the sky. Up into the source of the chaos and death.

Jake flexed his hands. Then curled them back into fists.

Shibby had been right about what killing did to your soul. Maybe for him that dark cavern inside had already been opened and couldn't be shut again, the damage already done.

Shibby herself was dying now. Jake felt guilt shut off his air, felt the night sky pressing down.

Blessed are the merciful, Shibby used to say at the dinner table or while teaching one of her kids to cut the grass with the push mower, its reels clattering. *For they shall receive mercy. And fresh lemonade.*

If all the world could be run by Shibboleth Travis, Jake had to admit, mercy might rule the day—the world, even.

But his soul had been battered, as battle-worn as his plane, which had finally gone down in flames when he'd parachuted from the cockpit.

Maybe my soul, he thought now, *also went down in flames. Maybe there's nothing left of it now. Nothing salvageable on the inside.*

He knew now that he'd hurt Shibby cruelly with the lie of not coming back. Amie had been right about that.

But he'd be damned if he'd stand here knowing that she was dying, knowing who'd tried to kill her—who'd probably succeeded at it—and let the bastard get away with it.

Whipple, he thought. *Charlie Whipple.*

As soon as Jake got to a phone, he'd call Whipple at the *Globe* and offer help. If reporters there wanted the facts on Fossick, Jake could give them what they needed—and more.

The double doors of the inn were easing open now, that British concierge standing there in the opening with that pasty face and that trusting, innocent smile that told Jake the concierge had not been in the war.

"Welcome back, Mr. Darnay. May I 'elp—?"

Plowing past the reedy man without speaking, Jake tightened his fists. He had a job to do.

He was defending Shibby now. He'd hurt her himself—but not like this. Nothing like this.

Shibby would beg him to think of the healing work of forgiveness—the wide-open arms of love. And to please, *please* not do this rash thing.

But she wasn't here to stop him.

Jake knew when he found Fossick, he'd make him pay. And ask questions later.

Chapter 41

Amie was trying to run toward a ladder leaning against the white clapboard. But her legs would not move.

She tried screaming for someone to help. But her voice would not sound.

A line of silver rungs stretched up into the clouds, and near its top, just under the clouds, stood Shibby, leaning out a high window.

And then Shibby was falling.

Amie reached out her arms to break the fall down from the clouds.

But she was still rooted in place—her feet had grown tendrils that snaked into the soil.

Shibby kept falling.

A man far below the high window looked up once at the human form plummeting down. Then looked straight at Amie.

No emotion. That's what she saw on the man's face. No emotion at all.

Jake only shrugged. Turning, he walked quickly away.

Amie woke with a start, her body gone stiff with cold. Her eyes sprang open—to a room that smelled of wood smoke and fresh paint and old varnish.

Raising herself to her elbows, Amie tried shaking her head to clear it. As she squinted against the sun streaming in, she could make out railings and, beyond that, tall windows that stretched two stories and, beyond that, steeply pitched rooftops and pines and a widow's walk. Beyond that lay a thin strip of water.

The loft of the shop, that's where she was, with scents of coffee and brown sugar and cinnamon from Fáilte next door wafting now through the air vents or walls somehow. A world of improvement over mildew and wild-animal urine.

Something stirred to her right. In the rays of dim yellow breaking through the windows, she could make out a small head of hair.

Rising quietly, Amie kissed her palm, then brushed it over the top of his head—an old habit of Shibby's.

Shibby had taken to kissing her palm and brushing it down the back of Amie's head, too. Even when Amie as a teenager was sulking beside the farmhouse steps. Even that last time before she'd left town.

Little Chester stirred, the edge of the covers shifting under his chin.

Tiptoeing to the percolator, she began measuring out grounds from the tin of Maxwell House she'd bought two days ago at Provisions. She was having trouble shaking the image of Jake from her dream—Jake alive, unconcerned, and walking away. Or the image of Shibby splayed on the flagstone, a halo of her own blood, and begging Amie to *care for Chester. Also for Jake.*

Amie made Chester cinnamon toast with scrambled eggs—more cooking than she'd ever done in this galley kitchen. He gulped it down.

Chester dressed himself in the one change of outfit she'd brought. Amie would go back with the leather satchel to the farmhouse for more today. She washed out her own toothbrush and heaped toothpaste on it for him. She'd have to go back to the farmhouse for that, too.

As he thumped down the stairs, he pointed at one of the photos on the far wall: Nubble Lighthouse on the coast at dawn. "Glad for," he said.

"Well, look who's playing the Glad For game now. Thank you, Ches."

Amazing that a child could absorb grief and, at least for a while, seem unfazed—maybe not deal with it fully until months or years later. She'd seen it happen with several of the kids Shibby had raised.

Amie tugged his cap onto his head. "You know, you can stay home from school today if you'd like."

Lord knows, you're dealing with enough already.

Chester blinked up at her above his bow tie. Shook his head. As if he were accustomed to carrying grief around like his lunchbox.

Children thrive on routine, she could hear Shibby say. *It feels safe. Secure.*

Amie safety-pinned a note to his coat that explained a bit to the teacher of what happened—though she also would have heard through the village grapevine. The note urged the teacher to call Amie through Fletch Osgood at Provisions if Chester needed her to come get him. It also promised to get a phone installed at Good Harbor soon.

Leading him through the shop and out the door, Amie stood with him in front of Fáilte to catch the school bus. The door behind them burst open, Ian thrusting two hot cocoas at them.

Her fingers already stiff inside only one pair of thin gloves, Amie reached for hers with a sigh. "Now *this* is a great way of saying good morning. But only if you'll put it on my tab."

"Already did."

"All right, then. But tell me this, Person Who Probably Knows as Little About Children as I Do: Don't kids get cavities if they have sugar on their teeth all day at school?"

Ian arched that eyebrow at her. "Some cavities are worth getting."

Chester hugged him around the leg.

"Glad for," he and Amie said at the same time.

"What's that?" Ian asked.

Amie gave Ian's arm a pat. "Just know that I'd hug your leg, too, but I'm too cold to bend."

"The tough among us just call it"—he turned to slip back through Fáilte's door behind him—"Maine." The door closed with a thwack.

Then opened a crack. Ian waited until Chester was looking away. *How can I help?* he mouthed.

You have, she mouthed back as the yellow bus pulled to the curb.

Amie took the remains of Chester's hot chocolate, hugged him goodbye, then watched his little shoulders rise stoically at the top of the bus stairs. He turned.

"Glad for," he whispered, "if I could stay with you today?"

Amie put out her arms just in time as Chester threw himself off the top step and down beside her.

The bus driver merely lifted his hand from the wrist and dropped his head in the signature greeting as he leveraged the door closed and drove away.

Amie leaned down to hear what Chester needed to whisper in her ear.

"I need to go bad," he added aloud. "But here." He pointed to the back of the bakery. "Not there." He pointed through the wall toward Good Harbor.

Amie waved at Ian as she and Chester walked to the back of Fáilte. "Yours is warmer," she called. "And probably smells like cinnamon."

Listening to the Glenn Miller Orchestra she could hear distantly through the wall in Good Harbor, Amie waited for Chester outside the bathroom door. The doorframe between this hall and Fáilte's kitchen appeared slightly scorched, no doubt from the small fire she'd heard the bakery had. An open container of trash sat nearby, which showed how busy Ian was today, his never leaving trash visible.

From old habit, and because Chester was in there some time, Amie scanned that side of the hallway and made note of the odd detail: the knot in a pine plank that was shaped like a fish, the wallpaper peeling along one seam.

Suddenly, her eyes snapped back to the trash. Sitting just below a discarded rag was a syringe, its needle attached.

Dashing from her post where she was supposed to be waiting for Chester, Amie skidded to the bakery counter. The owner of Daggerboard Gifts smiled back at her.

"Ian," Amie managed. "Is he—?"

"Had to step out for a minute. We do this for each other, my being just across the circle there. There's times, you know, he just gets these"— she lowered her voice— *"spells."*

~

Amie had planned on walking to the inn to ask questions. She needed the distraction of her body in motion, the jolt of cold in her face to help numb her mind from spinning like tires on ice. But with Chester . . .

"We need to go to the inn," she told him. "Where Mama Shibby worked—*works*. I could drive the roadster if it starts today. Or we could walk, but—"

"Walk."

"You sure? Because . . ."

"Walk."

Adding a layer of wool socks inside their boots, they began walking the half mile to the Promontory.

Holding his hand as they crossed the circle, Amie let her mind rotate through names—too many of them. Too many faces. Too many possibilities of what happened these past several days.

Days in which Seth Wakefield has been missing.

Did he administer the pentobarbital mix to Gwendolyn Weld? And why would he disappear if not guilty?

304

Chester jumped into a snowbank thick with sodden leaves, disappearing for an instant, then reemerging, his knit cap porcupined with pine needles. Amie reached to shake out his cap but left it alone. Her mind felt as if it were poking in as many directions as the pine needles.

Is Tess Michaud harboring secrets for something she did herself—or protecting Fossick, her boss? Or both?

Chester raced ahead now. Slipping, he somersaulted forward as Amie gasped. But he scrambled up, smiling.

Does Jake know what his boss is capable of? Could Jake in any way have helped Fossick in harming Gwendolyn Weld?

Chester leaped forward again, this time making himself slide on a long stretch of wet leaves and somersault, getting up each time to be sure Amie saw. She made herself smile at him.

How is Ian O'Leary connected with Gwendolyn Weld? Could that conversation they'd had have upset him so much he might've wanted to stop her? And why does Ian have a needle and glass syringe—smaller than the one in the barn, but still—in his trash?

And what does any of this have to do with Shibby's fall yesterday?

Now Chester stopped in his tracks to watch one of the Promontory's black Allards shoot past. Amie had been too distracted with her own thoughts to see clearly who was sitting in the back seat, but it didn't appear to be Fossick—who was supposed to be back in Boston anyway. Still . . . did they know that for sure?

Fossick.

If he did kill Gwendolyn Weld, or ordered someone else to, could he also have had reason to try and kill Shibby? What if he knew that Gwen had confided in Shibby and feared what Gwen might've revealed?

Together, she and Chester tromped through the damp leaves and snow, the last of autumn's sweet, mellow scents combining with the sharp, bright tang of winter. The sun through the pines warmed their faces.

Chester waited for her to catch up to him now and latched on to her hand. He pointed down to his boots. "Glad for," he said.

Amie pointed to his little bow tie. "Glad for," she said, making him grin.

She'd have rested in that, just seeing some of the shadows fall from his face.

But she had questions to ask at the inn.

So many questions.

Chapter 42

Tess turned slowly to face the young man—the handsome face livid just now. Mr. Fossick had warned her, of course, to watch out for him. She could sense him taking her in, the trim Dior pencil skirt, the silk stockings, the black slingback heels: a look both feminine and, she knew, subtly powerful.

Tom Darnay, he'd registered as, though that wasn't his actual name, she'd learned—because she discovered these sorts of things.

Now this *Jake Spitzer*—the name he'd grown up with—was standing before her, trembling with rage.

But she could see, too, that her looks threw him off guard. Just one more advantage to men being accustomed only to dealing with other men. Curves in a figure of authority just like curves from a pitch had them swinging at air.

Jake Spitzer lowered his voice. "I need to know where he is."

"Mr. Fossick left for Boston a couple of days ago now. I would've thought he apprised you of that."

"Oh, he did. But I believe he's still here. I've searched every inch of the property."

As if you could possibly know Fossick's mind as I do. "I'd be happy to tell him, Mr. Darnay—or, I believe, Mr. Spitzer—that you're looking for him when I see him next, though it may be a number of weeks."

"No."

She raised an eyebrow at the good-looking young man who'd snarled the word. "Pardon?"

"A word of advice, Miss Michaud. Never lie on behalf of a liar. I've done it myself. It's ugly."

Jake Spitzer whirled away from the hearth where she stood. Breaking into a run, he disappeared out the back door of the inn.

"You know," Fossick had said just yesterday, leaning so close she'd smelled the brandy thick on his breath, "that woman tried to manipulate me from the beginning, her claiming the kid was mine. Her being unfit, screws loose, and farming the kid out God only knew where. What sort of mother does that?"

"A desperate one," she'd answered. "Or a deranged one."

"That's it, what I've been dealing with now for years. The woman was deranged. Wanted my money, and what better way than to claim some bastard kid was mine?"

Tess had eased a step away.

"You know, Miss Michaud, I could question why you let that woman hide her car in my sailing hut here."

Tess had opened her mouth. But the excuse she'd prepared days ago wouldn't form itself into words.

The truth was she'd wanted to see Fossick squirm. Tess didn't mind wreaking just a little early revenge. Before the final blow.

Fossick had held up one hand. "But I know, given the relationship you and I have cultivated"—the hand he'd placed at the small of her back slid up and to her side—"I can trust you to make the car itself, and the memory of it, disappear. I want no appearance of connection between that woman and me. You and I are the only two people who know it was ever here."

You and I and Amelia Stilwell, Tess had thought. But didn't bother to add.

She did plan on working in this very place for decades to come, and someday—better sooner than later—she would see Fossick fall.

But she'd smiled as she'd ushered him to the door. "Consider it done."

Now Tess used the sleeve of her navy blazer to wipe clear a circle of fog on the back window to gaze out toward the sailing hut. If Jake Spitzer was out there, she couldn't see him. But he was the least of her problems.

As if right on cue, the door from the long corridor of guest rooms swung open. There stood Amie Stilwell herself, holding the hand of that pitiful little boy born to such a weak woman. A woman raised rich and privileged, yet unhappy. Married young, yet unhappy. Caught up in a torrid love affair years ago, yet unhappy.

Tess had no patience for women who took no charge of their lives.

This Amie Stilwell, on the other hand, was a problem of a different stripe.

"One of your housekeepers," the woman said as she charged forward, "allowed me to see the room from which Shibboleth Travis fell. Interestingly, its window frame is loose, and its rope-and-pulley system was tampered with."

"With these historic structures, Miss Stilwell, rot of the ropes and the wood is always an issue, I assure you."

"And yet, the guest rooms around it on the same floor have windows and frames that are perfectly maintained."

"'Perfectly maintained' is what I strive for in all things. As you may be aware, I was the one who instructed the maid Shibboleth

Travis to go clean that particular room's window, which had become inexplicably dirty. And, yes, I make sure our maintenance crew sees to all the physical issues of our lovely historic property here."

"But there are scratches on that window frame's paint that appear quite fresh. No dirt or dust over them. As if, perhaps, someone was working on it quite recently—perhaps trying to fix it but did a poor job. Or perhaps tampering with it."

Tess was impressed. Annoyed, but impressed. Here was another woman who at least knew how to assert some strength.

Not that Amie Stilwell would get anywhere with just strength. But Tess admired a bit of gumption.

"Not to my knowledge," Tess said. Which was technically, though not fully, true.

～

Tess had managed to field all the young woman's questions—without answering any of them. Now she was driving alone for her last task of the day.

Here at this curve north of Puffin Beach, still walking distance from the inn, the cliffs towered above the water, and the water itself was deep.

She would do as Fossick demanded, even while she reveled in knowing that Amelia Stilwell must already have reported the connection of the Bentley with Fossick.

There was a limit to what Tess would do for Desmond Fossick. But no limit at all, she knew, to what Fossick would do to protect himself. Every day appeared to give more proof of that.

Stepping out of the car, she bent to heave a thirty-pound weight from the Promontory gym—with its barbells and climbing ropes—onto the car's accelerator. Straightening quickly, Tess sprang back.

The weight stayed on the accelerator only an instant or two before rolling off, but it was enough. The car surged forward over the edge of the cliff until only air was beneath its lovely white-walled tires, its silver hood ornament catching the light, glinting.

Marveling at its beauty, its graceful lines, Tess watched the spoiled, rich, weak Gwendolyn Weld's Bentley plummet over the edge of an unfair world.

Chapter 43

Mechanically, Amie respooled the Deardorff's film. She felt as if someone were plucking a string here and there to make her arm lift or head nod—but no actual life surged through her body.

It was Chester's short, sturdy form trudging beside her that made her keep going. What she longed to do was curl up by a roaring fire in the gallery and give in to exhaustion and grief.

Amie went through the motions of the gelatin reliefs, the dye transfers. She wouldn't worry about getting the colors just right on these, though. She'd never frame them. But maybe there'd be a detail here that would help answer some questions.

A couple of the prints, she realized, she shouldn't have even developed. In her rush to finish before Chester got restless, she hadn't noticed on the negatives that part of a black sedan appeared in a couple, Fossick's name visible on its side—which ruined the shots. A shame, since the wash of various blues on the snow was lovely.

A tap on the darkroom door told her she was out of time.

"You're right, Ches. I told you we'd go see Shibby in just a few minutes. I'm coming now."

She'd hang up to dry what she'd done so far.

And study them later.

～

At the door of Shibby's room, Chester gazed up, eyes brimming. "She'll be better today."

Amie ran a hand through the thick of his hair. "That would be great if that turned out to be true."

He stared, accusing. Indignant.

She bent to hug the child. "Why don't we just step in, okay?"

The steel door swung wide.

There lay six beds. The first one held Shibby, unmoving.

Chester beside her, Amie bent over the still form and kissed the forehead. Out the window, frost-heavy birches and red spruce glowed.

A nurse's shoes were squeaking up to the door. Stella appeared, stabbing the sheets of the beds in the room back into tight, precise corners, adjusting the blankets.

Lastly, she approached Shibby's bed. "Good thing you're coming often. I'm afraid . . ." She looked away.

"Have you seen any improvement at all?"

"She ought by all rights to be dead, the way she fell."

"But the doctor seemed to hold out some hope."

"Hope," Stella repeated flatly, as if the word tasted stale on her tongue. "Doctors like to hand it out like candy because people crave it. Which leaves us nurses, who have to watch hour by hour as a patient declines, to tell the awful truth to the families." She shook her head. "I should've been a doctor."

As Chester inched away to lean over Shibby's head, Amie lowered her voice. "Are you saying she's getting worse?"

Stella held Shibby's right arm and felt for the pulse at her wrist. "It'd help if there weren't so many visitors tromping through here. Every last soul on the cape wants to come running to thank her and beg her to wake up."

"Who else besides former foster kids have come to see her?"

"People tromp in here from the inn, housekeeping, grounds crew, you name it—God only knows what kind of germs. That lady manager, she's been here, too, clopping around in those fancy high heels and that uniform." Stella smoothed the polyethylene feeding tube. Biting her lip, then turning to pat Amie's arm, the nurse left.

Amie lifted Shibby's hand, the palm calloused to the texture of saddle leather. Something about it made Amie's throat constrict.

Then she knew what it was: she'd never seen these hands still before Shibby's fall.

Chester squeezed in close to her. They stood that way together beside the unmoving form for several moments.

Footsteps thudded behind them.

Someone who walks like he owns the place, Amie thought, even before she'd looked up.

A short, powerfully built man stood there—but one whose energy seemed to fill the room, make it vibrate with tension. He swaggered forward.

"I'm Desmond Fossick." He drew back his head as if waiting for Amie to kiss his ring. Or his feet. Or whatever it was people kissed on this man.

"I'm Amelia Stilwell." She stepped protectively in front of the bed. "You're supposed to be in Boston."

His lips curled back from his teeth. "I'm touched that you'd know. I've just arrived back."

"Or never left."

"Don't tell me a pretty little thing like you suspects me of something. I assure you, I have people who can vouch for my leaving. And coming back."

No doubt. A man who can pay well for others' vouching for him.

"You shouldn't be allowed in here." Amie wondered if she should shout for someone to call Chief Roy from the nurse's station. This would be the perfect time for Stella to come walking back in. Surely even Fossick wouldn't try anything with witnesses standing here.

"I think, pretty thing, you'll find that when a man donates generously to things—hospitals and towns, for examples—they let him go wherever the hell he likes."

Fossick's eyes narrowed on Chester. Amie tried to read the face as she would have an aerial photo from behind enemy lines. Even with the nostrils flaring, the clench of the jaw, Fossick may have meant to ignore the child. But his eyes betrayed him, fixated on the boy's face.

Chester crinkled his nose at the man.

The marvelous thing about being six, Amie thought. *Expressing whatever you think when you think it.*

Amie crinkled her nose at Fossick now, too. The man glowered back.

With his left hand, Fossick drew up a bouquet of flowers he'd been gripping upside down. He punched the flowers forward.

A former boxer, Amie recalled. Lightweight champion or something like that. Ernest Hemingway, *Life* magazine's favorite writer these days, would love the guy, maybe invite him deep-sea fishing. She, on the other hand, was repulsed.

Fossick dropped the bouquet on the tray beside Shibby's bed. "I insisted on coming myself. Rather than simply sending someone."

"Like your man Tom Darnay?"

Fossick's head drew back again.

A cobra, Amie thought, *about to strike.*

"You know Darnay, then, do you?"

Amie felt the blood rush hot to her face. She crossed her arms. "I knew Jake Spitzer. The young man—the good person—he used to be."

Fossick snorted. "Actually, I'm told he's been looking for me, Darnay is—or Spitzer, if we're back to calling him that."

"I wouldn't know. I asked him to leave."

"I'm impressed Spitzer knows every good-looking broad in New England."

Amie met Fossick's gaze but refused to react.

Fossick took another step forward, and she felt the threat of him. But she did not blink.

"Spitzer will vouch for me, of course. Even in regrettable circumstances like this"—he nodded toward the form in the bed—"when employees are injured through their own negligence, Fossick Enterprises extends its sympathies."

Their own negligence. Amie's whole body went stiff with rage. "Is that really why you showed up? Not to bring comfort but to be sure your inn wouldn't be served with a lawsuit?"

"That, Amelia Stilwell, is awfully cynical for a pretty young thing."

"A worker in your employ"—Amie's voice had gone hoarse—"and the kindest person ever to walk the face of the earth, fell three stories under very peculiar circumstances. At your inn. And the best you can do is make sure there's no legal action taken against you?"

"To hell with 'peculiar.' She fell because she was careless. She also, I might add, had imbibed a good bit beforehand—didn't you hear? Inebriated. A shame. But a fact."

Amie's breath caught. How did he know that last? Had the doctor reported to him that Shibby had alcohol in her system at the time of the fall? Good God, had the chief?

Chief Roy had seemed so determined not to consider Fossick a suspect in Gwendolyn Weld's death.

Fossick's lips pulled back from his teeth again in what he might have thought was a smile—more menacing than it was friendly. "You appear surprised I would know that. What I also know is that Shibboleth Travis had a long-standing habit of drinking on the job—every afternoon, as a matter of fact."

"That is not true!"

"Oh, but my information, sweet thing, comes from a *very* good source. One who would know."

Amie felt the words like a punch to her gut. "If you mean Jake, he's lying." *Again.*

"Understand this." Fossick's words came like more jabs, to her face, her chest. "Miss Travis leaned too far out, misjudged because of her long-established weakness for drink. Hell of a shame. But a fact."

"Jake would *not* have said that."

Fossick sneered. "But would Tom Darnay?"

That she couldn't answer. "Regardless, it's not true."

"Yet, you do recall she had a drinking problem, yes? Everyone in town seems to have known that."

"Because Shibby herself told people—part of why people loved her—that she knew what it was like to struggle. But she'd gotten sober years ago, before she ever took in children."

"Yet, for all her nobility, must've lied to the state authorities about her past so she could be approved to foster. Let's be honest: we both know that people who've had issues with drinking always have issues with drinking. More concisely"—he leered closer into her face—"once a drunk, always a drunk."

Amie sprang toward Fossick. As his lip curled, she felt her arm rise to slap him.

Chester tugged on her sleeve. With effort, she lowered her hand and fisted it onto her hip. In her fear for Shibby and her fury with Fossick, she'd honestly forgotten the child was standing right there.

"Not now, Ches. Please. I need to set this man straight." She did not take her eyes from Jake's boss. "You should know, Fossick, and please do relay this message to that right-hand man of yours since I doubt I'll see him again—"

Chester tugged again, harder this time.

Patting his shoulder, Amie waved Desmond Fossick toward the hallway. "I think you and I had better discuss things out here, where this sweet child's ears won't have to get blistered with what I have to say to you. And I'm asking the police chief to post a guard by this room. To keep *you* out."

Amie took one step to follow Fossick to the hall. But Chester held on to her sleeve and would not let go.

"My name," he whispered. "She said my name."

Chapter 44

Heart pounding, Amie tried not to replay the scene in the hospital.

"Chester," she called across the gallery to the little boy now. "I apologize again for not listening to you the first time about what you heard."

She said my name, Chester had claimed. But the doctor had come to inspect. Had insisted there'd been no change in the patient at all.

Amie herself doubted it happened. Still, it broke her heart that Chester wanted to hear Shibby speak so badly that he would imagine it.

Amie squinted at the print she'd hung on the line—one of the photos she'd snapped of the inn two days before Shibby fell. The prints were still damp with developing fluids and dyes, so too early to stick them side by side under the stereoscope. But there might be something to look at more closely. As in any photo, the light had reflected off the camera's mirrors and onto the film, but on one of these prints, the early morning sun had fallen angled on the Promontory's elegant front. On the third floor, at the very spot where Shibby would fall two days later, a swath of light fell unevenly across the glass—a shadowed figure behind it, perhaps.

Amie had brightened the swath still more in developing. What it meant, though, if anything, was harder to say. Maybe no more than a maid from the inn cleaning the room—perhaps even Shibby herself.

Still, it was a bit strange that with no other figure visible in any other window of the whole inn, someone had stood close to that very one—with the room unoccupied, Amie had learned, for several days before Shibby was called in to clean it.

Maybe, though, a maid just stepped to the window of that empty room for a moment of quiet and looked out at the view.

Amie stretched the tension out of her arms and back.

Chester was amusing himself now at the record player, putting on one LP and single after the next. The older and more tattered the record cover or center label, the more likely Chester was to like the music impressed on its disc. Just now, he was singing along to "In the Good Old Summertime," then reverting back to "Tea for Two."

Amie sang along with him, Chester moving to hold her hand.

Just tea for two, and two for tea,
Just me for you and you for me alone . . .

Sadness shot through her—this time for his aunt Addy, who'd been raising this child so swaddled in secrets.

And for Gwendolyn Weld, so detached from the son she'd borne—and from herself, maybe, too—that Chester must not even have known who it was driving him into Pelican Cove, this stranger asking him to tell no one.

As the harbor-buoy chime over the door sounded, fresh snow tumbled in tiny avalanches from Chief Roy's hat and coat onto the floor of Good Harbor. Without his current scowl, he might have been a cheerfully melting snowman.

"Got something urgent to say. Though first: What the hell's with all the snow this early?"

Amie stepped away from the line of photos—and wondered if she should show the chief what she thought she'd detected. "I'm anxious to know what you found with the fingerprints in the room where Shibby fell." She motioned him to sit on one of the couches—away from where Chester could hear.

"I can tell you what I'm allowed to. No more'n that. First, I got to ask some questions about Mrs. Travis. Since you knew—"

"*Know.*"

"Yeah, sure. *Know* her well."

"And it's Miss."

"Miss Stilwell. Yep. I know."

"No. I mean *Miss* for Shibby. She never married."

He raised an eyebrow as if he knew something he couldn't say. "Not even before she moved here?"

"No."

Amie said it with confidence. But what did she really know about Shibby's life before she became Pelican Cove's patron saint of unwanted children? The article in *Yankee* had played up her singleness as if she'd been Saint Teresa of Ávila, choosing not to marry or bear babies of her own, only Shibby's trading out silence and contemplation for sticky fingers and chaos. She'd rolled her eyes at the article's "hallowization" of her, as she'd coined the word.

But she'd never, now that Amie thought of it, addressed the facts.

The chief pursed his lips. "So she raises all those kids that weren't hers . . ."

"They were hers in how she mothered them—*us.*"

"Did she have any enemies that you knew of?"

"*Does* she, you mean? No. None. Shibby would give a stranger the shirt off her back along with a ham sandwich." She stopped there.

"What's that pause mean?"

"Actually, she could rub some people the wrong way at times—mostly when she felt she had to confront someone. Usually one of us kids in the farmhouse for being unkind. But you know yourself from living here: for all her kindness, she wasn't afraid to be painfully frank— if someone was about to hurt someone else."

Amie ran a finger around the rim of her coffee cup. "People who don't know Shibby well only see the kind soul, the gentleness, how petite she is. If you know her well, though . . ."

"She had—*has*—a tough side."

An old memory flickered in Amie's mind. Jake covered in hay, hammer in hand, mending the chicken coop.

"Wanna study together?" she'd asked.

He'd marched to the wheelbarrow, begun hauling aged manure to the vegetable garden. "Still got hours more chores."

Amie matched her stride to his. "What'd you do?"

"Told her I'd gotten the eggs this morning. Hadn't."

"You *lied*? To *Shibby*?"

Amie had watched him dump his next load. "Oh, Jakie, you idiot."

The radiator clanged as the chief's chuckle rose, then ebbed away. He squinted at her. "How often did you see her drunk?"

"*Shibby?* Never."

"Her coworkers tell me she had a cup of something every afternoon at three or a little before."

"She did. Coffee. With two sugars. Like clockwork. For years."

"Sure it couldn't have been spiked good with something else all those times? There's the lab results to say she'd had more than a nip the day of the fall. Plenty enough to increase dizziness. Vertigo. Slower reaction time."

"Not possible. She's made a tradition of taking a shot of"—Amie made quotes with her fingers—"'Texas whiskey' on New Year's Eve. But even that was really just Coke. She missed it a whole lot, she said—the other. But she was afraid to touch it again."

"Damn legalistic, I'd say. Sound to you like it does to me—like someone with a past drinking problem?"

"She was—*is*," Amie said, "upfront that she did in the past. 'Blessed are the cracked and chipped,' she used to say, 'for nobody's scared to walk close-up to them.'"

The chief harrumphed. "Ask me, get too many cracked types around and you got yourself a damn mess. So how'd you explain her blood alcohol level at the time of the accident? Sounds to me like a relapse. Possible, right?"

It's possible, Amie thought, feeling her own disloyalty like a punch.

"Impossible," she said. "Someone had to have spiked her coffee that day with something like vodka that didn't have a taste. Shibby doctors her coffee with enough sugar to cover even the most bitter stuff, so I'd bet she wouldn't have noticed any slight change in taste. Now my questions for you: What did dusting for fingerprints show?"

"Several things."

Amie found herself holding her breath. When the chief didn't immediately speak, she couldn't help plunging back in. "You saw for yourself, the window frame in that guest room was so loose that part of it came away from the wall when Shibby reached for it. And the old rope-and-pulley system operating the window: someone must've changed out the lead weight to something lighter, because the window wasn't balanced properly, so it was unstable, too. And you saw those scratches from where someone recently worked on or tampered with it—scratches not covered in dust or dirt yet?"

"Yup." He ambled to one wall to inspect one of her seascapes. "Nice."

"Thank you. But did you . . . ?"

"You aren't so much on patience, are you?"

She crossed her arms. "Never struck me much as a virtue."

"The fingerprint thing can get complicated."

"I would assume there would be quite a few sets?"

"Yup."

"I'm guessing you and your men inspected the other guest rooms. To see if they had the same maintenance issues—loose frame, a window sash improperly weighted." She paused to see if he'd discovered what she had—no point in humiliating the man. When he only stared back at her, she added, "But they didn't. That was the only room. And the only room with a suddenly dirty window."

"Hold on, now. Who let you in that room when it was closed off for police?"

"My being close to Shibby Travis meant the other maids were happy to give me access to the whole floor."

He leaned back to survey her. "I got to say, I hope you're clear on who the professional in crime is here."

"Perfectly clear," she assured him with her best, and least genuine, smile. "What's less clear to me is why Mr. Fossick doesn't seem to be at the top of your list of people who might have arranged for Shibby to fall from that—"

"Assuming somebody arranged it and she'd didn't just topple out her own damn self. Even *if*, though, it wasn't just your standard accident on the job, and her having a good blood alcohol buzz in the head by then, which we *do know* she had, Mr. Fossick was out of town. If you're going to pretend to be a professional in crime, little lady, you'll want to get your facts straight."

Or someone convinced you, Amie thought, *that he had left town.*

"I won't pretend, Chief, that I have access to the resources you do. All I bring to the table is . . ."

What, exactly?

He gathered his mouth to one side. "The typical female nosiness?"

She raised an eyebrow.

"Or, Miss Stilwell, is what you're wanting to hear more like *an eagle eye*? Or like *razor-sharp analytical skills*?"

"More like that," she said over her shoulder as she walked toward her drying prints.

Someone had to have spiked her coffee, she'd just told the chief.

Even then, though, someone had to have learned Shibby's habits. And, harder, someone must have orchestrated all the other factors that allowed Shibby to fall. And someone must have been in that room to startle Shibby, perhaps even give her a final push.

Could Desmond Fossick have done it himself?

Or had he arranged it to be done by someone with an outsized loyalty to him?

Amie pushed the thought of Jake away.

"I wonder, Chief . . ."

"What is it, Lieutenant?"

He was mocking her, of course. He might not want her help, while also being uncomfortable needing it. But the ruffled ego of the village cop wasn't going to convince her to let someone blame Shibby for her own fall.

"I wonder, Chief, if you've gotten to know the general manager there at the Promontory."

Her conversation with the chief scrolled through her head as she stirred, up to her elbows in the plaster of Paris she'd purchased at Provisions a few moments ago. Fletch kept it in stock for the children of bored summer tourists, but Amie had only ever seen the stuff used with deadly serious purpose.

Chester scurried back to the record player to put on a single of Ethel Waters before plunging both arms into the wet, gooey mess. "Glad for," he said, beaming.

"Me too, Ches. Looks like white mud, right? Some coworkers of mine during the war . . ." She stopped there, wondering if he knew about the war that would've ended a year after he'd been born. "During a really hard time all over the world, these coworkers used this to make models of cities and . . ."

Arsenals. So we'd know where to drop bombs. She regretted now trying to explain this to a child. No wonder adults told fairy tales.

"Anyway, you can make little figures of the people here you've met or anything you like."

Humming "Stormy Weather" as Ethel Waters sang, Chester fashioned a person with an oversized head, a bow tie just under its chin, and two marvelous boots, the figure's midsection mostly missing.

"Excellent, Ches. You've got the idea." As she watched, the little boy formed a small ball with four smaller ones for legs, then added a tail and two long, floppy ears. Next came a two-legged figure with long arms and a huge cap with long, floppy flaps on both sides.

Chuckling, Amie knelt to see the figures closer. "Never thought about the two of them looking a little alike, but you're right. And once they harden, you can move them around."

Walking back to the prints that had finally dried, Amie chose one she'd enlarged of the third-story window. Light could appear to behave oddly when there was water involved, she knew, as when a straw submerged halfway in water seems to bend.

Two days before Shibby's fall when Amie had taken several photos of the inn, the weather had been misty. Was that why the light refracted in these photos off the droplets, appearing to bend in its arc across and through the glass? And with multipaned windows, light reflected differently off each individual section. In a second photo, the light fell so that figure behind the glass was ever so slightly more clear.

Just like during the war, it was the subtle changes from shot to shot that were clues to look deeper: the flattened blades of grass in parallel lines, the dark blots on an embankment that could mean a newly dug tunnel to an underground weapons construction site.

Something in the shadows, the seeming bend of the light of this second photograph, was different from the first. Something just around what might have been a shoulder.

Amie slipped two prints side by side under her stereoscope for a more three-dimensional view.

And stared. At what might be a shoulder, squared off, as with a man's suit or blazer. And below that, the faintest hint of an anchor.

Chapter 45

Shibby felt herself buoyed as if she were floating on the Frio back home, swept toward something she couldn't see but could already sense was welcome. Some sort of immense party, it felt like, all light and warmth and welcome.

She tried kicking her feet to move faster toward it, all that ocean of peace, but found she couldn't move anything, couldn't hurry her pace by an inch.

Now, too, something was holding her back: a voice, one she thought she knew, but deeper, sadder, more hoarse than she remembered.

The owner of the voice must be the one lifting her hand. She felt its warmth on her own, but she could not squeeze back.

"Shibby," the voice said, thick and choked, as if a young man were struggling with tears.

Jake. Dear God, it was Jake. He seemed to be needing her now. But she could not lift her arm to comfort him.

"I've come to confess. Though it's too late, much too late to make anything right."

He paused, as if praying for a response. But Shibby could give him nothing.

"A woman needed help, desperately. I didn't realize how much. Or maybe I did, deep down. Maybe I knew how fragile she was. God, who am I kidding?"

His voice shattered now, and Shibby longed to lay a palm along his face as she had when he was a boy, longed to pull him into her arms and wipe his tears.

"The truth is . . ."

He clung to her hand like a terrified child, just as he had years ago when he'd sat all alone near a blueberry bog and sobbed because no one had come back to get him. But this new fear of his was something else, something more. Perhaps something worse.

"Shibby, the truth is her blood is on my hands."

Chapter 46

Jake emerged from the hospital utterly drained from his confession to Shibby, and more determined than ever. Shibby, Stella admitted out in the hallway before he left, appeared to be slipping away.

If it was too late to change the past, there was at least time to make someone pay.

For all his frantic hunting, Jake had kept just missing Fossick. A man with people willing to lie for him could be hard to pin down. Now chasing Fossick meant following him out of town, tracking the snake where he'd gone. Jake had just confirmed with Fossick's office in Boston that he was headed now to Las Vegas.

Ignoring patches of ice on the road, Jake punched the gas into Dock Circle. He yanked on the Allard's wheel and barely missed the circle's central statue, that old Union soldier who wasn't.

Jake had been braced for having to face the parts of his past he'd despised. Instead, he'd found a hundred moments of remembered joy and connection. Shibby's face alone had cracked some sort of shell open, leaving him aching now, raw in a way he hadn't prepared for, vulnerable in a way he'd worked so hard not to be.

Double-parking, Jake leaped from the Allard and, slipping on the fast-freezing brick, slid to the threshold of Good Harbor. The door unlocked, he stood with its entrance bell still tolling like harbor buoys. It might have been a nice sound—the right kind of charming for this town—if he'd been in the mood for charming.

The only movement was a white ball of fur bounding forward, Amie's long-haired mutt with the cute face. Hopkins danced on his hind legs. But Jake didn't have time to dance.

He'd just opened his mouth to call out when somebody bellowed from the loft. *"Amie?"*

Heavy boots thundered down the spiral staircase.

The man running from the back of the shop wore a thick sweater, his cheeks stubbled and his hair mussed. His cheeks were bright red and chapped, as if he'd spent too much time outdoors. He was tall and broad shouldered, something about his face vaguely familiar—and also not. A scar cut from one temple across to the opposite jaw.

"Amie? Where's Amie?" the man demanded.

"How the hell should I know?"

Turning, the man was bolting for the door but stopped, rounding on Jake. *"You.* You're the guy who works for that bastard Fossick!"

Seth Wakefield, Jake realized with a start. Baseball star in high school. Brought home medals from the war along with that scar, someone at the inn had said. He was also the big guy in the high black boots, the veterinarian Jake had seen dancing that night in the Helmsman with Amie.

Jake shoved the chair that sat between them, sending it crashing to the floor.

"Just so we're properly reintroduced, *you're* the bastard who's been stalking Amie, then up and disappeared after a murder in your own barn."

Seth lunged for the door.

But Jake was just as quick, leaping to block the exit. "Stay the hell away from her, understand?"

A good four inches taller, Seth eyed him coldly.

Jake pulled himself straighter. "You won't get away. You realize the whole town's looking for you."

"*Let them.* Let them all look."

Jake swung, the punch barely connecting with a piece of chin as Seth jerked back. The fist that came in return landed squarely in Jake's chest, sending him reeling to the floor. Before he could scramble back up, Seth was gone, the harbor-buoy doorbell sounding like a warning.

"Everything okay in there?" somebody—not Amie—shouted. Through the right-hand wall. Or through a hole in the wall.

Someone had busted a hole the size of a munchkin door between Amie's shop and the bakery next door. Horsehair plaster hung in chunks, jagged, like bad teeth, from the opening. Jake ducked through, sweeping plaster dust from the shoulders of his coat.

Amie's neighbor, the guy perpetually in different shades of dark turtleneck, lifted a hand from his counter. "Pardon our mess. We're tearing down the walls that would divide us—apparently, whether or not one of us wants them down. My neighbor here is a woman who's never read Robert Frost, apparently. Or at least doesn't subscribe to his universal truth that good fences make good neighbors."

Jake bore down on the counter where the turtleneck guy stood with one eyebrow raised.

"I called to you," Jake said, "in the hospital parking lot. You had to have heard me. All you did was take off."

The baker's eyebrow arched higher, but he offered nothing.

Two women whose names Jake couldn't recall clustered near the cash register.

"I'm looking," Jake interrupted, "for Amie Stilwell. It's urgent."

"So maybe," the turtleneck guy murmured, "just a thought, maybe she doesn't want to talk with you at the moment."

Jake ignored this. "I need a coffee. Quickly."

One of the women shook her head. "You're right. It *is* little Jake. Got some rude on him, though. I don't recall that from when he was under her roof."

Jake threw up both arms in exasperation. "Look, I'm on my way to the airport. You people do know what that is, right?"

The two women exchanged glances. One of them shook her head. "If I was in as big a hurry as that, I'd have stayed home."

Jake slapped a bill on the counter.

"What's the word," the bakery guy asked as he took his time pouring, "on Shibby?"

"No change." That was all Jake could risk saying without his voice cracking.

But the three of them, the bakery guy and the two women, waited. As if there had to be more.

"She doesn't know anyone's there. She won't know I've left." His voice did crack now. Betraying him.

Please nod, he realized he was thinking. *Nod to tell me it's okay that I have to leave.* But they only looked at him. Then each other.

"I have to fly to Las Vegas."

Jake snatched up the coffee in its cardboard cup, a blurry lighthouse printed on the side.

Then hurtled out.

~

He punched his foot on the Allard's accelerator toward Portland Airport. Someone from the inn would come with a coworker later and pick the car up. Let that Michaud woman worry about it. She seemed to think she had everything under control.

Did Fossick realize women like her knew how to manipulate him— all while he thought he was seducing them?

Fossick had somehow managed to evade Jake at every turn here—hiding like the coward he was. But Jake would find him yet. Make him pay for what he'd done, and what he'd forced Jake to do.

A memory flitted into his mind.

"We love," Shibby had said, stroking the long wavy hair as Amie bent, retching, beside the stairs of the farmhouse, her party dress splattered and reeking. "And we hope."

But Jake had shaken his head. "You know how I got her here? Carried her out to my car. Pathetic. Her nothing but a puking rag doll. The hell I care."

Shibby ran a hand tenderly over Amie's head. "You did right in bringing her here tonight."

"Well, you know what? It's the last time I'll give a damn." He bent, grasped Amie's chin, and jerked up her face. What he'd meant to be a firm voice of decision came out a shout: "*You got that?* The *last* time!"

Shibby had reached for his hand. "This is our job. To love bigger than all the love she can't feel."

Jake snorted, his face turned away.

"Jake, listen to me. This is also our job: when she comes clear in the head, to welcome her home."

Jerking his hand from her grasp, he'd slammed the screen door behind him.

Jake pushed the memory away, along with the image of Shibby's face there in the hospital bed.

But neither the memory nor the image would go away.

We love, he kept hearing Shibby say as he drove. *And we hope.*

That night he'd brought Amie home from the party . . . that was the night he'd made a goddamn fool of himself by saying he loved her. That last night before she'd left town. Run away. Left him to walk the halls of Pelican High alone the rest of that senior year, the nerd with hand-me-down clothes and bad skin and no friends now that she'd gone.

Before he'd left town himself. Ignored Shibby's pleading. Marched into a recruiting office in Montreal and joined up.

That last night before Ames ran away . . . He'd rarely been invited to those sorts of parties in high school. Amie hadn't either until that last fall. She'd suddenly gotten pretty—too much so—her sweaters filling out and her skin going smooth. Suddenly, it hadn't been only Jake fumbling frantically with his locker's combination to go find her in the halls.

But that one night, that last night, at an empty summer beach house far out toward the tip of the cape, Jake had been invited, too. The record player—spinning mostly Duke Ellington and Glenn Miller—was cranked up to the point Jake remembered wondering if the bass drum would shake the boulders that hung above the beach and send them crashing down into the sea.

He'd pulled Amie out onto the dance floor, the two of them twirling and laughing. Then, on "Moonlight Serenade," he'd pulled her close, her mouth still open in a giggle. He'd pressed his lips to hers and murmured the stupidest lines of his life.

"Ames. You're not just my friend. Tell me you feel it, too. Amie, I love you."

She'd looked at him not with longing but with pity. *Pity.* She'd pulled back and placed her palm along his broken-out jaw.

"I love you, too, Jakie. I always will. Always. But not like that." She'd leaned back in, kissing him tenderly on the cheek.

With pity. The humiliation of it.

Then she'd walked away.

Nursing his third cup of gin, Jake had felt peevish, pathetic, and frothing, rabid-dog mad.

Amie had been dancing on the first floor with three guys no one else knew, boys from a hockey team up in Portland. *Three.*

Jake had tossed back another drink as he'd watched the skirt of her pink dress rising as she lifted her arms, calves still tanned from her summer job at the Promontory sailing dock. She'd laughed as she'd danced and raised her arms overhead, and she'd twirled, the boys gawking and falling into each other and reaching for her.

Even now, Jake could feel the fury rise in his veins. Amie being so stupid. Amie glowing with good health and good looks and all that attention. Amie, head thrown back and still laughing, letting herself be led by the hand upstairs.

Even now, Jake felt sick.

But here was the part Jake hadn't let himself relive since it happened—and even now, he could recall it only through the mist of the past and the buzz in his head that night.

He'd followed them up the stairs at a distance. The last of the three boys had sneered, "Hey, Amelia, your little lapdog Spitzer's trying to tag at your heels."

"Jakie," Amie had slurred. "Jakie's my *friend.*"

A bedroom door had slammed behind them. The three boys and Amie.

From there, though, it was blurrier still. Laughter like barks. The sound people make when nothing is funny at all. Laughter that competes with itself to be louder, and louder still. Some banging around of some furniture, maybe. A shout or two.

Jake had collapsed out on an Adirondack chair on the upper deck overlooking the beach and hated life. Hated Amie. Hated the boys she was with.

Maybe—this was blurrier still—she might have called out.

"Jake!" she might have said, and she might have been crying. And maybe, later, had the pink dress been torn?

She'd gotten out of the room before they could hurt her, he recalled vaguely. Hadn't she? She'd walked or maybe run out okay after not too terribly long, wasn't it? Though her dress had been torn. They hadn't hurt her, he'd been fairly sure.

Although . . . he'd been so angry, and the gin had done its numbing work. How much time had really gone by?

Come to think of it, he'd said something to her as she'd run out.

There it was: the memory bay doors opening and the bomb dropping.

"Slut!" he'd shouted at her—so loud he'd hoped Amie would not only hear right then, but be hearing the echo for the rest of her days.

He'd been so angry, the world rocking like a boat on the waves.

The stars that night had been nothing but smudges of light, his head going dark, too. He'd slid lower down in the chair and thought of the sand two stories below. The waves pounding the sand. The sand just lying there. Just lying there, crushed.

He'd sat slumped in that chair until a few hours later when he'd found Amie alone, curled up on the floor in a corner, and brought her to Shibby.

Jake, he heard again now as he gripped the Allard's wheel. *Jake!*

Slut? Had that really been his response?

Dear God, did I really do nothing at all?

Maybe it hadn't been the three hockey players, whatever they'd done or not, who'd hurt her, as much as her best friend who'd betrayed her.

But here was Portland Airport, his boarding time now. Right now. His hands gripped the wheel.

That was all in the past. He had places now in the present he had to be. He might have done his own share of harm—back then and now. He might have been Fossick's puppet. But this next thing he'd do for Gwendolyn Weld.

For Amie, too.

Swinging the Allard into a spot where someone from the inn could retrieve it, he sprinted with his crumpled ticket through the airport and out onto the tarmac. At the top of the stairs, a stewardess stood beaming.

"Well, if it isn't your lucky day. I was just about to—"

But Jake had already flashed his ticket and was pushing past her onto the plane. He must appear rude, he realized. She couldn't know that he was catapulting himself forward out of a need not to look at the plane's wings or its cockpit, a need not to trigger that roar in his ears, the visions of burning beneath him.

So far today, he'd held off memories of war.

But these memories of Amie, dredged up from so long ago . . .

Standing in the aisle on board, a second stewardess, her voice chirping above the engines, lifted something metal into the air. "Ladies and gentlemen, you'll find a safety belt at every seat—not to alarm you, but just as an added measure should you choose to use it."

She beamed pointedly at him. "We must all be settled in our seats before taking off. *Not* standing." Her tone was aggressively perky by now. "*Not* sauntering down the aisle, if you don't mind, sir."

Jake walked slowly toward his seat. One foot at a time. Stopping now.

His head was pounding, full of the sound of waves from that night long ago, and of Amie's voice. *Jake!*

His body slumped in that Adirondack chair, unmoving. Making no sound but to hurl the word *slut* into the house and out into the wind. So loudly she'd never unhear it.

Is that the way it had been? All these years,' he'd nursed the hurt, convincing himself he'd been so beleaguered, abandoned by her at the party, his love and pathetic longing flat-out rejected while she danced with the jocks. Then he'd hauled her home drunk, nearly unconscious and rumpled, her hair smelling of sweat and of rum, and left her vomiting beside the farmhouse porch, Shibby trying to say something to him.

What kind of boy turns his back on his best friend, even if he's been embarrassed? What kind of man makes excuses for what he has done in the name of *just following orders*?

"*Sir,*" came the flight attendant's voice, its cheeriness replaced by annoyance now.

He turned. Stood still, hardly hearing, hardly seeing as the stewardess bore down on him.

"Sir, you *must* take your seat."

Chapter 47

Her mind still churning over the photographs, Amie tried to concentrate now on the little boy. She smoothed Chester's curls back from his face. "It's not that I didn't believe you at the hospital when you said Shibby had spoken something out loud."

This wasn't exactly the truth. After she'd finished with Fossick, she'd *wanted* to believe the child, but she hadn't.

"Tell you what, Ches: We're almost there to the hospital. We'll remind them again about what you heard. We'll ask them to check really well every single thing they can check, to see if there's even a tiny bit of improvement."

But nothing in Shibby's face had altered, not even remotely. The doctor Amie dragged from the hall to check Shibby's vitals only listened to his stethoscope, counted heartbeats, examined her coloring—and pronounced the patient unchanged.

The doctor, white-headed and kindly, patted Chester on his head, and looked as if he might pat Amie next. But she drew back and straightened.

"One hates to disappoint," the doctor explained again. "But sometimes we wish so hard for a person in a coma to wake up, and we watch so long in the same room with the same walls, we begin to hear and see things that didn't occur. It happens all the time, actually. The mind can create what it desperately wants to be true."

When Amie didn't respond, he added, "Additionally, there is sometimes just before death what appears to be an improvement but is only the body's organs giving out their last effort." He patted her hand. "I will note on her chart what the little boy said. In case a change occurs later, we can look back and see the boy thought he heard something."

"Not *thought*," Chester countered. "I *hearded*."

But the doctor only turned, walking slowly away, mumbling to himself, "Now, where did I put that number?"

His shoes squeaked a few strides down the hall, then Amie heard him pause. "Nurse, wasn't there someone besides Miss Stilwell who asked to be contacted if there was a change in room 12?"

"*Has* there been a change?"

"Just a kid who thought he heard the patient say something. I'm not taking it seriously so much as I want us to make a note of it. Do let whoever asked for the update know that there was this one child's report—but that my professional opinion is, I regret to say, that the body is preparing for death."

～

On the ride back to the shop, Amie explained this again to Chester—how easy it was to hear what you wanted to hear, out of a good heart. But he only sat in the passenger seat of the roadster, back to working again today, with his little arms folded fiercely over his chest.

"Oh, Chester. I don't blame you for being mad. I'm upset, too. Mad and sad and confused. But I can't make Shibby wake up, much as I'd give my right arm to do it."

The little boy only stared back at her, tightened his arms across his chest, and buried his chin into his neck, pale eyes resolute. Defiant.

"Handsome," came his muffled voice, his chin still bolted down.

"Handsome? You sure are, little guy."

"No. *Handsome.* Handsome and Gretel. Gingerbread house."

"Ah. We could read that story again tonight if you'd like. Or you can tell it to me right now from memory."

Something, at least, to keep his mind occupied. Instead of on what the poor kid thought he'd heard. Or, God knew, anything from this past week.

"Two little children," he said, gesturing with both arms, "lost in the woods. Scared. Then finded their way home with pebbles."

Glancing right, Amie wondered what she was reading on his face. Did he have any early memories at all of the woman who'd given birth to him? Or was he missing his aunt Addy just now—was that *home*?

"Then bread crumbs." He shook his head ruefully. "Birds ate up all the bread crumbs. Poor Handsome. Poor Gretel." He raised his arms, palms out in a gesture of despair. "Bread crumbs all gone."

"Bread crumbs all gone," Amie agreed.

But the words on her own lips made her think. What other paths in her own mind might she be missing? What other connections should she have seen?

Slowing, she guided the roadster around Dock Circle to pull in front of Good Harbor.

Maybe there would be a bread crumb or two.

~

Unlocking the door and letting Chester bound ahead to greet Hopkins, she walked to the photographs hung to dry on the twine she'd strung up. Distractedly, she scanned each one. She was missing something somewhere, her gut told her.

Back at the record player, Chester pulled out a Glenn Miller album that Amie helped him put on the turntable. Glancing at the order of songs, Amie swallowed as she skimmed past "Moonlight Serenade," its connection with Jake and that party at the beach house so long ago too painful. Carefully, she set the needle down on "String of Pearls." Chester held Hopkins's front paws as the dog stood on his rear legs, the two of them dancing.

Smiling, Amie turned to where she'd hung the photos she'd developed. One showed the maples in front of the inn, the last of their deep crimson red leaves dusted with snow. Snow that would be knocked off as Shibby fell.

Amie's eyes welled.

No crying, Jakie. Remember. We said.

What she and Jake used to say to each other.

Was it possible he was nothing more now than some sort of hired gun who did Fossick's dirty work for him?

Amie's imagination flew scattershot as she tried once again to piece Jake into the story. Had he really become someone who'd do anything to protect his boss? Or himself?

And the general manager, Tess. Who seemed to want two things at all costs: first, to protect the inn from scandal and increase its prestige, and second—maybe even more importantly—to maintain her position of what she must view as power.

Blessed are the quiet, Amie thought bitterly, quoting Shibby in her mind, *for they shall hear God—and also when they're called for dessert.*

But not in the real world. Surely in the real world the quiet got outshouted—and trampled.

Amie looked more closely at the photos hanging from the line. Cocking her head, she stepped closer to the two shots of the inn's front where she'd seen what looked like an anchor through that third-story window. She'd blown them up far past the point of sharp and well focused. If only she'd had her camera aimed at the third-floor window two days later at the very moment that Shibby was falling, or about to.

These were the ones, though, from when she'd been merely trying to capture the charm of the inn. Sliding them under the stereoscope, she saw what she'd spotted before: enhancing the depths and dimensions, the scope showed a figure in some sort of square-shouldered dark clothing, the hint of an anchor over the chest.

Meaning whoever had been in that unoccupied guest room two days before Shibby's fall was not a maid. It had to have been one of the blazer-wearing members of staff. Or the owner himself.

It could, in fact, be Fossick with his peculiar habit of dressing like his staff when he was in town, even as his behavior put them all in their places at every turn. Or Collin the concierge in the same blazer, about the same height. Or any of a score of bellboys.

Or could it be Tess Michaud? She seemed to loathe Desmond Fossick, though. Hardly the person who'd commit a crime for him, surely.

Unless Tess had her own motivations.

Straightening to clear her head for a moment, Amie rubbed the back of her neck. Then bent over again to the scope. Probably there was nothing more to see here than the anchor.

Although . . .

Her hand beginning to tremble, she focused the scope over the figure's jaw—what little could be seen of it. Nothing but shadow, really. Nothing of facial features that Amie could see, even enlarged.

But there, on the side of the head, where the light fell, the shape of the ear. And at the lobe: a glint. A minuscule spot of light she'd not been able to see before.

An earring.

Amie froze where she'd bent over the scope.

"String of Pearls" still spinning out from the record player, Chester and Hopkins paused in their dance to land, tumbling, at her feet. Amie did not straighten from where she was staring.

"Well, fellas," she murmured, "this does narrow things down."

~

Amie drummed her fingers on the Provisions counter frantically, the telephone cord tethering her need to pace as she waited for Chief Roy to pick up. Ring after ring.

Finally, another voice answered. A deputy whose name Amie couldn't even make out, so thick was his accent from rural upstate.

"It's urgent. I need to reach the chief right away."

"Ayuh. Gone to arrest somebody in the Weld case," the deputy offered cheerily. "Probably shouldn't ought to tell you that. But one less of her type—foreign, if you know what I mean—on the streets if you ask me. Call back later, eh?"

Foreign? Amie replayed the words in her head. But that couldn't be right.

He must mean Kalia.

"But the chief can't possibly have any evidence."

"Well, now, having two witnesses testify they saw her walking onto the farm property where the victim was found just before the coroner's estimated time of death, that'd be pretty good, eh? Also, her likely being one of Desmond Fossick's women, if you know what I mean. Her being jealous, no doubt, of the one she knocked off."

"That's absurd. If—" She heard her own voice rising, desperation edging it.

But the deputy's cheeriness did not wane. "I'll tell Chief you called. Bye now."

~

Chester beside her in the roadster, Amie swung into the Promontory. She'd checked the Tipsy Porpoise, but another waitress shook her head when Amie burst through the front door with questions. "Kalia was out delivering a couple of blueberry pies to the Promontory. Manager ordered 'em." She checked her watch. "Should've been back a good half hour ago."

Now, with Chester at her side, Amie sprang out of the Aston Martin and waved the Promontory's valets away. "We'll only be a minute!"

There in the middle of the central parlor, close to where the vandalized portrait of Fossick had hung, stood Kalia Clarke, her right wrist cuffed to the chief's, both sleeves of her dress rolled up so that the tattooed *You Must Remember This* and the Celtic cross and thistles were visible. She was not resisting arrest or even protesting, her expression resigned—as if she expected no one to believe her in this adopted country of hers.

Amie raced across the parlor. "Chief! You've got the wrong person!"

"Half-dozen different clues say I don't." He began ticking them off on the fingers of one hand. "The Jamaican dame here, she was seen by not one but two witnesses who've testified they saw her walking, almost running, away from the Wakefield farm soon before the coroner's estimated time of death."

"That doesn't mean—! Look, Ian O'Leary was there, too, and, for that matter, so was I, but that's not enough evidence to—"

"But neither of you are—how do I say this for a lady's ears—consorts of Desmond Fossick and likely to be jealous of the victim." He cocked his head. "That I know of, at least."

Kalia looked the chief in the eye, then away. "I'd rather die a thousand deaths than have that man touch me just even once."

"Are you standing there denying, Miss Clarke, that you were seen pouring a whole pitcher of beer over the man's head in the establishment where you work?"

The ghost of a smile swept over her lips. "No. That I did."

"Or that back in the kitchen, you said to other staff members that Desmond Fossick's reputation ought to be trashed, and that you'd be happy to do so yourself?"

"No. I do not deny it."

"What better way to do it than what you did, knocking off another one of his mistresses and trying to place blame on him?" Before she could respond, he held up his hand. "You deny you were on the Wakefield farm early that morning of Gwendolyn Weld's murder?"

"I do not deny it."

The chief held out an arm as if presenting a prize. "There we go."

"The house that I rent, it is nearby, just beyond the property. I sometimes cut through the fields on my way to work."

"Mm-hmm. Very convenient, Miss Clarke."

"Just," Amie broke in, "hear me out." She glanced around for Chester, who'd curled up in a padded armchair, knees tucked under his chin. "You have to see this." Amie thrust the two key photos at Chief Roy. "I brought this if you need to see it more closely." She held up her stereoscope.

The chief scowled from her to Kalia and back. "Seems to me my job here's done. What the hell's this?"

She'd enlarged the photos of the inn so much at this point, the shadow of a figure through the pane of glass was hardly more than dark fuzz. Except for the faint outlines that told more of the story.

"These photographs are from two days before Shibby Travis's fall, I'll grant you, but hear me out. You mentioned in private that you thought the Weld case and Shibby's were connected somehow."

"Hell, I maybe did. That is, I do. But—"

"And I agree. Chief, from what we can see of the jawline, whoever this is in the *unoccupied* guest room at the inn, the very one where Shibby would later fall, has lighter skin than Miss Clarke. The person could have come to an unoccupied guest room just to admire the view—or, perhaps, could have come to tamper with the window's ropes and pulleys and frame. Then or even a day or two later, maybe, the same person could've dirtied the panes. If you look closely, the person isn't part of the housekeeping staff there just to tidy the room. See the square shoulder of a dark jacket and the anchor?"

"Huh." Frowning, the chief stroked his chin. "Still, that's a whole other crime."

"But we both have a gut feeling they're related, right? At the very least, you don't have enough on Miss Clarke for the death in the barn to haul her in at this point. Granted, this person in the shadows of this picture could be any number of employees here—or even the owner, who wears the same blazer when he's in town. But look here."

Amie positioned two photos on the nearest coffee table, with the stereoscope over them. "Look at what appears to be the bottom half of a face—a piece of it, anyway."

The chief bent over to squint into the scope. "Can't make out a damn thing who it is from the face."

"True. But follow the jawline up. To the earlobe. Where . . ."

"Well, I'll be . . . Hold on. I'll be damned. An earring." The chief's eyes had gone round as he looked up. "Tess Michaud?"

"Looks like it."

"But how the hell does Tess Michaud tie in with Gwendolyn Weld and . . . ?"

"Maybe loyalty to Fossick, or to her job. Or isn't it just possible there was some jealousy? You weren't wrong about Desmond Fossick's affairs. Maybe a love triangle involving Fossick, Gwendolyn Weld, and Tess Michaud?"

Even as she said it, though, something didn't sit right.

She'd followed the bread crumbs, but what if this wasn't the only trail of them?

Chief Roy nodded slowly. Then gave a shake to the handcuffs. "Well, now, Miss Jamaica, you might get to go free—just for now. Only where the hell's Tess Michaud? Hey, you there, concierge or whatever the hell you're called."

Walking past, Collin snapped his head around. "Miss Michaud? She's left just now for the hospital. A doctor it was that called here a bit ago now. Said Shibby Travis took a turn for the worse. Dying, he said."

"Oh God." Amie drew a sharp breath.

Chief Roy was stroking his chin. "If Michaud's gone to the hospital . . . Even if Miss Travis hasn't passed yet, Michaud's got the perfect cover . . ."

But Amie was already sprinting across the parlor to grab Chester's hand. "Chief," she called back, "can you send men to block Tess Michaud from the hospital?"

Even as she said it, though, and even as she ran beside Chester, Amie was certain she'd missed something key.

"Ouch," Chester whimpered as he tried to keep up.

Amie realized she'd been wringing his hand in hers. "I'm so sorry, Ches. Here's the car door open. Can you dive in?"

Like Superman, Chester positioned his arms in front of his head, fingers touching, and leaped into the passenger side. "Faster than a speeding bullet!"

"That's right, Ches. That's right." She said it soothingly.

Her panic, though, found its way to her right foot. Dropping into the driver's seat, she found the gas.

With snow beginning to fall again, the Aston Martin shot forward.

Chapter 48

Trying frantically to think, Jake dropped his head into his hands, nearly touching his knees.

They'd been delayed on the tarmac for a half hour now, and this gut feeling he had to go back to Pelican Cove was growing stronger with every moment. Going back, though, would put him dead in the cross-hairs of guilt. He might belong there, but why in hell let that happen?

Help, Jake prayed. Which was pathetic. Probably didn't even count as a prayer to whatever divine accountants kept track of these things. You probably didn't even get heard if you were showing up cold.

Especially if you'd been asked the same thing yourself, *Help,* and did nothing. Worse, in fact, than nothing.

We love, Shibby had said, *and we hope.*

But Jake was no good, as it turned out, with either of those. He stood back up.

The stewardess was back, her perky smile going flat. "Sir, I believe I've asked you to sit down. *Several times.*"

Jake stepped toward her.

"Sir, you will *not* become aggressive with me!"

"I just need to get off."

"You can't do that. We have already closed the cabin door and are ready for taxi. We suggest—but of course do not require—the use of your seat belt. We have provided ashtrays for your conveni—"

"My luggage is with me. I'm getting off."

"You absolutely may *not*—"

He swung his leather bag up from his feet.

"*Sir!*"

He fixed his face into the expression he used for reporters: the cool, steely gaze—with just the right touch of sympathy for the person who would, without any doubt, accede to his will. "I'll be needing that door open."

The stewardess stood before him—*valiantly*, he'd give her that.

"Not once have I opened a cabin door after the plane is ready for taxi." She held up the sample seat belt between them, a weapon. "Don't make me get tough with you. *Mister.*"

Sitting to Jake's left, a passenger with a French accent murmured from behind *Le Monde* lifted in front of his face. "There was once a time I had the . . . how do you say, *douleurs à la poitrine*, the chest pains, yes? After I had boarded the plane."

The stewardess glowered. "Don't. Even. Think about it."

She and Jake took each other's measure as the other passengers looked on with interest.

Jake placed a hand over his heart. "Ouch," he said slowly. Deliberately. "What do you suppose this terrible tightening in my chest could possibly be?"

Chapter 49

Sleet was falling fast, and Amie was negotiating the turns too quickly. Ice covered the lane ahead already.

The roadster fishtailed out of the next curve. An Oldsmobile in the opposite lane was drifting on the ice over the center line. Its driver, panicked, yanked at the wheel.

Brakes locked, the vehicle spun into a doughnut, stopping with its length blocking both lanes, both shoulders mounded with plowed snow.

"Chester, cover your head!"

Even knowing the crunch of metal was coming, Amie was not prepared for the sound.

Chester shrieked as the newly pounded-out front of the roadster crumpled.

Amie whirled toward the passenger seat. "You okay?"

"Ouch." The little boy peeked up from under the arms he'd wrapped over his head. "For the car." His eyes saucered at the tangle of roadster and Oldsmobile.

Ramming the roadster's gearshift into reverse, Amie heard the engine roar, the tires spin. But no backward movement, the two vehicles locked together by twisted metal.

The Oldsmobile's driver leaped out, sliding on the ice. "You okay, lady?" His accent was thick and Deep South. "Awful sorry. I got no idea how to drive on this stuff."

Tugging Chester's hat low on his head and grabbing his hand, Amie scrambled out of her car. "We've got to get to the hospital."

"Lordy," the other driver called, "the *hospital?* Is the kid hurt?"

"We're fine. Other emergency." She flung her keys toward the startled man. "We're sprinting the last stretch. You've got my keys when the tow truck comes. I'll be back."

∼

"Ches, I'm so sorry I have to ask you to run faster. Please, can you?"

The little boy's snow boots thudded a few beats faster. "I *think* I can, I *think* I can."

"Just like the Little Engine That Could, that's right. And it's going to be fine," she told him, lying. "We just have to hurry."

"Fast as our little legs'll go?" He was trying so hard to be brave. "Like Handsome runned from the evil witch?"

Amie made herself smile down at him. "That's right. Just like Handsome from the witch."

Except we, she thought, *are running* toward *the evil witch.*

She lifted her face to the wind so Chester wouldn't see the fear pinching it. Chester lost his footing, pitching to one side, and she stumbled to break his fall.

"That's the way, Ches, to get up and run."

Pictures flashed through Amie's mind: The photos she'd made of the inn two days before Shibby's fall—the ones she'd been focused on. But also there were the ones she'd snapped on Ocean Avenue that very day as she'd made her way to the inn to meet Chester's bus. The hemlocks and the maples, the ocean, and the light on the snow had been her aim. But the backdrop of one of the shots had included a black sedan, one of the Allards.

She'd taken no more photos during or after Shibby's fall, of course. Had even left her camera where she'd dropped it at the front of the inn. She'd had to retrieve it from the front desk later.

But she remembered the clump of people gathered just outside the entrance. Amie arranged them all again now in her mind. Tess Michaud turning to manage the noise, the story. The ambulance-hearse screeching in from the road . . .

Amie thought of what she'd learned during the war. *Look for the subtle changes. For what wasn't there that had been. Or what there was suddenly more of: a patch of trees that hadn't been there last week could mean camouflage over something crucial. A rocket launcher, perhaps.*

In this case, she'd looked dozens of times at the photographs of the inn's third story and the shadowy figure there with its Promontory staff blazer. Though they'd been taken earlier in the week, they'd at least included the scene of the fall. She'd set aside the photos she'd snapped from the day of, since they included none of the inn.

Think, Amie. Focus on what's there that wasn't. Or what wasn't but is now.

In one of those pictures she'd taken on the way to the inn that day, she'd accidentally captured one of the Allards in what was supposed to be a shot of blue light on snow. The driver in his blazer and hat had been hunched over the wheel. Nothing unusual there.

Except, now that she thought of it, there'd been more than one of the black sedans coming and going on Ocean Avenue from the inn during that time—or one making several consecutive trips. Odd, since you typically didn't see but one or two of those cars pass during a whole day around the village off-season.

Pay attention to even the subtlest change.

And, come to think of it, they must've left from the back lot where the fleet parked and not swung by the front to pick up a guest, since no Allards came or went from the front during the crisis of Shibby's fall.

Also, in Fáilte's back hallway, Amie had been fixed on the syringe she'd found in the trash, which seemed to point to Ian somehow. But she'd also noticed the scorched wall from the fire in the bakery that day. A fire that might have simply broken out in the kitchen. Or a fire that might have been perfectly timed. And set.

A clump of people had milled about on Dock Circle as someone put out the fire.

A clump of people . . .

An old memory clicked in Amie's mind. *To the river and back.*

A clump of children milled about near the woods, the children jeering as they clutched their rocks.

One voice screeched above the others: *Nobody wants you, Bastard Jew Boy!*

The vileness of the words had felt even then so at odds with the smile.

It was as much intuition as fact for Amie at this point. But the story's pieces were falling fast into place in her head.

"Oh, Ches," she said, nearly stumbling as this newest thought hit her—hard. "I've been so blind. Right there in front of my eyes."

The little boy's cheeks were scarlet with his effort, his breath coming in heaves. "Whatsa . . . matter?"

He wouldn't understand, but she said it out loud anyway as they struggled forward, the words exploding from her chest. "Oh God. I think I know what happened."

Chapter 50

Shibby realized her eyes must be open. Blotches of light and dark swimming above her, the blotches began forming themselves into objects: a light fixture whose glass globe was cracked, a water stain on the ceiling. And now a face loomed into view, its eyebrows arched in surprise, its lips a straight, angry line.

I wish, Shibby tried to say to the face—there was so much she needed to say. But her mouth was stiff and unwilling. *I wish . . .*

"Jesus," said a voice that must've come from the face, but all the blotches kept shifting as Shibby tried to focus. "This could've been so easy. What is it about you that you've always had to make life so hard?"

Life is *hard,* Shibby wanted to say. *It just is. That's why we walk through it together.*

"Anyone else would have died in the fall. Your being only almost dead and dying slow, that's been, quite frankly, a pain in the ass." The voice paused like it was waiting for an apology. "It's not like I *wanted* you to hang on like this or suffer. All you had to do was keep your mouth shut and get the hell out of my way. But, no, you couldn't do that. You've never been able to do that, have you?"

I wish, Shibby thought, but no more than that, her head still not clear. *I wish . . .*

"But just like you taught us, there was a bright side. Blessed are those who wait, right? Gave more time for me to make extra sure they pinned everything on just the right guy. God knows he deserves it. I see that now, the beauty of his going down for it all. I am *so close* to arranging it to the final detail. You, though, *you* had to start waking up."

The fall, Shibby thought. *I think I remember. I had a conversation that day that was hard, and even before that, what was it that I was afraid had . . . ? I was worried about that death in the barn. I was so worried that . . .*

"If Gwendolyn Weld hadn't pulled you into the mess. If she hadn't shared all her dirt with you. That weak, sniveling mess of a woman."

Gwendolyn, Shibby thought. *Yes. She told me her story. Not all but part. Poor struggling soul.*

"I never wanted to involve you, you know. If you hadn't come to me that day, you and your questions about—what was the quaint way you put it?—the nature of my connection with Desmond Fossick. God, then, *then* the way you stood looking at me. Like I never measured up in your eyes."

No, Shibby tried to say, forcing her lips apart. *It wasn't* my *eyes. You never measured up in your own. Poor struggling soul.*

"If you'd just kept your questions all to yourself, everybody'd been a hell of a lot better off. You'd have saved us both this whole charade, saved me having to do what I have to do now. Jesus, if you'd just quit trying to rescue people."

I wish . . . Shibby had nearly made sound come from her throat. Almost.

"You think I *want* to have to do this now?"

Something white blocked out the light above. A cloud. Or a pillow, maybe. Lowering toward Shibby's face. But her arms would not move.

"I wish . . ." Shibby heard her voice rasp as the pillow descended. "I wish you'd known you were loved."

Chapter 51

If only, Amie thought desperately, running, sliding, flailing as fast as she could through the snow and holding tightly, too tightly, to Chester's hand. *If only there were some way of letting Chief Roy—or anyone, anyone—know who to stop.*

Because Shibby might, in fact, have taken a turn for the worse today. But what if she's actually taken a turn for the better? What if there's been some reason to let her linger there in a coma, since she didn't die in the fall from the window? What if Chester has been right all along and Shibby is showing signs of waking up? In which case the final flourish could have been relaying the message that Shibby has worsened before making sure she actually dies . . .

"Good, Chester," she managed, breathing hard. "You're doing so well. Keep running, Ches."

Amie could see now more pieces of what had been missing: her second night back at the Orchard, the dinner at the farmhouse. Everyone hugging Shibby—big, crushing bear hugs of devotion. But one person leaving with a tepid thank-you. No kiss. No hug.

Shibby, who worked next door to where this person lived. Shibby, who knew, and sensed, things about everyone—but especially the people she loved. Shibby, who would have confronted this woman in private if she sensed any sort of deceit.

Everyone called you "the smart ones" in the house. Like the rest of us weren't . . .

I should've been a doctor . . .

"The beautiful one." In a small town with few ways to feed the one part of herself she knew to be worthy. No new men here to dazzle—except for the wealthy tourists.

And, perhaps, the owner of the inn next door.

Her. The one person besides Seth who could've handled a shot full of pentobarbital with ease. Perfect features beneath a mauve hat—the one she'd let blow away when she'd leaped into the ambulance—a convincing touch of theatrics that made her look so concerned. As gorgeous as she'd been in high school, but no longer the queen she'd once been, she was now just a beautiful woman in her early thirties, ambitious and smart—and bitter.

I'm seeing someone quite seriously now. We'll be getting married soon, I feel sure, she'd said at the farmhouse that night, but without much conviction.

What if the man was a millionaire connected to this very village, a volatile man but a ticket out, a change of scenery, the promise of some other future?

What if she'd been suddenly jealous or scared that Gwendolyn Weld's appearing back on the scene, and apparently trying to talk with Desmond Fossick, meant a division of Fossick's attention—and fortune? Gwendolyn Weld would've had every right to both, especially if she'd decided to name Fossick as Chester's father.

Even now, the little boy slipped on a patch of leaves and ice, Amie reaching to steady him as they both plunged on.

"We're almost there, Ches," she told him between gasps. "Almost there."

What if it had been this person that Shibby had left that morning early to confront?

This person had been walking to her house that sat next to the inn—her parents' old house, she'd reminded Amie. The house from the days when her father had been a contractor who built sprawling summer homes for tourists smitten with the cove—back before she'd landed for that one year at the Orchard. In the home of a builder, it might have been natural for a kid growing up to pick up some basic knowledge: how to leverage a length of board loose, or how to manipulate the ropes and pulleys of an old window.

Never awkward or ugly as a teenager, maybe that girl had not grown strong in the kiln of early rejection like other people.

Maybe, Amie thought, *too much beauty and too little struggle make a person brittle.*

Amie forced an encouraging smile at Chester as they ran on, both of them too winded now even to speak.

How could I have seen the pieces but not put them together earlier?

Truth always lay deep in the details of a picture and this was no different. The black sedans were so much a part of the village that anyone donning a navy blazer and hat could have blended into the background of life, gone unnoticed, even making several trips back and forth within a few moments as Stella had done. A blazer could have been so easily swiped from the closet, the car keys hanging on hooks for the staff there in plain sight.

A green truck was hurtling past now, the face of its driver so frantically fixed up ahead he didn't even see Amie or Chester a few feet away on the path.

Seth Wakefield.

Amie, with Chester beside her, ran on. They were nearly to the hospital's front doors, only a few dozen yards to go, and the shortest way not by the circular drive but straight ahead. "Chester, we should stay to the—"

But she thought it, and said it, too late. Amie's foot plunged through a smooth crust of leaves and snow that covered the boulders in the hospital's garden. Pain shot from her ankle clear through her head as she heard a bone snap.

Chester's face, fearful, appeared beside her.

Just yards from the entrance, she collapsed to one side, the pain washing everything dark.

"Amie!" she heard somebody shout. Running. Boots crunching on the snow.

Then arms around her. For a moment she thought it must be Shibby. The way her head was being held, like when she'd been sick all over the pink dress, the one with the V-neck that had gotten savaged. She'd thrown up for hours that night, and Shibby had cradled her head. That night before she'd run away.

Shibby, she tried to say. *Chester.*

Someone pressed a rough cheek against hers.

But she had to get up. She had to stand. Again, the pain ripped through her whole body, her foot trapped between boulders.

"Chester!" she made herself shout through the pain. "Chester, run to Shibby! *Run,* Chester. *Don't leave Shibby alone with anyone! And, Chester . . ."*

The little boy turned.

"Chester, you have to scream 'Stella, stop' at the very top of your lungs. Understand? Now, *run,* Ches, as fast as you can!" The pain so intense. Everything blurred. "Chester?"

"He's gone, Amie. He ran like you said."

"Thank God." She closed her eyes.

"But you're trapped. Your leg. The bone."

This was Seth. The vet. That much she could manage to think through the hurt. "Please. Help Chester. Shibby's room."

Her vision cleared just enough to see the *No* in his eyes as he pulled away from her cheek.

"Please," she managed. *"Run.* Don't let anyone touch Shibby. *Especially not Stella Lapierre."*

Seth floundered to his feet in the snow and ran.

"It's too late," Amie cried, sinking back into a gray fog of pain. "I'm so sorry, Shibby. Shibby, I'm sorry."

Chapter 52

⁓

Jake had screeched to a halt at a hospital side door, a nurse just stamping out her cigarette on the doorframe and heading back in.

"Wait," he called, diving out of the car, leaving the Allard in what wasn't even a parking space. But that wasn't his problem anymore. Nothing to do with Desmond Fossick was.

Jake was through the door before the nurse had time to protest, even if she'd wanted to. "Thank you. Sorry, it's just that my mother's in there not doing well, and I left too much unsaid."

The nurse frowned, but stepped aside. Maybe she'd seen her share of *too much left unsaid* here.

He'd waited too long already to set things right. Too long to call back the courage he'd had to have as a pilot.

If only it's not too late. Jake moved to a fast walk up the hospital corridor toward room 12. The door appeared to be fully closed. Which it hadn't been at any point earlier.

Jake's chest tightened still more. *What if there's been a death in the room?* He stopped where he was. *What if . . . ?*

From behind him, someone was yelling. A kid. Screaming as he hurtled down the hall, the ice on the bottoms of his boots making him skid and slide as he careened into a cart.

"Stella!" the kid shouted. *"Stella, stop!"*

Jake stood still, bewildered. The kid was Amie's Chester, hat pulled down to his eyes and cheeks flaming red as he smashed into the door of room 12, throwing it open.

"Stella!" the kid screamed again. "Stop!"

Doctors and nurses were running now from every corner of the little hospital. From the front entrance, Seth Wakefield came barreling forward.

"Stella!" came the little boy's voice from inside the room.

Jake did not move from the bedside. He couldn't.

He could see Amie, on crutches, in the corner of the hospital room trying to talk with the police chief and Seth Wakefield about what had happened, but she could hardly speak through her tears. Every few moments, she returned to Shibby's bedside to hold her hand and kiss her cheek.

Hardly coherent, Amie got out various versions each time of "You're awake. Dear God, you're awake and you're alive."

In the corner close to the chief sat Stella, looking sullen and peeved. If she would struggle some day with remorse, that day was not yet.

Someone—maybe Seth Wakefield, Jake realized—had gone outside to bring Amie in once Chester's yelling had stopped—and once the chief had cornered Stella. Bless the kid, he'd done his job.

Chief Roy appeared not to have solved the whole puzzle yet, but on instinct he'd figured there might be a reason for a six-year-old to burst into a hospital screaming one particular name. So the chief had held Stella there until he knew more.

"Your leg," the big-animal vet was saying to Amie. Jake really disliked the guy—though just now didn't seem to be the time to take another swing at him. "I'm fairly certain it's broken."

Amie waved this away. "Then I'm in the right place to fix it—later. It won't get more broken for waiting a couple of hours." She went on trading facts with Chief Roy and, still teary, hobbling back every few minutes to Shibby.

For his part, Jake stood unmoving beside Shibby's bed and held on to her free hand as if it were a rope she'd tossed while he was drowning.

"I've been a bastard," he said.

Shibby smiled at him before she spoke, her one word coming slowly and cracked. "Yep."

But her eyes sparked, so much love there and even mirth that he laughed.

Jake stood quietly by Shibby's bedside just holding her hand. The chief left with Stella in the handcuffs he'd thought he was bringing for Tess Michaud. Seth Wakefield made Amie promise to get her leg seen by someone.

"A *real* doctor" had been Jake's contribution—and his jab at the vet.

But Wakefield had only tipped his head, then offered to take Chester, the hero of the day, for ice cream at Scoops. Doctors and nurses had returned to their rounds.

Amie hobbled back now to Shibby's bedside and faced Jake across it.

Shibby herself fluttered a hand. With effort, she croaked, "I'll just rest now. You two can talk."

Jake felt Amie's eyes on him—and they were not particularly friendly. "I thought," he confessed, "it was Fossick who'd killed Gwen. And tried to kill Shibby."

"Me too. And I thought it was a good half-dozen other people at points."

"Including me?"

Amie opened her mouth, probably about to say no. But she gave a half smile instead. "Let's just say I desperately didn't want to think that. But you were awfully changed."

"The truth is I had a hand in Mrs. Weld's death."

Shibby, looking exhausted, gave only a single nod, but was listening.

"I was the one sending letters for Fossick. Trying to convince Mrs. Weld to accept the measly amounts of money we sent—hush money, I guess it was. I transcribed what Fossick told me, his denying paternity for her kid."

"You knew, I assume," Amie said, watching his face, "that her child was Chester."

Jake shook his head, looking from one to the other of them. "I assumed Mrs. Weld's kid was a baby since she was just now, as far as I knew, coming after support. I was slow putting the old pieces of her and Fossick together, figuring out her kid was Chester. As penance for my stupidity"—he made sure both of them were looking at him—"I'll do everything I can to be sure Chester gets to stay here with you. Fossick is out of the question. He doesn't want a kid anyway. Gwen's family . . . who knows how they'll react. But it was her wish that Chester end up with you."

Watching Shibby's face as the eyelids drifted down, Amie lowered her voice. "From that night at the barn, I gathered Gwen was fairly cut off from her own family or her husband's or both in Brookline. Turns out that's why Seth—"

Jake scowled.

Amie saw it and raised an eyebrow. "Not a fan of large-animal vets?"

"Just not that one. You were saying?"

"That's why he left town after he found the body and made an anonymous call to the police. He stopped in to the bakery, thinking he'd tell someone what he'd found, but he couldn't. He and Gwen had bonded over horses, and she'd confided in him."

"I bet she did." At a look from her, Jake sighed. "Sorry. I'm in no position to talk."

"Seth knew enough, at least, to assume maybe Fossick had killed her because of the affair they'd had and her making demands on him again. So when Seth showed up at the Promontory Inn right after the murder, demanding to know where Fossick was, Tess Michaud was happy enough to give the location."

"In Boston," Jake said.

"Exactly. Seth had no idea Gwen had a child. Nobody did, including Ian. Apparently, she left town for the pregnancy and birth, then her aunt Adeline, who'd always wanted children but never married, became Chester's sole guardian. Everyone in the family—except maybe Gwen's husband—thought the baby had come from some wayward teen and that Addy, whom they all thought of as eccentric, simply took it in."

"And the husband?" Jake asked.

"Apparently knew there'd been an affair, and was enraged to the point of violence, Gwen had told Seth. Another reason Seth took off for Boston: he was convinced Gwen's killer was somewhere in the city, either Fossick hiding on Beacon Hill or Gwen's husband gone back to Brookline."

"So he thought he'd just anonymously call the police, then take off and tell no one where he was going or why?"

Amie raised an eyebrow at him again.

"Okay, fair enough. It was impulsive, what Wakefield did, and stupid, but maybe not criminal." He sighed. "I was the one to give that poor, broken woman the impression that Fossick was softening, wanting to talk. I knew, too, that Fossick had some other woman on the side—but he always does, so that wasn't news. I just didn't realize one of his women was from here and was someone I once knew."

Jake's eyes rested on Shibby's face, eyes peacefully closed. "Someone who'd been cared for by the same big heart."

They stood for a moment in silence, both watching the face on the pillow.

Amie kept her voice low. "From what Stella told the chief a few minutes ago, Fossick had been at her house that evening those twin foals were born. They fought about Gwen. After Fossick went back to the inn, Stella sent a message to Gwen signed as Fossick. The note asked Gwen to meet him at the barn since he was too well known anywhere else in town."

Jake gestured with his head toward Shibby. "She figured part of it out, didn't she?"

Amie nodded. "I'm still putting it all together myself, and Shibby can correct me later or not, but here's what I think happened: Gwen was staying at the inn or at least had come several times there to talk with Fossick, and in a moment of wanting to start all over again, poured out a good bit about her affair to Shibby."

"The person," Jake said, "everybody confides in."

"But Shibby had seen Fossick slipping over toward Stella's house next to the inn any number of times over the past months. After the death in the barn, Shibby started connecting the dots, enough to decide to confront Stella. Maybe Shibby thought she could convince her to turn herself in, so that possibly there'd be some mercy."

As Jake held the small hand on one side and Amie the other, Shibby's eyes blinked open again. Her thin cheeks were still sunken, but her smile now made them plump up.

"I'm so sorry," Jake said again. "For being AWOL. For being a bastard."

He felt a slight pressure, Shibby's squeezing his hand.

"I need," she managed shakily, "to say something myself."

Amie leaned forward. "You rest. We've probably been bothering you talking like this. We should step out while . . ."

But Shibby, for all her still waking up, would not let go of their hands. She pulled Jake closer toward her so that she could make her rough, still-weak voice heard. "My telling you not to come back if you fought in the war, that was wrong."

"You were just . . ."

"Wrong." Her voice was not loud, but it may as well have been, full of a kind of weight. "Very wrong. Withholding welcome is a crime against God."

She pulled him closer still, seeming to gather the last of the day's strength for her next handful of words. "It took courage to stand up to a tyrant. I should have said that before." Now her eyelids began sinking again. "I love you, dear boy. Welcome home."

Jake ducked his head so that Amie wouldn't see his eyes welling. But the tears fell just the same.

He stood there by Shibby's bedside and thought of a time years ago on the porch of the old farmhouse with its peeling paint and its warm glow from inside.

Jake choked as he tried to speak. "'We love,'" he said, quoting her. "'And we hope.'"

Chapter 53

Three Weeks Later

Before she'd even turned, Amie heard the laughter fizzed down into quiet, the ting of champagne glasses stilled, the conversations slowing to murmurs, then silence. Shibby and Jake must've arrived.

Amie held Chester's hand as together they stepped toward Good Harbor's front door, her right leg in its cast and her crutch thudding beside it.

Thump and drag. Thump and drag.

Intermixed with the standing sculptures and hanging sea glass, a square card table covered in sailcloth heaved with lobster rolls in their split-top buns and barbecued beef, Texas style. On the next table were fried plantains and blueberry scones and French Acadian ployes—warm, spongy crepes—along with beans in maple syrup and bacon. On one table set off by itself were three rounds of warm blueberry pie.

Applause began at the back of the shop and spread. The crowd in Good Harbor formed a semicircle around the entrance as Jake maneuvered the wheelchair with its cane-woven seat indoors. Thumping forward to greet them, Amie glanced over the crowd. Even Fletch Osgood, if not smiling, stood there with the lines at the corners of his eyes crinkling harder, shooting back under the plaid flaps of his cap.

Lifting her hand to guests she'd only just spotted, including Eunice Kennedy, who'd driven up from Cape Cod, Amie paused to adjust the string of lights outlining the little arched door between Good Harbor and Fáilte. Passing the record player, she turned up the volume on the song "Tea for Two."

Amie and Chester embraced Shibby there in her chair, other villagers surging forward to do the same. Her color had improved every day of the three weeks since she'd become conscious again, and tonight she was beaming, if still weak. Ignoring Jake's eyes on her, Amie relinquished her place.

Chester, spotting Ian O'Leary holding a bowl of whipped cream, ducked away from the crowd to the table. But as he allowed his mug of cocoa to be piled high with cream, he turned his head back to glance shyly at Amie.

"Just me for you, and you for me, alone," he sang, his voice high and reedy, but surprisingly strong.

Amie joined in with him.

> *Nobody near us, to see us or hear us,*
> *No friends or relations on weekend vacations,*
> *We won't have it known, dear, that we have a telephone, dear.*

They lifted mugs of cocoa to each other.

Bending down, the little boy scooped up a circle of soft white fur, except for the black nose and eyes. Hopkins turned sideways to reveal the dog had on a sweater, its knitted lines uneven and lumpy, changing colors from blue to green and back.

"What Mama Shibby made," he said wonderingly. Shifting the dog away from his chest, he revealed his own sweater, matching Hopkins's.

Right down, Amie saw, *to the dropped stitches and uneven lines.*

"Perfect," she said. She touched the blue scarf at her own neck. "You know what this means, though, right? We're family forever now."

The boy nodded earnestly.

"You know, Ches, I need someone to help keep Hopkins company. Especially on days when I'm all distracted with adding up numbers for sales and bills"—she wrinkled her nose—"which is the not-fun part of a business. A dog like this needs extra love and attention. If you know of anybody . . . Wait, is that a hand I see, Mister Chester?"

The child, raising one hand from where both arms cradled the dog, was grinning. Amie kissed Chester on top of the head, then the dog. "All right. But you'll need to swing by to see him—and me—here at the gallery every single day."

"Ebery. Single. Day," Chester promised, squeezing the dog, who licked the boy's cheek.

Kalia nodded sagely to Seth. "Our sweet little Chester thinks he's the hero of the whole thing. I told him he's right."

"Nobody can yell like a six-year-old boy." Seth raised a glass. "Or dodge every last doctor or nurse who tried to stop him."

A small sea of glasses was raised. *To Chester!*

The boy beamed, whipped cream mustaching his upper lip.

Now that the crowd eased back toward the tables of food and champagne, Amie made her way again to the wheelchair and steadied the cocoa in Shibby's hand. "You still doing okay?"

Gazing the length of the room, Shibby smiled. "Never better."

She tried to push herself up then, but Amie held up a palm. "You're not getting up to serve anyone. For now, you're sitting right here and being served. Right now, for example, I'm getting you blueberry pie. Don't try and stop me."

Refusing to meet Jake's eye, Amie squeezed her way through the crowd back to the food. The chief, sidling up beside her, raised his glass. "Guess you'll be wanting all the damn credit for—"

Amie lifted a glass before he could say more. "To teamwork!" she said.

Other glasses around them lifted. *To teamwork!*

"Cheers to that," Kalia said, standing nearby. Then, her smile fading, she shook her head and lowered her voice. "Poor Gwendolyn. So she had an affair years ago with that awful man, yes?"

Amie nodded. "She'd been up before in summers and stayed at the Promontory. That's how she and Fossick first met. It was only coming in autumn with so few people here that she stood out. Fossick had apparently told Stella there was a woman trying to extort money from him. She only found out who that woman was when Gwen appeared, desperate this time, here in the cove."

"But who," Kalia asked, "made that god-awful portrait of Fossick worse?"

"That was Gwen. She'd tried getting Fossick to admit paternity. The last thing she wanted was a scandal. So she did what people do when they haven't felt heard—she went public, or as public as she could without scandal. She tried to make Fossick look to others as slimy and despicable as she saw him." She shot a look at Jake. "As he actually is."

The chief gave a nod. "Damned if the oil of the portrait didn't turn out to match the chemical breakdown of that British hoof oil, Carr and whatever."

"Interestingly," Amie added, "it appears that Tess Michaud might have known about it, Gwen's vandalism of the portrait, but did nothing to stop it. Maybe she shared Gwen's opinion."

From her wheeled chair, Shibby raised a glass. "Y'all know I'm not one to judge by appearances much—except, of course, when it's helpful—but I've never seen a man I wanted so bad to roast on a big spit as I do Desmond Fossick."

From where he'd been standing alone at the window, Jake moved toward her, shoulders sagging.

That, at least, Amie thought, *is a start.*

Patting his arm as she passed, she started to turn, pie in hand, toward Shibby.

"Amie," he said from behind her. "I want you to know I quit. The job with Fossick. I officially quit."

Pausing, she cocked her head. She knew this already. But she could hear in his voice it lifted a weight from him to say it directly to her.

"No idea what I'll be doing now, or where. But I quit."

She reached a hand out to him, which he took. "To the river and back, Jake. Always."

"To the river and back," he murmured. "Amie, I—"

Pulling gently away, she turned and delivered the pie to Shibby. Then, aware of Jake's eyes still on her, she walked slowly back to him.

"Amie, about the night of the party in high school. At the beach house."

Amie felt her whole body go stiff and cold. She'd not been prepared to think about this tonight. Or ever if she didn't have to.

"Ames, you don't have to tell me what happened, obviously. Just know that I realized I'd blocked so much out. Or was too drunk that night to know much. Or too angry with you for rejecting my unbelievably pathetic confession of love . . ."

Amie couldn't stop one half of her mouth from lifting at that. "It was sweet."

"*Sweet.* What women say when they're rejecting a guy. My point, though, is that I blew it—as much as a friend can. I didn't come back you up when you needed me most."

Amie looked away and then back. Made him meet her eye. "You made it worse, Jake. Their hands all over me, all inside my clothes, my thinking I was going to be raped by three drunken guys I'd just met, that was all bad enough. But my best friend in the world didn't come to help, then called me a slut."

"Amie, I'm so—"

She held up her hand. "I was no angel that year. We both knew that. I was a mess. But I didn't deserve to come out of that room with those cretins and hear that from you."

"Amie. I'm so sorry."

She studied him for a moment. Jake's eyes were actually moist. She leaned forward and kissed him lightly on the cheek. "We both had a lot of learning to do. Let's leave it at that now and move on, what do you say?"

From behind her, Ian leaned in beside Amie. "A *grand* opening."

His face above the gray turtleneck relaxed into a smile—the first real one she'd seen from him. "*Céad míle fáilte.* A hundred thousand welcomes to you."

"Now *that* is a good welcome, Ian O'Leary." She lifted her champagne glass. "So, it must be rough, being a baker who's diabetic."

He raised an eyebrow. "Impressive detection. I don't recall telling anyone here. Didn't need to add to my story of pity. How'd you know?"

"First, I never saw you eat your own creations, which is more than just self-control—it was superhumanly peculiar. Second, though, the syringe in your trash. It made me wonder at one point . . ."

"If the syringe in the barn was mine? Hardly blame you, my being there just after it happened and all shaken up."

She clinked her glass again to his. "Here's to a beautiful friendship, Ian O'Leary. And, someday soon, to our trading stories. Full stories. *Real* stories."

For a moment, he locked on her eyes. Then nodded.

But now, the grin returning, he gestured toward the cluster of people at the gallery's center. "I'm curious, though: How'd you figure it out?"

She shook her head. "I should've seen it sooner. All those years of training how to spot camouflage, and I didn't see it here—didn't recognize Stella's grief as flimsy and fake. I passed the closet in the

Promontory where they keep the blazers, but didn't think early enough how easy it would be for someone just to take one. For Stella to drive a car to your bakery where she made sure she was seen having a pastry, then set a small fire—"

"A wonder she didn't burn the place down."

"Drive back to the inn and scamper up to the third floor, wearing the blazer again, sabotage Shibby, get down the three flights to drive back to the bakery where she was seen again, the mauve coat over the blazer, I bet. She drove part of the way back to the inn, she admitted, and left the car at the Captain Smollett house—a nice touch to throw guilt my way in case it was spotted. She walked from there so she'd be on foot again when she came racing up to the ambulance."

"Elaborate plan. Didn't know she had it in her."

Amie shook her head. "She was smarter than people gave her credit for, sadly. Even the details of spiking Shibby's afternoon coffee or wearing the blazer and a hat so she'd be mistaken at a distance for a staff member. Or knowing enough of Shibby's past that she could quietly spread news of the lab report of alcohol in the bloodstream and make people think Shibby had relapsed and fallen out the window on her own. Honestly, she had me all on the wrong track. I half figured things out, half stumbled onto the truth."

"Yet stumbled on the right person. In time."

She shrugged. "I should've paid more attention to Stella's resentment, the depth of it—how the very thing that made her top of the heap in high school, her looks, hadn't created an adult life she loved. Bitterness, you might've noticed, rarely leads anywhere good."

"I might've noticed," Ian agreed.

Amie waited until he'd raised his eyes to hers. "And your connection with Aunt Addy. You know, I first thought it was just a circle on Chester's leather satchel. But I'm guessing now it was an *O*. For Chester's mother's maiden name: Gwendolyn *O'Leary* Weld."

Ian gave a single nod. "Gwen wasn't like everyone else in the family. Guess she had enough of her own secrets to not be too rough on mine. That's all I knew: that she had her secrets and that they were making her miserable—sick, even. I had my own, so who was I to judge? I swear I'd have spoken up if I'd known there was a kid involved."

"I believe you."

"When she showed up that day in my shop, she had news from my father: that he was demanding I come back home and be the rugged, rugby-playing, skirt-chasing, pint-packing Irishman that my brothers all are."

"That you're not," Amie said gently. "And shouldn't have to be."

"There was no mention of Chester—whose kid he was. *Is*."

"I'm assuming Stella wrote the note, the one supposedly from Seth, that sent you to the barn that day?"

"Setting me up, it would seem, to get caught there at the scene looking guilty, and Gwen already connected with me. In case it wasn't enough to leave the syringe in the stall that pointed to Seth."

Amie let her gaze wander to Seth's back across the room. "Odd, you know, too, how well Tess Michaud played into Stella's hands: Tess's drive to keep all hint of scandal from the inn, Tess's loathing of her boss. It made her look guilty, too. It was Stella who insisted to Fossick he offer his old lover the use of one of the Allards—another finger pointing toward Fossick or Tess."

"So, then," Ian said.

"So, then," Amie echoed. They exchanged smiles.

"Seriously, Amelia Stilwell, where do you go from here?"

"Just trying to keep food on my table. Though, come to think of it, I don't have a table. In my belly, then. Luring your customers to wander through that quaint little door and come buy a wall full of photographs or a floor full of sculptures."

"The customer-poaching I was assuming. What I meant, though, was . . ."

He nodded toward Seth and Jake standing a few feet apart, two bulls eyeing each other, horns ready, even as they pretended to toast. "Looks to me like you've got some man-sorting to do."

She shook her head. "Nope. Not any time in the near future. Got too much else I'm needing—and also wanting—to do."

Her gaze swung over the gallery, the stone hearth, the lights from the birch branches and rafters, the seascapes and sculptures and glass birds, her whole shop gleaming and glittering tonight. The whole village had gathered to kick off the gallery's life before tourists began arriving in spring.

But now, right now, was good, too. The fire blazing in the hearth, the warmth and the community and the laughter here, amplified because of the cold outside.

A gathering place.

After all those dark years of war and death. The gut-wrenching loss. The grief and despair. The heart-weariness that said you couldn't go on.

They'd hurt already beyond what a person could bear.

Yet they'd survived.

Those years were so vivid still. And also a blur.

Amie walked to Shibby and squeezed the small hand, hugged and chatted with Eunice for several moments, then stepped to the gallery's front door. Slipping outside, she shut it gently behind her and stood for a moment alone, the light spilling gold from behind her onto the circle. The air was full again of pine and salt air and fresh snow.

From the firs that lined the north edge of the harbor came the call of the loon, his three-note *I'm here, here, where are you?* that she'd heard her first night back in the village.

This time, though, came an answer: a three-note call in return. *I'm here, here, here I am.*

Amie's eyes filled.

Craning her head back toward the faces gathered there in the shop, Shibby at its center, Amie felt warmth surge through her limbs, even down through the cast. Cheeks flushed, she lifted her face to fresh snowflakes just beginning to fall.

Thank you, she turned to mouth to Shibby, who looked up from her cocoa just then and smiled. Amie laid a hand over her heart. *Thank you.*

Through the door, two figures, one tall and one very short, emerged to join her out here in the cold. But only Chester trotted forward, Seth hanging back.

She knelt to put her arm around the little boy, her eyes out toward the harbor. "You know, I used to be angry about it: not having a mom or really a dad to raise me."

Chester turned his big hazel eyes to her.

"But I look back and see Shibby and Fletch and Mary O'Kelly and so many more. I realized I'd been looking at what felt like a dried-up pond where family was supposed to be. When, in fact, I had a whole ocean of people who loved me."

What we remember, she thought, looking out to where the lights of the shops played over the harbor, *is so much like that, bouncing and refracting, leaving some things bright and glittering, some things shadowed and blurred.*

Even that, though, could be healing and good.

"I miss Aunt Addy," Chester whispered, and put a hand on his chest. "It hurts. Bad."

Amie's eyes filled again as she hugged him to her. "The hurt never quite goes away, but it gets less awful, I promise. Other people come along who love you so much. That won't erase Addy, just add to all the love." She put a hand over his little one still splayed on his chest. "Tell you what. You and me, we'll go day by day. You can always tell Shibby or me when you're sad. Or angry. But also every day, you and me, we'll point to things we're glad for. Like that cormorant there."

Chester pointed back toward Good Harbor. Or maybe to Shibby. Or maybe he also meant the hot cocoa and cream. "Glad for." He put his mittened hand into hers.

"We'll freeze solid out here, you know," she said.

"Make statues of us," he agreed and struck a pose.

Amie threw her head back to laugh. When the little boy began to laugh with her, she hugged him to her again.

A few feet away, Seth stood there still watching, waiting to see if he should join them. Amie waved for him to come.

"It's great to see you smile, Chester," she whispered, touching his mouth. "Glad for."

"Glad for," he echoed.

Author's Note

Readers who have been lucky enough to visit the southern coast of Maine will no doubt recognize the layout of Pelican Cove as being based loosely on the actual town of Kennebunkport. I decided to create a fictional village in order to combine bits of history, as well as the quirks and charm of several of my favorite coastal towns from Camden going south. The layout of the fictional Dock Circle, for example, is a tribute to Kennebunkport's Dock Square, and the unlikely statue of the Civil War soldier meant to honor the Union dead but actually wearing Confederate garb because the town refused to pay for a new statue actually stands in the town center of York. F.O. Provisions is based loosely on H.B. Provisions (though moved to the Upper Village), a perfect spot to grab all things needed for locals and tourists alike. The fictional owner, however, is based not on the current wonderful owners but on my old friend and mentor Fletcher Allen, as gracious and gentle a man as the fictional Fletcher Osgood is gruff.

Amie Stilwell's former profession as a photographic interpreter (PI) during World War II was fascinating to research, an area about which I was completely ignorant before planning this book. This was an arena in which women contributed essential work to the war, and earned a great deal of respect. The actual women PIs on whom Amie is modeled include Constance Babington Smith, probably the best-known PI; Henrietta Williams, who received the Air Medal for aerial reconnaissance; Virginia Stuart; and Marion A. Frieswyk. Using a slide rule, magnifying glasses, and stereoscopes, female photographic interpreters contributed significantly, along with courageous reconnaissance pilots, in spotting camouflaged arsenals and weapons construction sites, discoveries that helped determine strategical planning. Operation Crossbow (Peenemünde) and Operation Overlord (the Normandy landing), among other efforts, are prime examples.

Eliot Porter, mentioned as an early pioneer in color photography, is a historical figure, and I so enjoyed learning of his methods. It was his photography of Maine that I surrounded myself with many days when I could not be there physically but wanted to be reminded of spectacular landscapes and seascapes and close-ups of lichen and leaves and birds.

Although I don't currently live in New England, I loved getting to reside in and around the Boston area for nearly a decade. My husband and I made frequent jaunts up to the Maine coast, and now living a good thousand miles south, we still find our way back as often as possible. The novel's fictional Promontory Inn is a combination of two of Kennebunkport's historic inns, the Nonantum Resort and the Colony Hotel, as well as imagination.

Having read an intriguing article about Eunice Kennedy Shriver and realizing her dates for briefly attending Radcliffe fit with this story, I was pleased to get to include her as a minor character. I salute the remarkable work she began as founder of the Special Olympics.

Inevitably with each book, I end up leaving some issue of historical fact versus imagination unanswered, no matter how hard I try to anticipate questions. But that makes for part of the fun of book club discussions, remote and in person, as well as email.

For readers and book club members who enjoy dropping down research rabbit holes as much as I do, below are a few of the books I learned from, and I am so grateful to their authors: Joyce Butler's *Kennebunkport: The Evolution of an American Town*, vol. 2; Jack H. Coote's *The Illustrated History of Colour Photography*; Elinor Florence's

Bird's Eye View; Christine Halsall's *Women of Intelligence: Winning the Second World War with Air Photos*; Paul Martineau's *Eliot Porter: In the Realm of Nature*; Eliot Porter's *Maine*; Constance Babington Smith's *Air Spy: How Nazi Secrets Were Uncovered from the Air*; E. B. White's *One Man's Meat*; and Colin Woodard's *The Lobster Coast: Rebels, Rusticators, and the Struggle for a Forgotten Frontier*.

Acknowledgments

Although the fictional town of Pelican Cove is based only loosely on Kennebunkport, Maine, I did a good bit of research on the town (a partial list of books is in the author's note). Additionally, the good folks at the Kennebunkport Historical Society, including executive director Kristin Lewis Haight and others, were generous with their time in sending pictures and information.

As always, Elisabeth Weed at The Book Group is the best literary agent in the business, hands down—wise, insightful, and fun. I've so enjoyed working again with the team at Lake Union, a group of consummate professionals and genuinely kind people. Thank you especially to my editor Danielle Marshall, who is extraordinary in knowing how to champion and also push writers in ways we need—at least I certainly do; copyeditor Wanda Zimba (whose in-depth knowledge of Maine was such a gift); book cover designer Tim Green; production manager Jen Bentham; author relations manager Gabriella Dumpit; marketing manager Rachael Clark; art director Adrienne Krogh; proofreader Nicole Brugger-Dethmers; and so many more. Thank you also to friend and editor Blake Leyers, who is such a resource for brainstorming early ideas on a novel and dreaming with a writer about what it might grow into.

I am so grateful to the pretty darn brilliant beta readers on this novel who were not only graciously encouraging but also provided invaluable questions and feedback. It turned out to be a far larger group than I'd intended because far more of you than I'd anticipated said yes—but every single person ended up offering something fresh and important. Truly, this is a decidedly better book because of each of you—and life is richer with your friendship: Yael Abrahamsson, Janet Byers, Betsy Christie, Angela Deane, Fran Gary, Beth Jackson-Jordan, Olivia Jackson-Jordan, Diane Jordan, Julia Jordan-Lake, Shelby Huskey Jordan-Lake, Laura Kantorowski, Susan Bahner Lancaster, Kelly Moreland-Jones, Robbie Pinter, Suzanne Robertson, Elizabeth Rogers, Kelly Shushok, Lucinda Stewart, Tambi Swinney, Angie Tune, Mary Vaughn, Liz Waggener. Thank you to my Belmont University interns Kendal Cliburn and Isabelle Kanning, who are both so gifted and such a pleasure to work with. Ongoing thank-yous to my CiC group of women, the Discovery class of BUMC, and so many other fiercely loving friends, as well as to my kids' godparents, Ginger and Milton Brasher-Cunningham; my brother and sister-in law David Jordan and Beth Jackson-Jordan (and their wonderful young-adult kids); mother-in-law, Gina Lake; brother-in-law Steven Lake; and my mother, Diane Jordan, who demonstrate the best of welcome, authenticity, and family.

I'm so grateful, too, for so many invaluable writer friends who share struggles and celebrations honestly. I would begin listing you here, but since I'd be sure to leave someone fabulous out, I'll stick with loving the chances to give shout-outs to you and your books on social media and to anyone who will listen. Just know how much I value you in the community of writers.

As always, thank you to my husband, Todd Lake, whose encouragement and willingness to join me for crazy writing-research adventures never flags, and my young-adult kids, Jasmine (who drove all ten hours on a road trip so I could meet a deadline on this novel), Justin, Shelby, and Julia Jordan-Lake. I feel so privileged to learn from each of you in your own areas of passion and expertise, and so incredibly, unbelievably, grateful to share life with you.

Finally, thank you to the readers of this novel. I never take your time for granted, and I'm always so grateful to be able to share the journey of a story with kindred spirits who love books as I do. Stay well and stay in touch.

About the Author

Joy Jordan-Lake is the #1 Amazon bestselling author of nine books, including *Under a Gilded Moon*; *A Tangled Mercy*, an Editors' Choice recipient from the Historical Novel Society; *Blue Hole Back Home*, winner of the Christy Award for Best First Novel; and two children's books. Raised in the foothills of the southern Appalachians, she lived nearly a decade of her young-adult years in New England, which she still misses—and jumps at every chance to visit. She holds two master's degrees and a PhD in English and has taught literature and writing at several universities. Now living outside Nashville, she and her husband are startled to find the kids in college and launching careers, with only the ferocious ten-pound rescue pup still living at home full-time. Joy loves to connect with readers. You can visit her at www.joyjordanlake.com.